The Matter of Absence

World Writing in French
A Winthrop-King Institute Series

Series Editors
Charles Forsdick (University of Liverpool)
and
Martin Munro (Florida State University)

Advisory Board Members
Jennifer Boum Make (Georgetown University)
Michelle Bumatay (Florida State University)
William Cloonan (Florida State University)
Michaël Ferrier (Chuo University)
Michaela Hulstyn (Stanford Univesity)
Khalid Lyamlahy (University of Chicago)
Helen Vassallo (University of Exeter)

There is a growing interest among Anglophone readers in literature in translation, including contemporary writing in French in its richness and diversity. The aim of this new series is to publish cutting-edge contemporary French-language fiction, travel writing, essays and other prose works translated for an English-speaking audience. Works selected will reflect the diversity, dynamism, originality, and relevance of new and recent writing in French from across the archipelagoes – literal and figurative – of the French-speaking world. The series will function as a vital reference point in the area of contemporary French-language prose in English translation. It will draw on the expertise of its editors and advisory board to seek out and make available for English-language readers a broad range of exciting new work originally published in French. This series is published in partnership with the Winthrop-King Institute, Florida State University.

Patrick Chamoiseau

The Matter of Absence

Translated by Carrie Jaurès Noland

Liverpool University Press

First published in English translation by Liverpool University Press 2025
Liverpool University Press
4 Cambridge Street
Liverpool
L69 7ZU

The Matter of Absence was first published in French as *La matière de l'absence*
© Éditions du Seuil, 2016

British Library Cataloguing-in-Publication data
A British Library CIP record is available

ISBN 978-1-80207-209-9 hardback
ISBN 978-1-80207-210-5 paperback

Typeset by Carnegie Book Production, Lancaster

Translator's Note

Carrie Jaurès Noland

Patrick Chamoiseau's works of fiction, philosophy, and memoir consistently draw from diverse verbal palettes, making the task of his translator a complicated and subtle one. In a letter Chamoiseau wrote to the translators of his award-winning novel, *Texaco*, he acknowledges this challenge: "I try not to forget my Creole language, my Creole imagination, my Creole conception of the world ... I do not sacrifice to transparency."[1] Although he writes in French, Chamoiseau has managed to retain his Caribbean perspective, in part by embedding Creole expressions and invented portmanteau words into his prose. In doing so, he intensifies and expands the possibilities of the French language to create a language uniquely his own.

However, *The Matter of Absence* (published originally in 2016) is strikingly different from other works by Chamoiseau that have been translated into English. Here, the target of creolization is not simply the French language (although the reader will find many examples of resistant beauty in these pages); Chamoiseau also sets out to creolize *genres*. He braids together a wide variety of linguistic registers and generic conventions in an effort to tell many stories

---

1 *Texaco*, translated by Rose-Myriam Réjouis and Val Vinokurov (New York: Pantheon, 1997). The letter is translated by Carol Volk and appears in her "Translator's Note" to *Childhood* [*Antan d'enfance*] (Lincoln: University of Nebraska Press, 1999), pp. vii–viii.

at once. First, and above all, *The Matter of Absence* is the story of the author's mother, Man Ninotte, who died on January 1, 2000. Chamoiseau, who was born in Martinique in 1953, begins this narrative by recounting a visit to his mother's grave with his sister, "the Baroness." He then proceeds to evoke in rich detail the nature of his mother's existence after leaving her rural village to move to the *En-ville*, or "big city," of Fort-de-France.

But that's not all. The mother's story is quickly juxtaposed with both the history of slavery and the history of the entire human species! Along the way, Chamoiseau also explores various phases of the Black arts—storytelling on the plantation, the development of Caribbean dance forms, the jazz of Miles Davis, the poetry of Aimé Césaire, and the more recent florescence of painting and sculpture—while also contemplating the latest evidence concerning the evolution of life on earth. In addition, Chamoiseau weaves through this memoir of what he calls "our various humanities" a set of philosophical reflections that rely on a heightened vocabulary of abstract nouns and neologisms drawn from the works of his predecessor Édouard Glissant. In the course of translating these passages, I sometimes despaired of being able to find exact equivalents for Chamoiseau's noble abstractions. At other times, I was hard-pressed to capture the succulence and precision of his descriptions of everyday life. I hope, however, that I have managed to convey at least some of the nobility and some of the succulence of Chamoiseau's prose in English. His creolization of discrete genres, his cosmic perspective on existence mingled with his meticulous attention to the most piquant details of his mother's person, challenge us to rethink what a memoir is. Where, we might ask, do we place the limits of an individual subjectivity? How large, or small, is the story of a single being? Where does history—or her story—begin and end?

***

At the end of the text, I have placed a Glossary of terms that may be unfamiliar to the reader. I have included in this Glossary the French words "nègre," "négresse," and "négrillon," which appear throughout the text. But I also want to draw attention to them here to underscore the fact that there is no correct way of translating them into English, since each one has a long history in the languages of French colonialism. For an illuminating discussion of the various meanings of "nègre" (as opposed to "noir" ["black"], for instance), I refer the reader to Brent Hayes Edwards' "Translating the Word *Nègre*" in *The Practice of Diaspora: Literature, Translation, and the Rise of Black Internationalism.*[2] For a review of contemporary debates in France, see Grégory Pierrot's "Nègre (Noir, Black, Renoi, Négro)."[3] In this volume, I have chosen to translate the word "nègre" as "Black" or "Black man" and "négresse" as "Black woman." For the most part, I have kept "négrillon" in the original French since it is used as a nickname, like "the Baroness." My choices are inevitably imperfect. Nonetheless, I hope that the context will, in each case, allow the reader to sense how—ironically or affectionately—the word is being used.

I would like to acknowledge my deep gratitude to Christopher Beach, the brilliant translator of Annie Ernaux and Tristan Garcia, who offered sage advice and read the manuscript many times over. Charly Verstraet and Jeffrey Landon Allen, the gifted translators of Chamoiseau's *Crusoe's Footprint*, responded to my numerous questions with alacrity and good humor. Itati Villanueva and Allessandra Flaherty, two wonderful students, began the process of translating with me—I am very grateful for their insights and their comradery. Ann Rosen and Alex Gil generously assisted me in sorting out several enigmatic passages. An astute anonymous reader clued me in to infelicities that I hope I have been able to repair. Finally, I wish to thank Patrick Chamoiseau, who showed exemplary patience with my many queries. *The Matter of Absence* has a particular meaning for me, personally. I met Monsieur Chamoiseau at a book fair in Lyon soon after the death of my own mother. Perhaps this memoir about his mother, Man Ninotte—parts of which he read at the fair—was his gift to her. In a similar spirit, this translation is my gift to mine.

---

2   Cambridge: Harvard University Press, 2003: pp. 25–43.
3   *Small Axe*, Vol. 26, No. 2 (68), July 2022: pp. 100–7.

The Matter of Absence

By Patrick Chamoiseau

Translated by Carrie Jaurès Noland

For Mireille Chonville,
who was so very kind.

All passes and all remains.

—Antonio Machado

I do not portray being, I portray passing.

—Montaigne

Reality cannot be overcome, only elevated.

—René Char

Table of Contents

The Matter of Absence

IMPACT

But here is where the Baroness slips into philosophizing on the mystery of old folks

LEGENDARY OF THE GREAT AGE – "Those who live for a long time are nourished on absence," my big sister the Baroness confides as we pass by the entrance to the cemetery. "Their gaze remains fixed on what they no longer have, on what's lost. Submerged in wrinkles and lit up by child-like smiles, their pupils reflect as much tender vulnerability as greedy innocence. And these mournings, these ruptures, these losses that attack our ordinary survival and that destroy us in that way, seem to them like the impressive wake of a moving force that advances only by drifting out over the entire course of their duration. They grow rich from this wake, as though it were some impossible source that only their magician-like memory could transform into a substance. And this wake, my dear, is a celebration."

"And yet," the Baroness goes on, "those who live for a long time are gnawed away by absence. They grow dense with invisibility, no doubt because their body—all that can be seen, all that emanates from what they are—begins to fade away. Old folks turn into a substance that erases them (a black hole of losses, ruptures, and lacks). From that hole, they bring back the startling paradox—and the fragile triumph—of their long lives. And so, dear *Négrillon* (that's what she calls me), those who have had a long life draw ever closer to a mystery..."

I sigh. My dear Baroness, we are always afflicted by absence. I think of the moment of birth, this emergence into orphaned lights after the uterine cocoon. I think of the attachments that make you who you are but that, no matter what, eventually fade away. I think of the friendships that sustain you and that you lose, of these men, these women, these animal or vegetal existences that constitute our familiar landscape and that slowly, bit by bit, fall away. And then I think of the growing mass of deferred dreams that offer no escape, the intangible ruins of hope, the gutted but tenacious promises in their trembling rags, all these desires that are never fulfilled yet at the same time are never abandoned, and which accumulate, unseen, around lost illusions. All that carves out a hollowness that feeds on itself, that persists in everything that comes our way. And if our lives are still tossed about in a flow of abundance (so much light, so many fruits and songs, so much overwhelming feeling, so many renewed hopes), nothing can truly compensate for the immensity of these losses. They reveal strange passageways, forever open, at the edge of which we remain, silenced. What song are they singing, these placeless, gaping holes that only open toward us, inside us, and for us? And what do they whisper to the most sensitive among us? What is this thing that memory produces around what is missing, this pearl with no known quintessence that still inhabits us and that we inhabit?

"Those who have lived for a long time no longer need to ask these questions," replies the Baroness. Just like our mother, Man Ninotte (*Oh may all grace still be bestowed upon her!*), they have known the battering of sufferings and joys. The backdrop of their existence is a collection of triumphs and failures catalogued in a singular tongue, a speech with no alphabet. From every wound there springs only the dew of an unalloyed naiveté. These old folks lack everything, and yet they are given everything; they are as much what they've lost as what they've managed to retain. That's why I've tried to watch them so often, and when I do, sensing their strange substance, that accumulation of dissipation even in the intensification of life, I ask myself: *good God, what is this mystery?*

And I seek an answer.

"But *Négrillon*, those who live for a long time don't need this answer. They advance in a round that, at each turn, grows more acute and precise but in a temporal duration that doesn't seem to move forward. This duration has no beginning worth remembering and no predictable—although awaited—end. And so, the absence that nourishes them could not form a question, and even less so a response. If it were up to them there would be no story to tell, nothing to write. They are at once the masters and the victims of absence."

I say to her: Baroness, since our mother Ninotte's death—that ultimate loss, that fundamental absence—we have sustained her, and we have shared her. What have we made of this absence, this painful nourishment? All right, so let's forget about the questions and let go of the answers, but all the same, let's try to enter this still wide-open circle, to risk saying a few words there, without requiring that anyone respond, just trying to breathe and to smile, in harmony with the breathing of something that doesn't exist anywhere but that nonetheless lives on.

"I have nothing to say, and I don't much care!" the Baroness lets me know.

LEGENDARY OF THE RETURN – I had always thought that one day Man Ninotte would come back to visit me in a dream. In the legendary of the old Creole beliefs, it is said repeatedly that those who have gone will come back to leave signs—a sign after the burial to signal well-being or to inflict punishment; a tranquil light or a vengeful twist of fate to bring you down.

But Man Ninotte never did return.

Two or three times before her death, when the collapse of her spirit and the wearing down of her memory had already shattered her, we had no choice but to confront a powerlessness that disarmed even you, our Baroness, our almighty, omnipotent older sister of the highest majesty. We had to take Man Ninotte from her house and entrust her to the safety of a medical establishment that she was conscious of only intermittently. Do you remember? She had only brief moments of lucidity that made her whimper with confusion. She would arch her eyebrows and glance about her in slow terror. She didn't understand what was happening to her; and above all, she didn't understand what she was doing in this unfamiliar place. She demanded that we, the strangers that we had become in her eyes, take her back to her home so that she could rediscover once again her furniture, her possessions, her life. All these things that we couldn't give back to her—we, who were ready to sell body and soul for her. I believed, then, that she would come back to reproach us through the detour of some old dream. But Man Ninotte, truly departed on the first of January 2000, did not return.

Although I didn't really expect her, I was still surprised that she didn't come back to visit me. It took me many long years to become aware of this. Eventually, what was fully revealed to me was an expectation that I hadn't admitted to myself, one that I couldn't admit to myself. In my defense, I have to say that during a good deal of my childhood I had been paralyzed with fear of a thousand different zombies populating an invisible realm. No one had ever seen a zombie, but everyone knew someone who knew someone who had, and everyone—without ever having seen one himself—held the strong conviction that there were plenty of others who had seen a zombie.

But let me tell you more about these zombies.

There were three kinds.

First, there were the living ones that were accountable to some ancient pact with a slew of demons; they could plunge night and shadow into a state of malaise—or terror. There were also the dead ones that came back in the form of spirits from who knows where, or else the inexhaustible ranks of ancestors who had no name or address, bound genealogically by a jinx to all the living, and who sometimes played the role of angelic guardians and sometimes that of conscientious executioners. During my childhood, because of those zombies, no living being could ever truly be alone. Surrounded by the dead, by maleficent zombies or by a host of ancestors, each living being existed in a fog of intermingling spirits whose tales, untimely intrusions, and putative interventions gave meaning to all the connections, all the links along the chain of ordinary life, links such as duty, family, country, identity, providing reasons for being scared, reasons to hope, and explanations for every misfortune. Not a single link in the chain of what we believed was missing from its place in some ancestral lineage. If a few rebellious hotheads tried to extract themselves from that chain, if they tried to contest its hold on them, each one would be solidly re-inserted into this prefabricated life as though it were something reassuring... —"And why not?" the Baroness shoots back. "Life isn't easy, and crutches like that are welcome! Illusions are too. And as for the kinds of truths that come down to us from the past, the best thing to do is to just watch them wear out, without going to battle, without struggling, without worrying!"

As for the zombies, it was the Creole tales that mentioned them the most, but without furnishing precise details. The Creole storyteller never depicts anything, not a single landscape, and above all, no characters. He tells his stories without psychology, without explorations of the soul's depths. What constitutes the story can be found more in what he doesn't say than in what he does say. For instance, if he wants to put a luxurious house in his story, he'll say: *It had thirty dozen thousand bathrooms!*... and that's all you'll learn about it. In this house that has suddenly become a wonderland, if the least noble of our bodily functions can be so well accommodated, just imagine what an outrageous amount of care could be expended on our *most* noble functions. From the moment we hear of it, that house fills our entire mental horizon! To evoke an evil person, the storyteller would be satisfied with bringing him to life by means of a phrase: *a song that tastes like absinthe*. That song, its bitterness and its dangers, would incarnate the person, and, conversely, the person would be, for us, the song! A very beautiful *négresse* would be outlined by means of repeated variations on just thirteen notes: *She was so beautiful, beautiful, beautiful such that she went beyond beautiful; she left beautiful behind!* Or better yet: *If she were ugly, I would have shouted about that, and if she were bandyleggèd I would have sung about that too, but if I say nothing, damn! it's because looking at this perfect earthly creature has left me speechless…* Whatever was admirable about this person would emerge in a tempest of sound spread out against a background of the unsaid! And whatever was left unsaid by the storyteller was suggested by gesticulations in space that compelled you to dig deeply into yourself to find the feeling—horror or delight—that suited you best. In this way, he turned you around and around in circles until he left you to figure it all out on your own.

This was even clearer in the case of the nomenclature of the ordinary zombies. There were dozens upon dozens of them: *Soucougnan, Ti-sapotille, Diablesses des acacias, Tèt sans kô, Ti-mons, Lanticris…* And yet no one could describe these sinister creatures. They gamboled about in the mind, evoked by the gestural repertoire mobilized by the storyteller to announce their arrival and to send us into a feverish state. Since zombies weren't really anywhere, they were everywhere. And since no one knew diddly squat about how they look, they could be seen in front of us, behind us, and in strange creatures silhouetted by the night. The zombies that traumatized us the most, the ones that made me wary for the longest time, were the *Bet à Man Ibé*—the Beasts of Man Hubert. You could imagine their horror, but trying to figure out whether you were dealing with real animals or with nightmarish monsters would make you go over your ancestral fears again and again until you mixed them all up—and then you would go and invent even more! As for this Man Hubert, she owned these zombie beasts and would set them loose on you in the rascally night. And although none of the local stories could make things worse by adding more details to the picture, you couldn't help but experience their unfathomable, limitless hideousness... —"Ah yes," sighs the Baroness. "I see what you're trying to get at: the *Bet à Man Ibé* and Man Ibé herself brought on panic from nothing at all!"

The old storytellers were masters of all this nothing about nothing. They managed to convey more than the unsaid; they took on something unspoken and labored over it with care. The storytellers emerged from the slave plantations, and it is widely known that their words were a clever, indirect protest against that legalized crime. Under the yoke of total oppression, of an immeasurable dehumanization, they sketched out a horizon that owed nothing to the slave order. Thus, in their stories there was no realism, no description, no context, and not a single decipherable character. There was nothing transparent and, above all, nothing commonplace. In the dominant order of the plantation, everything was skewed, falsified, extended out over the trap of dehumanization. Thanks to the obscurity of this discourse that imploded on itself, our first storytellers were able to invent another world; they brought it to life without any instruction, divulging other lands beneath the canefields, indicating where these lands were located without having to point them out, and letting them do their unpredictable work. It was a meticulous and very wise *detour*!

Édouard Glissant has explored for us this notion of the detour. It speaks to the resistance, invisible and secret, of those who had to make their way through the slave plantation without ever giving the impression that they were challenging its ignominy. They exhibited a sweetness-and-light docility, yet all the while they resisted by means of imperceptible attacks, the effects of which emerged only as deferred, in the sadness of nightfall, in the amazement of morning, and in various other forms, such as fire, sabotage, the poisoning of cherished animals, and even the poisoning of the master or a pillar of his family. Poison became a specter that insinuated itself everywhere, unraveling confidences, troubling friendships, denaturing acts of obedience or fidelity. The great terror of the slaveholders was just that: being poisoned! It was impossible for them to predict when it would strike, to know what its nature would be, to determine from where it would come. Detour is a slow-moving form of rebellion that extends beyond the visible, an almost intangible *marronnage* that nonetheless fills in and haunts what seems real... —"That's nothing at all!" the Baroness replies, frowning beneath a pair of suspicious eyebrows.

The strangest thing is that the fear of being poisoned would move beyond the sphere of the slaveholders and spread throughout our society, traversing the ages and attaining the status of a tradition. In my childhood, before going out to carouse with friends, many people used to absorb a counter-poison made with a cloverleaf and a plant with special powers. This concoction was the go-to of the antidote shelf enthroned in every home. At a baptism, a marriage, or a party, before putting your lips on the cup, you would right away wipe the glass and cleanse the rim with a rub of lemon. For the noon-time punch, you would choose the crystalline white rum and not the aged rum, which could hide things in its caramel robe. In the world of cockfights, at the heart of the pits, the fear of poisoning created a ritual. Before unleashing the cock for combat in the arena, each cock owner would wipe off the feathers of his champion, lick his head and beak, and suck each of his spurs. We weren't just scared of declared enemies but also of the jealousy of our best friends (always possible) and the resentment of our closest allies. Sickness was approached first as a potential case of poisoning. Death itself was suspect! Any abnormal behavior, even the inebriation of love, might have begun as "a something" you were given to drink. No doubt the rivalries between the slaves in the Great House and the slaves in the fields—those everyday conflicts and vexations of the heart—spread the practice of poisoning as a way of severing the Gordian knot. Poisoning was an invisible accompaniment to human relations, a merciless possibility that, every instant, exposed your future to the whims of chance, keeping you in a state of constant vigilance.

But let's get back to those famous zombies. The living creatures who were in communication with the devils appeared in forms you could see (coffins that moved, dogs with fried fish for eyes, bulls without horns, beautiful ladies with hoofs, and so on). But others (who surged forth from an invisible realm) would appear as flickering fires or spectral lights, as rapping sounds with no cause, as wingless things that flew about the house, as laughter lacking an amygdala, as curses and dirty language—and as tuneless sounds unknown to musicians and acoustic bibles. These haunting distortions of the real populated your waking nightmares—which are the worst kind because they blossom in the day and hang on at night like assassins in your dreams. Although I was never able to see or hear any, I knew not a single second of childhood, not a single experience of fear, that wasn't populated with this insubstantial brood. During the day, the zombies coming from nowhere bothered no one: the day demystifies, and shadows are held down by the earth. But at night, things get blurry, shadows scatter like marbles of mercury. Some of them rise up, the visible begins its circus in the invisible, and the invisible suddenly releases its undesirable offspring. The night that erases everything turns this everything into something a thousand times more palpable, in limitless volumes and detestable shapes.

The old Creole storytellers who spent their time constructing these nothings about nothing—taking on the inexpressible on its own turf—only told their stories at night, in the glimmer of those torches we call *sèbi*. (In their trembling flames, *sèbi* ceaselessly outline forms.) Custom forbids storytellers from telling stories during the day under the threat of being transformed into... baskets!

—"Into baskets?"

—Yes, baskets!

No one knew where this somewhat ridiculous punishment came from. The Baroness, as I'm explaining this, is disturbed. "Among the panoply of Creole curses," she muses, "there are a lot worse. They could be changed into syphilitic mosquitoes, or bulldogs with suspenders; they could be afflicted with the head of a seabass or a case of scabies that would last seven years, or they could be made into *Maximilien-gros-tête* and Black men on mobilettes with no seat!

But a basket!!?

Why a basket?!!" she asks indignantly.

All I can do is admit she's right.

This story about the basket was at once disappointing and inexplicable. How could a basket become the instrument of a curse? And those whom I was able to ask, experts at the University, Doctors of Creole Studies and other such curiosities, had not the slightest idea. And so, it remains an enigma.

Nevertheless, being turned into a basket, while not the most despicable thing in the world, is also not that interesting. In fact, though, no self-respecting storyteller, from the dawn of these traditions up to this unprincipled age, would risk transgressing this rule... *the basket is scary!* I say to her after a long silence. Annoyed, the Baroness lets out a sigh. "I see your game: you're trying to make things more complicated than they are! The basket interests you because, first of all, it's only a hollow, a kind of void. Its only purpose is to be filled. And so, in that way, it expresses a kind of hopelessness if nothing is entrusted to the space it offers. A basket that falls from the night—a storyteller who has been demoted, no doubt—would receive nothing from the day. He would be condemned to be nothing, and condemned by nothing. Damn!..."

It's custom that absolutely forbids the telling of stories during the day. And everyone obeys. Custom isn't enshrined anywhere; no one has ever seen its judges or its armed enforcers. And yet, no storytellers, young or old, are known to have gotten around this rule. It is passed down by the stories themselves, which take it up in a thousand variants and patiently spread its decree. Each storyteller is careful to remind us that he is upholding the norm. It is even more crucial to celebrate the norm given that the most audacious storytellers never stop transgressing it. If the rules of the slave plantation, or of the colonial or postcolonial order, were disrupted by the stories, the rules of the vigil itself remained untouchable, as though they had become the guarantor of a much more precious liberty. And so, you might consider this fact: the storytellers, free spirits, and anarchists of the slave order nonetheless respected the authority of this custom. *No words by day!* They knew that it's difficult to fashion the invisible in the accentuated visibility of daytime. Nighttime is far more propitious, inhabited by shadows, by living stars full of creatures of the mind and colored by the prolific reddening glow of the *sèbi*... "At night, it isn't Reason that sees, it's everything else! And it's not the visible that dictates, it's all the rest..." the Baroness sighs.

It is also true, I tell her, that in the beginning, storytellers on the slave plantations produced their stories during funeral vigils. They spoke facing the night, but the night stood *facing death*. And so, the night contained many more invisible presences churning in a mill of ecstasy and terror. To speak before death, or in the presence of a dead person, is to find yourself suddenly at the very edge of an abyss. You have to deal with that abyss as best you can, because you're pretty much fighting for your life—for life itself! The task of the storyteller is to say: *Come on over to the side of life!* And life was not on the side of the dead body, and above all, not on the side of the slave order. You understand?

The storyteller's task opened onto an arena that was neither easy to enter, nor easy to exit. As he approached the end of his task, the storyteller who wanted to leave the circle of the nighttime vigil, to stop recounting his tale and hand the stage over to someone else, had to say so explicitly. He had to signal that he wasn't comfortable there anymore, in the circle; he had to shout to be taken out. A storyteller in the audience would then respond to him, declaring that he would carry on, and it was only his entrance into the vigil's circle that offered a way out to the one who had been presiding up to that point. Continuity was essential: what had just been recounted had to be looped back into the woven net that remained suspended. It had to be developed further without any break.

Death could not be allowed to find the least little tear in the weave of life.

The new storyteller would find himself facing the abyss of death, the vertigo of night. He had to manage to keep life going. The great storytellers of the burial vigils were called *Majolè*, Majors of the air. The *Majolè* were the champions in this dance of combat called the *danmyé*. By extension, the master storytellers were also considered *Majolè*, and the circle of the vigil was like an arena for storytellers in battle.

They faced each other with the word, with the breath, with—you could say—the invisible.

Their weapons were made of air and skill alone, but they could annihilate with as much violence as any other villain.

This combat of the air was also a struggle against the symbolic abyss that a death opened in the midst of the living, a struggle against this impalpable thing that the night and the *sèbi*, the prayers and the tears, forced into consciousness, into the world. The domination of the slavers was also the work of invisible forces made from that same invisibility that broke your spirit and led you to interiorize the merciless dehumanization they imposed. The primordial struggle could only unfold against this invisible force. Damnation at that time had taken such a strong hold that even in escaping the plantation—if you got to escape, to take refuge in the woods or in the foothills, like a maroon, or even if you had the benefit of obtaining your freedom papers—you were still trapped in this curse. Whatever you did or said, whether you were in chains or not, whether you were resistant or docile, simply by being alive in a black skin, you remained a slave—that is, dead, while still catastrophically alive... The only way to get out: transform your imaginary! Switch imaginaries! ... Become a Warrior of the imaginary!... —"Sometimes it seems to me that *you* present yourself in that way," the Baroness interrupted me. — You're right, and I apologize because it's just vanity! Such powers are still to come...

It could also happen that a storyteller would ask to leave the circle where he had just spoken, and no one would reply. Or, more precisely: *no one dared to reply!* To go on at the point where a previous storyteller left off, that would be like acting as if you could do better than him. In fact, to tell tales during a vigil the storyteller has to get the space so enflamed that no one wants to reclaim it. Someone so reckless, someone who would take on the risk of surpassing such a moment of verbal prowess, might be plunged into inescapable ridicule. It would be like shifting over (even if symbolically) to the side of the dead body. People in the audience would question the newcomer. They wouldn't respond to his efforts to start things up again. If he asked, "Is the court asleep!?" then spectacular snoring would be the response. People would shove each other aside to take his place, just as cattle do when a fence has been lowered. The one deemed inadequate would have to flee from the circle in the face of such mockery and hostile pressure. So, a great storyteller could turn about in the circle of vigils, chanting *Get me out of here, I don't feel right here!...* and savor the silence that hollowed out the crowd, bearing witness to his now uncontested triumph. That storyteller could then abandon the narrative and start joking, monkeying around, telling riddles and other proverbs like those dispensed by the minor players, the second-class raconteurs. For everyone, it was as though death had been vanquished, brought down by the Master of the Word alone. No one could succeed him. From that point on, the Master of the Word was more sacred than human: *Majolè!* You could say that the *Majolè* is a storyteller who, simply due to the quality of his artistry, is capable of vanquishing death itself and putting life in its place, or, instead, you could say that he transmutes the void that death generates into a space of life!... The *Majolè* brings into being what one might call the Warrior of the Imaginary!... The Baroness looks at me attentively but remains expressionless.

There's no account of what happened to the storytellers who recited their stories by day, and no one has ever seen a moaning basket abandoned by the side of a road. And since it's not conceivable that humans wouldn't transgress a law if they could, you can assume that dozens and dozens of storytellers must have told stories during the day. It's just that their words would have been lost in gatherings deprived of mystery, without shadows, without spectators. It's also possible that a dead man exposed to the sun, without the threat of night to conjure the immense void that he reveals, would become a triumphant corpse, one capable of gobbling up the most powerful stories without leaving the smallest remainder. Custom, then, annihilates and commands respect without expending any effort at all.

The Baroness, who seems interested in what I am mumbling, says to me: "If I've understood you correctly, at night the storyteller confronts two things. First, night itself. Second, a combat with Titans in which the entire mind is brought into play. And, if I follow you, this combat would involve grasping the invisible, the unspeakable, and making it into a story, giving it meaning, grabbing hold of death, stripping it of its horror, leading it—from one bit of mirth to the next—toward a celebration of life. It would involve constructing an instrument of knowledge. Your ingenuity," she goes on, "would make this storyteller confronted with the night, with the face of death, into a hero, into a *Majolè*. Next to his authority, the daytime storyteller would appear to be nothing more than a sort of entertainer, a jokester, taking no risks and receiving no glory..." I reply: Exactly. Nights are always fecund, the Arabs say. Only the night can, in one fell swoop, dissipate the certitudes of the day and prepare the world for the splendor of dawn. This is night as I experienced it long ago in my childhood. But there was something else too...

In those days, cemeteries were the site of a tragic enchantment. They established the lines of silence between life and death. Their walls, thought to protect us against contamination, contained spaces that no normal person would want to traverse or dispute, allowing just a glimpse of a few elaborate crosses on the tombs of the rich or the *békés*, silhouetted against the sky like emblems of victory. The white lime covering the ramparts and tombs provided a serene and placid surface for the multi-colored wreaths of recent burials or for the bouquets of those plastic flowers intended to lend a cheerful note to catastrophe. This collection of plain white tombs against the backdrop of such a shimmering land produced a breach that the radiance of the sun intensified into a single flame. At night, the whitish reflections made the lines of the crosses tremble before fading into the dark, highlighting them, so that they seemed more alive just before they were lost in the shadows. Fort-de-France had two cemeteries: one for the rich (White-French *békés*, mulattos, and a few fortunate blacks), and one for the poor (the rest of the country). Not a day went by when someone didn't come to fill them up, bringing people who were deprived of their last hope. It was as if, like a clandestine fisherman, the cemetery had sent out lifelines bearing hooks that could drag in a catch of victims. As opposed to our fishermen, though, the cemeteries never came back empty-handed. They never ceased siphoning off life's debris, accumulating bones, piling up memories, welcoming processions of sadness and tears. All was arranged so that the dead would remain behind. They were accompanied en masse by people dressed in the most beautiful clothes, taking little steps (as in a ritournello by Brassens) to show they weren't in a hurry. Fantasies in marble and cement were erected for them. They were surrounded by grillwork worthy of Spanish castles. The black hole of the crypt would be sealed with immense care. The guardian would receive his beggar's change. The crosses and the virgins would be distributed, sanctifying the site and justifying the fact that they would be rooted there forever. Candles and friendship flowers were provided, manifestations of frank goodwill, and the most flattering photo would be placed on the tomb (embellished with a *you–will–forever–be–missed* in gilded calligraphy). The dead had what they needed to pass the time, spying on those who were still alive and endlessly rereading testimonials of the love bestowed on them. As soon as the first shadows appeared, the doors would be locked.

The cemetery for the poor didn't offer the same degree of comfort, entrusting the remainder of the deceased to a bit of earth, simply turned over and topped with a hodgepodge of crosses and a crown of conch shells. Such sobriety could easily be justified: he who, on earth, had known poverty and whom poverty had known would have less desire to return, and could easily be contained by ramparts a good deal less spectacular.

Coming back from the cemetery, we invented a route of right angles, different from the route we had taken to get there. That way, the dead who were rich and the dead who were poor wouldn't come after us, and we wouldn't find them again upon reaching home. We also needed to make sure that we dusted off the bottom of our pants and our polished shoes so that the dust belonging to the cemetery didn't end up settling here in the house. The town stood still as the processions departed the cathedral to join, inch by inch, the security of the cemetery. If you were ill, you had to stand erect as the funeral procession passed, or else be carried away a few seconds later. If you were in good health, you had to be quiet, look around and salute—because you never know... You always had to keep a cheerful countenance in the face of death as it passed you by.

But that wasn't enough.

The dead left their tombs.

They insinuated themselves among us and used all sorts of pretexts: shadows that were too still, moons that were too bright, reverberating mirrors, reflections on the windowpane, dust forgotten beneath the bed of someone dying, the badly disposed-of waters of the last funeral bath... The flowers, epitaphs, enameled photos, and chiseled regrets could certainly, with the favors bestowed by the night's magic, allow them to be active again in the world of the living. Obsessive thoughts, passionate affections, and inescapable griefs constituted for them strong moorings to that world. And so, each disappearance filled with its substance all the places that the disappeared had once loved. And since people loved all sorts of things and places, the dead were everywhere. Even outside of cemeteries, it was better to keep them at a distance so that they wouldn't mix the troubles of death with those of life. It was better to try as much as possible to capitalize on their goodwill and to profit from their clairvoyance so as to thwart the mischief of bad luck or bewitch chance.

But in its essence, this story is very old. Consider the dawn of our many diverse forms of humanity: envision that hominid who suddenly becomes conscious of the death of one of his own...

This is our origin, the very first!

Imagine the mind of the poor fellow who accidentally discovers this brutal void, this suffering and violence, or simply the turn of ordinary events leading to a moment when someone he knows becomes permanently rigid. This hominid could have been content to see there someone asleep—someone sleeping a sleep longer than the other sleeps, the mother of all sleeps—or else maybe a voluntary repose with no limit, a voyage out of time in the cosmos of dreams. And that must be what our hominid ancestor saw. But next would come the moment when the corpse was divided up by a swarm of animals. The worst would be the horror of such decompositions, and more, the drying out to the point of disintegration of that drama of dust. This revelation, soon repeated, would inaugurate a permanent tragedy. Death would become, from that point on, a generative enigma. The immensity of this disappearance, this void, so total and sudden, this slide toward the unbearable, would fertilize the ground of his mind. Beneath this stellar lightning bolt, the hominid mind would find itself forced to broaden all its convictions. To confront the senseless, to come up against the inconceivable, to face the unspeakable—such experiences propel neuronal activity beyond its limits, opening the mind onto expanses from which will be born the fulsome and reflexive consciousness of Sapiens, a species capable of seeing the world and seeing himself in the world. He will see the Other and he will see himself in the Other. Once identified as a double, the double begins to exist in the one who now perceives him—and simultaneously perceives himself. The death of the Other spells the death of the one who has become conscious of that death. What will follow from this residual shock is an immense creativity that Sapiens will ceaselessly exalt.

"Whoa, there, *Négrillon!*" the Baroness interrupts me. "The elephants, the chimpanzees, and the bonobo monkeys are aware of death! In the face of death, they fall silent, they act with compassion, like most mammals. And so, the perception of death exists even before reflexive consciousness comes to titillate the noggin of hominids or inflame the big brain of your Sapiens! Before Sapiens, there was 'consciousness,' my dear, and not only among hominids!"

I tell her: In life, dear Baroness, there's no true beginning in that sense. There's only an alchemy of blind mutations, unpredictable emergences, proliferating combinations. And so you're right, the reflexive consciousness of Sapiens didn't come out of nowhere. Almost all animals have 'states of consciousness,' more or less prolonged, more or less accentuated, more or less intentional or individuated. It's like a property of life that emanates from everywhere, that blossoms forth as it will, and that, at a given moment, and supported by a mutating loop, finds in Sapiens sufficient amplitude and constancy. Sapiens himself will be the fruit of a potential disseminated among hundreds of hominids, each of which will adapt according to his own individual potential, asserting that potential now here, now there, up to the point where it can be transmitted and conferred to all those who are capable of realizing it... From that point on, the question remains: Could there be glimmers of consciousness in the psyche of plants? Another question left unanswered: Could there exist a greater level of consciousness, say, a cosmic consciousness, that would traverse everything that exists and to which we would have access? —"*Alea jacta est*," the Baroness scolds me. "There, you've dipped your toe in the Rubicon!"

The grave will begin the task of filling up the void; it will be the creative confrontation with the mystery of death. The grave will be an innovative protest against infringements on life, the basis for what is no longer just a senseless annihilation. Dying will become the "inevitable and mysterious passage" toward what cannot be known, but which Sapiens will undertake to invent. The first graves protected the head, the face, and the belly of the deceased. They had to keep intact the most significant substrate of what the deceased had been, help him to remain in an incomprehensible elsewhere. He had to be equipped for this voyage into the unknown, and then a set of instructions had to be transmitted by the inexorable means of ritual. The ritual recapitulates the known, lets us imagine what we don't know, and determines what we would like to know, anticipating, in the name of those who remain, what the deceased will soon learn. Ritualization also means that this active proximity with the great mystery now serves to reinforce a collective order, supporting the emergence of an authority imposed on the living. Except in extraordinary circumstances (and even if the graves themselves are reserved in certain places solely for notable persons), nowhere on this planet—except during the Slave Trade, North American Slavery, or in the Nazi camps—will the deceased be abandoned without a hint of enchantment, or without serving to shore up some form of authority. The abandonment of even insignificant remains will itself be the object of ritual. Everything will be conducted in such a way as to ward off decomposition: the grave markers, the pile of stones, the pigments, the shield of swaddling, the womb-like jar, the basket, the uterine cave, the deep nourishing maternal earth, the purifying pyre that renders you consubstantial with the flesh of the world, the immersion in the original ocean genesis or the fertile lime of the marshlands, the exposure to the alchemy of winds and sun, the mummifying grasp of a fragment of eternity... Some will even go so far as to devour the cadaver so as to conserve in themselves the best part, to prolong it in the form of an earthly power. The death of a fellow human being now holds the promise of a regeneration. Disappearance becomes emergence. The fear that death inspires also serves to combat unpredictable disruptions within the group; the invisible is mobilized to bestow meaning and order on the visible world... A good part of what makes the human being human will be born from this brutal confrontation with a life that opens onto death (both in itself and in the world) as an intolerable *beyond*. One can only confront death with imagination's redemptive effervescence: the sacred, the divine, initiation rites, symbols, structuring archetypes, sacrificial fertility, diverse metempsychoses, art, art, art, and a thirst for knowledge that has become insatiable!...

—"All right," the Baroness grumbles, "you mean, the imagination has a horror of the void, that it is from the void that its life-force is born..."

During my childhood, the aura of the gravediggers reinforced the stark void of the cemetery, its charge of fresh sadnesses and faded sufferings, its silence almost completely undisturbed by birds. These gravediggers seemed to have been initiated into ominous mysteries. Some of them recounted that the most active deceased were those who were still remembered, whose tombs were kept clean with fresh flowers and candlelight. These deceased had the force of significant powers at their disposal. The least powerful were those whom no one remembered, those who had no one to love them or hate them. They came to resemble those futile roots that trees perched above cliffs tend to develop. Their tombs, abandoned to random vines and fissures, would float like phantom gumtrees. When a tomb disappeared—it could fall into ruin, then be finished off by City Hall—the deceased would join the public ossuary. Thus, an archive of forces and invisible forms would come into being, composed only of what forgetting had succeeded in taking away.

The gravediggers themselves seemed half-effaced from this world. A boundary crossed over them, which conferred upon them a sort of power. They seamlessly entered and exited the tombs. They touched the bones and the caskets without coming back trembling. They tolerated the deafening silence of the graves without losing their hearing. These gravediggers kept the registry of the tombs, and they knew which of the dead had reached the state of dust and which ones still persevered in a parchment-like aridity, with nails like a dragon's and an ever-growing head of hair like that of a beast. They stood by the bedside of those infants who had lost their way in life and departed early on. Their tombs were austere, with a makeshift crucifix and a clumsy inscription, light enough to be swallowed up completely by the wild grass and the earth. Their brief parenthesis of existence didn't have enough weight to make immortality necessary. Alongside the gravediggers, the sorcerers sold coffin nails, skulls with their jaws attached, wisdom teeth with seven branches, and other bits of bone or skin required for magic spells. The gravediggers, those masters of the cemetery, had the power to seal the tombs with gestures at once terrible and protective. Terrible, because in sealing the cave the gravediggers cut the last tie holding back that other mystery of life; protective, because they lifted the deceased out of the hands of the sorcerer vandals, thus conjuring away—with a perfectly sewed-up seam—any desire the deceased might have to return and sow trouble among those left behind. And so, reigning over the void, the loss, the lack, and the silence, the gravediggers set up their camp at the front lines of an utterly invisible battlefield.

Today the cemeteries are somewhat deprived of mystery, exposed under the light, equipped with barbed wire, criss-crossed by health and sanitation services, standardized by stacks of low-rent vaults. They still lend themselves to magic practices, but no primordial fears protect them. Certain tombs are transformed into meeting points for the hordes of dealers, or into hiding places for the booty of bandits. The homeless sleep there and do their business there; the land of the dead no longer repulses these types... "It's because they're already dead themselves!" the Baroness states with sudden vehemence. "These creatures are empty, just like our cemeteries, which are now inert as they wait to serve some other purpose. You know, they've twisted the railing on the tomb of our Man Ninotte!"

As for zombies—they weren't just the dead; they were also the ancestors, the immemorial lineage of those who lived on the other side of the real, or the other side of the world. It was customary to accord them the first drop from the rum bottle, or leave them a plate to the left on the family table—and that's not counting those everlasting candles that would diffuse a redemptive light for some group of hypothetical survivors. They say that most of our ancestors were derailed by our massive uprooting from the coast of Africa.

They even say that this drama constitutes for us, the other Antilleans, a second origin!

They say that in this deportation there were too many brutal ruptures, too much destruction of foundational myths and principles of decency. They say that there were too many dead thrown howling into the Atlantic with far fewer niceties than one would accord to trash accumulated during the voyage. They say that the surviving captives of the slaveships, upon disembarking in these hellish islands, had kept the memory of some ancestral lineage, a vague recollection transmitted for better or worse to what would become an uncertain progeniture. They say that this transmission took place blindly, in an ad hoc manner, without rituals or methods, that a debris of memories must have been dispersed in the chaos of this Caribbean history dynamited by too many genesis stories, too many myths, and too many cosmogonies. Also, by too many minglings of uncontrollable individuals, isolated men and women swept along by their legends alone, individuals who coupled without respect for the Absolutes. They say that the African ancestors mixed with those of the Americas and of Asia, and that they met up with those phantom armies that penetrated the conquering vessels and the masters' houses. The ancestors from everywhere who took offense at such a confused muddle were numerous, one might even say innumerable. Not knowing where to go nor where to return to, these ancestors populate the depths of our spirit with bitterness... *Oh, what chains, my cherished one!*

Most of our ancestors, those who were wrenched out of Africa, found themselves flung into a frail state of dysmnesia. They were maintained in a state of instability due to the compulsive memory of the body, which exulted in the songs and dances of the drums. Obscure mixtures of songs and dances bound together antagonistic ancestral lines that were confused or poorly defined. The slave masters forbade all figuration. The slightest sign could be established by means of secret amulets, dangerous talismans, diabolical scapulars. And so, over the course of generations of these modified lineages, everything—the drums, pottery, utensils, tools, doors, walls, skin, and clothing—all remained empty, lacking inscriptions, lacking relief, evoking nothing. A disenchanted nudity. Our African ancestors must have had to keep afloat without even the symbol of an attachment capable of re-grounding them, without any path toward the tranquility of an Absolute. Still today, those ancestors constitute, alongside us—the other composite descendents—a past left behind, a past that comes back, a past that dies again and yet does not pass away.

The artists of our Americas are familiar with that deep wound: the original interdiction against all figuration. That interdiction is like an imposed, ultimately interiorized erasure that our artists still have to take into account. The enslaved Africans could—and had to—project themselves into the master's signs and symbols: his coat of arms, his cross, his icons, his songs, even his genesis stories and tales of domination. They were refused the right to develop the least form that might have reanimated lost gods from a tenebrous African past. In the disquiet of the master's mind, every inscription, every cultural form, harkened back to Africa. And every version of the sacred coming from Africa was dangerous to the slave order. The reminder of spirits and gods was part of an effort to re-humanize. To put it plainly, such a reminder was a form of resistance. If music, dance, and stories were from the start lively forms in the Caribbean and the Americas, it is because the gods who dance and sing and tell stories always seem to find a way to accommodate loss and suffering, to disperse tragedy by means of merriment. Merriment is light, like the breeze of the tradewind; it harbors no menace. In contrast, the form—drawn, molded, sculpted, engraved, evoked—which is self-contained, which is immobile and silent, which suggestively makes what it holds or touches shine forth, this form can make use of anything, the worst as well as the best. It can accommodate as it sees fit what the artist wants to project into it. Whereas the dances, songs, and stories could be displayed without too much difficulty through the detour of joyful merriment, the figurative arts would be assigned to the corolla of something impossible and the chrysalis of something unformulable. The artist capable of fabricating forms would be reduced to doing so without the aid of the sacred. And worse: the artist couldn't get to the *work*; he had to sacrifice himself to the *task*. The creative gesture of the artist—Antillean, Caribbean, or American Creole—still confronts this impossibility.

In what has been erased
Each Trace spells out
Each Trace calls out

The re-conquest of Africa (the re-conquest of the sign, of the symbol, of the lost form—in short, of the *erased*) would generate the artistic energy of the Caribbean and American plantations. This energy would also preside over the dynamics of the literary—the novel, poetry, and the theater. Dance and music would not have to embark on this quest: the memory of the body had from the start reinstated an impossible Africa in the rhythms, dances, and songs. The sacred remainders, the specters of ancient forces, were themselves invisible within the drums and work songs. Unless these remainders became excessive, they shocked no one: they were commingled with the tasks of the slave and didn't get in the way of their full execution. The rhythms, songs, and dances were part of the general ambiance of every plantation. Examined more closely, however, they all appear to constitute a kind of detour, one that seems inoffensive at first. At every revolt, at every burst of liberty, each time the glance of a singer started to be inhabited with life, each time the face of a dancer stopped being expressionless, what had seemed absent would instead declare itself: the persistence of a humanity that could not be tamed. What had been obliterated stopped haunting the lacerating wound and started to roar.

Forms submitted to the outline of detour
Shadows waiting
Intention watching over what has been deferred
The Trace informs

The signs, symbols, and forms would manage to persist in the practices of those clandestine resistants known as *quimboiseurs*. These healers had maintained—no one knows how—a science that gave them access to the ancient divinities, and they worked relentlessly to reanimate these divinities in the gods imposed by the master. They were able to achieve this through their creations, antagonistic associations, syntheses, and other transmutations of a compound magic. However, the objects of these surreptitious practitioners would remain denuded. Their spells would not be written down. Their conjurations would mix vestigial intangibles in derivations and blends and their formulas would be re-copied letter by letter on inelegant supports. Nonetheless, when the healers had to fabricate their *quimbois,* these would undergo the work of form, they would inspire the sovereign emergence of the sign.

Quimbois are small assemblages, more or less inspired by Vodou (effigies, bones, plates garnished with ritual objects in the place of spirits, sacrificial animals), that condense so as to disperse more effectively the evils that the *quimboiseurs* seek to vanquish or to direct toward a specific person. The *quimbois* settle at crossroads, hang from trees, and are buried in certain spots... Today, these small "installations" are the only ones that capture the popular imagination. Composed of all sorts of things, organizing intensities of intention and projection, *quimbois* transmit with fear, respect, and awe an obscure grasp of the real. They ordain the real. They impose visions. They bestow authority. They produce artistic shudders. It is from this magic clamor, from this certitude, that the real can be transformed, a real in which there will be born other resistants, such as dancers, musicians, singers, storytellers, and, in the end, our visual artists! *Quimbois* liberated other possibilities for all the other forms! —"Everywhere art appeared, art traveled in the wake of magic," the Baroness reminds me. —Exactly, I tell her, then art stopped being foolish and started to reflect on itself...

No matter what I say or do, the *quimbois* that I see at the crossroads still produce in me the shock, at once ancient and familiar, that is associated with the popular imagination. Despite myself, I fall back into a suddenly distorted reality. Time contracts, the ancient healers rise up from the shadows not yet dissipated by daylight. For me, they are like a cry of memory, a historical reminder, an imperial order to confront a rush of unknown possibilities. I fall silent, I take some distance, or I freeze. In them, beauty can be sensed. I enter into a state of attentive concentration. There I am, before a collection of invisible forces, a concretion of energies that are impossible to identify and that fall into patterns without becoming fixed. They radiate out without dispersing, subjugating me all the more. I pass by the *quimbois* but take care not to get too far ahead of them, just as Césaire advises.

Passing forms and shapeless shadows
Recite to the four roads past and to come,
Lending order to spaces also in the state of becoming

The works of our first true visual artists would have to go in search of an identity. They would organize themselves in groups and schools, making use of ostentatious signs. *They had to overcome that primordial erasure.* They had to reduce the impact of the amputation. The signs, symbols, and forms of Africa, the Amerindian signs, and even the devices of Vodou would, for a long time, provide the battle standard for that search. These remainders permitted artists to ground an esthetic discourse, to take root and become part of the land. *To assume the lack while trying to make it disappear.* But many came to understand that the *fundamental lack* and the *structuring erasure* resist—like a pack of deaf devils—such simple negations, and that denying their existence would mean leaving behind a fertile zone of confrontation only to flail about in insignificance. It was clear to the most talented of these artists that lack and erasure were the first things they had to take on until they could be overcome. Consider, then, this challenge posed to our artists: not only to deny the lack, not only to assume it, but *to make of it an immense horizon*. To express without revealing, to show without showing, to say without formulating the least little thing that might be audible to the appropriate ear. To point out the formlessness necessary to form, its *undecidability*, its points of emergence which became increasingly like beginnings. Thus, the root can become a breath, an amniotic fluid, an erasure that is carried forward, that starts to link everything within reach.

Semblances
Gradual suggestions
The imaginary, alert with possibility

The past of slavery isn't remembered in the way one remembers other things. Certainly not in the way one normally mourns in our lands. Beyond the major uprooting that millions of human beings experienced, the artist sees in the memory of slavery dispersions of shadows, configurations and flows, opacities that sustain and sweep away. The space that's created can be seized at all different levels and let go in the next instant. The figures that flow out of that space can be sketched out and liberated immediately after. Each form establishes itself like a small genesis, produced and still producing itself; each form, when encountered, seems to be in a state of becoming. It is like a warning, the energy of which must be captured very quickly. Consider this: In the dehumanization that was our foundation, that was *our second origin*, the human (this resistance) generated a thousand variants under a thousand different inventive forms, initially indecipherable to us. Our most significant artists and poets remember this impact, this mystery; in everything they achieve, they are informed by it. Ultimately, the perspective that emerges is one in which this vast crime becomes for all, with all, in the name of all, a vast experience.

To inspire the possible
To authorize variation
The butterfly of a nuance

And so, in my childhood, which was exposed to this legendary, this inexhaustible collection of legends about the formed and the formless, the dead were there without really being present. You know about that, dear Baroness. The dead visited people in their dreams, set off alarms, were prodigal with counsel. They showed up in more trivial ways to redress wrongs, to deliver reprimands. Anyone who has had a foot tugged by death retains the white marks on his ankles or tibias. If I never saw the dead—that great never never—I always lived as a child in fear of these recurrences with no rhyme or reason. Dear Baroness, you remember, you saw me leap at times onto your mattress because of nighttime terrors or who knows what kind of unspeakable vision. My dreams were hallucinations. The rooftiles of the house trembled under the passage of... I know not what. The northern wood of the walls on the old framework underwent strange contractions. I could hear the galloping of three-legged horses. The screeching of the AntiChrist's claws on the Syrians' rolling metal curtains. At night, I thought I perceived the limp of a female devil trying to make the clip of her hoofs sound like high-heeled shoes... I am still trying to decipher those nights, to be an expert in the psychology of shadows, bursts of intuition, and luminous tremblings. My intellect has never formulated this precisely, but the person I have become has been affected by this dreadful bewitching of the world. Since then, counter to my own desires and beliefs, I have waited for an oniric visit from that immense disappearance.

Except that for me, our Man Ninotte has never returned.

That, in itself, isn't normal.

As the last one to be born, the mythical frail one, puny from birth, I have had a hard time conceiving that she would not be concerned with what I have become since her momentous departure. I started imagining that she had invited my other brothers and sisters over without my knowledge: Paul, that mischievous musician whom she adored because of his lost-sheep side; or Marielle, the champion basketball player whom she seemed to prefer to everything else on earth; or Jojo l'Algébrique, who sent her into ecstasies because he was so brilliant, and, of course—to each queen her honor due—the Baroness, her alter ego, the only one who looked her in the face at the same height, and whom she couldn't but secretly admire.

The Baroness was the eldest sister. That meant that (if you'll forgive me), having gotten the bad spot in line, she was soon sacrificed on the altar of duties, tasks, and responsibilities. No doubt, she never had the time to dream, to make mistakes, or even to imagine (if only for a second) that life could be as sweet as a bowl of tapioca pudding. She must have had to learn her lessons and those of all the others, do her school exercises and those of all the others, take on tasks (which consumed the entirety of our lives), watch over the execution of the remaining chores that fell to others; take care of herself a bit and take care of others a lot, night and day. She had to be ready to take on the work of Hercules because (in a burst of admiration and, equally, concern) Papa had quickly named her "The Baroness," which meant, in his language, a haughty carriage, chest up, back straight, chin high, a gaze without a trace of weakness, total authority, an aptitude for action, the art of productivity, resistance to wear and tear. If Man Ninotte owed an update to anybody, it was surely the Baroness.

But how to ask her this question?

Not easy.

She was not the type to hold discussions about that sort of chimera. A great pedagogue, highly rational, an escapee from the periods of family poverty, she looked at life as a matter of efficiency, of lack and waste, of justice for all, privileging a concerted solidarity and the application of good sense in all things. She left nothing to chance and distrusted good luck. Whoever deviated from these coordinates attracted the welt of her wrath; she would do no matter what to set you straight. The entire world was accustomed to obeying her, and if her orders didn't transform the world, still no one triumphed through disobedience, and the world retained the mark. To broach with her this business about oniric visits, I had to evoke at length the return of the dead to the people of the earth, the domains of the formed and the formless. I had to tell her that there is beauty in these doubles of the self, that Sapiens had struggled to prolong himself beyond his limits, that there was a neat trick for transmuting any dead person into an ally, a witness, or a foot soldier of eternity's promise. With a considerable amount of verbiage, I told her how the spirits invade the world of graves, how they escape from them like surviving pearls to bear witness *urbi-orbi* to the fact that death is the beginning, that the void is full, that other worlds palpitate beyond this one.

There's not a single group of people on this planet who aren't surrounded by spirits. Spirits accompany daily life, mingle in family affairs, officiate at initiations, sexual rites, cooking methods, fishing, and the how-tos of hunting or agriculture. They reign over the inextricable flow of past, present, and future. Spirits supervise wars, and assure the harvest, govern over enormous cataclysms and extraordinary misfortunes. There exists not a single people for whom spirits do not permeate the world to the point of profoundly humanizing it. With these spirits, nothing is inert, and not a single inch of this planet can be considered vacant. The old trees become envious creatures. The rocks concentrate within the energy of old souls. Anger, gladness, emotion, vengeance, and jealousy all become characteristics of the sun, of stormy weather, of climates, mountains, and forests... There's not a single place where you wouldn't be subject to one of these ghostly presences. Thus, no animal or vegetal creature—not a worm, or an egret, or a flea—can be counted out. Thanks to spirits, our species could extend on forever, electing unusual affinities among all that exists. To grasp his shadow, each individual would see himself flanked by a radiant double. At the moment of burial, the double would begin a voyage into the dense materiality of the living or, alternatively, would haunt the environs to be reborn among the newborns as an animal or even a plant. We have always lived within this swelling wave of disappearances and reappearances, an alchemy of impossible possibilities that everywhere crowns the inescapable Feast of the Dead.

I reminded the Baroness that the graves where the dead lay in the fetal position were the most numerous, that the baptismal rites of certain burials invoked the amniotic fluid, or that old ocean which had undergone stellar fecundations and volcanic inseminations in an astonishing eruption of life. I argued that there had always been this intuition concerning the generative importance of water to the forging of these doubles. As proof that no one is alone, one need only think of twins and imagine Sapiens faced with such a phenomenon. How could one not see in those twins an extension of the miracle of the identical? Imagine that the shadow had come alive? That the reflection had been triggered without the mirror? That the same was suddenly detached? This strangeness, this uncanniness, became a symbol, a knowledge or power. Everywhere twins would inspire a wondrous respect. Everywhere they would be deemed capable of seeing both sides of the world, of becoming the greatest builders or those who have the wisdom of the founding word... And so, dear Baroness, our diverse humanities have lived with this belief that the dead always return to us in one form or another, as though to signal that death and life together nourish each other, and that we must wait for an alliance of all dissociated things, as in the grace of those moments of insight when shadow and light come close to being the same thing—as Saint-John Perse, now gone, sings to us.

Thus, in those early times, death seemed an enchanted thing. The original terror it evoked was strongly present in the expanding minds of young hominids, who countered it with an intensity of enchantment that survives even to this day. And yet, in westernized lands, death is gradually dying, bit by bit. Death is being de-sacralized. The fire of cremation is replacing the nourishing maternal envelope of the earth. And this fire is not the enchanted fire of archaic bonfires or the fire of the glowing pit, but rather the fire of the electric meter in its fumes of mercury and lead, its residues of phosphate and calcium. In the nudity of electric cremations, we seem to lose both death and its double. The old abyss of the beyond that consciousness has confronted yawns open once again. Small rituals, shorn of the sacred and the divine, are recreated in the bewildered hollow of funeral halls. Already new hopes are stirring up the still sterile ashes of our tremulous lucidity. We don't know what will come to replace the double, but it is certain that the void and the nothingness frighten us. From the ashes that we scatter (and, soon after, from the powder of liquid nitrogen or the hydrolysis of pulverization) there arise new doubles that will go in search of a meaning inherent to the living intention of the cosmos... —"I understand these realities," the Baroness replies. "The abyss always emerges once more; you must try to leap over it! But consider this: the double we imagine is no doubt a reflex; it can come with a secular salubrity, an austere atheism, and a stubborn agnosticism! All the double indicates is that there will always be something mysterious in the world, especially where death eternally passes and passes again."

So, I still haven't dared to ask her the question—for one thing, to avoid the risk of knowing that she actually has received this precious visit and, for another, so that she won't have the impression that this matters to me. I simply repeat: Exactly. This old wives' tale is antique poetry. That's what I wanted to say…

LEGENDARY OF THE ANNOUNCEMENT – The Baroness, as the respect owed her required, had been the first to receive the message. On the 31st of December, after attending our family get-together on the cusp of the new year, she had left to go to bed. She had plumped up her pillow and turned off her light and was getting ready to lift the covers over the shelter of her eyelids when she was submerged by a premonition of the worst. As she was attempting to decipher it, the telephone started ringing. Premonition is a kind of carnal vision, a thunderbolt of sharp precision with cavernous echoes. It informs your whole body, tetanizes the nerves, and brings into play that part of your attention not ruled by your conscious self.

The Baroness stopped short at the edge of that void. That's how she found out, even before knowing and understanding what the nurse was channeling into successive warnings from the other end of the phone line. Premonition revealed to her that Man Ninotte had moved on to an irreversable fate. What she already knew—but refused to admit because it was impossible—was what she had to decode from the embarrassment of the nurse as she resolved in herself that she would submit to fate's iron chains. *Oh, what chains!*

When we found ourselves around what remained of Man Ninotte, when we had to confront together—her two daughters and three sons—her fulsome immobility, her absent, mineral passivity, that silence without beginning or end (just as when we had made a circle around the casket that we had to seal shut), we must have understood that a good part of the world had now shrunk, that the horizon had suddenly become deformed, leaving irruptions of emptiness and invisible devastation. A good part of who we were had slipped out of space and time.

Why had time stopped, leaving us adrift like commas on a white page? I don't want to say something wrong, dear Baroness, but I believe that, at the moment of the announcement, *the instant had swallowed us up*. We had been plunged into the greatest depths.

We aren't used to being engulfed in an instant that fuses with us, an instant that we absorb and that utterly absorbs us. No one has that ability. Confronted with this instant, we generally remain just before, or just after, or slightly to the side, and often completely outside of it. But to find oneself in a moment that has to be lived through with no distance, with nothing deferred, with no illusion possible, without a desire that could let in a bit of oxygen, forced to hear everything, perceive everything, feel everything without any order or proportion, is something that stops time short and annuls space... Prudently, the Baroness looks at me, lifting an eyebrow: "There are two questions underlying your rambling, the question of life and the question of time! If you join together two endless labyrinths, you're sure to get lost!..."

I tell her: Borges didn't like novels. He said it was a waste of time to build interminable labyrinths; it was sometimes even impossible to traverse them. In contrast, in the short story (sober, brief, and balanced) there is the possibility of saying precisely what needs to be said with the greatest possible efficiency. That can be done even if your intention is to convey a species of infinity to the reader. Vincent Message[1] explains that after reading *Finnegans Wake*, Borges illustrated his esthetic of the brief and the efficacious with a tale of an Arab king who is plunged into a labyrinth by the king of the Babylonian Isles. During much of his life, an immense labyrinth is being constructed for him, with a complexity that proves bewildering to all simple minds. Our labyrinthed king nearly dies there because the labyrinth has been constructed in such a way that it is almost impossible for him to find the way out. *"Like a novel by Joyce!"* Borges would have grumbled. The king escapes, threatening to make an even better labyrinth for his torturer. A while later, this vengeful Arab succeeds in devastating the kingdom of Babylon, seizing hold of his executioner and giving him some of his own medicine by sending him in turn into an unusual labyrinth, a very Borgesian labyrinth: *a desert!*
He had to confront the complete void that is the desert!
The worst of labyrinths!

---

1 In "Les deux rois et les deux labyrinthes. J. L. Borges, J. Joyce et l'idée d'efficacité romanesque." *Littérature*, 153, special issue on "Narrations," 2009: p. 209.

The desert concentrates everything nowhere, like the center of a slow explosion. It always seems straightforwardly accessible, traversable, but it unfolds without offering any signposts in the oceanic infinity of the sands. At first, the desert seems more effective in that it allows, at least, for hope: it presents neither an entrance nor an exit: it has no stairs, no spiral hallways, no galleries, no impervious walls or monotonously replicating doors. All is clear and open. Nothing interrupts the horizon. The desert allows the creative expression of potential routes without any points of departure. As for ordinary labyrinths, they eliminate all perspective; they spell out the impossible, requiring you to blindly find your way out. In the labyrinth of the Borgesian desert, the problem is to get from one end to the other of a self-renewing infinity; you reach an aperture that opens only onto itself in an inexhaustible explosion in which you remain attentive, in a state of desire. The king of Babylon, who needed the support of a visibly complex interlacing of doors and hallways, couldn't stand it. He should have known that in the overcrowded labyrinth, the kind found in the novels Borges disliked, the problem wasn't to find a way out, but rather to experience (while still desiring serenity) the infinite density of the journey, the mystery, the uselessness and pointlessness, the adventure of the senses, of language, of imagery, of the fire of the mind and the vertigo of the endlessly fecund void. The problem was to annul, in the sudden surging up of a paradoxical desert, the exhausted landscape of habits and the sterile earth of ordinary blindnesses. There's no need to escape from the hallways; it's useless to hurry across the sands. The art is to make an art of the labyrinth, to make it the site of a wandering without triumph, an eternity full of extraordinary and thus savoured moments, a continually unquenched thirst for experiences, oriented by these principles, with no entrance or exit, nourished by intimacy with an impossibility accepted in tranquility... Whatever they might be, labyrinths must not be feared. They oblige us to live intensely.

But let's linger a while on the unfathomable nature of that announcement. On May 8, 1902, just before Mount Pelée annihilated the city of Saint-Pierre and its thousands of inhabitants, a few people had a vague intimation of what was coming. During the preceding months, the mountain had been letting off smoke, erupting with trails of ash liberated from the tombs of the lahars.

Crabs, snakes, birds, and rats were all leaving the area. The countryside (like the city) was already buried in a lunar shroud. No longer was there a green forest, a blue ocean, or rays of sunlight; there was only the beginning of a gray obliteration that the governor of the land (arrogant and sure of himself) believed he could master. He set himself up on the site in grand official pomp with his family. Before that fatal day, many inhabitants of Saint-Pierre had taken off without looking back.

They were driven by fear.

They left, not because they could anticipate the inconceivable force moving toward them, but because they were afraid of dying. Just before the burning cloud that would wipe everything away a few seconds later, there was this strange intimation that spread among the inhabitants. They wandered off; they withdrew. In confusion, they began to complete a task that would save their lives. Some of them left the city without knowing why, taking the last boat before the fateful hour. Others, for the most part those who were isolated, took to the road on foot or on horseback, bringing nothing with them, not knowing why but simply compelled by the need to get away. I imagine that some didn't understand what their intuition was shouting out to them; they stood still and stopped to question themselves and check the everyday reality around them, which indicated nothing out of the ordinary. They didn't budge, but their innermost being sensed what was going to happen, so that by the time they were annihilated by the eight hundred degrees of rock and ash, they already knew they were no longer of this world. When they left that world, they were no longer part of it…

—"Well, that's a pretty thought," the Baroness retorts, "but the evening before something not so banal after all had happened: the eruption of a magnetic storm had rained down on the town, with Dantesque glimmers and the roar of a forge. So, it's possible that this famous intuition you're talking about was nothing more than a final resurgence of fear!" I tell her: Intuition always feeds itself on fear, never on well-being. The clairvoyance of intuition propels itself beyond fear. Those I'm telling you about saved themselves *in extremis*… they glimpsed the beyond advancing toward them!…

Where do the chosen ones come from? How can they, at some point in their life, perceive what is impossible to perceive? Is it a singular faculty of their mind, an acuteness of the reptilian brain, that draws forth from a gene pool thousands of years of vigilance and anticipation focused on survival? Like this group of Sapiens that set out on the mystery of the ocean and made it to Australia? What signs, what birds, what odors, what string of little islands, or what prescience indicated to them—no doubt to only one among them—in the yawning stretch of the horizon, at the other end of the ocean mystery, the generous abundance of an entire continent? For a long time, without being at all sure about it, I pictured these beings as capable of harnessing the disaster, or, alternatively, of sensing the riches, even before they appeared. I pictured this Amerindian who was the first to see a European vessel glide between the bays of his island, who initially heard the immense clamor of genocides and felt the tipping of the world, which, with this first ship, would eventually meet up with its fate. Did he exist, this obscure visionary? Did he howl against a wall of incomprehension, or did he take refuge in the silence of his intransmissible knowledge?

I also imagined this King of the Congo who, from as early as the 16th century, had declared war on the slaveships. I like to think that he had had a premonition that what was taking place there in the Americas wasn't the enslavement of war prisoners—as his people had been practicing for millennia—but instead a barbarian practice totally unknown to all barbarians, an abyss that would for a long time absorb the attention of a good part of humanity's conscience. For a long time, I also imagined these 13th-century Manden hunters in Mali who, when faced with regular attacks on their humanity, produced the first formalized declaration of human rights.

Hunters declare: Every life is a life...
Every life being a life, all wrong caused to life requires reparation.
Consequently, let no one injure his neighbor gratuitously, let no one cause
harm to his neighbor, let no one make a martyr of his fellow man, let
each man watch over his neighbor.
Consequently, hunters declare:
From now on, each person disposes of his own person, each is free in his
actions, each may make use of the fruits of his work.

Such is the oath of the Manden people addressed to the entire world![2]

Many receive the announcement; many discern (beyond the confines of their own absolute convictions) the near totality of the world, and in this totality, a new generosity, often framed by a halo of disasters. And many pass it on, sometimes in silence and incredulity. I imagine them compelled to live with that: the doors of another possible world suddenly opened wide before the astonished hollow of their mind... —"This charter of the Manden is very controversial," the Baroness tells me. "The Mali of Soundjata had nothing like a land of perfect humanism... and even if Unesco has added it to the list of the world's precious possessions, it remains suspect in the eyes of many of those who are in the know..." I say: You have to pity those who are suspicious of poems, or who remove the smallest possible glitters from the firmament of human experience! Whether it comes from the past, the present, or the future, no matter: it came to us!...

Early in the morning, the telephone rings. It's the Baroness, letting everyone know. The news does not come as a surprise but as a total aberration of the possible-impossible. It was expected and it was impossible. It was desirable and it was unacceptable. It was in the nature of things and at the same time it was an abomination. Beneath this shattering of our world, our recourse is to imagine that Man Ninotte is finally breathing the nascent oxygen of deliverance and easy repose, taking those little sips of leave-me-be tonics. That thought helps us contain both the spiral that is sucking us up and the abyss that is opening before us. In that early morning, the birds are beginning to show their customary signs of vigor. They sing the light, you could say. They call forth the light, comfort it, disseminate it to the four winds for the well-being and hopefulness of all. The world that rises out of the shadows seems to want to ignore the news and continue on without us. It's the Baroness who sounds the alarm. Death has become the sun of this day, but the birds continue singing.

---

2 Youssouf Tata Cissé and Wâ Kamissoko, *Soundjata, la gloire du Mali* (Karthala-ARSAN, 1991).

Consider the poetics I subscribe to: *Each form not like a beginning but like an in-beginning.* To give the impression that each thing is beginning, never that something is coming to an end or established for good. To offer the instant of beginning seized in flight, maintained in suspense, deconstructed, in an extraordinary relation to the open all-is-possible. To create a generic space in which agglutinations start to move forward toward evolving organisms, complexes that will have to adapt to times and spaces that have yet to be born. And, on the way, to mobilize archetypes, signs, and symbols, all the varieties of markings, without being able to identify any of them. They are simply invoked, suggested, seized— or better yet: *rigorously poeticized.*

It is as though Being (the consciousness of existence) had lost its absolute meaning so as to stay close to those incessant becomings of the beginning of things. (This is a very fluid, very available, and very open way of existing). This achievement and suspension of all that exists ends up producing a *concentrate* which, in each of its qualified forms, invents its own music and diffuses its own movement.

Under the immense impact of the announcement, we begin by freezing up, like creatures at the first sign of danger. It isn't only the body that is stilled, but also the world as the mind conceives it. The links with all that exists are neutralized. A major suspension contracts the field of perception into itself. Immobility looms up like an ancestral rampart erected in the face of death. Immobility tells death to pass by, tells it that no living thing stands a chance here, and thus there is nothing for it to steal away. Immobility imitates death in order to make it believe that its work here has already been done. Confronted with great crises, almost everything on the great chain of living things makes use of this imitation of nothingness, this sudden tension in *disappearance.*

Who was the first person to use the term "*disparu*" to refer to someone who had died? Who first abandoned the idea of "sleep," of "journey," of "eternal repose," of "passage" to another shore, to land on "disappearance"? Never has a term seemed as appropriate for what it is meant to describe. Instead of letting us deny disappearance (like a certain species of monkey that lugs around the little body of the miscarried offspring until it falls to pieces, an outcome that finally manages to penetrate the wall of instinct, forcing the monkey to integrate that which seemed inconceivable), the corpse simply proclaims to our consciousness that there is no longer anything beyond this skin, these eyes, the flesh of this body—nothing, no person, and above all, not the irreducible existence of the one we loved. The truth that the corpse maintains, what it attests to, is what, even more than what has gone, has suddenly disappeared in the very essence of what remains.

Man Ninotte knew how to decode signs. A spider in the evening would be the promise of sorrow; a large fly in the afternoon confirmed a visit. Mirrors and broken glass told her an abundance of tales. If the palm of her right hand started to itch, money was en route to her wallet. Sometimes a sign of who-knows-what sufficed to impel her in the direction of the lottery booth. A ringing in her ear revealed to her a far-off whisper concerning her own person. I saw her predict with exactitude the advent of bad weather at the apparition of a bunch of winged ants or from the way a large brown cockroach took flight. The black cat, like a *chien-fer* or a nighttime butterfly, presaged nothing good. On the positive side, the left hand wasn't worth the right; the hot required different precautions than the cold. As for colors, their various vibrations triggered a whole set of possibilities... She lived with this dashboard of the sacred. But a negative sign produced in her the same effect as a positive sign: her determination was redoubled. She would leave the house with the same defiance, and the angle of her gait would evoke that of gumtrees in the wind. Man Ninotte, like other adults of my childhood, above all the *manmans* fighting for their brood, kept a lookout for what would come next. Not only bad luck—that old unbaptized enemy—but also the lucky breaks, the thrill of a happiness, the little trifle capable of enlivening the rest of the day. Nothing was settled in advance; if you were attentive, you knew how to apportion the sweet, the spiced, and the bitter. She approached each instant as the occasion for a portent and, like that Zen sage, would lift a finger at the least diversion, suspending everything that was taking place in the vicinity and thereby arresting the continuous flow of our blindnesses.

In terms of the land, it is the conch shell that proclaims with its roar each time someone falls victim to "mortality." I love the way the Creole language names death: *mortality!* Suddenly, that named thing yawns open and threatens everyone. The conch shells were prepared according to an Amerindian practice allowing one to produce and modulate the sounds. After abolition, the former slaves, our matricial ancestors, were afraid that they'd rediscover once again the indistinction of the group that was the general rule on the plantations. Rather than form villages, they scattered in isolated huts on the crest of the *mornes*, the foothills that, over time, gave birth to quarters[3]... To compensate for this dispersal of our huts to the minimal benefit of the hillside communities and neighborhoods, a sense of solidarity was formalized by rites, such as helping someone to raise a home or someone else to plow a rocky slope. The news of these important events had to be transmitted to everyone. They were shared on Saturdays at the marketplace, or Sunday after Mass. For major announcements (the coming of cyclones, catastrophes, wartime conscription...) the signal of the conch shell would be emitted in the manner of the Amerindians to echo in the hillsides. When announcing the passing of a "mortality," the conch almost immediately inspired a gathering. One blast signaled the death of a man; two indicated that of a woman. For the death of a child, no particular pattern seems to have been selected (but that would have to be verified). The sound that signaled the mortality of a human being was grave, powerful, profound. It expressed the wrenching out of something that had been strongly rooted, ceasing *bam!* as if in midflight,

---

3   The French colonizers had organized the land into villages, plantations, and quarters. The word "*quartiers*" first designated the military stronghold; then it was applied to what wasn't a village or that didn't emerge from a plantation. It is often topography that allows us to circumscribe a group of houses under the name "*quartier*." The Creole Quarter is not the village of the first cultivations: the Creole Quarter reaches out in all directions. The village, in turn, gathers around itself a central, almost totemic space. The village surrounds a symbolic structure in which the importance of the individual remains subordinate. The quarter organizes the experiences of individuals in an ensemble of interconnected networks, at once antagonistic and in solidarity.

creating suspense. Then a silence would fall from the entire sky. That silence was part of the call.

The sound of the conch modulates very little. At first, it can appear cursory. However, linked as it was to a system of information, it transmitted all that had to be known about the deceased. What was known of the disease or the weakness of someone in this or that quarter found its missing complement in the conch's tone. The signal reverberated from one foothill to the next, from one quarter to the next, in a radius that would be that of an ordinary person walking, since during this period everyone always walked, everyone walked far, and everyone walked for a long time. After the sonic alert of the conch, the word, as it traveled, would furnish the details. Over the course of several hours, walkers, pedlers, merchants, eternal wanderers, and occasional voyagers would all add further details and spice up the gossip. Finally, there came the "burial announcement," the funeral notice, written or unwritten, that took off at a run along the roads, thanks to the labors of the town criers. Everyone felt involved—whether they knew the person who had been struck down by mortality or not. One simply had to identify their domicile and go there at the close of day. At the first sound of the conch, people nearby would run to the house of the deceased to be of help to the family—as if to reinforce life's resilience when confronted with *that thing*. The hut of the deceased would fill up very quickly; no one could conceive of leaving someone to face such a situation alone. When mortality started to circulate on the earth it was channeled through ramparts of lively solidarity and through bursts of cordial compassion that held in awe its contaminating power... Out of this, there came those who possess the science of washing the dead.

Washerwomen of the dead!
These were ordinary-looking women. They didn't hold your attention at all until you learned the nature of their art. From then on, what was ordinary about them didn't stop being so, but not a single inch of their person left you indifferent. Like gravediggers, they were stationed at the unstable border between shadow and light, inside and outside, the comprehensible and the incomprehensible. Their profession forced them to be solitary their whole life long. They came to it by who knows what series of accidents and

never left it behind. It was said that their children would become seers and that they tended to lose their purpose in the midst of life.

It was not in the city of my childhood that this practice was revealed to me. There, the sound of the conch shell remained far away in the distance, in the crests and the ravines, while in the streets and on the sidewalks, all that resounded were fragments of words that Saturday merchants managed to distill concerning disappearances that had occurred in remote corners of the land. Sharing the news of a death constituted a vital knot in the social fabric of that time; denying death was established as a collective duty. During a vigil, it was as a collective—among friends and enemies, neighbors and strangers—that the mortal rupture could be repaired. You had to be there; you had to be one of them. The demand was so strong for this social cohesion that the radio would take up the relay, instituting long funeral announcements as the conches fell silent. This practically imperative call to assembly was transformed into a simple news item on the radio; it was up to every individual to figure out what should be done. And yet, at 1 PM, the countryside (already quite urbanized) fell still once again as people listened to the frequently interminable list of the deceased.

Depending on the heart's nature and the ear's desire, that list could resound either like a death knell of misfortune or, alternatively, like the chiming of deliverance.

Here the shadow is not cast
Does not cast itself
Like a trace, it brings and carries away

Everyone is impressed by a giant conch shell—with its crown of points, scalloped pavilion, and rosy mother-of-pearl spiral. The conch emanates true majesty as it ages and its forms achieve balance. Amerindians consumed the flesh of this mollusc but elevated its shell to a means of passage from this world to the invisible one. A few conch shells placed around a tomb sufficed to guarantee a communication between the depths of the earth and the spheres of the sky. By making use of them, one addressed the living as well as that ocean of the dead. To augment the power of a *quimbois* object, all you had to do was present it in a conch shell, at the base of its spiral. The object would acquire a considerable power of attraction and the ability to repulse certain evil spirits. A shell "charged" by its magic object could be buried under the threshold of a hut or planted in a Creole garden. Or else it could be positioned in such a way as to stand guard over a buried pot of gold. Some used ordinary shells as weapons or as materials for a dike to tame a river. Others mixed shells with ingredients from the lime kilns to make cement. It was the surviving Amerindians who transmitted these customs to the colonizers and the African slaves. Passed down to us through accidental minglings and the clash of encounters, they slowly lost their lofty meanings. Even this species of conch is now of declining significance. Its shells persist among us, hardly enchanted anymore, due to an absence of folklore that wears them down. The ones we still get a glimpse of seem to announce their own disappearance. Dear Baroness, examine closely each shell: each one bears within it a world that has lost its public; each one bears within centuries that have fallen silent.

In what the shadow outlines
The Trace dances
The Trace sings
Peaceful and without limits, the Trace bends us its way

In our neighborhood, the washerwoman of the dead was almost always the first to arrive at the home of the deceased. She would identify the "master of the dead" and would do nothing further without his approval. That title always intrigued me. At a certain moment in one's life, one might become a "master of the dead," standing at the helm of the terrible ship, responsible for the conditions in which the dead could pass over to the other side, but also accountable for the actions that had to be taken to avoid contamination. This "master," without ever acting on his own, had to watch over the preparations of the house, never taking his eyes off the washerwoman as she worked.

I must tell you about the work of these women who washed the dead.

The intervention of a washerwoman was never as simple as just washing the body: the dead had to be *prepared*. A washerwoman had to extract the body from its miseries, organize what it had lost, equip it so that it would be ready for whatever came next... The body had to be made presentable in the appropriate way for the spirits and for the people attending the wake. Not a single drop from the bath could be lost or remain behind. The washerwoman had to watch over the body's flawless disposal. The dust of the room had to be gathered up then carried away the next day to be eliminated by someone trustworthy and according to a special method.

And that was the simplest part.

The most difficult was this: it was the quality of the deceased person's life that determined the way he died. It was said that those who had prayed a great deal during their lifetime displayed a luminous tongue, fingernails of virginal blue, and a face whose wrinkles vanished on their own. Those who had never prayed—or who had been very naughty, causing significant damage to the entire earth—would find themselves disfigured by grimaces, with eyes of ember carbonizing their eyebrows and eyelids. Some, at the arrival of the washerwoman, would spit out their evilness; it emanated from everywhere in substances difficult to describe and even harder to clean. Some tried to escape from the treatment imposed on them: their bodies would be covered with a nauseating paste, legless bugs, or sulfurous ashes. These became impossible to manipulate in any way. We saw bodies with mushroom skins or covered with scales that had to be detached, one by one. We saw bodies with the down of ortolan bunting sprouting from their armpits, or with little branches of basil growing out of their ears... Faced with certain catastrophes, some washers would make their escape, crawling away on their stomachs; others would start to cry like burst cisterns. These had to be whisked away as quickly as possible, and a matron a bit better prepared, more experienced, would have to be found. A rare few of the disappeared were the blessèd sort: they displayed movie-star faces to the body-washers, fairytale smiles with the innocence of Le Petit Prince, beatitudes that the washerwoman could only caress and, with humble propriety, render a little less glamorous...

—"I see what you're trying to insinuate," murmured the Baroness. "The washerwoman was leaning over death's senseless abyss. Using all sorts of nonsense and visions, the best ones could make it bearable. Those who ran away didn't have the strength of imagination to compensate for the great void that sucked you in..."

I reply: The best ones were undoubtedly artists of the mystical—or better: poets of an ancient dimension...

But let's try to get to the crux of the matter.

During the period preceding the burial, the "master of the dead" would stand right at the edge of the abyss. Every moment, he had to feel the glacial breath of the one storytellers call, in familiar terms, *Bazil*.

Bazil, for us Creoles, is nothing other than death personified.

Storytellers, washerwomen, those who cast spells, diviners, and sorcerers... no one could describe Bazil. There was no scythe, no black veil, no cart spiked with tibias, no bony orbits hidden in the back of a hood. Just his name. And, also, there was the fact that he was pale, due to his kinship with slave masters. All the initiates treated him with the distant familiarity that you would show to a nasty dog you couldn't get rid of and that wouldn't let you go. The fact that he was never described reminded us that he opened the door onto nothing but a void; he was a brusque reminder of the beyond... To find oneself "master of the dead" was to enter precipi-tously into a tête-à-tête with Bazil; it wasn't about drinking a cup of punch or slapping down dominos or having a chat. You couldn't attend to anything else—no sudden gestures, no useless words, no embellishments to your teeth, no crumpled linen or sloppy appearance. The only admissible attitude was silence, slowness, dignity, and maximum concentration on the beating of one's heart. We had seen one master of the dead remain completely speechless as a result, with veiled eyes and hair gone white. But we had also seen some masters of the dead grow in strength and wisdom; they would become interesting people from then on... The body-washers bowed down before the master of the dead and didn't lose sight of his slightest gesture. He became the point around which everything in the house pivoted, like a silent navigator, standing erect at a helm he didn't touch and fixing his eyes on a horizon that nobody else could see. The master of the dead remained in this state for several months after the coffin was placed in the vault, that is, for the time it took the body to complete the first of its transformations. From then on, this master of nothingness (who could sense the uncomfortable frontier of things, there where the immense vertigo of the beyond starts to quiver) was able to rejoin, sincerely (and with relief), the reassuring side of life.

At the break of day, as soon as we heard the announcement, we each started out for the hospital. The lonely elevator. The empty corridors, half-lit. We were each welcomed upon arrival by the Baroness. It was as though she were holding out to each and every one of us a supportive buoy. To see her standing there, full of energy, almost smiling, still confident about I know not what, indicated to us, with auratic authority, that it was possible for us to be confident too. Each of us went to the bedside of Man Ninotte's last repose to assess once again what we already knew, and to discover the weight of what we didn't yet know. It was like grabbing hold of a handle of something just about to escape, finding it in your hand but not really knowing what to do with it.

We created a circle around her.

We created life around her.

We created love, sadness, distress.

We created refusal, protest, resignation, loss.

We created courage and cowardice.

We did everything one does when one doesn't know what to do.

Everything in us strove to restore to her what she had given to us, and thus to ward off the abyssal immobility that wasn't her, but was the last support for what remained of her...

There is that gesture of lowering the eyelids onto the defunct mirror of the pupils that are now fixed upon the inconceivable, lost in the nothingness... pupils that will never be inhabited by anything again.

To frequent the impact
There, where the Trace inaugurates its stories
At the swerve of the formless and its in-beginnings
And the obligatory relation to blank horizons

How could we not check to see if something had changed in the order of the world? But all was in place. Attenuated, and as if anesthetized, but bristling with sharp, almost unintended clarities. The crystalline sun of January... An odor of disinfectant... one of the last bumblebees under a bell-shaped flower of the thorn apple... Warm asphalt, the dead wood and rusty roof tiles... The anolis lizards exposing their cold flesh to the warmth of the gates... The wan breeze already announcing the asphyxiation of the dry season... The dews beading wonders on the leaves of the laurel tree... Since it was very early in the morning, the traffic hadn't yet swallowed everything up. From the car, scrolling past on both sides, you could see the quiet calm of the gardens, the sleeping houses, a lightbulb's glow behind a blind, the edge of the route abandoned to wild grasses and small bits of trash... The town was shaking off its stillness in a swell of awakenings. Everything was in place. The scale of what had just happened to us was not such that it would trouble the normal course of things. No alarms. No trainwrecks. Except that we were let loose, floating, ejected from an ultimate innocence, a bit uprooted, with the sensation of being utterly unique and altogether insignificant in the midst of the impassive flow of life.

These moments were so completely joined to me that I couldn't reach them. To be so pressed up against the present, to find yourself as though hemmed in by it, is something that prevents you from putting off what you can't avoid, while still making it impossible to admit to yourself that it has happened. Now, after all these years, with this necessary distance, I try to examine these moments once and for all, sensing to what a great extent I had been swallowed up by them, and yet how much they were lost to me. All that remained was a slowly unfolding amazement, an immobilizing fright. Not the suffering of the child that enflames you to the point where you can't breathe nor the suffering of the adult, who only confronts brittle rigidities, but a complete stupor, the kind that engulfs and consumes horizons.

The birds were still singing.

Those birds that did not sing were in a state of wonder as they hopped in the abundance of light. The entire day, as Césaire put it, had the taste of childhood.

THE EJECTED

*But here is where the Baroness presides over the
adventures of all kinds of survivors and survivals*

Man is made of what he has and of what he lacks.

> —Ortega y Gasset, cited by Edgar Morin in
> *L'Humanité de l'humanité*

The lord whose oracle is at Delphi neither reveals nor conceals but gives a sign.

> —Heraclitus of Ephesus

LEGENDARY OF THE GROUP – Gathered around her memory in a tight row, we approached the abyss, and, in silence, like a lost tribe on a voyage with no shores, with no movement, just the spiraling of a mind at the mercy of what was now a collective howling, we bowed under the irruption of a new order that deformed things and removed meaning from where it had once been found.

But access to the lost tribe begins with a sudden solitude.

Sucked under the wave of this terrible news, we had all, in some way, become aware of ourselves, become aware of the absurdity and the fragility of our own existence. If she, our Ninotte—so strong—if she who had protected us from everything, who had proved herself capable of conquering almost anything, if she could be broken and then disappear like that, it meant that the abyss was at our heels. And that it was inevitable. So much strength, so many nighttime vigils, so many hopes, so many struggles from the moment the day began, had suddenly contracted violently to come undone at the impasse of suffering and the stillness of oblivion... Swept away without remainder: our dreams, our ideals, our lovely certitudes, what animated us day after day under the trellis of illusions! What mattered most was suddenly obscured. We all found ourselves wading in the ruins of what had abruptly become pointless, and that lay prone all around us.

As long as she was there, it was still possible for us to be children.
    The archive remained alive.
    The option still existed, even if the desire to resort to it had never been awakened.
    The fact that she was there preserved for each of us the most intimate part of the illusion. Day after day, she would stitch back together the rifts in its fabric. She was the shield that protected our backs, an anchoring buttress on the slope of our lives. She preserved for us the possibility of regaining this universe that she had made for us. Now, an entire backdrop had been swept away, the great landscape of origin summarily erased. Her disappearance exposed us to violent winds. We each found ourselves forced to be what we had become and to persevere, pursued by the abyss. Thus, she closed off our childhood, all of a sudden, without warning.

To name something ruthless, merciless, and pitiless, the Creole language says it is "without a *manman*." The language's most terrible insults are directed solely toward the mother. At school, no fight could get started without a slur concerning someone's mother. That's where the energy of rage could be found.

In the school courtyard, when two combatants faced off and, despite the eagerness of the crowd, were actually not so keen on getting their butts kicked, all you had to do was take two stones that would then represent their respective mothers and set one down near one combatant and the other within reach of the opponent's foot. The bloodthirsty crowd had to invest a lot of meaning in those stones. A simple kick from one of the protagonists at the stone of his adversary would trigger a deadly combat. The *manman* could inhabit anything—a sound, a word, a rock, a sketch, a bit of whatever. The idea alone conferred maximal force to a thing. For the old-timers from around here, the *manman* is the origin of all that is best: kindness, tenderness, love, dignity, honor, pity, and compassion. When this origin disappears, life can be swallowed up by bitterness, or else the heart of solitude can gain the upperhand, leading one to locate in one's own self the foundational source, the essential principles.

Now, we found ourselves reassembled once again. This proximity brought her back, Man Ninotte, the vast body that was her and that embraced us all: the Baroness, Marielle, the second sister, Jojo l'Algébrique, Paul the musician, and me, that last little spark of her womb. We composed ourselves into a horde, a clan, a tribe, by once again becoming part of her... But, more precisely, we became a tight *group* of the same blood and the same torment. This collective located our newfound solitude under the benevolent protection of a far vaster wing. Willingly, we flowed back into this original comfort, as though dissolving in a trance. We were no longer ourselves, but *the children of Man Ninotte*, and, at the same time, because of this clustering together in the face of danger, we each felt affirmed in our irreducible singularity. Man Ninotte had made us, had made herself with us, and without her we had to pursue what she had made, what she and the lineage that preceded her had made. To be grouped together saved us from losing our way; it brought us back to a dominant order that swallowed up what each of us had individually become. We were divided between this instinctual refuge in the group and the irrevocable isolation that was about to befall us.

But once again, the origin of the human could be found right at the heart of what we were so spontaneously doing. When you think about it, you realize that Sapiens—and the clump of hominids that remained on the sidelines of Sapiens' ascension—must have organized their initial survival in groups composed of around twenty individuals. This way of forming a cluster of individuals was fluid; it was a gathering of adult women and men, the elderly, and children, brought together by procreation or circumstance. To be more numerous would have made displacements, rapidity, and the effective organization of necessities more difficult. To have been less numerous would have worked against the ability to respond to the exigencies of the hunt—the windfalls or the brutal losses. Before the family, clan, or tribe, there emerged the tactical and operational group. No doubt, this formation was reinforced by the imitation of animal groupings. It permitted them to be stronger when facing the enigma of the world and its dangers. Since the world was empty, filled only with swarms of animals, vegetal creatures, mineral wonderlands, and elemental forces, each individual had to cling instinctively to those who shared the same concerns—or, let's say, the same fragilities. Somewhat in the way that the magnetic force of a wave concentrates compatible atoms in the midst of the immensity that surrounds it.

All around that prehistoric group, space unfolded, immense. To meet another group was quite rare. Even before the dangers and practicalities of the situation could be assessed, the surrounding emptiness itself required clustering for survival. Children were raised collectively by all; the father didn't exist. Sexual functions, subject to the dictates of space, ensured, perhaps on their own, a healthy mixture of genes. The leader was a contingent figure and could be exchanged for someone else. Power was only established with the emergence of the community and its symbolic restraints, which were useful for allowing a large number of people to act in concert. Wandering was a way of inhabiting, and this way of inhabiting was slight. The rule was: a fluidity of recompositions in relation to encounters and departures. The group could be split up to achieve operational agility or to resolve an internal misunderstanding. Thus, the group could be reborn in an altered form that reinforced its spirit. Individuals nourished the group, but the group existed perhaps without the members even being conscious that they formed one. In the engravings and drawings that the Sapiens and their precursors have left us, there are practically no representations of the human, only the display of an ensemble of select animals—not even all animals, not even those that were most frequently hunted. We often see the same animals again and again, those which constituted vehicles for fantasmatic projections. The few human silhouettes that appear here and there, much less polished than those of animals, are ancillary or indeterminate. Among the millennia of engravings which have been found, we find no sun, no stars, no moon, no landscape, no insects, and not the least depiction of daily life. The world seems to have been erased under the hegemonic force of the strongest or most desirable animal. The group couldn't see itself, and the group couldn't see the individual, who also couldn't see the group.

It is said that the imprints left on the ground by the desired prey, the sought-after prey, the unknown prey, provided the forms for the first alphabets. These imprints could be read one by one, and they could be combined to the point where they could be arranged in a series of stories to form, eventually, a library. The prints, their forms and their depths, introduced the possibility of a complex system.

The imprint, which became a mark, might have inspired the use of signs within the group.

The mark must have preceded the sign: the mark must have a meaning to achieve the status of a sign.

The mark is not really thought out consciously, whereas the sign rises out of an intention.

The mark inaugurates, whereas the sign expresses.

The mark functions as an indication, whereas the sign recounts.

The sign captures the invisible.

The sign is a silence that speaks and constructs.

The sign could recall the visible when it was no longer there.

The sign accentuated what passes. Indicated dangers. Revealed things never before seen or encountered. Signs oriented. Invoked. Convoked. Threatened. They constituted over time the archive of what was not there but continued fully to exist. The antici-patory hominids, but above all Sapiens—that terrible, creative force—placed on their arms, bones, oars, boulders, cliffs, and skins a plethora of signs to express the inexpressible... The sign imposed itself on the enigma of the world. It created the idea, the individual, the emotions, the particularity of sensation. It captured the fluctuating; it was the first shudder of the imaginary still trapped in the bedrock of magical thinking. It established orders, prayers, desires, and organized the senses of the mind, and it constructed a friendly landscape within the still menacing landscape. Groups of Sapiens lived increasingly in their signs, projecting themselves into them. These signs protected them from the disquieting silence of existence. Immediately after the animal imprints, handprints must have been among the first marks to be raised to the status of signs. Handprints continued to serve as a means of expression on the walls of caves, rendered in positive color or in negative shadow. The hand-become-sign bears witness to the shudder of a muse individuating itself from the deepest deposits of the collective gangue, which still dominated completely.

Fine rains
Fern leaves
Car windows
Pearly streams and glistening gardens
The texture of a plenitude

Now, consider this paradox: almost none of the signs that Sapiens and his cousins left out in the sun have come down to us. Only those engraved in the dark womb of the cave have survived. The expressive intensity of these walls suggests that there existed an equivalent outside in the sun. A profusion of marks, signs, representations, and gestures must have covered the enigma of their world. This visible mesh placed on the invisible-of-the-visible constituted us; it still lives on with us. What was offered to those wondrous kingdoms of shadow could only be incantatory, a quasi-religious outpouring. What was offered to the light must have concerned the prosaic part of life: necessity, action, the ordinary expression of each person in a communal space. That is precisely what was obfuscated in the light: the prosaic. Now, all we have left is the sun. The darkness of the caves must have suggested a reunification of unknowns—dream and emotion, desire and fear, lyric ecstasy, a solitude in solidarity, the extreme intensification of time and space, the very substance of the possible and of human sensibility, all the promises of a fabulous realm of conception.

The day dissipates; the night concentrates.

Human groups used to live in the light, on the threshold of the caves. Their depths were the domain of seers, shamans, or of those whose lineage was very close to the poets to come, those whose enterprising imaginations would become a way of knowing. The wall of the cave provided a sort of skin, an antenna, a resonating membrane, for the ensemble of mysteries. It allowed direct contact with the substance of the non-visible. Numerous hands would be placed upon it. Innumerable points, stripes, lines, implanted teeth, and bits of bone... Repeated throughout millennia, and forever indecipherable. The archive of the inaugural question, of the founding desire to understand, of the vow to make order out of the mystery—all this can be found there, in the unattainable depths of the shadow. It is the shadow that transmits to us in enigmatic form a hint of what the light withdrew from us. —"And so, the shadow teaches," the Baroness says hoarsely. —Let's put it this way: daytime exalts the human and nighttime takes him even more deeply into himself...

Think of those two stones in the school courtyard that become *manmans*: they come to us from so far away! Of course, Sapiens always accorded to mineral majesties the magnitude of a veritable existence. In numerous mysticisms, the density of stone represents the utmost concentration of light, shadow, and symbolic possibility. But this faculty of projecting a mental universe onto whatever can lend it support, this ability to transmute an imaginary, will come to constitute an uncanny power. It is by this means that the group will be transcended, that the hundreds, then thousands, then millions of Sapiens will be simultaneously exalted and horrified, carried away or inspired, solely by the construct of an imaginary landscape. Some lives will be swallowed up by this imaginary landscape; generations will lose themselves in it, body and soul; gods and devils will emerge from it; and heroes will come to incarnate it. Sapiens will put many things in the place of these stones. When such supports become useless, the same effects will be provoked just with the expansion of an idea into a system, which will then be able to galvanize every single one of our bodily cells. There is not a weapon, not a wall, not a bit of barbed wire, not one of our disasters, nor one of our marvels that isn't borne by this transmutation.

A walk under the guavas
Counting the cocoplums and the blackbirds
And the great inhalation at the crest of the foothills
Every day

The slavers made sure to mix together different ethnic groups in the hold of their accursed boats. They feared contacts that might lead to orchestrated revolts. But this dispersion wasn't sufficient. Secret communications took place all on their own.

There, again, groups formed.

The group transcended the efforts to disperse it, engendering aggregates of desperation or of elementary survival, mimicries of total annihilation or strategic outbursts. The formation of the group sustained the captives who hurled themselves overboard all at once in one movement, or those who were found dead, smothered all at the same instant by swallowing their own tongues. The group formation was the matrix of those indignations that permitted the captives to summon the individual members to take hold of the deck and sometimes the helm and the sails, to massacre the sailors of the crew, or to survive a shipwreck... Over the centuries, the primordial instinct of the group outwitted the deathly safeguards of the slavers.

Numerous Africans were able to escape from the slaveships as they approached the islands or arrived on the banks of the continent. Losses. Wrecks. Epidemics. Revolts. Juridical muddles forcing the release of a shipment. These escapees found themselves alone or in groups on the *chiquetaille* of islands, the solar bays and the tortoise-harboring sands. They disappeared into the dry brush or the humid forests. They encountered Amerindian peoples who lived there. The Africans were taken in, even welcomed. The Amerindians had undoubtedly not yet integrated black beings into their mythologies of evil; their social structure, still somewhat close to a loose grouping—semi-nomadic, mobile, reactive, relatively open—must have taken care of the rest. The escapees mingled freely with those who had saved them. They constituted those clusters of "Black Caribbeans" that the colonizers must have confronted among the other Amerindian warriors. Imagine the terror of these sailors when Black Africa surged forth like a ghost of vengeance from the depths of the *kanawa*, those long Amerindian canoes. The Black Caribbeans vacillated, partially hovering in the margins of the communal structure that had adopted them, and partially existing in the impossibility of returning to any community inspired by the ancient ways. Their mixed phenotype and their fragile memory, unburdened by the weight of ancestry, constituted the basis for an African impossible, an Amerindian impossible, and an indecipherable future. Some must have forgotten Africa; others must have known the torment of the desire to return, and most built new existences between the lack and the gift: the lack occasioned by a lost land, and the gift of a natal earth... From that point on, they were to produce no foundational myth.

Nothing gets in the way of the instinctual cohesion of the group: it is nascent oxygen and vital energy. Very early on, the prehistoric group was open to the crucial intermixing of genes; it absorbed them, made them reverberate on into infinity. During their territorial conquests, the Sapiens mingled with all the hominids that they encountered: Ergaster, Erectus, Neanderthal... And that's not even counting those which haven't been identified yet. Sapiens is fundamentally a mestizo. All of us have these genes, these names, these histories, these worlds: these *disappearances*. The prehistoric group speaks the matricial language of all languages, inaugurating much more weighty and complex modes of organization, such as the nations, states, and empires, from which will rage the unbridled will of Sapiens.

The Creole group, arising from the contact of cultures and civilizations at the time of the colonial violence, built itself on random composites of diversity. Not only through a mixing of cultures, but also through a *culture of exchanges and contacts*. The Creole group opened up onto a community never known before, introducing a diversity of interminglings, the transformation of lacks, losses, and emptinesses, with the unpredictability of a flux that was relational, accelerated, massive and intense.

The plantation was structured around the enslaved mother and her children. The father—the authority, the law—was the master slaveholder. He possessed all the power. Over the women, the children, and the entirety of the livestock. The progenitors of the enslaved were dissolved into the herd. The women were organized around their progeniture. Alongside the mother, there stood the *manman-doudou*, or grandmother, the sisters, and the first cousins. A second ring could be composed of cousins and allies met along the way. This enlarged coalition was organized in an impromptu manner: in the absence of a functional male father, the coalition of women distributed the functions of authority, tenderness, fusion, or discipline among the nebula of women. However, that coalition was not considered a viable family. Around this core, there swirled the men. They provided the most urgent necessities and, at times, some welcome surplus. But they remained temporary residents, more or less voluntarily temporary, beyond the group that was composed of women and their children. This core was supple, open, fluid, as opposed to the closed nuclear family structure of the master or of other immigrant groups.

With respect to the family, the Creole formation is infinitely open. When I was a child in the streets of Fort-de-France, the adults who wanted to identify me after I'd done something naughty would ask me: *Saki manman'w!?* "Who is your mother?!"… The mother alone situated you. When the father was a stable presence, and when he could be named, the mother was given his first name: Man Ninotte thus became *Man Joj*, "Madame Georges"—a way of saying: the wife of Georges, my father. But the given name of the father remained no more than an appendix to "*Man*," solitary and solar.

Of the song in the marinades
Of the joy in the Calalou
And of the sweetness in the Féroce

When they took flight, there was no space for enslaved Martiniquans to form tribes, villages, or communities based on former practices. Mount Pelée, rising abruptly, full of impracticable ravines, was the scene of hunts led by slavehunters and packs of watchdogs. To survive, the fugitives had recourse to the instinctual organization of the group, that informal formation—light, fast, continually adapting, coming apart to reconstitute itself a bit later, and leaving no visible impact on the ecosystem of the woodlands. They planted a few roots, or several plants that vanished into the vegetal profusion. Their makeshift shelters were of light bamboo; all that could subsist in their encampments, only partially visible, were ashes of a hearth and some scattered rocks. To detect their traces was an art form. They were the invisible inhabitants of the great woods, just like the zombies or those Amerindian divinities, the *maboyas*. For the most part, the formlessness of the group permitted them to maintain a state of patient survival, and to constitute at the right time a dangerous striking force. On the large islands of the Caribbean, or in the Guyanas, tribes of escaped Blacks could take advantage of a vast back-country where they could reform several operational elements of their original communities. But on the smaller islands, the clustering of the maroons offered another way to resist as a collective, one that, at the propitious moment, could ritualize the encounter, thereby producing a union that was useful to all. The group formation leaves each individual some space to manoeuvre. These spaces connect without one ever canceling out the other. Nothing can be cumbersome; everything must be made from hardly anything, the almost nothing of subtle intensity and of desire. We come from that.

In the cities, the enslaved Blacks reconstituted what they were able to recall of the former communities. They created associations called *Nations, Powers, and Convoys*. Flush with several dozen members along with a set of protocols, they possessed a king, a queen, princes, princesses, squires, counselors—a multiplying hierarchy. These trifling dignitaries strolled about in great pomp during religious festivals or under the extended license of the *carnaval*. Hats with plumes, epaulettes, gold buttons, crests and banners, and tutelary colors maintained the decorum... In this display, which was sometimes considered grotesque, none of the masters discerned what was an attempt to re-humanize, a refusal of the degradation they had imposed, an indefinable resistance that harbored pride. It was the way the enslaved Blacks developed to exist in a community that was at the same time impossible to realize, a way to inscribe their intention in a form that had disappeared.

At the beginning, these associations were constituted on the basis of identical ethnic origins. But since the members of the same ethnic group were of insufficient number—because they had been dispersed over the ensemble of islands in such a disorganized way—the groups integrated those who wanted to be integrated, those who agreed to adopt the rules and who aspired to a clandestine dignity. *The Nations, Powers,* or *Convoys* crafted ostentatious protocols, but they had no brace of symbolic beliefs, they were in no way paralyzed by the suns of genesis stories or foundational myths. These associations existed in an inhabited void. In a generic lack. At that point, despite their spectacular decrees, they too found themselves animated by the energy of the group, an energy that transcends all the ruptures to form the spearhead of a renewal.

The revolts mentioned in the colonial chronicle were sporadic. Far more common, more part of the ordinary course of things, were the poisonings, fires, and assassinations. A Creole formula (surely invented by the masters) states: *Konplo neg sé koplo chyen* (the plots of Black men are the plots of a dog)—meaning that they are noisy, inconsequential, predictable. Many a revolt must have been thwarted, but some still unexpectedly occurred. *The Nations, Convoys,* or *Powers* never orchestrated visible revolts. These were the result of individuals who suddenly coalesced into a group, united by the urgency of an identical anger. That same exigency transcended individual situations, transforming the revolts into dramatic flare-ups. Historians recount only a few small events, scattered throughout the archives of the tribunals. It has been difficult to make them admit that these human conflagrations acknowledge the continuing presence in us of uncontainable flashes of lightning and thunder.

It's not a hindrance
If the night is greater than the star
The star is there

On May 22, 1848, in the city of Saint-Pierre, a slave uprising forced the governor to proclaim, in anticipation, the abolition of slavery. The decree coming from France would arrive in the country a bit later. There was an exchange of fire. Houses were burned down. The Martiniquan Separatists made this date into a national holiday, a founding moment; they raised it to the rank of a "revolution." A historian from Martinique protested against this designation, which he judged abusive. He said, basically, that it had been nothing more than a peasant revolt, that it involved only a couple of dozen individuals from one part of the country, the rest of the enslaved population having remained perfectly silent in a posture of wait-and-see. Here, the historian, bent over the altar of his discipline, brandishes the model of European revolutions and seeks to apply that model to the explosive actions of the group.

There exists a profusion of names around the family title of Man Ninotte. There is *Oliny*. There is *Solbiac*. There is *Balthazar-Christine*. There is *D'Artagnan*. There is *Daribo*. There is *Marlet*. In all these names, we find the name of the progenitor, of the adoptive father, the imponderable liaisons of blood and of backgrounds among the quarters of La-Bélème, La-Belfort, and Vieux-Pont. The name with animal and bird resonances came to her from her husband, our papa Georges, who comes from a similar intermixing. And that's not counting the string of surnames and diminutives. The Baroness spent a good deal of time trying to untangle this impossible genealogical tree. Personally, I like it when the different branches mingle, when the twigs lead nowhere, when I find leaves unattached or flowers that are impossible to identify. Mysteries, too. Just like the objects, the furnishings, or the horses, the enslaved person had no name. Just a nickname or a surname. The business of naming was for masters and for persons whose existence was sufficiently legitimated to possess the status of personhood. For us, in the formless form of the group, it isn't the branches and roots that legitimate the names, the given names, the family names, but rather the stories that bear witness to a link of kinship or adoption, proximity or companionship. The group created a kind of haze of solidarity, of inextricable effusions and contaminations, that the officers of the civil state had a hard time untangling when they had to give a name to the members of these masses presenting themselves after abolition. They labeled us with all sorts of designations, sanctified the surnames, transformed them into first names, got swamped in nicknames of proximity, and associated us in assemblages born of chance and imagination. When they'd had enough, they would grab a name from mythology, from botany, or from the resources of whatever lexicon, to inflict it upon us in mockery. Our unusual names and our sonorous surnames are due to this initial lack, signaling it, reminding us of it. They give names to what they cannot encompass. They recount what they cannot say... —"Ah," the Baroness looks at me, wrinkling her eyelids; "Answer! No stammering! Behind this title that you have taxed me with and which you beat into my ears is there some kind of intention?!!"

A good dry swig of happiness.
Three madous of health
The domino of friendships
(It is given, and given well)

In addition to the religious festivals that provided a perfect alibi, the *Nations, Power, Convoys* also paraded during *carnaval*. In the Caribbean, *carnaval* is a moment of intensity: there are mimes, dances, clowning around, and music—an extraordinary concentration of expressive forms from the most somber delirium and inflamed sexual obsessions to demonstrations of hope and fine words. The energy of *carnaval* has traversed the centuries, gathering us together, as before. The illicit gets a seat at the table; the forbidden is at the helm; outrageousness keeps company with the most delicate of sensibilities; the shadow surges forth in all its manifestations; Africa prowls around; gods and devils return to the surface; insult, contempt, and malediction wander about in chains. In the midst of the total frenzy, desires and losses suddenly rise to consciousness: *you can hear them howling*. Among the fascinating creatures that emerged during carnival, there was *Marianne Lapofigue*. She appeared beyond the parade and started dancing inside a ring of onlookers. You couldn't see anything of her aside from a braid of banana leaves that covered her body, pointing to an outsized derrière that she would shake every which way. Her skull (much smaller than her large body of leaves) was swathed in rags. Her face was covered with a store-bought mask, or else her head would disappear beneath the banana leaves. As a child, trembling as I watched her, I didn't find her naughty or dangerous, just a mystery that was pleasant but also ridiculous; she was celebrating something unknown to the rest of us. I know now that Marianne came from an obscure memory of the great masks of Africa. No doubt, it was that obscurity that gathered so many people, for such a long time, around this strange creature. We were contemplating something unearthed from deep within ourselves.

Also, there was *Caroline*. This was a personage wrapped in a pile of rags. She was hidden behind an imperturbable mask and lugged around on her torso or back another creature as strange as herself that gave her two heads, four arms, and four legs. All she did was dance with her double, whose legs hung down and jiggled. We all circled around her without asking ourselves what it all meant. What was she carrying? Who was she carrying? What kind of longing or lack was thus manifested in the permissiveness of the Mardi Gras? And where did it come from, this fascinated pleasure that we felt in her presence? Man Ninotte was not interested in *carnaval*. Even now, this attitude remains a mystery to me. I saw her sit, imperturbable above her sewing machine, while in the street, just under our windows, there barged by a parade of people cursing and singing, or else a sedate procession of people in hats and lace. It is possible that the shared laughter and elated dancing only reached her ears in the austere form of a singular, continuous lament.

Yellow morning
Young light
All joy is a bird

The group formed a reflective surface around Man Ninotte. We passed on, one to the other, our attitudes and our emotions. The pain of one of us, expressed or deferred, affirmed or hidden, reinforced the same feelings in another. The Baroness transmitted her boundless strength to us all. The least show of weakness would have terrified us. Her fragility was nourished by ours, but she made it into a strength and then gave it back to us. Usually, when Man Ninotte was absent, it was the Baroness who, without any instructions, ruled over our universe. It was she who gave the report when Man Ninotte came home. When we got bad grades, when someone showed up with an old report card, Papa raised an eyebrow, ignored us, and turned to her to inquire: *But, Madame the Baroness, what's all this about? Didn't I tell you to keep your eyes open?* She had to be up on everything, explain everything, have a response to everything, be responsible for everything. After our Papa hadn't been around for a long time, Man Ninotte suddenly left the Baroness a large, unredeemable space, a liberty that was hers in full. Its fresh air reached us a bit attenuated, through her mediation. Before Man Ninotte, the horizon was empty: before the group that we had become, there was still the Baroness, that absolute rampart, that energetic core.

Now, faced with this ordeal of her death, we no longer needed individual confirmation, but instead sought to share a community of experiences and behaviors located well beyond our individual sphere. Without hesitation, we submitted ourselves to that ordeal through the reflecting mirror constituted by the group. We each watched the others. We each sensed the others. We did together what had to be done. Our telephones rang together and together we gave the same explanations. An outpouring bore us together in a single stream, but this stream maintained us within reach of the firm bank of life. The most extraordinary thing is that we nourished ourselves with Man Ninotte herself, with her gestures, her manners, the attitudes she would have had in a similar situation. An explosion of reflections flew through the group. Each of us transmitted to the other the bit of her that was reflected in him, or her. We shared what we had found in her and that, over decades, was re-emerging in the strategies we had adopted, each in our own way, to cope with that great abyss.

The Sapiens child has no claws, no fangs, no immediate strength. There's an unfinishedness of his being that requires a long maturation. Everything is missing. He is nothing more than a void, a hollow that calls out. A few innate gifts of the species allow him to confront immediate necessities: latching on, sucking the breast, crying in order to evoke the sympathy of providers... But he has to assimilate everything, even before being able to understand or speak.

Weakness, in contrast to strength, can learn.

That is why the Sapiens child becomes an insatiable mirror.

He reflects in his cells the knowledge of his mother, who passes on what happens around her. He drinks in as much as possible. When the other hominids, the most gifted animals, will stop learning, will harden their understandings, Sapiens will retain this opportunistic relation to all variations. *He will be in a fusional relation, constant and immediate.* To reduce the phenomenon of "imitative contaminations" between differing groups, communities will sacralize prohibitions, erecting ramparts of symbolic absolutes.

Despite these measures, all individual contact (with humans, with hominids, or with animals) will produce change, will present new possibilities. Certain peoples begin to believe in reincarnation when there appears among them a newborn who seems to possess a thousand years of accumulated wisdom. These infants display talents as mature as those of an earlier being who has returned to earth. The first groups must have developed a capacity of imitation so powerful that they could explore the entire tree of life and capture several millennia of both useful and useless knowledge. The mirror-effect may even have been at the origin of the erratic mutations that animate living things. When we examine a newborn infant, we approach the immense potential of the species, indecipherable like a great landscape blurred by its own light.

To escape from the petrifying power of the Gorgon, Perseus contrived to look at her by making use of the mirror's oblique protection. That is how he could vanquish her while deploying her terrifying ability to destroy his enemies. Perseus thus became a hero, simply by manipulating a mirror, by submitting it to his own will. The hero is always individual, separated from his community; he is extraordinary, beyond norms. It is this larger-than-lifeness—and thus this solitude—that establishes his heroism and makes him admirable. Heroes show us the path of individuation, shaking up the rules of the community. If the individual submits to his community, to his species, to his culture, he becomes a pretty rock or a lovely coral. His experience of life extends no further than the horizon of his community or his unique species. But if he uses the mirror of Perseus to capture and compel everything to serve his own experience, then he perpetuates life, he *experiences* via a plethora of sources. In addition, the mirror creates a distance, a lightness that preserves him from the weight of seriousness. He captures everything in the play of a reflection and finds himself in the movement of a beam of light... —"All right," murmurs the Baroness, her eyes laughing. "But heroes spent their time demolishing monsters, and thus eliminating everything out of the ordinary. In this way, they normalized the world. They put an end to many individualities, many diverse forms! Just think what our biodiversity would have been like today if we still had that Beast-of-Seven-Heads that our Ti-Jean L'horizon demolished, the astonishing bull of Minos that furious Hercules massacred, or even the great serpent, swallower of comets, that the foolish archer, Yi, whom the Chinese venerate, pierced... The heroes impoverished the world!..." Exactly, I say cautiously, the hero of ancient times in fact served a norm for which he was the model. He made things move forward, opened up other possibilities, and it was salutary in most cases. He also achieved a certain truth. Today, neither hero nor truth is possible, nothing but the distribution without end of experiences, poetics, and forms of intelligence... in a play of reflections and lights... We are all heroes!

The mirror-effect also played a role in relations of domination. The slave reflected the master. The dominated takes in what he can and even what he doesn't want to. The system works in the opposite direction, too: the West, which has spread itself throughout the world, has in turn been marked by the world, and enriched in that way. The mirror-effect pollinates in all directions and produces something unpredictable in its glimmers and reflections. The difference between the immense plantations of the southern United States and those of the Caribbean islands is that on the islands, because of the exiguous space that separates the house of the master from the slave quarters, the mirror-effect functioned even more effectively than in the immense plantations of Faulkner's country. But in one case as in the other, masters and slaves affected one another, mutually undergoing change, but at differing intensities. Beyond any will or desire to make it happen, the contact takes place, change is initiated, interaction is activated, the mind is transported, without being able to imagine or even know that it has occurred. The difficulty here is to bring this to consciousness and to try to nourish it with a poetics...

Flows of fleeing laughter
And seeds to give away, seeds you don't want to lose

Our childhood unfolded between the authority of Man Ninotte and that of the Baroness. An old Creole proverb says that two valiant crabs cannot survive in the same hole. When there are strong personalities involved, co-habitation is difficult. And so, Man Ninotte and the Baroness waged a little war of competing affections. Malicious gossip, disputes, undeclared opposition, and sideways looks. Together they constituted for the rest of us a unified instance of power, but between them there reigned only an affectionate discord. Man Ninotte rarely called her the "Baroness." Instead, she called her "Manmzelle Anastasie"—the "Manmzelle" being a way of putting her at a patrolled distance. Often, she would say to Papa: *Your Mademoiselle Anastasie did this, your Mademoiselle Anastasie did that!...* It's true that Papa accorded to the Baroness a particular attention, full of admiration and concern, woven with constant formalities (*Have I not told you...!?*) or exclusive and precise tasks. When he said to her: *I have a word to say to you...*, that often meant she would find herself in the afternoon charged with treating the outbreaks on his skin. She was the only one who could clean out his *vers bleus*.

Now, let's examine the differences between them.

Man Ninotte seemed to be at war with life itself. During that period, misfortune was the dominant theme. What she forced on us, in a rough manner and without reprieve, seemed to be the collateral effect of this daily struggle. The Baroness, for her part, applied a code of discipline, obligations, and duties, the necessity of which seemed to derive from her will alone. Make the bed. Dust the shutters. Clean a burnt pot. Do this, do that. She let nothing go and kept us in line, constantly watching over us. Man Ninotte, for her part, yelled all the time, but after a stroke of bad luck, she yelled even louder than the bad luck so as to be heard. Her shouting told us what we had to do. The Baroness didn't shout; she would rope us in with a gesture, and this gesture would submit us to the task. And so, if Man Ninotte always handled the bad luck, the Baroness always handled us—without a shred of leniency.

It will take me many years to get past this impression, to comprehend that the Baroness, too, had to stand tall in the face of bad luck. As the first born, she had known the harshest phases of the war Man Ninotte waged against worry, against poverty, against troubles. She had traversed the thirty-three nuances of the worst-case scenarios, known nighttime in full daylight, known how everything could scorch you, how the impossible could be coiled up in every little detail of the ordinary. For you, it must have been hard not to measure the dangers we faced each day, day after day. Baroness, you felt more than we did the importance of eliminating the least waste, of neither failing nor faltering. You had made your own this total preoccupation of Man Ninotte's: that her children should have access to weapons that life had not planted in her own garden. Better than the others, you knew what Man Ninotte didn't tell us; you saw what she hid; you no doubt heard the sound of the tears she held back; you knew the extent of her strength, the immensity of her weakness, because you had to grow up so fast, too fast; you had to keep all that inside of you without being able to explain it to anyone, and even less so to us, we who could receive nothing from you other than that decisive imperative. What Man Ninotte succeeded in doing each and every day in an instinctual bodily combat with the dog's life she led, you prolonged by foresight, attention to detail, organization, method... —"What bad luck?! What poverty?! Don't exaggerate!..." the Baroness sighs, exasperated.

The signs say that there will be seagrapes
Kaleidoscopes of butterflies
That for you, the water will come alive

The Baroness did what she wanted in the house. That might seem straightforward, but there was nothing obvious about it. Our family was essentially matrifocal: the decisive authority was Man Ninotte's. Papa constituted a sort of semi-distant stellar ring; he maintained the lookout on the outer limits. While Man Ninotte tried to involve him in some activity or other—the children's communion, somebody's birthday, an indispensable purchase— he was content to take on an inspired air before letting out the identical one-liner: *Very well, that's something we should have expected and been prepared for!* His participation in the business concerned ended right there. The expanse of the house thus belonged to Man Ninotte, and since she had no tendency toward being a mother-hen—as she reminded you at the least occasion—there was no softness, no kisses or hugs. No question of making yourself at home *chez elle*, of planning to take root there or imposing one's own law. She would explain to you more or less gently that you had to get your own house if you wanted to exercise the possibility of raising your voice or imagining *Missié-a!* a single wrong move. And so, no one attempted to raise a flag.

Except the Baroness.

Man Ninotte didn't cut her off.

A slap meted out by the Baroness (the most terrible slaps in existence) only led to two or three more from Man Ninotte herself. The Baroness roamed the topography of the house with the step of General Mangin, following lines that criss-crossed those of Man Ninotte without ever provoking a frontal collision. No one would have thought of complaining about some severity of the Baroness's. As for the rest, Man Ninotte simply watched her do it: the Christmas decorations, the doilies, the Sunday cakes, the arrangement of our apprenticeships, the initiatives involving the sewing machine... When she started working for the National Ministry of Education, the Baroness introduced into the house a stove, a refrigerator, a kitchen cabinet, a television and a pressure-cooker, a pile of extravagant objects that Man Ninotte contemplated without saying a word. Sometimes she looked askance at her, shook her head, made the sound of a *tsk–tsk*, as if to ward off evil fate; but she left her to her own devices. I never had the impression that there was a mirror-effect between the Baroness and Man Ninotte: they were so different from each other! Man Ninotte, round and massive, chiseled into a brute force; the Baroness, slender, majestic, with the allure of a gypsy queen fallen down to earth on a holy Friday... They seemed to share a complicity in nothing. Baroness, it took me many years to discern in you the spectral ripples of Man Ninotte. A subtle aura emitted by your silhouette almost completely replaced her and established a version of her inside of you that also inhabited each of us in a different way... —"Still, you mustn't exaggerate!" the Baroness says firmly with impatience.

With what changes us:
Seven corn seeds
Seven orange seeds
And the flowering lentils

The group gave us the illusion that Man Ninotte was still there, that she had been prolonged in this totality that we had become. The group was what our woman warrior had protected all her life, both as a collective and as individuals, a totality that constituted the sweetness of her existence. So many awakenings before dawn, so much laundry to do, so many shopping excursions and meals to cook, so many life strategies and survival strategies, so much shame undergone and fleeting moments of pride, so many failures and so many successes... *not even celebrated in the clamor of day!*

Who remembers?

The instant the announcement was made, the flowers of the market should have begun to sing again! There should have been a parade of flamboyants around the cathedral! The sky should have let loose a single quiver of butterflies above our street! Clusters of mamoncillo, chocolate buns, and bushels of vanilla should have been planted all along the Levassor Canal up to the heights of the college seminary! The streams should have splashed each letter of her name and the sewing machines should have embroidered them in the tablecloth's lace... All these things she could have experienced with true pleasure, without worrying that she'd lose respect. Pressed tightly together, we managed to produce a distillation of all that. We reawakened what animated her look, what inspired her smile. We disappeared into that collective, one that simultaneously underscored the solitary nature of our distress.

Who remembers?

One can imagine Césaire and Glissant asking themselves this question as they looked upon the land's hollow gaps. Their incredulous dives into colonial history led them to glimpse miraculous reservoirs. Revolts, defeats, resistances, and chaotic uprisings lay there with no one to see them in the dust or between the lines... *so very many!* So many obstinate refusals lodged in the rhythms and the dances. So many vigilant glances in the clarities of rum. So much desire under the thick mane of the sugarcane. Behind the escaped slave who proclaimed his refusal there could be found the obscure resistance that accepts, the acquiescence that refuses, the madness that searches, the patience of those who endure on the plantation. The slaves wove dreams, they unraveled anguishes, they plaited lunacies, they tried to conjure life under the arcana of gesture and from the tissue of signs. They started fires to nourish the ashes. They broke tools to contain suffering. They braided wishes and sorrows with the leaves of the vetiver bush that they deposited here and there in their gardens. They knew how to take to the hills just as they knew how to conquer the villages, the towns, and the cities. They managed to work life into death, to plant there something that holds fast and that never lets go. Here, the tally of heroisms had no one to record them. The landscape had no witness. Nothing was judged and nothing pardoned. Nothing was celebrated and nothing forgotten. Everything was buried

deeply in tombs of wind and in the earth's counterless memory.
Who remembers, if not the stones that might have cried out?

In the carafe
Dreams to drink
And freshness at the pleasure of drinking straight from the spout

Leading a troupe of five children doesn't allow you to practice
nuance. Man Ninotte's orders were collective, as were her
reprimands. Get up. Wash up. Sit down to eat. Do your work.
Brush your teeth. Go to bed. Say your prayers… Whoever ran
off like a maroon or a highway bandit would get a personalized
punishment; but aside from that, we would all be considered
responsible for everything, and the Baroness represented all of
us when faced with a case to judge. If dishwashing wasn't done,
if blinds were poorly cleaned, if a plate broke, if a meal burned,
or bread was wasted—any of these would let loose a thunder of
babbling and bad humor that chased us all over the house. Even
the Baroness got the brunt of it. No one was spared, no one got out
unscathed. As for sweets, the same thing: a soda had to be divided
into five parts; an apple and a pear, too. *Idem* for a simple slice of
mortadella. On Sunday afternoons, when the Baroness concocted
a big cake, each of us only got a puny triangle, an unjust portion,
rarely replenished…We lived, then, with the sense that the world
was certainly over-populated, and that no calamity could surpass
that of being born with brothers and sisters. One by one, in the
order of our ages, we have spent a lot of time struggling against this
lack of distinction: first, to be noticed by Man Ninotte, to regain
some semblance of advantage when it came time to distribute the
candy, to grab a little bit of personal tenderness amidst the bolts
of lightning intended to educate us; then, in order to become the
person that each of us is. An increase of our individuation had
distanced us from the group; but the shock of that day brought us
all back, delightedly, to that initial cocoon, that first indistinction.
  The children!
  We were forced to recognize that who we were was linked to the
group, that the group had created both the most conscious and the
most hidden dynamics, that the group was in us, and that we were
in it, as though sunk in a deep archive. To find our equilibrium, we
needed to be in the group and also outside of it. And we needed it

even more when in shock: we needed to melt into the group while distinguishing ourselves from it.

Some memory, lost in us, had already known.

Can you see how our origins stand before us every time?

I felt with great force what the captive Africans would have felt in the abyss of the slaveship. The original community, its sacred framework, was dissolved in the shadow of the hold and the crushing of the chains. Anything you could have been in those chains was crushed as well.

No longer anyone there: only livestock, cargo, a load of ebony wood.

No longer any name: no origin, no history, no future.

Not a single plea was heard.

Not a single prayer brought comfort.

The slaveship's hold allowed for only one magnetic bond from which there emerged at times the active, coagulating energy of the group. Those who could nourish themselves entirely on this effusion multiplied their physical resistance and their ability to survive. To survive the crossing was to fall into the ardor of rebirth, but without hope of ever finding again the lost community, or even of reconstituting a new one. At the other end, upon arrival, the slave plantation extended the phenomenon. It didn't permit the creation of the slightest bond with others, only individual survival, which had to happen according to the codes that the plantation furnished, and that the Creole storyteller, that founding-refounder, would so beautifully transcend.

During the vigils, the Creole storyteller assembled the lonesome survivors around a kind of composite language in which all could recognize themselves and through which all could participate. Around this language, there would be born an ensemble of groupings that became conscious of themselves as such, despite the unusual diversity of belief systems and the lack of shared symbols.

The stories he told would be available to be taken up by others.

He made them evolve in response to the make-up of the audience, its state of mind at that moment. He asked questions to which all of the listeners had to reply. He stopped at each fork in his long narration to decide along with the audience which path to pursue. He absorbed the pools of emotion that the assembly loved to wade through. At that time, our storyteller was above all an *improviser.* He came from neither near nor far. *He rose from the depths and reigned over the now.*

He founded no lineages with his tales; he invoked no totems. But all the possible avenues for the survival strategy of each person were unfurled, and each person, by committing himself to these interactions, by responding to and thus orienting them, joined the others in progressing toward one destiny, all while affirming a personal path. Each person constituted, so to speak, a *singular rhythm*, which accorded itself to the various rhythms of the others and flourished with them. So that the vigils of the storyteller, and the voice of the storyteller, were carried along and reinforced by the imperial polyrhythm of the drums.

The *tambours-ka* and the *tambours-bèlè* were permitted by the master during periods of intense effort, or during free time on those long Sunday afternoons. The drums brought joy, laughter, and danced encounters between men and women. Solidarity around deaths, around the building of huts, around ways to reinvent gardens in an earth where *only the tough soil was arable* constituted so many pretexts to take out the drums. People worked and sang together, but *each one was alone in this togetherness.* The drums were the expression of this complexity. The master couldn't have guessed that in this drumming there was the leaven which would germinate the negation of his domination. After abolition, the large central factories reassembled many former slaves. They went there to earn their pittance. At the end of weeks of drudgery, the paycheck would uplift existence. During that period, in the gatherings that went on for a long time in the vicinity of the grocers, the drums would surge forth like totems of sound. All the fever born of payday, of rum, and of long frustrations crystalized around this roaring god, this melancholy god that led back to nothing sacred but only to the polyrhythms in which all emotions could fuse. Rather than evoke a god, the drummer, or *tanbouyé*, would take into careful consideration the slightest *dispersion*, each one adding a rhythm attentive to the rhythm of another, each one nourishing the other in a strategy of improvisations that are as complementary as they are antagonistic. When one would suddenly get lost in his own personal inspiration, the others would hold on to the basic rhythm, the rhythm that would bear them along, composed of a chaos of

singular rhythms, and together they would feed his loops and swerves, carve out his moorings. Polyrhythm diffracts; it doesn't gather together except to prolong a perpetual diffraction. That is why Miles Davis would turn his back to the public and face the drummer, nourishing himself at the source of the rhythm master...
—"If I follow you," the Baroness interrogates me with the air of a schoolmistress, "polyrhythmy came from an infinite number of solitudes entering into solidarity with one another?!" —Yes, I say, in a slightly lower tone. Polyrhythmy was nourished by these thousands of possibilities, but it is open to only one round of them. It is this openness that remains the determining factor, an openness that offers lightness, not the heavy plenitude that we seek when we attempt to work together. But, of course, that might very well be subject to discussion. What's important is not to simplify things...

There is this fine bath begun
That one takes only
With three leaves of one's last three dreams
(And all the rest is limitlessly given)

I always keep an eye on the traditions of the *bèlè* dance. In that dance, you can sense the hypnotic force of the drums. I arrive a bit in advance for the pleasure of seeing the audience gather around the drums, as though around a portal to remote powers. The singer and his respondents create a background narrative: wrenching pleas that tell a tale on a swell of tonal variations. Two *tanbouyé* drummers stand before them, seated at their instruments, flanked by those who keep the rhythm of the *tibwa*, those two sticks they strike on the slats of the drum. The cadence of the *tibwa* makes a stable rhythmic surface on top of which the two master-*tanbouyé* improvise in alternation. The circle of men and women dancers forms, and then, one after the other, each couple separates, approaches the drum to salute it as though it were a divinity. Finally, each couple begins a joust of conquest-seduction. It will end with the domination of one by the other, or by their contented and blissful union. If the singer, the respondents, and the *tibwa* create an invariable rhythm, the *tanbouyés*, in contrast, improvise. They saunter across the five rhythms. They unleash sounds. They glide along the rumbling. They provoke crystalline fractures, a shellfire dynamics. All is recalibrated to the rhythms of the dancers before them. Their bodies underscore what the sounds are telling them, moving in twists and turns. The solo *tanbouyé* deciphers the desires, inspires the strategies of each male dancer so that he can dominate his tender adversary. The singer, attentive to the evolutions of the couple, sends out tonal sheets that will reinforce the decree of the drums. Each dancer tries to capture the soul of the *tanbouyé*-soloist, to attract his energetic beating. The *tanbouyé*-soloist can then abandon one dancer for another if the latter succeeds better at a creative symbiosis with what he is expressing. The ideal alchemy occurs when one of the dancers manages to incarnate the sonorous architecture of the drum, *to become the lost god*, which makes him invincible, out of reach, affectionately triumphant—at that point—over the other. The same structure applies to the dance of combat called the *danmyé*, but there we find no tenderness, just the salience of the gesture, the rhythms now war-like, the implacable pulse of the drums neutralizing the adversary without mercy.

In the plantation, masters, slaves, Amerindian survivors, immigrants, and travelers were all forced to live together and, whether they liked it or not, to create the new world. The human group that the Creole storyteller would reveal was not a community like the former one. It had no sacred system, no hierarchical authority structure, but rather was nourished by a *chiquetaille* of references that Glissant will come to call *Traces*. The Trace is a vestige come down from the great sign systems and symbologies, a bit like what arose all around us after Man Ninotte disappeared. The Trace is fabricated like a pearl in the shell of the wounds left behind when the great sign systems and symbologies are removed from the everyday lives of survivors. It is in this sense that the *bèlè* drums can be considered magnificent Traces. And the songs and the dances are also magnificent Traces. The sonorous conch is another. The Creole garden, with its mixture of medicinal and symbolic plants, is yet another... In the land of the American Creoles, here in Martinique, our ancestors lived in a seedbed of Traces. These Traces made possible an explosion of individual rebirths.

Now, we must understand how that happened.

The Trace is essentially composite, fragile, and uncertain. The Trace is unanchored. It is apt to take off on a tangent, joining in emulsion and in synthesis with other remainders. In the field of Traces, each enslaved person could take his pick—creating, improvising, developing a purely individual survival strategy. The drum of the plantations holds the memory of all the drums of Africa, of their symbols and their gods, but these gods are dismantled, these symbols fall back to earth. *It's the free imagination that gathers them up, and the talent that improvises with them.* The drum-become-Trace can only offer to the survivor the possibility of creating something new. Henceforth, the Trace no longer founds communities; it founds *individual possibilities* which reinforce themselves by associating in a sporadic manner. The principle of the Trace will traverse the centuries. Think of those musicians that Parker, Miles Davis, Coltrane, or Monk gathered together in the studio, simply because of their singular chemistry. Together, in the chaos of African polyrhythm-become-Trace, these solitary figures unleashed their improvisations, their *personal wisdom*; they captured the moment, digging deeply into it, in a proliferating grace that allowed each individual's riches to be realized in a communal richness, a sublime occasion. The alchemy didn't occur every time. Nights in the studio could be sterile, drowned in alcohol and heavy drugs. But at certain hours, the miracle was produced. *Powerful manifestations of human genius surged forth instantaneously!...* In the same way, around the Creole storyteller, around the *bèlè* dance drums, those who respond, who dance, who tell stories are in that instant nourished by the infinity of these moments. No millennial force directs them; they advance in a collective composed like a bolt of lightning that, from one vigil to the next, realizes the fulfillment of their shared experiences. Thus, they never cease being born into a world that lies in the wake of the ruins of the former, essential one; they never cease being born into the fervor of that fundamental lack.

They are born alone, but *with*.

Solitary, in solidarity.

That is the power of the Trace.

The *bèlè*—its songs, drums, and dances—is an archive of bodily memory. The survivors of the crossing disembarked, stripped of their previous existence. They took off again in search of their humanity, relying on the only archive that remained to them: *the memory in their bodies*. The dancers (right after the sorcerers, to whom they are very close) will become the first to resist the slave order. Those who wanted to be reborn began to dance what the former symbolic systems had inscribed in their flesh. Gestures became weapons. This occurred to such an extent that, in the Creole language *fè jès*, to make gestures, came to mean practicing a magical activity that could modify reality and the world. The great masters of the *bèlè*[4] have identified two instances that encapsulate the human treasure contained in the *bèlè*: *lespri jé, lespri jés*. The spirit of play, the spirit of gestures. The *bèlè* dance is a collection of games—for the feet, the hands, the shoulders, the torso, and the face. Each gesture opens up a family of bodily articulations from which the dancer can draw at will. To teach these gestures is above all to transmit the *spirit of play*. "To play" (to play with the arms, the legs, the feet) means that precision doesn't come from above but from the capacity to experience what is happening, to capture the sounds, to *put yourself in the sound*, to sense the rhythms, to anticipate them in the increasing intensity of your desires. That's why polyrhythm and improvisation (which characterize the musics of the Caribbean and the Americas) create above all a space of play.

Lespri jé—it's the individual who is authorized to create the self.

For each dance, the individual composes and recomposes a self without end.

Gestures are the other treasure.

The experts in *bèlè* have inventoried dozens of these gestural combinations. Gestures also involve the arms, the legs, the torso, and the posture. Having the spirit means putting to work, at the moment of dancing, an esthetic of movement, of its cadence, its grace, its precision, and its emancipating power. It is an art that unites the mind and the body, and that flows just as much through the dancers as it does through the *tanbouyé* drummers and the singer. The spirit of play opens up a creative void, while the spirit of gesture is born from the carnal depths of the imaginary. These two forms give structure to an invisible form in which the performer, hewing closely to his greatest imaginings, actualizes himself... Cautiously, I ask the Baroness: Do you understand what I mean? —"I think so," she sighs, not truly convinced. "But the important thing is that *you* understand what you're telling me!..."

---

4 Association AM4, *Tradition danmyé-kalennda-bèlè de Martinique* (K Editions, 2014).

There is a magnificent work[5] that reminds us of the spiritual dimension permeating jazz from its inception to its latest developments... Most of the great jazzmen, with the exception of Miles Davis, laid claim to a sort of divinity. They thought of themselves as borne by an inspiration that came from God, a force thrusting them into an experience that could be considered sacred. This creation-jazz, captivating and open-ended, tuning itself to all melodies, bearing them elsewhere, seemed to emerge from a place where no other music had ventured before. For musicians deeply plunged into this phenomenon, the music always emanated from a lost divinity, an immanent sacred source. This creation-jazz, the spirit that flows from it, would be a sort of fervor in the face of divine splendor; it allowed Black populations to stand tall despite a de-humanization raised to the order of a system. However, where others assumed there was a god, a great impassive immanence, Miles Davis saw the void, the abyss, vertigo. His intuition was correct: systematic de-humanization propels you into a beyond.

Not only into a "beyond" but also a "beyond the conceivable." Rather than awaiting a response from this awesome silence, this space with no coordinates, Miles started to "make art with it" (as René Char would say); to search in its company; to remain erect before it, without a veil, without any concealment; to make of it the matter of life's creation. The joyous anguish of the gospels, blissful and frantic, transformed itself in Miles's work into a severe anguish, demanding and courageous, which held itself up as a demi-god in a solitude he accepted, a vertigo that remained wide open. What the spiritual-jazzman called "God" was, I believe, this vertigo of the beyond breached by the annihilating, *all-denying spittle*[6] of de-humanization. This is what polyrhythmy offered to his talent.

---

5 Imbert, Raphaël, *Jazz suprême. Initiés, mystiques & prophètes* (Paris: Éditions de l'Éclat, 2014).

6 TN: The phrase "all-denying spittle" comes from Aimé Césaire's play *La Tragédie du Roi Christophe*. The full line is "la vaste insulte que tous, ils ont reçu, plaqué sur le corps, au visage, l'omni-niant crachat" (in Arnold, A. J., ed., *Aimé Césaire: Poésie, Théâtre, Essais et Discours* [Paris: Présence Africaine, 2013: p. 1028]). The line appears in Ralph Manheim's translation, *The Tragedy of King Christophe* as: "the total outrage that we have suffered, the all-denying spittle plastered on our bodies, spat into our faces" (New York: Grove Press, 1969: p. 42).

The beyond remains intolerable for an identitarian approach that habitually covers it over with the sacred, with cosmogonies, and with origin myths. Archaic communities refused the asphyxiating discomfort of what surpassed their understanding. Faced with the beyond as it emerged in the "Black condition" in the United States and the Caribbean, the only thing that could stand up to it was individual experience, solitude forced to create its own sources and its own foundation within itself, *to take the turn toward improvisation*. Jazz possesses this spirit, one that can be found in the biguine, *bèlè*, salsa, reggae, calypso… all the Creole musical forms of the Americas and of the Caribbean where improvisation reigns.

In essence, the jazz spirit is a religious spirit. I mean, it is something that *links things together infinitely* and, in that way, liberates them: in the implosive alchemy of the instant, in the improvisations that are ceaselessly re-fertilized. For that reason, one should approach improvisation as a solitude that soars toward its own plenitude and that, from the movement of self toward self, of self for self, founds fluid solidarities, essential fraternities, each one with the others, with all possible musical forms, with the world these various musics disclose. Here, the collective is born of the individual realizing his full potential. It is a collective that only has relevance for the thriving of each and every one.

To read in the astonishment of the stones
To preserve a few as friends

Around the body of Man Ninotte, we were stupefied, as though confronting a total aberration. If a part of us knew and recognized that aberration, if a part was moved by it, had dreaded it, had been more or less prepared for its blow, nothing could prevent our minds and bodies from sinking into a stupor. An inescapable sense of guilt reigned here and there among us, becoming more acute in one, rebounding off another. Each of us asked ourselves if we had been sufficiently loving, sufficiently present; we attempted the never-ending calculation as to whether we could have made more of an effort to be near, to be tender. We also felt the full extent of what we had lost, what we hadn't known how to experience fully. It was clear that we hadn't taken enough advantage of what we had been given. Something deep inside us makes us forget death, refuse its existence—and it was even more true in this case. This death constituted, so to speak, the most decisive lesson, the ultimate experience that established in our consciousness the fact of our own disappearance, and, equally, the desire not to disappear when our turn comes. My mind, merged with that of the group, twisted and turned in all directions. We were alive, life blinded us, life was in us, and it was life that set the hard flint slab of this day across an indecipherable abyss.

When I discovered Émile Zola's *Germinal*, I was struck by the everyday existence of the Maheu family, this family submitted to the ferocity of extractive capitalism. The soups, the baths, the meals, the restless children, the petty order of the days in the narrowness of the domestic space, between the blows of the workday and the persistent dreams. I had found, described in this work with surprising precision, a bit of the universe of our own household: the kitchen, the lamps, the candles, the cloud of worries, the soothing alcohol, the miracles accomplished by the women, the serious conversations between the papa and the mama, the poverty ever renewed, fought off inch by inch, insistent, never-ending. The Maheu mother made me think of Man Ninotte, especially when it was her turn to descend into the mine; and the Maheu father reminded me in so many ways of my Papa. Zola revealed to me the universe of the modest poor around me: merchants, fishermen, dayworkers, street vendors, salesgirls… They suddenly appeared to me shot through with an unsuspected heroism. Submerged by difficulties, these brave people knew how to be joyous, how to get the most out of small moments of happiness. Except that what I perceived in the poverty around me was clearly distinct from that of the miners in one way.

Something not visible animated all that I saw.

Something unpredictable shuffled the dominos and dealt the cards. The real wouldn't stay fixed within the lines. It stagnated in troubled pools, pulsated from muddy streams, flowed from bizarre distortions. Many of the people inhabited places located in their own minds: the Syrians, camped out in front of their shops, fixedly contemplated the cedars of Lebanon, disturbed by the fires of the desert. A couple of poor buggers sang unknown refrains on sidewalk corners or tried to find something of themselves in reflections in the windows. One would leap two or three meters above the gutters if you looked like you were going to grab his butt. Another went running away across the market at the slightest sound of a certain syllable. For yet another, the simple mention of the name of the battleship *Émile Bertin* would make him burst out like cannon fire on the porch of the church. One woman declared her piety and sold cones of pepper while rubbing her string of rosary beads. Yet another distributed to the children of the boarding school hibiscus flowers and little flags. And that one over there openly babbled with herself when she wasn't insulting the mannequins in the shop windows showing their tits. There was so much fear of the *quimbois* that every single shopkeeper hallowed his doorway with alkali and disinfectant. One business owner rejected the sidewalk on the left side and the shadows of ladders; others threw stones at the *chiens-fer*; and the majority avoided black cats and those mantous crabs that popped up in the drains. We offered saccharine smiles to the priests out on a spree, fearing that they would shake their robes at us. Someone sang dirty biguines or church verses, then mixed them all together. Someone else stared at the very dark-skinned people she found on her path and stood stock still, grimacing with her hands on her hips so that they'd go away. More than one crossed the street to show off a blouse in nylon, a pair of pants in Tergal; another went on her way floating in a cloud of that perfume known as *Ploum Ploum*. Some honked their horns to signal that it was they who held the steering wheel. Another laughed too much; another never stopped crying; and yet another had only her anger to live on. They cursed for no reason, cursed at length, cursed to say what we didn't dare say. They honked again. Everyone said hello to everyone, and everyone expected to be greeted. You had to make room for the stream of sound coming from the guy carrying the radio; you never got involved in bitter disputes between the *femmes-matador*; and you never lingered on the sidewalks where the *quimboiseurs* passed... The honking was perpetual... it went on and on. No one was ever entirely there—*I saw you, I didn't see you!* Everyone kept a bunch of stuff around for making things. Nothing was simple or simply logical. Everything remained at every moment imaginable. And anything could be made from anything else.

Within the Creole marvelous, there can be found this trembling of the ordinary. The teller of the origin stories knew that the real was rigged, that the order of the world, put in place by the masters, offered no good news for anyone or anything, that this slave and colonial order was something immanent—in the sky, on the earth, in your blood, your skin, your bones. He knew that men and women had created for themselves, under that dehumanization, a double of their body, and that this double lived in a universe of constant emergences. An emergence is a bank of fireflies; it flickers everywhere, lighting up without indicating the path, without revealing the landscape, but still establishing lines of flight in the thickness of the shadow. In a poem, Césaire exclaims, when thinking of this phenomenon, *il ne faut jamais désespérer des lucioles… Never despair of fireflies.*[7] He meant that the fireflies do not exclude the night, but that with their light, their flickering, the entire night can become something else.

In *Germinal* (at the end of the gray winter, the carbony blackness of the mines, and the painful revelations of the strike), the coming of spring in nature accompanies an awakening of consciousness in the mining people. There is a sort of linear advance. In contrast, in our world—from the slave plantation to the universe of Man Ninotte—there was a chaotic germination that would appear intermittently, shimmering, from day to day, even in the midst of misfortune. I say to the Baroness: To understand this shimmering, think of that scene that Glissant proposed as an archetype: the Black man born in Africa, deported to the Americas, who at the time of his landing took off for the deep woods. He nourished the hope that he would discover a way back to the lost country. His journey would come up against the quasi-fatal instant when the inconceivable, tearing his illusions to pieces, would establish an insurmountable limit as

---

7   TN: Chamoiseau has slightly transformed this line from Aimé Césaire's "Vertu des lucioles" [Virtue of Fireflies]: Césaire writes: "Ne pas désespérer des lucioles," which translators Clayton Eshleman and A. James Arnold render as "Not to despair of fireflies." I have slightly modified their translation. See *The Complete Poetry of Aimé Césaire*, Bilingual Edition, trans. A. J. Arnold and C. Eshleman (Middletown, CT: Wesleyan University Press, 2017: pp. 826–7). Unfortunately, this edition is not complete; it is missing alternate (and sometimes definitive) versions of Césaire's poems; therefore, I will occasionally modify Eshleman's and Arnold's translations, using versions that Chamoiseau himself might have used. All modifications on my part will be noted.

violent as a wall: There is no going back. There is no path. There is only the invention of the possible. Only the living of the possible.

And that is where our story begins.

Against that wall, our poor hero will shrivel up on the spot. He will remain immobilized. Or else, by a sudden impulse of his spirit, he will cover the wall with flickering light. *Our bank of fireflies.* Galvanized by these specks of light, he will once again take on an infinite journey, transmitted from century to century to us and beyond us, *bringing with him that flickering wall of light.* Without having had to run for the woods, the teller of origin stories will, from the start, invest with meaning this strange wall where the flickering sets off small horizons in the mesh that has no horizons. Alejo Carpentier saw there the magical real; our beloved García Márquez did too, and they were both right. But you can also see the truly wondrous phenomenon, this refraction made of lucidity that is madness but that also watches over us, a disenchantment that, despite everything, enchants, that weeps and smiles, that closes its eyes and yet sees everything, that knows everything is beyond reach and still renounces nothing. This is how Man Ninotte lived.

Here is the new age:
The lovely mornings of the cinnamon-apple
The adamantine dew like an offering on your hands

LEGENDARY OF MEMORY – The disappearance of Man Ninotte began with the wearing down of her memory. The old memories remained, the very oldest, but the others entered into a wobbly waltz, with lifts and falls, absences and hypermnesia, of which she was intermittently aware, and which threw her into a terror, the extent of which was not immediately clear to us. Someone who loses the power to remember experiences a terrible defeat; it is as though a part of oneself had begun to sink into a void, and one finds oneself, day after day, in an increasingly unfamiliar place.

They say that certain Benin kings, just before delivering their captives over to the slaveships, had them walk around an ancestral tree. This circular walk took place before the menacing ocean, in the city of Ouidah.

That tree was the Tree of Forgetfulness.

The women would take seven turns around it; the men nine, I believe. This disparity in itself is surprising: Did women have less memory baggage than the men? Was the part of memory they were aiming at more extensive in men, or was it necessary for them to erase it more radically? Was it a favor accorded to women, a small hope of returning? The legend is well established, it is often repeated, but it doesn't answer any of these questions.

The practice was supposed to make those who were being sold into slavery lose the memory of their origins. Why? No doubt, to prevent the captives sold by their very own brothers from holding resentments and transmitting them down through the millennia. That must have worked. I spent my childhood and a large part of my youth without ever hearing anyone speak of that aspect of African history—my history—nor of that sale of prisoners by the African kings. And, as for me personally, I don't feel any resentment about it. The other reason I can imagine for this imposed forgetfulness is that it must have relieved these unfortunate people of their shared belief systems so that they could survive the terrible hold of the slaveship and then confront the need for an almost total and individual rebirth at the other end.

This practice is rather stupefying.

It seems to presume that an archaic community would agree to erase what constituted its very legitimacy (genesis stories, cosmogonies, origin myths, rituals, gods and demons, ancestors and spirits, philosophies and knowledge) and that some of its offspring would be deprived of it all. Which was the worst of damnations. To find oneself "ejected" from all of that meant, according to the imperious communal womb, that they were destined for annihilation.

It could also suggest that what was about to happen in the Americas was alien to the approved charters, something beyond their reach—and that it would be necessary to become an entirely new person if one were to find some kind of future there.

Finally, the practice of circling an ancestral tree assumes that no return would be possible. *The journey binds, sweeps all roads away!* Césaire would write in *Ferrements*.[8]

---

8   TN: The original French is "Le périple ligote, emporte tous les chemins." Clayton Eshleman and A. James Arnold (2017) translate this line from *Ferrements* as "The periplus binds sweeps away all roads" (529). Translation modified.

Since, from the very start of the journey, the tree of forget-fulness erased all the paths, all the ties, and all four horizons, those who were carried away over the coral reef were no longer anything but a biological relic, or, at best, an intensity in a state of becoming. Since they kept on living, they couldn't even adopt the cocoon of the communal ancestors. They were branded as soon as they left the irons of the barracoons for the irons of the boat and all signs of the past were taken away—jewelry, bracelets, objects that could reattach them to their original understanding of the world. All that was left were the scarifications—and to get rid of them would have required removing their skin. But scarifications have no meaning on their own. They need to be immersed in a community. So that is how everything began for us: *with an imposed forgetfulness...* —"Yes," the Baroness tells me. "To forget is already to begin something else, which is what permits you to insinuate that we, offspring of the survivors, were not going to 'start again,' but rather, right away, 'start' something else..." —Which explains why we haven't been able to formulate any kind of genesis or origin myth... I respond. Our beginning is an explosion that Glissant will call *Digenesis*, a genesis that doesn't assign you to a community, but instead initiates a becoming... —"Glissant is a Papa Legba," the Baroness sighs. "He ensures the crossing!"

The African kings couldn't have known the bottomless depths of dehumanization that would occur in the hold of the slaveship. Such a thing was beyond the inconceivable. As for what would happen on the plantations in the Americas, it was in fact the *ontological damnation of the Black man*, with no reprieve up to this day, something no instance of slavery, ancient or contemporary, from Africa or elsewhere, had attained. No instance of slavery had "racialized" or "essentialized" its infamy to the same extent. Yet the Tree of Forgetfulness materialized a terrifying premonition of this racialization. It erased the former canvas without creating a new one. For those men from the great land, this ritual could no doubt be justified by the fact that they were sending thousands of their compatriots into the total unknown. It matters little in the long run what they had in mind: all premonitions remain in part obscure. Today, in Ouidah, artists symbolize the situation as two doors: one of no return, which represents the passage from the African soil to the slaveship; and the other, that of the return, which marks if not an actual return of the descendents to their ancestors, then at least their re-unification, restored despite the rupture. These doors have no frames; they are porches that allow passage in both directions—the passage of glances, and of the sea, sky, and dusty winds.

Those who arrived still alive at the end of these thousands of voyages number between twelve and fifteen million people. And that's just an estimate based on the current state of knowledge, which is insufficient. It is estimated that at least two million captives died on the crossing for multiple reasons, often for the worst reasons, and these ended up in the abysses of the Atlantic Ocean.

This ocean can be approached in three ways.

We can see it as a junction between Africa and the Americas.

We can see it as one of the most successfully forgotten cemeteries of the world.

We can also see it as a world of plains, mountainous silences, and unknown lives, just as intense as those which stand in the sun, already fertilized by a tragedy that ought to oblige us to be better than we are. Alas, even in this moment, what is happening in the Mediterranean—where an immense cemetery is being dug beneath the flow of migrations—demonstrates that "The Atlantic Experience" remains a dead letter... The conditions and the context are of course different, but even in the vibrancy of a global awakening on a similar scale, the general indifference is nonetheless identical.

But let's talk about these dead Africans in the Atlantic.

No doubt there are those who, during the crossing, committed suicide because of a too active memory, a memory that resisted being erased, those who were dismayed by their inability to make sense with the means at their disposal of what was happening in the hold. And there are those whose memory had indeed disappeared in the circles executed around the famous tree, who believed that their memory had been erased and thus found themselves facing an insurmountable existential nothingness. What is it that best allows one to survive in the hold of those monstrous ships? Memory urgently maintained, or loss of memory? —"It's a subject worth discussing..." says the Baroness, prudently.

So, let's discuss it.

First of all, one had to be persuaded that these circles around the tree erased all memory of origins. That is plausible: these captives came from extremely powerful symbolic systems. What they were told took on the allure of incontrovertible truth. For us, even today, it is practically impossible to live without a system of beliefs. At that point, did those who were convinced of the efficacy of that tree and who ended up in those boats already feel like orphans? Did they sink right from the start into that "black melancholia" that the slavers and planters feared? According to this hypothesis, the erasure of memory was like a poison that killed—*bam!* right away—or else it exterminated slowly.

Next, let's examine the case of those who didn't believe in that erasure.

These Africans kept their collective memory. Collective memory is a powerful machine, but it is also fragile. Its absolutes must have been derailed all the more easily when the hold of the boat could not be integrated into those categories of worst-case scenario. Up to that point, such a damnation of the Black was unknown to the historical record. As a result, the catastrophe into which that damnation plunged these Black Africans was bottomless, horizonless. Collective memory thus functioned in a vacuum, and violently, but without providing a response, without offering any oxygen, with no support other than the flesh and spirit of the ones who still straddled both worlds. And so, that memory also killed or immobilized in an inescapable rancor those who managed to maintain themselves through its use. To be enraged helps one to survive, but perhaps less so to live. In both cases, with or without the power to recollect, death was often the result.

One doesn't decide to erase one's memory. It is memory that is structured by forgetting, and that, with forgetting, decides what will last. All memory is a form of coordinated forgetting, a necessary forgetting. Someone unable to forget would find himself as helpless as someone who forgets *everything*. In the horror of the hold, memories remained more or less vivid, depending on the individual, and more or less virulent or soothing, depending on the personality. The force of the collective was subject to the liquifying shadows of the hold; the individual was precipitated to the front line, left starkly alone, in sudden and extreme nudity. There was a terrible transformation, like that of a butterfly turning back into a caterpillar to start from zero all over again. The difference between those who got out and those who drowned can be found in this: *a capacity to be born, or not, out of individuation.* —"If I understand you, individuation begins with a void?" the Baroness asks me. I tell her: In that case, yes. At the time, the collective identity filled all spaces and all horizons. The hold of the ship was the site of a massive dynamiting of that communal identity. One had no other choice but to be born there to oneself, and in a completely novel way. In this awful history, forgetting is the architect of individuation, and the tree of Ouidah is its foundational song!... Today, things are different: the fundamental given of the contemporary world is individual experience, and it is the memory of the new collectivity that we must patiently invent.

I give you:
Relation as the substance of a private Genesis

The greatest hero of Creole folklore, the one that the storyteller of African descent would invent in the slave plantations, is named Ti-Jean L'horizon. He is small, young, weak in appearance; he inspires neither confidence nor a desire to condemn without trial, but he upends all obstacles, and manages to create for himself *ways out.* There are only monstrosities around him, the material realization of all the wounds of Egypt, and the seven capital sins. He is not in a fairytale; he's in the time-without-*manmans*-or-papas of slavery. *He is a stranger.* All that can sustain him is his cunning and his resourcefulness. The solutions that he comes up with are not collective solutions. He invents and invents himself at the same time. He brings out contingent possibilities and activates conjunctural energies. He generates perspectives and lines of flight. He advances by creating horizons. He is a beautiful hero with no memory.

There came a time when Man Ninotte's memory was so shredded that she could no longer recognize us; it was as though she no longer possessed a full consciousness of herself. She was sinking into a slow detachment from her own person, which made her forget the gestures of walking and the reflex to swallow. Old emotions, inscribed in fossil neurons, brought back memories like bitter absinthe, memories of angers, of childhood enemies that she began to discern everywhere, memories that awoke in her the behaviors of someone besieged. She fought with the void, struggling in the gaps of space and time. The forgetting that memory does not choose, about which memory is clueless, opens the door to the muzzle of that devil Bazil. In the rubble of her memory, what was left for us was the most visible aspect of her power: her body, still massive for a while longer, her face but without its familiar expressions, and her gaze, which no longer lit up at our approach. There was nothing left of that light that had enveloped us for such a long time, that fine pleasure she took in seeking us out, in just looking at her children, and that we sometimes glimpsed in the midst of the tempest of her shouting and injunctions. What remained to us was only what was visible, what howled out to us that it was not the essential, that the essential was elsewhere, that Man Ninotte was already gone. With what remained of her, we saw what didn't remain of her, and that was what still identified her for us, more clearly and more successfully than ever.

The captives who survived the slaveships brought ancestors to the islands with them, and thus all that they knew of Africa. But this freight was submerged in the liquifying pocket of forgetting. The structure of their memory had been tested to the limit by the terror of being forced to experience the hold, that unknown without limits of the ship and of the "immense journey." As Glissant says, these Africans were the only *naked migrants* who landed on the Caribbean islands and the Americas. Without clothing, without weapons, without baggage, without tools, without a library, without the smallest instrument. The only thing they brought were "Traces."

A thousand apologies, but we must go back once more to consider the Trace.

The combinatory power of the Trace is infinite. The culture that arose on the slave plantations (dances, music, codes, principles of survival and of life) was a combination of Traces, mixtures made in haste, marks that were never monumental, signs and emblems that drifted off, producing entire landscapes. A culture of shock, of encounter, of all the moral, immoral, and amoral ways of being in relation. That culture produced a heritage that we had to learn how to identify, in ourselves and around us, a culture that bore witness to a completely unprecedented American Creole adventure: encounters between continents, minglings of cultures, echoes of languages, deviations of phenotypes, maelstroms of antagonistic experiences, all open-ended and shared... The Trace came from that. This culture is therefore a *nothing-universe that subsists*. The result is something subtle, light, trembling, always becoming, something that intermittently lights up another possibility in the ruins of past symbols and lofty certitudes. The Trace is much closer to a question than to a response. The Trace is Creole. Jazz is a Trace.

For Glissant, the Trace is also that by means of which a very particular way of thinking can be grounded: a way of thinking that trembles. Trembling thought is not fearful or timid; it is the youthful openness of a conception that is saved from systems of thought and systematic thinking. To tremble is to frequent doubt and uncertainty, to expect the unpredictable, to live with the inexplicable, to take on the beyond, and to attempt to remain there as humanly as possible. It is what poets do. The Trace transports and magnifies this trembling. Under the prohibition of the plantations, the enslaved left more Traces than flourishing displays, more open and fragile aggregates than triumphant syntheses, more searching and mobile hesitations than proclamations. The Trace opens onto the infinite. Glissant reminds us that its fragility is what constitutes its resistance, and that its transience is what guarantees its duration.

The Trace is in conformity with the hindered nature of our artistic expression, of our esthetic, which was from the start that of the *detour* (of the disguise and the secretive). It was necessary, in this extremity of de-humanization, to survive and resist, to express without showing, to exist without fighting too hard, to hold tight without slackening, to act clandestinely so as to transform life itself. That's why the speech of our deepest thoughts was never literal and couldn't be. Neither direct nor plain, never spectacular but always opaque, condensed and circuitous, always in the horizontal prolongation of a thousand dozen different meanings.

Always in Traces.
It is in this formlessness, and through it, that our most important artists have emerged from the places where they are located. They

are Martiniquan, Caribbean, or American Creole through their capacity to magnify the formless. And it is through this very formlessness that they rid themselves of everything else, thus confronting the world's intractability. *Artists of Traces, artists in Traces...*

In his beautiful book, *Roots,*[9] Alex Haley endeavors to create a mnemonic continuum. His hero, the enslaved Kunta Kinte, has preserved a rich corpus of memories. He even locates the village of his ancestors, returns to the time before the original destruction, negates it, and reconstructs it. This way of perceiving can be found in the lineage of Marcus Garvey, who, for Black Americans, is responsible for forging a Black consciousness, an Absolute that erected Africa as a source, the land of return. Garvey organized their migration back to the land of origin. In the Americas and in the Caribbean, there were many individual attempts to return to Africa, to the original density of being, in order to escape from the turmoil of the explosive intermingling that had engendered something unintelligible and, from then on, unliveable. During slavery, the first generations of those who fled from the plantations, the famous escapees, or *"nègres marrons,"* were always haunted by the desire to return to Africa. For the enslaved who were born there, in the Americas or the Caribbean, and who sought their liberty, this urgent desire was transformed into a profound suffering, a vivid impossibility. Among those who managed to remain for a long time as maroons, there were some who ran aground on this dream of a lost Africa. This lack would determine the direction of their gaze, the current of their dreaming, and the paralysis of their life in the lands of Creole America. Césaire's poetic majesty developed out of this longing for a phantasized Africa. He made it into a source at once intangible and open to the world, and in its loss, in its omission, in its lacuna, he created one of the most superb poetics of the twentieth century. Césaire successfully transcended our initial lack. In contrast, the "return," when it is literally put into operation by Marcus Garvey's ships, opens onto an impossibility, no doubt exhausting itself for that reason. When memory only serves to immobilize itself, forgetfulness ceases to structure

9 Haley, A., *Racines*, trans. Maud Sissung (Paris: J.-C. Lattès, 1993).

the present, to give breath to the possible. The healthiest memory sees nothing but the future and opens only onto becoming.

As for jazz, it wasn't going to return to Africa; it was going to *embark on a vast expansion of possibilities.* Fed by African polyrhythms, by all the potentials of sound and melodic exchange, jazz is a music of the great encounter. That is why jazz will never settle on a part of itself, why it will explore all of its origins as far as it can—as I do now—without exclusivity, not contributing a desire to start over, or grieving for the same or for the intangible, but instead reaching for the infinite of the all-possible, which is born of ruptures and lacks that have been kept alive. That is why jazz is a Trace. Past-present-future; land lost—land gained; dream country—real country. These are in every Trace at once, ceaselessly reinvented by a process of becoming in which no anguish can paralyze the movement forward.... —"I see what you're insinuating," the Baroness tells me. "The door of no-return and that of the great return must in some way leave a place for the door of an expansion"... —Yes and no: the expansion wouldn't have a door, I stammer, nor even an archway. It opens onto everything, everywhere, from the start.

Since she no longer had any memories—neither there nor here nor elsewhere—when she became a memory without horizon or perspective, we became living memories; we sought memories in the way one seeks a fictive treasure.

Each star
Witnesses an impossibility that we were able to dream
And every firmament is but an order unto itself

On the slave plantation, art is not in the service of something sacred; instead, it draws out the sacred from itself, from a thousand Traces. Thus, in the most extreme forms of domination, when what is originally sacred loses its oxygen and its meaning, art sacralizes its own expression. Art is nourished by a sacred that is unsure of itself, trembling and free, fluid and available for all adventures. The blues, gospel, jazz, and the *bèlè* all depart from the dominant sacred to go further and create indecipherable forms of sacralization that verge on disorder in its most generative aspects. The biguine, which grows out of a popular culture that is hardly contestatory, would nevertheless institute disorder, rupture, and unpredictability in an alienating form of sacralization that utilized the instruments of the master. The biguine would de-sacralize the violin, the piano, the clarinette, in order to re-sacralize them in a way that can't be defined... —"A sort of secular sacralization?" the Baroness asks, worried, raising an eyebrow. I tell her: Sacralizations in which nothing is worshipped but in which something is vivified and liberated...

The Haitian "naïve" artists know of the Creole patchwork cosmogony of Vodou. The painters of the Saint-Soleil community told André Malraux, who marveled at their art, that they were assisted by the Loas, the spirits. However, they took from Vodou not submission to a divinity, but rather a multiplicity full of candor and precious innocence, capable of glossing over the frightening real, adorning the world, transfiguring it and recreating it in a sacralization-without-the-sacred of a lost paradise, of a possible paradise. Perhaps certain Loas carried these artists along, but the Loas did not dictate anything. In that same space, though, Vodou art continued to celebrate the signs and the forms, the irruptions and the powerful interweavings of the divinities.

In these extreme situations, the creation of artworks ushered in the liberation of the mind and body, the empowerment of spirits and the enlargement of consciousness. The sacred is there—in the encounter that augments you, that changes you without denaturing you—but the gods don't address art anymore; they no longer lend art its order. It is humans who speak, who advance rebelliously, as in the subtle evolution that, from *The Iliad* to *The Odyssey*, resulted in the gods' retreat, leaving the intelligence of Ulysses to act and decide in their place.

When the rains are violent and storms beat against the shore, you can see the bones resurface, an entire bed of remains that come from the Amerindian peoples who are now gone. Certain of these vestiges belong to our enslaved ancestors; their suffering also permeates every inch of this land, but their survival was so hindered, so diverted, and so fragile that what it produced often dissipated without leaving a remainder or was maintained with no testimonial. It is the memory of the colonizer that marks out our territory. All the rest (just like the experience of immigrants from India or China) would disappear from the official chronicles, subsisting only in the earth, in the ether of sounds and words, in the creative enigma of Traces, or in the fossil-memories of impossible witnesses. The land is punctuated by so many moments of stasis, so many stupors and dissipations, that Césaire regarded each blade of grass, each mountain, each ravine as a site of memory (as did Glissant). In short: he regarded the land as though it were a Trace in which you could sense the outline of impalpable monuments. To access the experience of being from these islands, to find, to understand, and to enrich oneself with what exists here, to transcend the blindness that the splendid landscape produces, one must be sensitive only to that which is lacking.

All these lacks join together and mutually inform one another.

All these lacks mark out and, together, expose other levels of consciousness.

All these lacks initiate.

After the departure of Man Ninotte, I found myself more than ever attentive to old stones, to the ruins of dungeons, to the rusted metal of factories and plantations, and to the Amerindian ceramics that you might trample in the sand. I contemplate the gray wood of the Great Houses and the huts, the profundity of the trees that have lived for so long. I attend to stories and songs, practices, customs, and manners. I listen to silences. I reflect on shadows and dust. There, where the colonial monument intrudes, the Trace calls out. There, where the monument crushes and reigns alone, the Trace diffuses and invites. There, where the monument shouts, the Trace sings. To remain sensitive to the Trace is a way of envisioning the reality of the world, giving it, if not its truth, then its mystery. By which I mean: its life.

For those who sing
Who live in laughter
Not only does time pass
It also obeys

When her memory was no longer able to control what had to be forgotten, and when Man Ninotte began to fade little by little from the world, a swarm of inert things took over. These things, accumulated over the course of a lifetime, and that seemed to us somewhat insignificant, had to be saved as this life was being extinguished. With the passage of time, they took on a peculiar consistency. When it was no longer possible for her to live alone—when it was necessary to arrange another life for her within a medical context, to gather the affairs of her entire existence into boxes, bags, and valises, which were divided up everywhere among her children—I discovered, among the things she had allocated to me, the fragment of the bladder of a dried fish.

Man Ninotte had drawn on it a child-like head.

The square block of the head, the eyes, the nose, the frown of the mouth. I found it and looked at it; that's all. I knew that the woman-warrior sometimes preserved shell-objects, the beads of the conch, the horns of an ox, dried gourds, and glossy seeds on which, in her meditative moments, she would scratch signs or draw forms. I knew she possessed the science of sewing, the secret of paper flowers, the technique for making candy, pâtés, and the decorated cakes for which she was legendary for a hundred meters around. But all this belonged to the chapter on industries of survival. The bladder, in contrast, with its parchment texture, its uneven cut, and its light-yellow color providing the background for the awkward design, this perfectly useless and gratuitous bladder hooked itself onto my life, resisted cleanings and avoided abandonment, maintaining itself in an aura redolent with tenderness. The bladder makes me think of those marks in the cave. No doubt, those marks are the acts of initiates, shamans, neophytes, temperamental poets, and spontaneous artists who placed their hands, scratched what they saw in flashes, responded to the dense form of a vision. These artists were a bit like Man Ninotte, who had drawn that head on this repurposed and flattened bladder and placed it in the sunshine to dry for a bit, a head meant to capture who knows what thought, what intention, what sentiment, and that ultimately expressed an unsuspected aspect of herself that life had never permitted her to express. I have always thought that my artistic tendency came from my Papa, that subtle reader of La Fontaine, the violinist who was awake to the pleasures of life and to what he found lovable in women. Of Man Ninotte I had only retained the image of an all-terrain warrior, the majoress of everything having to do with survival, without ever considering the moments she had devoted to minute creations, to those urges with no obligations attached, that her dreams and her reflections constantly produced.

There it is—that fish bladder.

Well over a century
If only for the freshness of the soul
(And a bit of freshness for an eternity)

The little bladder does not appear on its own: it transports the memories of Man Ninotte returning home with baskets of fresh fish. It contains the time she spent standing next to the basin in the courtyard for scaling, gutting, and rubbing the fish with lemon, preparing kilos of *waliwa*, *portugaises*, *daurades*, *marians*, and *koulirous* for us, but also for her trade networks on the street of the Syrians. It arrives with the fragrance of lemon, crushed red peppers, onions, parsley, thyme, garlic, and salt, the brine of a creamy consistency when the catch of the day could be found preserved with the *blaff*, a soup of small rock fish, with the stock, and the fried fish. It arrives with a host of fishermen who reign over the hustle and bustle of the market, the names, the shouting, the odor of fresh iodine, the scales that cling to everything, the dead eyes, the reddening gills, the intestines to be jettisoned, these moments of life, the time of succulences, spaces of sensation that pervade the heights of my memory and remind me to what a great extent fish were at the core of our ability to survive. The little bladder brings back to me the imprints, the crevices, and the furrows, until then invisible, the odors that my nose cannot capture and the flavors that are nowhere near my mouth, but that are still there, still everywhere. In that way I adorn that small bladder; in me, it takes up an abode.

Dreams that build
Patience that acts
Some flowering fronds in the mango-season

Our reflex is to think that there initially existed such a close proximity between art and magic that only the initiated could have the experience of leaving a mark in the depths of the cave. One needed to have a sure sense of purpose to crawl for hours in the cave's narrow bowels, illuminated by a flickering wick in oil, to confront the unknown, the inevitability of a landslide, to reach unforeseen spaces brought to life by light, and to take the time to imagine and then execute a drawing or a mark before going back. Such a journey naturally discourages crowds. However, in the caves that have been unearthed, the markings are innumerable; they pile up over decades. By creating a mark or a sign, a person could actualize a secret part of himself at the margins of the community. There, the initiate could display his singular talents better than anyone else. But it is also possible that cosmologies, origin stories, and dominant myths were assimilated and reformulated in diverse intensities and modalities by ordinary individuals, as is the case among the Australian Aboriginals. Each member of the community had to place markings on everyday objects—on sites, weapons, tools, the skin and the body; respond to collective challenges; deal with personal emergencies; comment on events; and embed these remembered events in a swelling tide of significant markings at different stages of elaboration, contraction, or expansion. The sacred and the divine, which mediated between the individual mind and the communal grasp of the world, nourished these spontaneous markings. You can still see them today in the cities of the world where successive waves of graffiti overlap over the course of what is now generations. What is it, then, that graffiti writers or street artists do, if not interrogate the disenchanted enigma of cities in their margins and forbidden spaces, project as personal symbols the question of their individuation on the great stage of the world? They reformulate many makeshift cosmogonies, contingent origin stories, passing mythologies, and hybrid urban legends that then migrate and connect. They form groups that cross oceans, languages, races, and frontiers. From prehistory to the neolithic and all the way to the contemporary world, generations of points, lines, hands and hatchings, scratching and stencils, and irreducible graphic enigmas are maintained by such mirror-effects, without completely detaching themselves from what makes them what they are. After the enchanted caves, the disenchanted and disenchanting cities offer to the human mind an unsustainable virgin page, an emptiness that must be animated or perhaps sublimated through poetic means. The graffiti writers, artists without divinity, explore such opacities.

Crawling through the obscurity of the earth's bowels with the intention of depositing a mark sparks in the mind of this original artist an exploratory fire, a will that encourages a confrontation with that terrible unknown. Once the mark is made, it enchants the person who then crawls toward the exit, confers an aura of singularity, and awakens the desire and the courage to return. The mark ushers in the individual who, slowly, becomes a person. This has enchanted us for thousands of years.

Some of the markings located in the depths of the cave seem to decelerate time and contain space. They take us back to primordial periods of fusion with the world and to our fascination with all natural forms, the splendor of which compelled Homo Sapiens to imagine them alive with forces and spirits. Even before becoming artworks, or being raised to the status of signs, these markings suggested a secret esthetics that the battle against death, the call of spirits (from lesser divinities up to a single great God) would eventually formalize. This fusion of human beings with the existing things of the world sometimes drove these markings toward fecund analogies, incantatory fixations, where vegetable, mineral, and animal forms would mingle with a variety of human forms. This hybridization transmitted an aptitude or desired force to the forms it modified. In this way, the world and its mysteries allowed themselves to be tamed. The hybrid form brought back the power of the old tree, the vibrancy of the animal, and the splendor of the formidable stone in condensations of meaning. Formal hybridization would disappear, but the force of the combination would remain in our imaginaries.

All artistic form is a concentration of presences previously dispersed.

That is why the slaveholders were so fearful of both forms and signs. Today, many artists abandon the frame of the painting to rediscover this kind of maximal concentration: for instance, the installation that locates its new significance in the very flesh of the world, its times and spaces. The forms that constitute *Les Mythologies de la Lune* [The Mythologies of the Moon] or *La Tribu Perdue* [The Lost Tribe] of Ernest Breleur are in no way hybrid: they are from before and after the metamorphoses—which is to say *beyond*... The formlessness that this artist works with (just like that put forward by Christian Lapie) suggests a variety of forms without letting them fully emerge. Their formlessness is a call: it spells out all forms, sorts out all forms, detaches all forms, and recapitulates all forms as though they were metamorphoses coming from nowhere—no place, no culture, no specific imaginary—but cognizant of them all. And that is their magic.

Sand yawns in the light
The day is a shroud over itself
A weary luster

Every Sunday, Man Ninotte, with the Baroness as reinforcement, made us clean the linoleum of the living room, the Persian blinds, the buffet, the table, and the four chairs. The procedure began with an orderly dusting. The house was located in the middle of town, which, always under water and under construction, subsisted in a permanent cloud of dust. The Persian blinds, just like the least little corner of our minuscule lodgings, were quickly covered over by a gray coat that snuffed out the light of everything. After tracking down the dust, fly droppings, roach eggs, and spider traps, we had to polish with that miraculous substance known as O'Cedar. With slaps of an old rag or a new chamois cloth we did our best to reawaken the mahogany glow of the wood on the stairs, the table, and the buffet. The Baroness supervised the work with her usual rigor: we all had to apply ourselves with equal energy, and the result had to be a bit better than just well done. To find ourselves together, with wet dish-towels, sponges, water, and soap, recreated the houpdila of a party atmosphere. The O'Cedar required a careful, even application, and then it had to be feverishly rubbed to a gleam until there arose, in a perfume of honeywax and mulled wine, a luminosity emanating from its depths. The chairs had to start reflecting the things around them, the tabletop had to proclaim its splendor, and the buffet under its slab of marble and zinc handles had to take on the allure of an immense enchanted chest. Once all that was accomplished, Man Ninotte took from the bottom of an off-limits suitcase a large velour tablecloth, thick and heavy, with pretty fringes in yellow gold, which might have represented the scene of a hunt, but where an unforgettable red of extraordinary flamboyance dominated. She covered the table with the cloth, smoothed it carefully so that the velour best captured the light coming from the windows, and there—wonder of wonders—she would place a bouquet of flowers she had obtained that morning from one of those nameless, placeless flower merchants who appeared on earth on the day of the Savior and on that day alone.

In the living room, Man Ninotte hung two paintings from the Syrians' shop. During this period of our childhood, my gaze often wandered over *The Angelus* and *The Gleaners* by the painter Jean-François Millet. It was almost impossible not to see them. I could spend months without looking at them, and then suddenly I would contemplate them for an eternity. In the two paintings, the fields extended far off into the distance with nary a hill, a tree, or a Black man at work. The horizon was strange, the clothes of the peasants remained an enigma, and the bales of hay were truly a mystery. Altogether, they constituted a world at once foreign and terribly close. For me, these people lived as though for an eternal moment, with no before or after, in an infinite present, total and tragic, at once full of a crepuscular hope and stilled without any perspective. Millet is a master of light. He doesn't make a triumph out of it, but instead subtly engraves it into a night that is just beginning, or a day with the texture of earth. In *The Angelus*, the night is there but light is everywhere. It rises from the ground, it falls from the sky, it reworks the colors on the fabric of the clothes. In *The Gleaners*, the night is still to come, but the day is already fading into a powdery clarity, drab like faded whitewash but softened by the divine light of three young peasant women in their quest for a godsend.

Why had Man Ninotte chosen these paintings?

That was not my concern at the time. It's only today, with no possibility of an answer, that I ask this question. Is it because they seemed exotic? Were pastoral scenes fashionable during the years when the city was beginning to transform lives? Or did they capture an energy launched against a poverty like hers? A will to get out from under poverty by mobilizing the forces of the sky and the obstinate vigor of the earth?

It is not time that gives life
It is living that gives life

Sunday was flower day. The flower merchants appeared in the deserted city with basins of arums, daisies, gladioli, poppies, bougainvillea, and all species of plant tucked into jam jars. They took up their positions along the Levassor Canal, on the sidewalks and along the parapet, and solicited the worshippers who were returning from Mass. And so, I have this memory which, over the years, has become an important one: every Sunday, Man Ninotte would set on the gleaming table a bouquet of flowers, mostly white. The façades of the houses facing ours sent back the morning sunlight, which rushed into our windows, was sliced through by the blinds, and magnified the radiance of the flowers. The bouquet remained for the good part of a week, long after the red tablecloth had been taken off and the room restored to its ordinary state. The petals accumulated on the usual layer of wax on the table, around the flowerpot, until the Baroness, suspecting that there were some mosquito larvae in the water of the fading flowers, got rid of it all. For me, this simple detail made Sunday into a day notably different from the others. Sunday was light without dust motes, a musical tranquility, a wonderland of glossy furniture, the red of the tablecloth projecting its pink hues on the wood of the walls, and the whole ensemble at the service of these flowers diffusing their vivid perfume into the far corners of the house. *A transparency.*

For decades, Man Ninotte created this Sunday poetry. It was an art of living beautifully. Such delicacy was quite surprising in a woman warrior. I wasn't aware of it until much later, not having thought about it before, and only thinking about it again when I saw a bouquet of white flowers caught in a particular light. Beyond that, she also made flowers in paper which, added to the candies and other Creole sweets, ameliorated her usual income. The Baroness had told me that before I was born these artificial flowers were a great success, that other mothers in her cohort would even fight over them. But the artificial flowers never took the place of her bouquet of fresh flowers, haloed in the faraway hymns of the Mass, of the bells swinging back and forth, of that bright burst of Sunday cleanliness. Without even thinking about it, I found that Man Ninotte started to exist, to still exist, in these bouquets of white flowers that traverse my life and give me access to that part of her that the rigors of bad luck and the sacrifices she made for us had never allowed me to see.

The *négrillon* that I was had never paid attention to these bouquets. The atmosphere of the room, perfumed with O'Cedar, radiant with fresh flowers, did not constitute for me a center of interest. My life, my preoccupations, and my explorations were elsewhere. The scene was set there, Sunday after Sunday, associated in my mind with the summons of the church, with the silent light, with the women who sold flowers, and with the aroma of eau de cologne coming from the worshippers. When the scene came back to me, it could have drifted off again on a tangent, tied as it was to nothing, floating around amid vague sensations worn down to insignificance. But something made me invent it, no doubt a caprice of writing, a poetic shrill note, and the scene remained in a slip of memory that served no purpose before coming to reinforce, like so many other memories, what I would then reconstruct of Man Ninotte in myself. The scene attained its total plenitude only in that relation. Things need to be linked.

But consider this paradox: For me, all bouquets of white flowers encapsulate an entire universe while revealing in this same universe the primordial geography of a lack. I am no longer seeing a bouquet; I am looking at myself. What sharpens our vision, what holds our attention, is what closes our access to a far greater sensible world. To look is not to see.

All that you know to invent in yourself
And this terrible happiness that obeys only you

As was the case with everything she did, Man Ninotte had wanted to initiate the Baroness into the commerce of those bonbons that had helped her survive. Preparing the confections is a delicate matter. The sugar is boiling hot, the fire omnipresent. You have to fiddle with the oven, manipulate hot pans, pull and knead the red-hot sugar until it can be sliced and modeled into dozens of striped candies. Melted sugar is brought to the right consistency, stretched out like modeling paste with added touches of color that spread out into multicolored lines. The odor of cooked sugar fills your brain and excites your saliva. Back then, we would all rush into the kitchen, ready, for once, to work hard. The Baroness, as always, held onto the first strands. Except Papa didn't want his *Mademoiselle the Baroness* to burn herself. He prevented Man Ninotte from engaging her in the dangerous phases of the infernal mystery. Officially, the Baroness was supposed to be satisfied with participating in the last phase of the process, cutting that coil as it was cooling down and extracting from it the dance of the bonbons. Unofficially, when Papa had his back turned, she would plunge right in, reproducing the smallest gestures that Man Ninotte was making between the fire and the burning sugar. It was also she who was in charge of delivering the bonbons to the grocers, butchers, or neighboring shops, or else to the houses of the city's mulatto women, who sold all sorts of things from their window ledges. As if time had folded back on itself, each time I see one of those saleswomen at a street corner, carrying that see-through box in which you'd generally find traditional cakes, *filibos* and coconut cakes, there is that gesture of Man Ninotte's (which cuts right through me), the gesture of extending from a nail on the door a long opulence of melted sugar—crystalline, sparkling, and whitening as it cools.

The Baroness is skeptical. She recalls the O'Cedar operation, the crusade against the dust, but she has few memories of that famous bouquet. She believes the bouquets were there only occasionally, and, as for the flowers, she doubts they were always white. She senses a fabulation on my part, which isn't surprising coming from someone who spends a great deal of time writing stories. She doesn't go so far as to suggest that I need help, but I can tell that she doesn't approve of letting one's mind wander about unchained in a savanna. I tell her: I have forgotten almost everything, dear Baroness. Often, all that remains is the poetry of things, the flavor following in the wake of an instant, the absurd epiphany of a Sunday...

(In this very simple happiness)
A few stones like friends
A landscape like a church
And the courage to still the silence

As a true native of the countryside, Man Ninotte kept the custom of accumulating plants. She had passed her childhood in the self-governing space of vegetable gardens, chicken coops, pigsties, and an abundance of fruit trees. In the *En-ville* of Fort-de-France, fruit trees were not desirable; people fought against the wild grasses, the dust, and the earth; they walled in, tarred over, and cemented everywhere. Upon arriving from her region, Man Ninotte found herself exposed to misfortunes, and thus the necessity of a garden, pigsty, and chicken coop. It was forbidden to have a garden in our two-room house in the city or in the cement courtyard common to all the families who were renting rooms in the house of the Syrians. It's important to understand that at that time, when everyone knew poverty quite well (except the *békés* and the mulattos), our survival strategy centered on accumulating. No one threw anything away. Everything was essentially polyvalent. Everything could be preserved, set aside in some corner, for years even, waiting for a new use to present itself. What ecologists today call "a virtuous circle" was then ordinary practice, even an obligation. The grocery stores didn't hand out containers and offered very few wrappers. Everything was sold in crumbs, in dust, in half-dust, and item by item. Butter, lard, and *roucou* were delivered on a square of Kraft paper. Flour, red beans, lentils, sugar—all were sold by weight in little packets that no one threw out. As for oil, gasoline, vinegar, or rum, you had to show up with any old thing that wasn't punctured. The demi-johns were like majestic queens. Bottles, always very rare, were charged a high deposit. You had to pay for them or bring them back for every transaction. Accordingly, all tricks would be employed to keep them as precious objects. The garbage pail of Man Ninotte was used only to feed the illegal menagerie she had started raising in the courtyard. The first little supermarkets would multiply packaging and fill the garbage cans with stuff no one knew what to do with any more. Practices changed, but Man Ninotte and the Baroness kept this aptitude for seeing a whole rainbow of possibilities in the least little scrap. Never did anyone throw out a vial, or any object made of glass or plastic. Not a jam jar, not a wooden crate, not a cardboard box, or a bag—nothing, nothing. You had to keep everything. Strangely, the house wasn't crowded: there was so much to create, to transform, to transport, to share, to stock out of reach of rats or roaches, that these hundreds of containers circulated at great speed from hand to hand in a calm, seldom-interrupted flow.

Ever since the time of slavery, when the masters controlled for the most part the ornamental gardens, Black men and women have accumulated around their dwellings medicinal, aromatic, and magical plants in what looks like an illegible jumble. Over the course of many years of experimentation, this practice has given birth to an ecological intelligence that has become the *Creole garden*. Man Ninotte, braving the interdiction, reproduced these timeless thousand-year-old practices in the communal courtyard of the Syrians. Like other families, under the shelter of the sheet metal roof she raised a Christmas pig, chickens, and ducks. But she also found the means to make her own garden. She arranged a forest of plants in a checkerboard pattern of jam jars, used-up basins, and plastic canisters. The construction sites nearby furnished her with earth that she would use to fill a milk carton here, a margarine tub there. The container was chosen with the specific plant in mind, one that she had procured at the market, from a cutting torn from the forest border, or brought back from a family visit to the area around Lamentin. The courtyard space was devoted to so many uses that all the room was taken up. As in a Creole garden, the plants had to be tightly arranged, some almost straddling others, on the side of a basin, in an available corner, or on the roof of a tiled shelter. During my childhood, even if I never paid any attention, I saw them all the time, like an indistinct mass, full of varieties. *Pieds-piments. Pieds-pois. Hibiscus. Ferns. Arums. Crotons. Atoumo. Brisée. Gros thym. Thé pays. Zeb-mouton. Zeb-mal-têt. Basil. Fleurit-noël.* Plants kept Man Ninotte company. Every so often she would throw a volley of water at them, remove a dead leaf, scrape at their earth. She paid no more attention to them than that, but not a week passed without her bringing back a new growth. The plants grew, gained strength, died, or disappeared into the hands of another local woman to whom Man Ninotte offered them. To give away plants was also a custom of the countryside that was maintained in this precarious cityscape. Every visitor who came from the foothills arrived with fruits and vegetables and left with fish, bits of fabric, shoes from the Syrians or, of course, with a plant in a jar that Man Ninotte had multiplied from cutting to cutting. Since the variety of plants is inexhaustible in number, and since each person wanted to possess them all, there was always something out-of-the-ordinary to exchange.

When Man Ninotte found herself forced to move, the Baroness had to divide up her plants among those who could adopt them. She took many of them with her. I, who had no interest in plants, also found myself with a bunch, which I placed somewhere in my house and then promptly neglected. When Man Ninotte became scarcely visible to this world, I started to fuss over her plants, to water them on my own, to watch over them without even realizing that I was doing so. After the great dispersion, her plants merged into the border of my garden and I forgot all about them, except when cleaning if I happened to bump into one of them, in bloom, magnificent, or all sad and sickly, an event that would send my thoughts back to her. There was a time when Man Ninotte could be found in her entirety spread throughout the plants in my garden. She stimulated my interest in them. She was at the basis of my infatuation with certain orchids. I could suddenly discern her presence in those that had belonged to her, and they would instantaneously radiate like lovely, unexpected treasures. Among the escapees there is a plant with brown leaves that produces over the course of a mysterious cycle small flowers of a very vivid rose-violet color. I don't know its name. I don't try to find out its name. I like it that it has no name, that it isn't catalogued anywhere, that it emerges out of this void. Released from its jam jar, it had grown at the edge of the terrace; then it detoured toward the earth beyond, at one side of the border; and then, after having disappeared for a long time, it started to become visible again and even presented itself like a lookout, a tender banner... —"I have the same one," the Baroness ends up admitting to me. "But it's puny and doesn't seem to improve with watering and fertilizing. Every day I ask her, and it's been years: *Hey Ninotte, my dear, you aren't doing well at my place?!*"

I saw the Baroness reign over the universe of the home, but I never saw her take care of the plants in the jam jars, as I did. Yet she inherited Man Ninotte's propensity to make vegetable beings into permanent friends: *langues-de-boeuf, langues-poules, crotons, hibiscus, red-plants*—all plants that chase away the bad Blacks; *roseau des Indes* with their properties that provoke abortions; and then that plant-your-luck that needs just a little water to proliferate into multiple vines of a green striped with white, which, at the Baroness's house, as on Man Ninotte's buffet, inspires in me waves of wistful admiration. There is something scandalous in the way the Baroness knows how to make the bougainvilleas flower, the way she gets the begonias to bloom and transforms no matter what dirty cutting into a remarkable plant. In her hands, insignificant thickets turn into splendid ornaments, and the plants that would grow old quickly anywhere else remain on the fringe of eternity in her home. Which almost seems unfair.

Man Ninotte had very early on been tossed out of the countryside so as to be placed, as was done at that time, in the home of mulattos in the city. I used a portion of this itinerary for my *Marie-Sophie Laborieux* in the novel *Texaco*. She was thrilled by the *En-ville*, just as she would have been by a promotion in status. Once she became a city dweller, she only rarely took us back to what were for us the foreign neighborhoods of La-Bélème, Jeanne-d'Arc, Vieux-Pont or La-Belfort. This was after I was born. But the Baroness claims that Man Ninotte went there frequently. No doubt, it was during the period when the Baroness, the first-born, was just an only child hanging from her mother's apron strings. For me, though, it was rare to take the rickety bus on that road to Gondeau, flanked with sugarcane fields and mango trees. I know there were a few people in the family who did visit on a monthly basis. But I am basically a city-person and know nothing of the countryside.

Everything about Man Ninotte came from her origins in the countryside: her Christmas pig, her raising of chickens to eat on Sunday, her medicinal plants, her spectacular laundry days, her sense of how to embellish time, her gifts and her transactions, her ways of getting by without making a fuss... The city that I knew preserved a lot of space for the butterfly grasses and the wild recesses watched over by mango trees. The neighborhoods were peopled with *pieds-fruits-à-pain, green mangos, pois d'Angole,* and other useful plants. Our band of *négrillons* would chase blackbirds, hummingbirds, and lizards, and we would lead colonial expeditions to streams where we could catch lapias. We held a registry of *pieds-zicaques, moubins, guavas, manjé-kouli*—all the fruits that you could eat without a knife. The proximity of markets bathed me in waves of vegetables, hosannas of spice, and aromas of the woods, to a degree of intensity that no child of the countryside could have imagined. Early on, the city was but a budding sprout in the interstices of a triumphant rural landscape. Ultimately, though, it was the city that vanquished its rural phantom. And yet for a long time the city retained, just like Man Ninotte, this superimposed invisible double.

Even the yam follows the cherry-picker
It is for you to trace the axis

We also had to divide up her jewelry. All Creole *manmans* have
their box of jewels. Man Ninotte wore very few, but most Man, on
certain occasions, wouldn't go out unless they could make a display
of chains, necklaces, rings, brooches—impressive, to say the least.
In that total annihilation that was slavery, one's appearance became
a primordial concern. All the Black folks of the plantation, when
they went down to Mass in the parade to town, made an effort to
show that they enjoyed the status of free Black, or at the very least,
that they were more than the color of their skin. Around each one
of the damned, good clothes, shoes (when possible), sumptuous,
spectacular fabrics, and jewels created a phantom double. These
jewels are now among the piquant notes and comforts of our
imaginaries.

Man Ninotte didn't have a lot of jewels.

She didn't invest much in displays or appearances. She would
sport her jewels at baptisms, communions, marriages, and
other ceremonies of a very special nature. The rest of the time
they remained at the back of her wardrobe in a *Vache-qui-rit*
box, crammed into a small suitcase, which was itself buried in
the wardrobe. It should be added that François-Arago Street
was intersected by two parallel streets, Lamartine Street and
Ernest-Renan Street, where a brood of jewelers proliferated. These
were phantomatic beings, lost in the penumbra of their workshop
and bent over black stones, with a magnifying glass hanging from
one eye or a mask protecting them from a sort of welding torch.
They came from a long tradition of more-than-ordinary slaves,
Black men with special talents who had found themselves free to
exercise their precious artisanal craft. Some of them even had the
luck to be sent to France to perfect their technique. Thus, there
existed from the start a few fellows who weren't really broke,
exceptional Blacks, so to speak. They weren't the type to just hang
around on the stoop with their mouths hanging open. They didn't
try to hoodwink you or to excite one of those desires that empty
your wallet. They were content to wait for those women (that is,
all of them) who knew that no life on this earth should be lived
without a bunch of jewels.

On the window of their small workshops could be found a display cabinet. There, you would discover marvels in gold and silver that could make you cry out with longing. Jewels were paid for according to a science of installments, cent by cent, in tandem with the small strokes of good fortune that might come one's way and held by the slim thread of a promise. Man Ninotte must have had to negotiate for her jewelry, exchanging various services—but there, again, her creative side would manifest itself. It often happened that she would melt down a bit of gold to extract from it something that she wanted. I remember a pair of miniature scissors that she would wear as earrings. I never knew, nor wanted to ask her: Why scissors? Was it because of her talent as a seamstress? Was it to celebrate all those little repairs that rescued our appearance? We will never know. What is left is the pleasure of imagining the expression of the jeweler who received such a request. *You said what, mââme Georges? Really? Scissors?!!* It has to be said that our jewelers were, for the most part, conservative; they had placed themselves exclusively in the service of tradition. They had been executing the commands of tradition for decades in order to satisfy our old instincts. *Colliers-choux, anneaux-créoles, chaînes-forçats* constituted the basic panoply of options deriving, if not from the depths of the ages, then at least from the time of slavery. The *béké* masters generally had at their disposal a favorite "*négresse.*" They would offer her necklaces made from links that looked like the links of an iron chain. They would also offer her beads of gold recalling a fairyland of pearls. The necklaces were formed link by link, bead by bead, lending these jewels a length proportional to the duration of the love that had inspired them. In the city of Saint-Pierre, these dominating women, these "matadors," held a string of fortunate lovers and pimps on a leash. For this reason, their jewels were innumerable and their necklaces boundless. The chain-link necklace bore witness to a desired bond, one that they hoped would be much less wavering than the bond attested to by the chain around the slender neck of the enslaved. And the hollow bead, that pearl of gold, signified through accumulation the extent of an affection that had been dispensed drop by drop.

The *béké* women (who definitely did not appreciate the existence of "favorites") never wore gold necklaces in the form of chainlinks or gold beads. They chose to display their haughty distinction with necklaces of real pearls. For Black women, jewels constituted—beyond the alchemy of sentiment—a treasure that could be mobilized to provide some emergency funds, to pay rent or to buy oneself a casket. In a way, jewelry gave us our first banks, and the first instruments of feminine emancipation that no ruffle-wearing Black man really knew anything about. For ages, jewelers reproduced very faithfully in gold the slave necklace, or *collier-forçat*, and the bead-necklace, the *collier grain d'or*. Over time, and due to the whim of the individual buyer, some novelties did appear: the *tétés-négresse*, the sugar-apple, the bees-nest, and the caterpillar, that reproduced in gold those forms inspired by living things. These had suggested themselves—no one knew why—to the satisfaction of all, and they were transmitted across the decades. But outside of this limited range, daring was rare. The jeweler from whom Man Ninotte had ordered the scissors must have choked: *But what are you saying, mââme Georges, you're really sure?!!* and resign himself, thinking that if slave chains or *négresse* heads had been imitated, then *why for Crissake not scissors!...* And so, for a long time Man Ninotte was the only one this side of the world's poverty to display these curious earrings. And the mysterious pleasure she took from them I find in myself at the sight of a pair of scissors of any kind.

This rumbling of the great rains
May the thirst of the foliage
Invent itself under full moons

I love the strange poetry of this jewelry. The chain-link necklaces evoke the alchemy of attachment and submission; they refer to the real chains of not so long ago. They are based on these chains; they signal that there is—in this relation between loved one and lover, in the links that I accept, that I assemble, that I wear—the strangeness of the sentiment of love, like an intensification and a loss of self. And they suggest just how much this loss arises from exaltation and rebirth, from a death that eats away, and a life lived to its fullest.

The chain link refers to the litany of shadows. Gold is a celebration of life!

It is also possible that each chain-link necklace, circling many times over the liberated throat of a woman matador, pointed to the absent chain, intimated that it was still there, that its persistence regulated in one way or another the most intimate aspects of our lives, our most profound access to small liberties. *Gold became a form of memory; it constituted an archive!* I also think of the wonderment that the first jeweler must have experienced when he imagined the chiseled form of a jewel in the troubling tip of a woman's breast, and sublimated it in that way, just like the other jewelers who immortalized the scaly form of a sugar-apple or the undulating mystery of a caterpillar, or, yet again, the minute texture of a simple bees' nest. The gaze of the artists who became enraptured by small things, even in the midst of all-encompassing shadow... Even if the shadow reigns without hope, this *love of seeing*, which mobilizes the tiny splendors of life in our ornaments, and which fixes them in gold, indicates to us the subtle paths that our survival had to carve out... —"If what you're saying is to be believed, gold transmuted these chains and sent us back to the side of the living?" ... the Baroness asks. I reply, cautiously: Maybe, or maybe not, but in these times of dehumanization, all creativity, even on the futile side, was, desperately, a form of resistance...

A sudden memory of the Baroness—There was a time when Man Ninotte wore a cross of Agadez to attract good luck.

Besieged by my evocations, the Baroness rediscovers a bit of her memory. She finally confirms my recollection of the flowers and brings me her share of clarifications. In Man Ninotte's home (*oh let it be preserved from infernal fire!*), the Sunday flowers were accompanied by an aerial shower called mousseline that made for them a bower of tender green. There were gladioli, daisies, anthuriums, sometimes lilies, but also branches of jasmine lifted from the balcony of one Madame Joseph, a mulatto woman of the area. The jasmine from this lady took over the railing of the balcony, dripping down into the street, within hand's reach. The other flowers came from Man Macé, a vendor at the vegetable market, expert in medicinal plants as well, who sometimes left our mother the unsold remainders. Man Macé, whom I don't remember at all, was located in that zone of the market reserved for the healers, those who had knowledge of the secrets of plants. It was from her that Man Ninotte received care when sick, whereas she would confide our health to the medical doctors from France. Although I often accompanied her when she shopped for vegetables, I never saw her negotiate with the healers. She must have only gone to see them when she had a persistent headache, a vague fatigue, an issue with a congested varicose vein, or some other small calamity that none of the children, except perhaps the Baroness, heard her refer to. We never saw her sick, but we could sometimes catch her in the act of sipping a mysterious tisane.

But let's talk about those healers.

They presided from their corner of the market over an extraordinary assortment of products: bushes, twigs, dried algae, pollen, seeds, flowers, roots, bark, unguents, brews... They officiated over this strange altar like Vestal Virgins breaching the sanctuary. Aromas rose from them continuously, like blankets of ether, penetrating the skin with a fierce persistence. These healers had access to another side of the world by means of who-knows-what vegetal portal.

They venerated plants.

They spoke about them as if they were people familiar with things far greater than us. They claimed that plants had invented this life in a small bit of blue algae, and that these algae had become acquainted with the sun and brought back its light so as to set off an intermingling of energies. They claimed that all terrestrial animals, ending with us, came from mutations of the algae and water as a result of solar chemistries. Plants could be found at the base of many beings found on the road to consciousness. Long before us, they had been able to meet up with bacteria, fungi, viruses, malevolent spirits, known oddities, and unknown ones. Healers claimed that in a time before memory, plants had known how to welcome deluges of dead stars and living comets, that they had been instructed there in the fecundation of marvels and calamities; that they spoke to one another and taught one another in a kind of reciprocity, and that they could protect one another even though they weren't the same species; that they knew how to kill, intoxicate, nourish, seduce, gently poison, put to sleep, awaken, suffocate, and carry off in perfume-flavors all the insects and all the animals; and that some had known how to domesticate men. Healers claimed that plants knew how to travel, perhaps at a slower pace, but in a much more fundamental way than our own, and that long before us they had undertaken forms of war and forms of love, forms of dissociated solidarity and forms of antagonistic association... They even claimed that certain trees were the tallest of living things, that they could live for millennia and shelter millions of existences; that among the trees, some were of a timid nature, reluctant to mingle their branches, but that others exuberantly intertwined with everything; and that their genes remained open to a thousand possibilities without ever being fixed on one of them. They claimed that the vines were concentrates of substances capable of provoking all the emotions, and that some could spread out over more than a thousand meters and retain more suppleness and consistency than a human substance could envision. At that point, one merely had to open the library constituted by these women without pages or print to enter into the most extraordinary of life's archives and follow its paths leading toward the future.

It was thus normal for Man Ninotte to have drawn together these vegetal memories of her own existence, to have put so many in jam jars right beside her, and to have coddled them and offered them as though they were her most precious things. Her approach was in no way utilitarian. She had everything she needed to take care of herself from the healers, fresh everyday and in profusion. All she had to do was show up. Or rather, what she accumulated with these plants was more like a joyous variety: flowering plants, plants in beautiful colors, plants for no purpose, plants with a curious allure that showed no desire to flower, and which were not expected to flower... While the healers had surrounded themselves with a battalion of allies of martial strength, Man Ninotte, for her part, placed herself within a motley band of fellow mothers and friends... —"I like this approach," the Baroness concedes: "Friendship applied to plants!" —I say: It's unlikely, but it's still possible that plants don't have the same way of seeing as animals do; their expressions don't look anything like ours, so we have a hard time seeing in them our ancestors, our parents, sisters, brothers, or mates. But there's a part of us that knows them, even recognizes them, and they identify in us immemorial genetic alliances, residues of old heredities. They detect the good and discern equally well the bad... That is why certain plants flourish at one person's house and not at another's; certain people are overwhelmed with their favors and their abundance and others (affiliated too closely with the animal) leave them sterile and as though indifferent... —"The mystical is keeping an eye out for you!"... the Baroness sighs. —But poetry watches over you... I tell her softly.

Each dream
At the temperature of the greatest ideal
Foundation of your survival

But let's return to the poetry of Sundays.

If there exists an expert in the art of sewing, it's the Baroness. Man Ninotte devoted her Sunday afternoons to prolonging the life of our shirts and trousers. She had become an ace at mending holes, covering up tears, taking up unraveled threads, giving new life to fabric. The ready-to-wear goods the Syrians had brought back to our land made her lose all desire to make new ones for us. She procured our clothing at their establishment, and then all she had to do was keep up their appearance despite the damage caused by our pranks.

Still, there were the household linens, the school clothes, and the Sunday clothes.

The house linens came from everybody's clothes—old togs, rags, and half-rags that had been stranded under mattresses, and that we could wear for our everyday antics whenever we wanted without inciting any reproach. As for the school clothes, they were the object of permanent surveillance. Man Ninotte scrutinized us when we returned from class, and the Baroness remained vigilant with respect to the state of our buttons. This clothing was submitted to hard tests. It was rubbed against walls, trampled by rushing mobs, subjected to ink wars and the rapid-fire splatter of stains. It was subject to premature aging caused by games of hide-and-seek and assaults against the enemy. Buttons didn't stay in place, and their stitching veered toward the langorous. The slightest offense against school clothing was received very badly, but what really had to be avoided was torn clothes.

A tear could not be explained away.

There was no circumstance that could mitigate its inadmissible existence.

It was a crime, and you were guilty.

And just as the guilty one assumes responsibility for his crime, frequently you'd be left with the torn pants for the rest of the week, exposed to the ridicule of the monsters of your kind.

The Sunday clothes were only for Mass and the service of communion. These clothes were more than "clothes" in the Creole style: in French, you would have said "garments." For me, they consisted of a pair of shorts made of gray polyester, a white shirt, and a pair of black shoes. This outfit was treated delicately and warily: you didn't hang out in it, and you gave it back to the Baroness immediately after returning home, just as you might return an object lent on consignment. As a result, the Sunday garb was less frequently worn, much less frequently worn, so it didn't get old. We were only relieved of it when we grew older, and then it was handed down to someone smaller. Man Ninotte and the Baroness were always pitiless with regard to ordinary linen, but to damage garments, to harm the Sunday clothes, this could send you straight to hell with no chance of return.

And so, on Sunday afternoons, in the dusty torpor of the city, the murmur of the pedals and the hiccups of the old sewing-machine would resound. The mothers of the street mended the miserable rags of the week and made clothing for future use. Man Ninotte would squeeze an infinite number of scraps of cloth of all qualities into the suitcases hidden above the closet. They served to fashion dresses, bedspreads, and nightwear. Our woman-warrior used ordinary cotton or otherworldly fabrics for the handful of ceremonies that would transform her into an impromptu queen, with a bearing suddenly almost as majestic as that of the Baroness. By osmosis or mirror effect, the Baroness wielded the same talent for dressing up any vestimentary wreck, drawing out something splendid from the least shred of cloth. For her dresses, she had perfected Man Ninotte's technique of cutting out from newspapers a series of patterns that she scientifically transposed onto Kraft paper. These helped her make outlines of decorations that were curious (to say the least), as well as mini-skirts, lowcut bodices, ruffles, and frills. Before such apparitions, Man Ninotte would close her eyes and Papa's busy eyebrows would crease. The Baroness would exhibit her creations at the Grand Ball of the girl's high school, or at the Ball of the Red Cross, those exceptional occasions when she took her place in the world's affairs. An excursion by the Baroness was first of all a day of experimental hairdos, special curlers, exploratory make-up, careful attempts, adjustments, and postures analyzed in a play of reflections in the mirror. The moment of the Baroness's departure was like the raising of a curtain in a theater, her return a feast of things to relate. During the week, the sewing machine remained in a corner of the room under a round wooden cover with a rectangular base; on Sunday, it occupied the table in the dining room. I heard that machine whirring so often. It stood as a centerpiece and was contemplated like a sovereign for such a long time that just seeing an old sewing machine in a film, or in the semi-darkness of a hut, can submerge me in a flow of long Sunday afternoons when Man Ninotte and the Baroness, busy with their fabric handiwork, would find themselves at peace.

Time is no longer a problem
It just passes
In the chaos of times linked together

There are also photos of Man Ninotte. I still have a large number with me, most often forgotten in albums. But some of them pulsate in a sort of halo. These are the ones that survived her move. First, there is a portrait photo taken I know not when, by I know not whom, that presides over my office next to the portrait of Papa. You see her in her valiant stance, hair nicely done, full cheeks, massive neck, and an amused look with a little hint of curiosity conceded to the photographer. She is holding the pose. I, who have never seen her other than moving at full speed, vanquishing tasks— brushing, washing, cutting, cooking, drying, ferrying, ironing—I look at this photo as though it were of a stranger. She's doing nothing other than standing there with the least hint of a smile. She's not sporting her wide-brimmed hat, her hair is styled, and her skin is not moistened by that eternal sweat in response to the sun. I tell myself that she's just stopped working a half-second before plunging back into her Herculean tasks. Yes, that must be it. She is immobilized, her mind free, for once, with an open gaze that seems to follow you everywhere and that nothing will be able to destroy again. Each time I look at that photo seems to have been anticipated by this mise-en-scène designed to make you believe that she could exist in any way other than under high alert.

The other is a photo where you can see her near the basin of the courtyard washing fish. You see her from head to foot, not sitting on a stool as she sometimes did before the colossal basins of codfish and sea bream, but no doubt standing on one of those occasions when she was preparing a quick *blaff* after a good catch of fresh fish gifted by a fisherman. In this one, she is smiling, as though taking a slight break that was respectful of the rushing river of her day. This photo is just right: it shows a stolen moment, a captured occasion opening equally onto what has happened and what is going to happen. It also shows a confidence, an *all-is-still-possible* testified to by the posture that charges her body with a beautiful energy.

The third photo was taken on her hospital bed. The old warrior is surrounded by her children; she's looking at the one taking the photo, and the others, I among them, are all around her. A moment of tenderness, of calm, of ordinary life, but one that, in the uncertainty of her look, signals that she's arrived at a frontier in her life, a tiny instant between the initial force and the weaknesses that would remove her from this world. A photo can release in me inexhaustible stories, but these only bring back waves of sensation; they are snapshots that I thought I had forgotten and that lie like underground streams in the arcana of my memory. They generate a space of sensation that I must have made use of in many descriptions; they are purveyors of impressions that I must have associated with certain characters or with those immodest reams of pages covered with writing. But I had never written about them, contenting myself with placing them under a frame on shelves that I sort through from time to time when a book calls out to me. It is not necessary for me to contemplate these photos for them to give me this sense of density—I was going to say this sense of *duration*—which fills me with the feeling of how excessively fleeting life is, a life that is borne along in an instant, impalpable but present, of inexhaustible eternity... —"You would place the 'snapshot' above the story?" the Baroness asks me, surprised. I stammer, worried: Where the story maims and simplifies the world, the snapshot leaves it as it is, the visible and the invisible, the familiar and the mysterious, the before and the after, a clarity and an ancient opacity, the explained and the shadowed-over, all woven together. The snapshot acknowledges the simultaneity of times and spaces; that's why literature is now more a matter of 'snapshots'... —"That's not clear," she says.—Precisely, but I will get back to that! I tell her.

There is nonetheless a loss of the moment in the photograph. The underlying idea of the one who takes it, or the one who poses for it, is to capture that moment so that it can be rediscovered later. That's already a way of giving up on being able to live it. What we get later is a new moment, of which the photograph is a part, but which it also takes away from us by bringing us back to the original moment that has been lost. In this way, before every photo that captures a feeling we've experienced, we perceive a lack; we experience a bit of the impossible; we reinvent an instant that we did not live and that we lost; and we lose the instant in which this attempt to go back in time takes place... The Baroness protests: "What the photograph gives us is less the moment in itself than the perspective of the photographer, and this perspective is a creation!"... —Exactly, I say. A creation based on a moment that the photographer considered not banal but rich, an instant that, for him and for those close to him, will remain definitively lost... —"Yes, but the creation is still there!"...—she insists. Of course, you're right, but perhaps the creation only has importance when one has lived everything there is to live... I tell her, guardedly.

Since later there will be more sadness,
Better to sing right away

On the kitchen table there was always that large gray basin that held the fresh fish in a thick brine. Around eleven o'clock, after her tour of the vegetable market, Man Ninotte would go off to tackle the Homeric *ouélélé* inspired by the arrival of the fisherman. She had her chosen fisherman. She had only to appear, to look down on the crowd and say: "Hey, Simon, I'm here, what do you have for me?!"... for the forementioned Simon to respond with a sign to be patient. He'd act like he'd forgotten her for a few seconds, then he'd cheerfully hold out to her his best catch of the day. She would receive his booty without having to pay right away, saying simply: *Thank you my son, may the good Lord bless you!*... Sometimes, she would ask him to add this or that fish with the succulent flesh, the one the fisherman would always try to hold onto for his own use. If an emergency called her back into the streets of the city, she would place the wriggling fish in the basin in the house; if not, she would clean it without delay because the house had no fridge. The fish would end up in a bath of brine, lemon juice, a heap of crushed garlic, salt, peeled red peppers, some cut-up greens. This mixture imparted to the fish an incomparable bouquet of aromas when fried in a sauce or in the airy subtleties of the *blaff*.

Her favorite dish was the *blaff*. White, red, yellow, or black, the rock fish were all plunged into a clear bouillon where there floated a green pepper, a knot of herbs, and a few things to tickle the palate. As soon as the fish were added, she would turn off the heat, cover the casserole, and let a subtle alchemy do its work. She savoured her *blaff* with a couple of ripe banana slices and a chunk of bread. It was her evening meal, with, for dessert, one of those glasses of milk to which she attributed the seven virtues of the world. I saw her, year after year, sitting at the table in front of her *blaff*, in the calm of a day's close, while the Baroness prepared everyone's bedtime, or in the calm of those solitary moments when the house had emptied out, once we had all grown up. The *blaff* was the moment for taking stock of the day, and, no doubt, the moment for preparing the battles of tomorrow. She stayed focused on what she was savoring, spoke not a word, and heard nothing. You could glimpse in the wrinkles of her forehead or the emptiness of her gaze a host of passing sadnesses, clouds of melancholy, flocks of worries or of small pleasures, their flight disappearing over a still unknown horizon. The most extraordinary moment was the end of her dinner: she would attack the head of the fish with particular care. It was as if there were much more substance in the head of the fish than in the rest of the body. Man Ninotte decorticated the head with the fervor of her faith in God; she sucked from it every last bit, hollowed out the cavities, explored the undersides, took apart the secret hidden spots, aspirated the grooves where there remained I know not what substances. When she had finished, she left only an abundance of little bones, grayish, clean, and immaculate, piled up in the middle of the plate. I don't know if the fish-head possessed a veritable flavor, or if it was just the desire to leave for her children the best parts of things. Whatever the dish was—chicken, rabbit, duck, fish—Man Ninotte kept for herself only the bony parts, the least noble morsels. Now, I tend to think that those meagre parts that we never liked, parts to suck more than bite, were ultimately, and without doubt, the best.

The Baroness, following her example, had become a specialist in bones. It was useless to try to appease her with slices of flesh. From a chicken, she would take the wings, the head, the feet, and the bones of the thorax. When it came to fish, she would welcome the skinniest specimens, the minuscule ones that exhibit mostly their bones and flippers, and, of course, the heads. The chicken in the oven on Sundays was often stuffed, since the Baroness adored the stuffing mixed with the carcass. That was her gala feast. Papa, to whom one served the fleshiest parts, didn't understand that a Baroness of her stature could find pleasure in wearing down her teeth on those pitiable little skeletons.

For the catch of your nets:
The rare garfish and the blue balau
And the most unusual of the black carangue

Among the arts of survival, the soup must also be mentioned. Since Man Ninotte and the Baroness would kill a rooster or two chickens every Sunday, the heads, wings, feet, and innards would find themselves thrown into an ever-renewed broth. It was kept simmering eternally, refreshed from one week to the next, growing quite thick because Man Ninotte added to it whatever vegetables happened to show up, as well as the rest of the rice or noodles left over from preceding meals. She could add to it the debris of no matter what carcass, ham bones, scrapings of fat or the meat from an ox's foot. The soup was served hot with stale bread. I consumed it without enthusiasm during my entire childhood. For me, it belonged, like the fish, to the ordinariness of poverty. Many years later, I found it, intact, of the same consistency and quality, at the house of my brother, Paul, the musician. This *yé-yé*, plugged into the avant-garde music scene, was the furthest you could imagine from Man Ninotte. I never saw him take care of a single thing at the house, and he interested himself even less in what was cooking on the stove. He was the type who would eat all alone, much more preoccupied with the adventures of his band than by the family drama. Yet a good deal later, he took pleasure in gathering his friends around this soup. He would concoct a similar marvel, which I tried out in a state of astonishment, and which let me recall (with regrets and remorse) what the original soup, unappreciated, must have been like. His guests went into ecstasies over this culinary success, one that gets better and better as the days go by, and even better when it has had a chance to rest in the pot. What is most extraordinary is to see the musician *yé-yé* preparing his soup in an outside kitchen like those in the countryside, with the same gestures, the same way of cutting the spices and local onions, of arranging the ingredients around the stewpot before adding them, remaining for more than a day by the bedside of this mixture where there floats, like magic, Man Ninotte herself, in her entirety.

The Trace is there
It is held in suspense
Not offering itself, not taking shape
Informing secretly and making secret

Here's another mystery from that time. In general, Man Ninotte cooked with the cheapest ingredients. Her network of fishermen assured her an abundant supply of fish that she circulated in a barter network. The country folk and the market-sellers brought her vegetables, yams, cabbages, green plantains, and a myriad of fruits. When vegetables were in short supply, she would go off to acquire some at the market. But it was usually on this semi-free foundation of ingredients that she would cook our daily meals.

Among the abundant vegetables, there was breadfruit.

The origin of the breadfruit tree dates from long ago. Introduced by the colonizers and used to nourish the enslaved, it became, after abolition, the "tree of liberty." The former slaves who no longer wanted to work on the plantations, and who constructed their dwellings in the back country, planted them all around. You couldn't die of hunger when the trunk of a breadfruit tree could be found within reach. And when you didn't die of hunger, you didn't need anything else, above all not a slave master disguised as a boss. So, to bring Black folks back to their fields, the planters proceeded to cut down that species of breadfruit. But that was a lost cause. In the landscapes of my childhood, all the huts, even those in the working-class areas of the city, were flanked by the trunk of a breadfruit tree. Breadfruit is normally cooked in large squares, in water, sometimes accompanied by other vegetables, and a bit of codfish. Man Ninotte adored it, like everyone else, but she had a special place in her heart for the *migan*. To make this dish well, you have to cook the chunks of breadfruit in spices until they melt and merge with the pieces of salted meat. For the final result, you would obtain a gluey consistency of a tender yellow color, which you could accompany at the time of serving with a hash of grilled cod. The *migan* (because of how often and inevitably it showed up when Man Ninotte had found nothing else to cook) was, for me, the very emblem of poverty. I detested this viscous paste, just as I detested all forms of breadfruit. If I declared that I didn't want to eat it, Man Ninotte would shrug her shoulders: *Si'w pa léy ou ké domi kotéy!* "If you don't want it, you can sleep next door!", meaning that you would go without eating entirely. As I grew older, I could avoid eating breadfruit in all its forms, but it would come back again and again like a calamity. Man Ninotte ate it in moments of solitude with as much appetite as she had for the *blaff royal*. The *migan* disappeared from my life until it returned, in my later life, as part of a ceremony of memorable flavors that today allow me to savor it as though it were one of the marvels of the world.

These are the images that move me: baskets of various vegetables, sweet potatoes, yams, cabbages, carrots, cucumbers... The assortment for the *blaff*: red peppers, packets of local onions, *bouquets garnis*, garlic, the salt box, pepper, and limes... The tablet of cocoa with which she concocted a thick chocolate and that could be found placed on the table in a large piece of Kraft paper. The rice and the lentils that had to be washed grain by grain. The dried codfish, flat and sparkling with salt, with its slightly disagreeable odor, giving rhythm to our childhood of *macadam*, fish cakes, fritters full of onions, and hot peppers with avocado... All these things were so frequently served they bored me no end. I awaited the rooster or the Sunday chicken, or those Saturdays when her pocketbook allowed her to buy us steaks that she would marinate in spices before cooking them, perfuming the house in the fragrance of happiness. I was forced to eat what she made, for to abandon a dish meant going to sleep at the neighbors' house for good. The least reluctance to eat one of her dishes shown by any one of us would torture the woman warrior. According to her philosophy of existence, children should be happy. So, she used more of the products we preferred, secretly watching over our pleasure, while assuring herself that the official order remained in place: *Si'w pa léy ou ké domi kotéy!*

Our meals were in perfect symbiosis with the fruits and vegetables of the season. Fish established the base; meat constituted a luxury. All had spent time in a marinade. Fried, *en daube*, or in a soup—the spices crowned with hot peppers established the very insignia of good taste. There was no fridge, domestic preservation of food necessitated salt, drying out, and the marinade. The ingredients had to do their best to keep some hint of their flavor in this effervescent base of spices without which even the best of meals strike me as hopeless.

She never turned off the transistor radio. It was a little box with batteries that was found on top of the sideboard, in the corner closest to the kitchen. When it was nearing the end of its life, we bought another. Whether she was preparing the meal of the day, resting, or sewing, Man Ninotte listened to it without really listening to it. She would lend her ear from time to time to capture something resembling the news. Not an instant of the day, or even the week, went by without the babbling of the transistor radio, its words and its music. From time to time, she would approach the radio, turn up the sound, listen to a snippet about a catastrophe taking place somewhere in the world, or a song sung by Tino Rossi whom she adored, and then she would go back to the task, leaving it on. Sometimes she responded to the device, entered into dispute with what it was saying, explained something to it or cursed it out categorically. I never saw her maintain the same relation with the television, which arrived many years later with money from the Baroness, who had become a teacher. Man Ninotte's time was that of the radio. Once her curiosity for images—in black and white, then in color—had passed, the television was never really part of her world. Any transistor radio I hear brings her back to me, instantaneously, in continuous visions of our everyday lives. There were incredible moments, such as the day when I heard her cry out: *Hébé bondié!...*, and saw her throw herself on the device as though it were a rat to crush with stones, then raise it to its highest volume and try to grasp what was being said, all the while refusing to understand.

The radio announced the death of General de Gaulle.

De Gaulle was a part, an extension, of the radio.

An invisible part.

It wasn't until many years later, with the arrival of the daily newspaper, and then the television images, that we had a clear idea of what he looked like. But we knew his voice down to its smallest details. His dragging syllables and spectral grandiloquence symbolized France. Ever since his June 18 call to action, the elderly locals were persuaded that de Gaulle was addressing them, that he had called them *directly* to his aid. During the war, there were dozens and dozens who hurled themselves into the storm to go save de Gaulle and gun down a few Germans.

They saw a bunch of Germans, but they never saw de Gaulle.

Even if they came back more or less handicapped, they transmitted to their children that veneration for the man who incarnated France with his voice, who had called them up, and thus who had *named* them, and who, for them, had vanquished Hitler. De Gaulle became, for nearly two generations, the good papa far away, a phantom who watched over us, *who made us visible*, and to whom, for that reason, one would have gladly given everything. The image of Man Ninotte, standing petrified next to the transistor radio, trying to convince herself that the untouchable general had left this world, that all, from that point on, would go very badly, that France would abandon us to the shadow, and that France itself would be invaded by hordes of barbarians—that image stays in my mind, and very often I have the impression that transistor radios are singing to me once more of the death of this Monsieur de Gaulle.

The devotion that an entire generation of Martiniquans felt toward de Gaulle is very real. Our enslaved ancestors had always believed that France was not really aware of what the white planters were inflicting on us. Any good news always got to them from the boats that went back to France. Even the Code Noir that Louis XIV and Colbert published so as to regulate the crime of slavery, to confirm it as an affair of State, could appear to them like a rampart against the extreme cruelty that the masters were capable of. The mulattos entered into politics in order to make themselves visible to France in a certain way: French citizenship was demanded as a means of exit from nothingness and shadow, almost as a kind of humanization. When, many generations later, the call of June 18 resounded from the Galena radio sets, the listening maroons, the thousands of colonized people relegated until then to limbo, felt as though they existed—and they were grateful for that for the rest of their lives. The mechanism of the "he who brings the good news" still functions. A prefect who represses the crowd by means of tear gas is denounced to France, which no doubt ignores the event. A minister or a president who comes to visit us has to be the bearer of something that acknowledges us a bit more as a point of reference and that renders us, by this fact, a little less empty, more visible to the world… —"You're exaggerating again. Everything that's excessive is insignificant!" the Baroness comments, condemning me in the process.

To live in immobility and silence
At the refined point of movement
In an unfathomable music

Joy! There is a fund of joy in these memories, an indefinable quality that hardships don't manage to disperse. The photo of Man Ninotte, standing up to clean her fish, clearly shows the glitter of laughter in her eyes. She is not simply smiling at the person taking the photograph, but also displaying a contentment with life that rises from the greatest depths, brought to the surface by the opportunity extended to her at this moment. A delight dwells in me then. Despite the memory of poverty that this photo so fully revives, I sense the persistence of joy.

We weren't sad!

Man Ninotte and the Baroness were not sad!

("Oh, come on," the Baroness grumbles.)

The old house opened to us a palatial universe. Every meal seemed to be part of a feast. The scent of a cake baking in the oven was felicity. The desire to consume didn't get the upper hand. The least acquisition was received as a stroke of good luck. Simple ordinary things became infinite by being lived to the full. Smiling, laughing, overt teasing, dancing, singing, partying, and taking pleasure were all subject to the law of the loot. Happiness was plucked even from the infinitesimal, in all its forms, over the course of hours, days, and weeks, a quest that was savored and always satisfied, worthy of the paradoxical abundance that was experienced by hunter-gatherers with their austere practices.

Life's plenitude palpitates around us.

It can be found in the evident contentment of the birds. It is in their twists and turns, woven with songs greeting the light. It is in the games that young animals retrieve from their inexhaustible instincts. All of these creatures know this vitality that rises up from the rapture of being alive, a vitality that comes from nowhere and that has no cause!... —"That could be explained," grumbles the Baroness, "by the fact that the most clever animals have been able to store up richer experiences; that this is how they have been able to survive better than the others. This spontaneous joy would have favored those with genes that incline them toward happiness from the start." —Exactly, I say, but all life is that vitality for living charged with an exaltation with no cause, no origin, and no contrary: the purest of joys. I discover it again in these memories like a felicity that has always been there, at lower or higher intensities, traversing trials and time. *"There was joy! – Deo gratias,"* the Baroness exclaims in exaltation, "and simply saying it doesn't express it enough!"

This solitude that does not isolate but gives
In ample relation with all human things
And a few others as well

LEGENDARY OF LANGUAGE – We had chosen the most beautiful of coffins, something lacquered that I've forgotten all about but that sported all sorts of gold trimmings and chiseled handles. Nothing was beautiful enough. It had to be something that could magnify for us what remained of her. The world, life itself should have stopped with her—and we too—but everything continued on. Everything was affected, but nothing had changed. Death drove us back to earlier convictions about immortality. It was the only way we could tolerate this beyond that, all of a sudden, she had unveiled to us. The Baroness claims that losing your mother places an abyss at your heels, an abyss that doesn't suck you in but that pushes you out as though outside of a nest, to inhabit what remains: landscapes of invisibility.

We tried to save what could be saved. She—so strong, so weak, so courageous, so terrified, so invincible, so exhausted, at once the conquerer and the victim—had been, in our eyes, an astounding manifestation of life. How could we imagine that nothing of her remained? Our everyday consciousness could not reconcile itself to this fact. But an age-old lucidity adapted itself to the phenomenon and indicated from deep down that nothing of what she had been existed anywhere, any longer, and that, in response, as a refuge, all we could do was celebrate life: the life in her, her in life, and life in the indistinct form that she had suddenly become. In this way, death unveiled to us compelling landscapes of heightened aliveness.

The wood of the locust tree sinks down
But in your name
And in your place that hails the world
The dream of the locust tree defies eternity

The undertaker signaled to us that it was time to reclose the coffin. We united one last time around what was no longer her. There was nobody there except a group of assembled children who didn't quite know what to do. Our pains and our strengths mingled; one became the other; all of us were nothing more than a prolongation of Man Ninotte. The ladies who knew the prayers and songs were not there. Only we were still there. The sorry fellow from the funeral home, who had seen so many others, patiently took it all in, discrete and polite despite everything.

There are things that are difficult to close.

There are open things that cannot remain open.

There are impossible things that we must let go.

There are silences that cannot be overcome.

It is true: there was nothing to say. Nothing to chant, nothing to cry out. From now on, things were beyond the reach of ordinary language. Touching her, stroking her cheek, arranging her collar, a fold of fabric. The gestures themselves seemed absurd. However, an *utterance* sought a pathway in each of us, a desire to formulate things, to seize the world with a bit of voice, a balm of words, a magic stroke of language. Sapiens must have had to improve language in the moments when the unspeakable inflicted frontal blows on the limits of his expressive capacities. The unformulable and the unsayable, true friends of the poet, are the treasures from language's peak.

Consider, dear Baroness, this hominid who stood up for longer and longer periods of time, who liberated his hands, who found himself facing a new horizon of possibilities. Try to picture him. His arms stir the empty space so that he can maintain balance. His fingers close on nothing; they spread, they come together, and they grope in the void. The hands that were shaped over the ages, and the genes that were preserved—these will determine the possibilities that will emerge onto the plane of accident and necessity, danger and desire. For a long time, I pondered that time when the hands of *Homo erectus* found themselves before the void, useless, available, directly in touch with the emotional and creative part of the brain. Among the things that could shape these hands into more complex instruments, aside from tools and practical objects, there was this *grasp of the void*, these signs that articulated space, that projected desires and that ordered, conjured, and palpated the invisible world, deploying impulses that formerly served for foraging insects. The hand gestures and the possibilities afforded by the fingers, which were simply utilitarian at the start, found themselves available for the accidental, the involuntary, the sometimes purposeless, in the wake of a dream, the shock of a delirium, or the progressive architecture of a thought. That's what's most precious: that grasp of the void, which configures what exists only in the mind, those inventions that give meaning to the world, or that ceaselessly configure what does not exist. And since words didn't yet exist, it was hands that dealt with the unsayable, that were the first to confront it. Those who still write with their hands remember those generative moments; the hand still possesses that memory, and even that consciousness. The hand outlines sounds, words and images, flavors, colors, and forms that have no other outlet. Thus, the hand models from nothing; it is stimulated by other hands that, all around it, are searching for the same thing, responding and advancing toward more and other experiences.

And for that night
No length of candle
Will limit the extent of my hopes

The poet Édouard Glissant wrote by hand. He wrote at night. Nighttime, he said, brought him into immediate relation with almost the totality of existence, with all possibilities, with everything invisible. No doubt the tropical nights remained his favorites. They were charged with sonorous lives, with the tremulous and the inextricable. What swept over him during this nocturnal creativity was surely the atmosphere of Antillean vigils, the circle trembling with the light of torches, the entangled voices of the old plantation storytellers and the singers of *bèlè*. It is likely that fear—the sacred fear that enriches all childhoods, just like the fear that is consubstantial with these torchlit nights—enriched Glissant's perception of the world. The world surged forth from the indecipherable impetus transmitted by those who were presiding. It surged up in him suddenly, in an always inexhaustible totality. He surely wanted to retain this initial terror, this ban on understanding, this thirst placed on alert, this abundant obscurity that would require the great suns of consciousness.[10] And so, he wrote by hand at night. If the gas lamp hung over his first writings, perhaps more than was needed, it was no doubt because it also flickered like the flames of the torches. It created an ambiguity, made the shadows speak, animated with incertitude the welcoming resistances of the paper beneath the gesture's grasp. Thus: the night, the night, the hand, the hand—like vectors of light and like vectors of Relation.

Next there was the pen, pen and ink, never the ballpoint as far as I can recall. In that too, no doubt, in the tilt of the pen, there was the memory of the thirst for knowledge on school benches, a memory that invokes a child's writing, still seeking itself, applying itself near the iron inkwells, learning to tame the Sergeant-Major pen. No doubt, there was also the memory of the almost imperceptible squeaking of this pen as it spun out the swirls of its ink, distributing thoughts, intuitions, and insights even more vast that his hand tried to capture in flight. And then this love of paper, not only paper, but of the notebook with, as I recall, those stiff covers, those black cardboard bindings that anticipated the book. And then this cramped writing, economical with space, a relic of an era when paper was rare, notebooks precious and impossible to find, when you had to optimize space, and then also, surely, the vow not to spread out but instead to plumb the depths, to excavate the silences, to orchestrate the cries, to make a seminal word rise from the richest vein. I remember having heard from Glissant that his first period of writing, the most intense, occurred in constrained spaces, with a notebook placed on his knees, and that he had always celebrated this initial discomfort, wanting to rediscover that

10 TN: Chamoiseau might be referring to the title of Édouard Glissant's *Soleil de la conscience* (Paris: Gallimard, 1997).

hindered desire from which all later expansions would have to be attempted. From the trembling of the torches, from the fragility of the hand, he will have brought back the trembling thought, the thought that pushes away all the totalitarianisms, the prison of systems, the explanations that impose themselves as definitive so that he could offer the openness of a poetics of indefinition, a poetics that supports the widening, deepening expanse, a poetics that allows for a vigilance over every instant in the wake of the uncertain, the splendors of intuition, the solitude that has become solidarity. From that which lies beyond writing, beyond genres, beyond linearity, beyond all ostentatious language, in the nomadic and unfamiliar languages, he had chosen the ever-subsisting mosaic of archipelagos. There was no need for an ocean that would furnish the link, just the work in its becoming, crystalizing from one writing to the next, itself diffused into all possible genres. From the primordial night, from the guiding hand, he will have brought back this capacity to confront, intact, the mystery of a world bound to its diversities, a world that is inexhaustible, vital. And thus, he will have modeled a tolerance for the indefinition and the incomprehension of the night, a refusal to fix it in an interpretation, no matter how generous that interpretation might be. He will prefer to privilege the act of listening, a participatory perception, a spiral of questioning, forever renewed, against a backdrop of Antillean terror, or, perhaps, against a backdrop of those commotions that animate outbursts of beauty.

His hand came before the typewriter. The hand, it's true, confers an organic connectedness to sentences, stirs up ideas so that they remain free. Ideas are held together by the movement of the hand, the *consciousness of the hand*. Since there is union there, in the magnetic grip of the hand, chaos can open up, hollow out, spread out, become vertical, practice detour—and all that at the same time. And when the mind, awestruck, confronts the mysterious, then it is these lines, drawings, and scribblings that take over, the free gesture releasing a form, the scribble desacralizing the universe of the sentence, the scarcely identified form signaling something opaque that transforms the page into a map of wandering generative forces—the Trace keeping company at all times with the inexpressible.

There was, no doubt, a care taken for the time-tested sheet of paper, a care that testified to the struggle that linked together the dissociated, a care that dissociated that which, by being linked together, violated the acute clairvoyance of things. Each notebook became weighted with a burden of formlessness, which surrounded the writing that remained just below consciousness. The space beside the lines created a materiality that could not be transmitted and that served as a support for the incisions the typewriter would later produce. Glissant carried each notebook with him wherever he went, holding it as close to him as possible. Each notebook was part of him, as in a Digenesis. If, at times, the ancient form of genesis works to contract things until they form a single unit, Digenesis diffracts absolutes and protects us from them. Glissant's manuscripts thus testify to a quest that was at first manual; it is consubstantial with the Martiniquan landscape, so completely charged with our nights, our sounds, and our moons that all the Martiniquan earth thrives in this alluvium that surges forth and offers us what we need to make the world fertile... This is a bit of what I see in the handwriting of Édouard Glissant.

Here is the gift:
To find the new in all ancient knowledge
And the plant-for-all-ills under the wise, giving grass

Jojo the Algébrique had the advantage of being at once a genius at math and an unlikely practitioner of the arts of poetry. He drew often—by which I mean: he interrogated the lines of the real. And it is he who would salute the sun each morning by reciting a few of Césaire's verses. He understood, I know not why or how, that poetry allows us, if not to understand or conquer, at least to humanize the world, and that poetry is not content with the possible alone. Poetry searches for foundations and for lines of flight.

So, it was he who knew, faced with Man Ninotte's coffin, how to access the impossible word.

He recited something that I found very beautiful, something I don't remember, but that set us free. The Algébrique has this ability, in extraordinary moments, to elevate his words to a higher level. The words are made distinct, like precious objects: they quiver with unknown meanings as the breath of an accomplished diction lends them distinction. Then the words emanate wavelengths that go from luminosity to tranquil clarity, all of them, together, borne in the swell of a hypnotic obscurity. Before the coffin, the pace of the speaker's voice slowed down, became more solemn, but in no way triumphant. It was like a prayer offered on one's knees in a field of ruins. The sobriety of his gaze became more profound, his arms rested at his sides, and his hands no longer found a reason to move. His words detached themselves one by one, sustained in a single vibration, the sentences emerging slowly, one by one, in the crystallization of a series of sensations, images, colors, and sounds... I no longer know what he said—poetry, prose, personal thoughts, or a composition taken from a school assignment—but it was what had to be said, exactly as it had to be said.

Language comes to the rescue of both the hand and the body. That which was only destined for a purely utilitarian use could also be used to indicate what doesn't exist, what emerges in what can be told. And what can be told will become a force capable of lifting up entire clans and tribes, spreading almost without limits the power of the creative mind. The inventions of gods, of devils, and of demons will take on their first consistency in language, and by means of language they will begin their journey; they will begin to enter into combat with one another or be transformed through exchange. The gods will be able to fashion the different tribes. These mythical constructions will assemble the hordes that until then had lived side by side without knowing how to join forces. The dissociated will be able to aggregate. The antagonistic and the irreconcilable will discover solidarity. Patchwork collectivities will succeed in moving and, equally, in being moved. Gradually, the ecosystem of mental productions will bring together groups of Sapiens to an extent previously unknown: chiefdoms, nations, states... No longer is it simply the functionality of the group that manages to keep it alive; from this point on, it's a matter of sharing an imaginary construction that one can inhabit, for the most part, as a collective. Since then, it's what doesn't exist that has supported us and transported us the most. We tell the story of the road we take; we inhabit what we imagine; we are what inhabits us and what we imagine ourselves to be. In an endless loop, we invent past, present, and future all at once.

It isn't enough to love
Make great joy from what you love

The colonizers thought that their language was the only one capable of saying things. The Amerindians and enslaved Africans thought so too, and they experienced the languishing of their languages, which had become useless. They believed that they saw their soul worn down along with their language, almost like a part of their blood. Memory gets rid of languages that no longer serve us. These languages start to wander "between phantasms and phantoms." The encounters among languages placed them in the relentless forging cauldron of language. Here, in Martinique, forgetting carried away the rubble of lexicons; it made them into fossils that steal into the stories and into the debris of rituals and chants.

The Amerindian languages collapsed into the abyss of a quasi-genocide.

The African languages expired in the inside-outside of the hold.

The language of the colonizer (dominant and thus blind) can only express his singular arrogance.

A real without alphabet emerged.

The inexpressible then reigned.

Enslaved peoples first confronted the inexpressible with the inaugural cry that resounded in the hold of the slaveships, and then with dances that spelled out the remainders of a sacred syllabary. Finally, the desire to speak, the obligation, also, to see, to hear, and to express oneself pressed together the surviving words, diffracted their sonorities, carried forward their meanings in mixtures and detours, until that desire produced this functional weave that was the Creole language. For us, the language identified as such was still French; however, our sensual grasp of the world was through the linguistic alchemy of Creole. This language was almost invisible to those who spoke it. It was undetected even when storytellers and singers elevated it to the fertile heights of a new genre of narration. It is important to understand that Creole was a language, unaware of itself as such, that it remained invisible to itself, and that it refashioned the world in all the diversity of its human palpitations. Within the dominant French language, the Creole language would remain like a terrifically active lack, a howling underbelly, then like *a mute who speaks*, as Jacques Coursil has beautifully proposed.

After the abolition of slavery, the Tamil language brought by Hindu immigrants to our islands was quickly asphyxiated. It descended like silt into the sacred rituals. The Hindus had the right to erect temples and to be consecrated in the votive cults of a few divinities who had survived this exile. The debris of the Tamil language became the fossilized phrases in the memory of the *pousaris* priests, disappearing as these priests disappeared. A few final words, like archives of emotion, light up intermittently in the incomprehension of many. Today, the language is brought back by Hindu militants, having been made a bit more available for study; but the most beautiful fragments remain in those few sentences and prayers that the *pousaris* conserve in a fold of their memory, where they can feel the vibrations—obscure, healing, and fecund—of what it is impossible to say.

I offer you:
Two-three sticks of sweet cocoa
And the grapefruit glacé

As soon as it appeared, Sapiens' consciousness was confronted with the inexpressible, that which cannot be articulated about life, death, and the world. Natural forces were noisy and sonorous, the sky full of hustle and bustle, and the earth howled from the mouths of its volcanos. No doubt Sapiens perceived in those forces prodigious beings, gifted with fabulous languages that his imagination undertook to identify. We should also try to imagine the moments of silence that accompanied the reigning splendors: sunsets, lunar wonderlands, seedbeds of stars that at times seemed alive, great landscapes where earth, vegetation, and water entered into inaudible and grandiose symphonies. It is still possible to envision the original silence, the inexplicable magnificence, like an injunction to consciousness to elucidate what is perceived. Consciousness would respond initially with the *feeling of the beautiful*: an unrest mixed with terror and fascination that will be lost in the idea of the sacred, or in that emotion supposedly inspired by the divine. In the face of such bolts of lightning, what can one say? And how can one say it? From where can one draw a language able to advance so far ahead? Some had to sketch out gestures, open up like blossoms to the generative force of the cry and to those ancestors of song. Others discovered themselves while dancing. Many simply had to be crushed by incomprehension. The inexpressible took root in human expressivity, constituting all at once an unknown source and an unattainable desire. Poets must have come into the world very early on, at the border of an obligatory silence, pensive, contemplative, often immobilized at the edge of this vertigo, executing gestures of conjuration or of grace, giving orders to the invisible, the sounds of their throats searching for meanings. Poets must have been born even before they knew what they were, from the dance, from the chanting, from writing or speaking. Poets are the ones who yearn for the inexpressible, not as a problem to be solved but as a source of sunlight in which to thrive.

Let's talk about the feeling of the beautiful.

Imagine this inchoate human consciousness opening onto three immensities: the threat posed by a human unconscious charged with all the forces of the animal; the omnipotence of nature and all living things; and the infinite dissolution of death...

Imagine what happens to this human being...

Consciousness begins to detach itself from the unconscious; it senses its separation from everything else in the world. It starts to perceive itself as subject while constituting its surroundings as object. It is buffeted by fear and incomprehension under the immensity—the furies and the serenities—of nature, the cycles of light and shadow and of sun and moon in their inscrutable movement... Danger is everywhere. To survive, consciousness must study the sky and the starry nights. It must endlessly and astutely observe nature, where the creative pulse of vitality is concentrated. It perceives at multiple intensities the infinitely large and the infinitely small, equilibrium and disequilibrium, the horrible and the sublime, the rotten and the splendor of the fresh, the sumptuous and the insipid, the bizarre and the pathetic, harmony and disharmony.

A concentration of major proportions; an expression that is total.

Besides the fear and the incomprehension, and in the face of an unconscious that threatens consciousness from the start, there will emerge fascination, astonishment, curiosity, attraction, and bursts of a chaotic sensibility that inspire in consciousness the idea of an all-powerful creator, the postulate of a great invisible architect, the premise of a cosmic intention, a divine intention, that would organize this immensity. There will emerge, then, the attitude of admiring submission, which is one of the first signs of an encounter with beauty.

Danger is everywhere. To survive, incipient consciousness will also study living things: trees, animals, insects, other hominids that live close by... It will know the deadly strength of the life that desires to keep on living, the material density of living creatures, their ferocity, their ingenuity, their innumerable languages. Consciousness will contemplate the silent mass of great stones, cliffs, mountains, and, above all: the mystery of the face of the Other Hominid and the animated depths of his gaze. All of that gives the impression not of a spectacle, but of an inextricable weaving together of *presences*, as Mr. François Cheng proposes in his meditations.[11] Faced with the flux of these "presences," our consciousness makes itself a "presence." The "presences" are both far away and close, attracting consciousness and repelling it, distinct from it while traversing, electing, calling for, and thus comforting it. "Presence" is the way to name the indefinable reach of living or mineral things in their most beautiful radiance.

This is the initial stage of the desire to know the Other. The Other, here, can be defined as being all presences—living, human, vegetal, mineral—the irruption of the elemental forces—wind, earth, water, fire... The Other is also oneself, that obscure, chaotic, profound self, the unconscious that works over the spark of consciousness with forces of madness and the deviations of animality, and which nourishes impulses, desires, and dreams. Archaic consciousness will perceive all presences as living: the elements, caves, stones, night, wind, sun... It will glimpse there an unpredictable, secret, obscure, invisible, and powerful being—that is, beauty. The radiance of the beautiful is in the intensity of an existing thing when it inspires in us the sensation of a presence.

The beauty of salt sparks
When the sea remains docile on the talons of heat

---

11 *Cinq méditations sur la beauté* [Five meditations on Beauty] (Paris: Albin Michel, 2006).

On certain evenings, seated before her plate of *blaff*, Man Ninotte would find herself submerged under a tide of worries. Worries about the day that had just passed and worries about the next day, which she was trying to figure out how to resolve. Too often, her task must have seemed beyond her strength. She never complained. She could cry with rage and impotence without making us bear the burden. The Baroness must have been aware very early on of her difficulties. She served as her second-in-command in ways that were far beyond the responsibilities delegated to her. Above all, she worked her butt off at school. She knew about the undeniable need to learn, and she established a direct relationship between what the teachers demanded and her future capacity to resolve a good number of Man Ninotte's worries. Jojo l'Algébrique also became aware of that pretty quickly. He put himself to work, knowing why it was necessary. If his grades, in whatever subject, were below an A, it was because there was a misunderstanding between the teacher and him. As for me, I wasn't aware of any of that. The only advantage of being the youngest is that the blows of misfortune fell first on all the others, and the strength of those blows dissipated well before getting to me. School remained a kind of task. But I was partially conscious of this difficult moment when Man Ninotte, before her *blaff*, would lean back in her chair, her arms folded and crossed above her head. She gave me the impression of having to get through all the nights of the world. To see someone cross folded arms above the head is, for me, a sign of having to shoulder the heaviest of burdens; it is one of the forms taken by distress. Some time had to pass before I discovered that this gesture has existed in Africa, as well.

Here is the offering:
A people of sea urchins
Of rare octopus
The star apple, impossible to find
(And the last pistachio cone)

In the ancient tombs are to be found simple objects, positioned with care around the remains: small stones, seashells, pollen, pigments, flowers.... Things that, all the evidence suggests, do not have a particular use (unlike weapons, food, the signs of social rank), but which must have allowed those who placed them there to express what hadn't yet been expressed by anything else, and that no other language could articulate for all eternity. The discovery of death is one of the first tragedies of an incipient consciousness, the source of its endless consternation. The dead visage lends beauty to the faces of the living. The extinguished gaze magnifies that beauty. Death always exalts the density of life; it always reveals life. The attempt to ward it off inspires further elaborations of the beautiful in rituals as well as in the gestures of magic, supplications, signs and symbols, religious conceptions of survival and immortality and rebirth in all their possible forms. Death constrains us to produce actualizations of our imaginary that resist time and that help us to live better. *Death opens us up to ritualization.*

No human mind exists without the sacred. The feeling of the sacred also arose from the inexplicable totality of nature, from the incomprehensible immensity of the universe, from the mysteries of existence and the desolations of death. The idea of the vast creator who gives meaning to everything is the ultimate completion of that process of sacralization. That is why, for so long, the beautiful and the sacred will be inseparable. Before inhabiting art, the beautiful will accompany the sacred. *The sacralization that gives meaning to what exists is the primal energy of beauty.*

The feeling of the beautiful opens onto the poetic state, that aspect of life that escapes obligations related to immediate survival. It is when the hunter observes a bird without thinking of killing it; it is when the warrior lingers an instant to gaze at a flower. The feeling of the beautiful is present in the one who gathers a useless green stone and contemplates it, as in Saint-John Perse's *Anabase.* The initial poetic state opens onto the feeling of the divine and the sacred, at which point it nourishes magnificent dreams, ideals, and natural values, as well as an ethics of sublimity. It can lead to psychic ecstasies of admiration, burning contemplation, and a type of adoration that one finds in the sacredness of religion. The feeling of the beautiful is always at the source of the feeling of love. As Edgar Morin explains, the amorous feeling intensifies curiosity, mystery, devotion, adoration, a resonance with the divine, the desire to know, the desire to possess, the desire and the quest... By giving birth to love, the feeling for the beautiful can reach the sublime. Love can associate the psychic ecstasy of adoration with the physical ecstasy of orgasm, a sublimity that only the relation to the divine, to magic trance, or to religious fervor can accord to individuals. Today, with secularization and disenchantment, it is love that concentrates all the profound energetic forces of the feeling for the beautiful. It is love that confers the greatest poetic intensity to individual existence. Sharing the secret of his music, Mozart said that he brought together notes that love each other. *The feeling of the beautiful opens onto the infinite languages of love.*

The feeling of the beautiful excites oceans of contemplation. Contemplation is not observation. It leaves necessity behind. It knows that water is illumination, and that night breathes in the opalescence of dreams, that there are universes in the knot of a shred of bark and an entire world in a corner of the balcony. It knows how to surprise the mosaic of lights on a rainy boulevard. It luxuriates with pleasure at the windows, on the heights of the foothills, and in the calm of the terraces. Its languor is intense, its immobility precipitates it toward all things. It penetrates what it looks upon and is penetrated by what it sees in return, until the lines of the real grow wider and a plenitude surges forth in all that contemplation perceives. *The feeling of the beautiful inaugurates a mode of understanding.*

The feeling of the beautiful can make us love a tree, worship a stone, or go off to encounter flowers and landscapes. It impels us toward *contact*. It is born of emotions and sets off emotions. It develops, from experience to experience, an emotional range that will become the unique sensibility of every individual... I say to the Baroness: The best of man is beautiful: goodness is beautiful; gentleness is beautiful; friendship is beautiful; joy is beautiful; devotion is beautiful. To us, generosity always appears beautiful... *The feeling of the beautiful participates in the humanization of man.* —"But then, what do you make of those Nazi doctors in the concentration camps who listened ceaselessly to the marvels of classical music? Didn't they also frequent beauty?" the Baroness interrupts me. —No, they patronize an esthetic, I mean: they patronize that which man has made of an old, de-activated, received notion of the beautiful, forgotten now, no doubt...

To beauty frequented

No infernal cycle

Let us remember that in the tales of the Creole storyteller from the time of slavery there was nothing that could save the hero. Ti-Jean L'horizon could not count on any good-natured prince. No angel accompanied his shadow. No good witch served as his fairy godmother. His universe presented itself as utterly pitiless; he had to get along on his own. That always made me think of the stance of Man Ninotte who, with respect to us, had recourse to yelling, orders, warnings, and anxious reproaches. Hers was an inflexible posture that never wavered and never debated. Hugs and kisses were out. Words of love were unknown. The only recompense, as in the Creole tales, was that food and sweets were never lacking when asked for. If by chance she wasn't able to bring us enough, she was pummeled by despair. She redoubled her efforts to find something ... *and she found something!* In the Creole tale, the ideal end, the ultimate treasure, was often a feast. Psychologists argue that the absence of the father required of the mother of our matrifocal families that she create a certain distance and, in that way, that she remove the risk of any definitive fusion with the omnipresent, omnipotent mother. It was often the grandmother or some aunt who would provide maternal affection, whereas the mother incarnated distance, the law, and decisive authority. To create distance, not intimacy—that was the battle to be won.

I love to compare the worldly language of the storyteller to the language I was able to experience in the shadow of Man Ninotte. The storyteller explained things with silence, with mime, with clowning, and with twenty different qualities of gesture. His body was a score that he could play completely from one end to the other. Sometimes, his voice recounted one thing and his body articulated another. His tensed body could contradict what his joyful voice was saying. His eyes, his eyebrows, the sounds that came from his mouth, from his throat, from his belly drew you toward an assortment of emotions with multiple meanings. The listener had to demonstrate an attentiveness to different levels of performance, to sense the danger in a veneer of sweetness, to struggle with the fear that laughter can spread. Before us, Man Ninotte, for her part, wore a constant frown. Only a vague nuance in her eyes would indicate that she was in a good mood, or, alternatively, that you'd better not be naughty. On good days, her gait was slower, more relaxed; she went forward attentive to what was happening around her, stopped willingly to chat with a friend, was available to the moment, to the useless activities, to the wasting of time. Otherwise, she was just a bulldozer going up and down the street, returning in a hurry to the house to deposit her purchases, then taking off just as quickly down the creaking staircase. Never did she make me think she pitied my fate. A plea for compassion had no truck with her; there was only her imperious injunction to be brave. When we were sick, her yelling abated. We were rubbed down, hydrated with cinnamon, nutmeg, tonics, and herbal teas, or brought with our complaints and sufferings to the doctor. But if the infirmity went on for a while, if a joker lingered between the sheets and hung out in bed, then exhortations would stun him with implacable force. The child who was just pretending to be sick had only one solution: to put up a fight. We were thus forced to decode that pitiless arsenal in order to identify her immense love, constant sacrifice, and infinite attachment.

I remember from those childhood meals the central dish, which was yellow plantain. Nourishing and sweet, it was cooked simply in water and served to children, mashed, cut in rondelles, or sliced. This dish could accompany anything; it went marvelously with fritters, rendering daubes, *blaffs*, and ragoûts sublime. I can still see Man Ninotte during all those years, leaning over my plate of yellow plantains, splitting the pieces she had served me from end to end, separating off the tips, devoting herself with more care than necessary to removing the central vein that was said to be dangerous. She spent several minutes doing that, focused, silent, available. At those times, her gestures were slow and deep, so generous that they could escape the shipwrecks of oblivion and represent the quintessence of a tenderness without limit, lodged at the heart of this constant state of high alert that she personified, and that taught us, day after day, how to live in this world in which nothing came easily.

Happiness of a wicker cradle to play the aristocrat
When well given, given for good

The most difficult moment for the African captives was when the boat raised anchor to move out into the open sea. The captives had known the life of *barracoons*. They had passed through the tree of forgetfulness and found themselves chained, head to toe, with people of different ethnicities and different gods. They knew nothing of their future. The general opinion was that the whites intended them to be eaten. But from where they were, they could sense the coastline, hear the hum of the forests, the rustling of the savannas. The odors were still familiar. The respiration of the nourishing earth still rose above the rumbling and spray of the ocean. Except that then, *manman*, there was the terrible evening when the captain surreptitiously raised the anchor to set sail toward the coral reef beyond which there loomed the open sea. The ship took off like that, cautiously and in silence. The captives in the hold, anesthetized by their heavy heart, didn't suspect a thing. The ship tackled the somewhat tumultuous passage, opening all its sails to the horizon's unknown. It was then that the captives felt the change. They no longer sensed the "presence" of the earth, its odors, its dusty breath, or else it might have been the rolling of the boat that signaled the menacing expanses. Despair crushed the suffering, the terror, all the deaths that occurred on the spot, the desperate leaps, *manman*, the horrible jolt that initiated the immense voyage. In the annihilation of all known languages, the scream, bursting forth a thousand times over, became a primordial cry.

Many centuries and many generations later, Césaire would write through the detour of a poem: *The ocean is the root of the lung of my cry.*[12]

The cracking of the hatch. The squeaking of the locks. The raising of stairs and passerelles. The tolling bell of the last anchor that was raised and that strikes the bridge. A week. Two weeks. Three, six, seven, eight weeks...

What remained in the oceanic night of the hold?

---

12 In "Éthiopie." TN: Chamoiseau writes: "*L'océan est racine du poumon de mon cri.*" The complete quotation is "À l'océane racine du poumon de mon cri" and is translated by Eshleman and Arnold as "at the ocean root of the lung of my cry" (pp. 800–1). I have modified the translation to reflect Chamoiseau's rendering.

What remained was the terrifying lapping of the open sea; the acid of incomprehensions; the suffering and the chains that knot together solitudes—and reinforce them too; the erasure of landscapes and points of reference. No object, no sign that remains, only a nudity that has become scorching despite invocations and incantations. Memories float like the debris of an old disaster; they come up against vile smells, volleys of saltwater, fumigations and pittances of food. Shadow has eaten away the time. Rays of light are lost in the rolling of the waves without troubling those who remain immobile. The lost country maintains its presence over the course of weeks in wrenching images and hallucinatory visions. They soon repeat; they are already fading. The spirit of each person is struggling, constructing oblivions, vivifying wounds, in a long mental anabasis, and a catabasis too, that opens onto death—desperate death, vicious death, melancholic death—or else the spirit is lost in the channels of fright, or else, unexpectedly, it attains that refuge of the living where certain existences are able to find themselves, maintain themselves, under the protective wing of an entire species.

There:
To invent the day that is coming
And all the others after, at the sole discretion of your dream

Man Ninotte had her fetish formulations. It is impossible for me to remember them all. Of course, there was this maxim that she repeated after the funeral notices had been transmitted by the radio, or just like that, for no reason, at any moment of the day: *Neither flowers nor crowns, only bank notes will be accepted!*... Or else, when one of us went off on a lark and she could find no way to oppose it, her maxim of conjuration was: *Go where you want, die where you must!* Or, again, the frequent exhortation: *Pa fè mwen ni a vini wè zot lopital oben lajol…!* "Spare me having to visit you in the hospital or prison!..." If a piece of good fortune came our way, she accompanied it with a chuckle: *For Black folks every day, for békés one time a year!*...

But the word that stays with me is: "categorically."

I said it to him like that, categorically!... I looked at her, ha!... categorically... I told her like that, categorically, don't let that happen to you again!... She put into this word firmness, menace, pleasure, a covetous tone, a revolt of the will, a call for strength, something that cut through the air and gave you the impression of an implacable boundary. Papa, who sipped the French language as though is were a sweet, aged rum, also loved to caress words. No doubt Man Ninotte had taken from him this pleasure in tossing off her "categorically," which glittered with tangential meanings, runaway meanings that she herself couldn't measure or limit.

Make a vow
To drink the bitter absinthe with three clover caterpillars
Until well crocked

Just before they sealed the coffin, in that swarm of images, objects, and memories that traversed us all, I realized that our relationships with Man Ninotte were not identical. Each one of us had our own history with her, and each possessed a unique story. For me, the last to arrive, it was suddenly clear that everyone else had known her longer, more deeply, in more prolonged circumstances, and in a different way from the way I knew her. The prize for longevity, of course, went to our Baroness, the first-born, witness of the beginnings, a second mother sacrificed from an early age to responsibilities, and thus exposed to a greater extent than we were to the enormity of what was opening or closing in the wake of such a coffin. What use would it have been for us to question ourselves when your memories, Baroness, encompassed our own, and surely went beyond them? I imagined how, as each bolt was tightened, another memory would be taken away from you, and how others would be constructed, or would be privileged. I realized how, as each bolt was tightened, thoughts were being set loose in my mind, initiating the revelation of what was going to be imposed on us and what was going to subsist in us or lie around us like debris from a great shipwreck... A bit of nothing: a plant, a word, a sewing machine, a doily, an old valise, a whole heap of rubble like seedlings that each of us would come up against and reflect upon at one moment or another of our lives. When the tirade of Jojo l'Algébrique was over, and we had to give in to the polite impatience of the fellow from the funeral home, there was the last look, the last vision, the last kiss, abruptly sliced through by the lid of the coffin, that cushioned *clack!*—categorical—that resounded for a long time in us and throughout the world, ushering in whatever there was of her that we would, from that moment on, preserve.

A young lady accedes to the title of "Man" when she has a child or when she gets married. *Man* means, quite simply, "madame" in French. In Creole, it is also exactly half of the word "*manman*," and it vibrates in a way that resists translation.

Here is your blood brother:
Who sharpens his dream
On the stone of his lucidities

If, like everyone else in the land, Man Ninotte heard the funeral notices, as far as I can recall she never went to any burial. She watched the processions with us from the height of her window. François Arago Street is situated between the cathedral and two cemeteries. The processions on the way to the tombs had to take this route, and during that migration the life of the Syrian shops was suspended. The Baroness tells me that the most spectacular processions were those that came out of a Freemason lodge, located just a bit further down the street. It was an impressive ritual in which the men would transport the coffin on their shoulders, advancing millimeter by millimeter in studied postures that added to their legendary quality. I don't think I attended the circus of the Freemasons, but I often saw these ordinary cortèges reach what one could call, at the very least, arresting proportions. People were still trampling on the steps of the church as the head of the cortège passed through the entrance to the cemetery. The instinct to accompany the family in mourning was strong; it was a constraint that didn't need to be policed. The funeral notices that had been transmitted by radio enlivened that old duty and that ancient call to order. The deceased would start to take on greater dimensions in proportion to the human emotion he had inspired. What remained of a life could be measured by the number of compassionate attendees. This number indicated the quality of the dead person's soul, the exact weight of his good deeds.

For a good person, a procession of good people.

For a dog on this earth, a parade of ants in an empty street.

A spring

Says that she is your surname
That her froth is your first name

It was the Baroness who composed Man Ninotte's funeral notice.
I was charged with taking it to be broadcast by the radio station.
I never knew who composed the burial announcements of former
times. They were disseminated in writing or through the voice of
the towncrier in the quarters and the foothills to round up people
for the wake and the burial. I had always been fascinated by the
tenor of these words that were at once conventional and tragically
intimate, words that called for solidarity in suffering, implicating
us all in that confrontation with the ultimate dragon. These
notices specified the maiden name beneath the married name and
the members of the family; there were details about uncertain
relations, the labyrinth of cousins; the dense tree of alliances was
displayed. Also specified was the place of work, so as to mobilize
the colleagues of the deceased, and the door was left open for
an informal expression of sympathy. Buses were even chartered,
which were stationed at strategic crossings, and which brought
people from related labor unions as well as friends. The funeral
notices of the *béké* were much shorter. They informed without
rounding up people: just the name was given, and the date of
the burial was barely indicated. The burial always took place in
the morning, almost on the sly, to preserve them from being
contaminated by the dregs of the country's undesirables. There
was a time when the nickname was more useful: it was always
better known than the last name and it identified the person
better. For Man Ninotte—better known as *Man Joj*, or as *madanm
gwan chapo-a*, "the woman with the big hat"—mentioning the
nickname would perhaps have been necessary, but the custom of
nicknames had already lost its force. So, the rallying cry of our
little tribe remained highly conventional.

We wanted her to be immortal, so we invented paths of light
for her, a bacchanale of memories, of concrete objects, relics, and
sensations. No doubt, she was above us, or else at some spot in
a place she loved, in the bacchanale of a vegetable market, at the
guardrail of the Levassor Canal where the flotilla of fishermen
were moored, or perhaps (given this everything-is-possible that her
new condition conferred on her) she went back in time, through
the ages, taking a tortuous route between the canefields, toward

the sites of her childhood. Then, surely, she once again discovered her taste for singing, a smile in her eyes, a joke, and a saying in a smidgen of French. *Ni fleurs ni couronnes, seuls les billets de banque seront acceptés!... Neither flowers nor crowns, only banknotes will be accepted!...* We never were able to determine if that was a last will and testament, or a pleasing joke.

CRATER

But here is where the Baroness
emerges from the cemetery quoting a poet

You can express the cry to the point where it meets up
with a structure.
You can also trouble the structure until it reaches the cry.
In other words, today there are no longer any poets or
novelists, there are only poetics.

—Édouard Glissant[13]

The poetic word is not a window
framed to satisfy the needs of sensation or to adapt to
our expectations;
it is a crack through which the silence of the outside
enters.

—His Highness, Guillaume Pigeard de Gurbert

---

13 TN: This is a quotation from an interview that, to my knowledge, has not
been translated: "Solitaire et solidaire: Entretien avec Édouard Glissant"
by Philippe Artières, in *Terrain: Anthropologie et sciences humaines*, 41
(2003): journals.openedition.org/terrain/1599. Accessed October 26,
2023. The original reads: "On peut pousser le cri jusqu'au moment où il
rejoint la structure. On peut aussi écheveler la structure jusqu'à ce qu'elle
touche au cri. Autrement dit, aujourd'hui il n'y a plus de poète ni de
romancier, il y a des poétiques."

LEGENDARY OF PARTICIPATIONS – The Baroness had left nothing to chance. Under her strict guidance, as soon as Man Ninotte was gone we put into action the customary care of her body, which had been repatriated to her house. The Baroness covered the mirrors and the clocks so as to bar all false ways out. The locks had been undone, leaving the doors wide open, and the knots had been untied. Later, after the cemetery, she supervised the organization of the nine days of the novena, oversaw the counting of the rosary beads, inspired the concert of sacred singers, and presided over the illumination by means of conjuring candles of the only possible route from the benedictions all the way to the exit Mass. We took care of ourselves by taking care of her.

At the church of Lamentin, the priest had used his time in a rational way. It was simpler for him to accomplish two services at the same time, so he found himself before two coffins, that of Man Ninotte and that of another person from the same area. Even the Baroness could not identify this final companion imposed on us by the priest's liturgical economies. Perhaps they had known each other, or perhaps they had simply crossed paths somewhere in this commune where they had both been born. But even if that hadn't happened, even if they had remained unknown to each other their whole lives, they found themselves there, side by side, twins consecrated in this last act of reverence. The two families filled the little church, the porch, and the few steps that led to the entrance. The choir of prayers and hymns, the symbols and the incense, the celebrations of light and flame, to which we had had recourse in the intimacy of our small group, now extended to the entire commune. They increased their number to about a hundred souls, assembled and fervent, applying themselves in unison. It was as though we had called for reinforcements from the four horizons and an army had come to reanimate our ranks. On the benches assigned to us we espied the silhouettes of friends—good comrades, allies, members of trade unions, buddies, and cousins—but most of the faces were unfamiliar. No doubt these were people who had known Man Ninotte personally, at one moment or another in her life, before we came into existence. These strangers reminded us that she had been more than our *manman*, that her life did not consist only of us, that she had had periods of youth, secrets, joys, hopes, dreams, friendships, and other histories that didn't concern us and that were condensed there, in presences without a name, at the edges of her final wake. We could make out those who knew the place, the habitués of the Church, of its services and its liturgies, from those who found themselves on unknown terrain, who had come simply to fill up the space that otherwise might have given room to suffering. The service was precious to us. Millennia of devotional practices were conducted there to bring succour to souls, an old wisdom accustomed to combatting that timeless defeat. The officiating priest distilled a form of solace with his singing voice, his hymns with their regular cadences, his epistles and verses familiar to the most ardent worshippers, his moments of silence and his moments of contagious fervor. It was as though an entire community had created a protective arch over us to contain the intrusion of Bazil—and it required every single one of us to do so.

The priest standing before the two coffins made me think of our original storyteller. He had found himself before this vast coffin that was the plantation, in the middle of the mortified flock of the enslaved. Imagine, once again, the very first storyteller, the one who possesses and carries forward a bit of the memory of the African griots, who still divines the ancient power of the word. Let us relive this inaugural scene. A slave dies, others assemble around him, and the drum and the dancers are there, reenacting a flow of obscure memories. A slave in the audience first begins to sing and then he suddenly feels the need to speak.

The song halts and the word is born.

There—that's him.

He doesn't look like it, but that's him.

He takes the stage and begins to speak at the center of this collective scene, one that he completes but that nothing delineates. There's neither a sign nor the slightest symbol, not the least command, merely the ancient mixture of emotions that he raises from his most profound depths, and that he projects before him in this space. Here are residues of millennial rituals and the reflexes of tradition. Those who are there are not tied together, nor are they tied to themselves. At that moment, the one who opens his mouth—this poet able to rediscover in himself what no longer exists—starts to thread speech through the rubble of words, of languages, of songs, of games, of myths, and of cosmogonies, to work with them without knowing them, lacking all gravity, imbued only with the virtue of the laughter that has become a necessity and the lightness that the mind is able to retrieve. To speak at the edge of this abyss where Bazil resides, to enlist every possible thing, to use whatever can be used—whether it comes from the master, from the Amerindians, or from the lost ancestors—to seize everything, as in the compulsive gesture of the shipwrecked, to mix all the possibilities of liaison and rupture, of the mark and of erasure, of synthesis and the refusal of synthesis, of that which is impossible to say and of the utterance that reenchants all empty horizons... *that is the poetics of our Creole storyteller!*... In the small church of Lamentin, the stage of the collective was not empty; the officiant dominated the assembly; the logistics were powerful and the ritual was one of the most ancient; the archaic traces fit together with the austerity of the modern; Creole ways were mixed with what we had been taught. Bazil found himself surrounded.

Man Ninotte had wanted us to have religious instruction. She imposed it on us up until the famous and somber communion, at which point we would receive the most delicious chocolate, heavily smeared on buttery bread of an incomparable flavor. The Baroness was charged with following the progress of the affair, but Man Ninotte still kept a close eye on everything with the intensity of a fundamentalist believer. You couldn't miss Mass on Sunday. Deserting the period of instruction at the presbytery for the back of the Pax movie theater on a Wednesday afternoon was out of the question. However, Man Ninotte never verified our exact understanding of the mysteries of the Holy Trinity, and she herself never set foot inside the church. To her, priests didn't seem like a breed worth frequenting. If a very pious neighbor pivoted around at the sound of the Angelus and chanted at the top of her lungs all sorts of *libera me, domine!* Man Ninotte replied with the songs of her belovèd Tino Rossi or some other jingles chock full of love and pleasure. Legend tells us that in former times she went to Mass, that in that time there were entire rows reserved for the important people of the town. They had to pay for the privilege. Their rows were marked with their names and reserved for them. The only ones who could sit there during the Grand Mass were those who rented them. During the era when it is said that Man Ninotte went to church, she could be found in one of those reserved seats. Inadvertently, no doubt: she wasn't the type to overthrow the world order. One time, the assigned people presented themselves and indicated that she had to leave, which the beadle must have seconded by pointing out the seats that remained in the rear, near the door. Man Ninotte, they say, got up, gathered her things, looked everyone up and down making that *tchiip* she made on a bad day, and left the cathedral so definitively that no one ever saw her again at Mass. Though for us, her troupe of natural pagans, this rule never applied. On the contrary, she considered it a duty to follow the Mass, and to do the two communions, just like the diplomas and the other hassles that led to obtaining a high school degree. Once the formal communion had been achieved, each of us was free to continue our religious education or not, and to dwell with God as we saw fit. She might speak of it from time to time, but she obliged no one to save her soul...

While the officiant was officiating, I imagined her in that church of Lamentin, the church of her childhood, toward which she must have descended from the neighborhood of La-Bélème to attend the Sunday service, barefoot so as not to ruin her shoes, stopping on that bridge over the Lézarde River, a few meters from town, to wash her feet and put her shoes back on. Jojo l'Algébrique remembers that bridge; he calls it *shoe-bridge!*... According to him, it belongs to the pantheon of landscapes left to us by Man Ninotte. I imagined this small, round *négresse*, entering the church in her pretty shoes, attending the service, no doubt listening to the priest just as she might during this last ceremony when she had to hear all the sacred words all over again. I saw her in the central bay near Man Manotte, her mother, or Man Douro, her grandmother, doing what there was to do, as it had to be done. But her mind was reaching out more toward the life of the street, the animation of the town, the opportunities of the city, than toward the quietude of the old mango trees teeming with blackbirds that provided the usual ambiance of her native quarter.

Times do not begin
Do not end either
(There are only attritions and calendars
In our renunciations)

The priest who was officiating seemed to hold a power over death. He was not afraid of death. For us, he gathered up each pocket of shadow to transform it into light. The elevations, the transmutations, the sacrificial humilities, the glorious offerings came one after the other in the half-darkness of the little church. The afternoon sun traversed the stained glass windows as though to complete the task. Shadow was allowed in, among us and inside us. The knot of our sorrow was untied until it dissipated over the whole country. Choirs had taken hold of our sorrow and were dividing it among dozens of hearts. They sent it out into the sanctifying echoes of the church, then through the currents of dust sweeping the streets, and then on into the wilderness, the meandering of birds, the bustling of crabs, the hollows of cliffs where the sea roared, into all that could disseminate, spread, dissipate, and expand. The officiant integrated the event into the order of what was, for us, tolerable; he secured it all with a key of hope. He was full of proud glory and frank humility. Submissive, and triumphant in the submission itself. He urged his freedom to worship toward a sublime obedience. He sanctified the gathering that we formed and, moving beyond our assembly, he drew himself up before the fundamental adversary, before all that lies outside of symbols, outside of the possible, beyond the reach of everything that might lessen the mysteries of life. Like a shaman, he seemed to follow the active force of a river so as to arrange the landscapes or mobilize the winds unfurling around our vision. The trees became tremors, the somber stones murmured. The statues, the stained glass, and the columns that hold up the vault began to rustle with forces; only one among them was named, but all were present. The officiant preserved for us the memory of the most ancient experiences.

He recapitulated them for us.

I saw the smoke of the incense rise alongside the rays of light; it bore away the hymns and the prayers, a whole convoy of sacrifices. Its perfume began to purify all things, recalling to my mind the Egyptian praises, the ecstasy of the Three Kings who presented their gift, the Arab treasures along the commercial routes. I smelled the fragrance of caravans transporting between oases aromatic olives, myrrh and frankincense, and the sweetness of linseed oil, Chinese cinnamon and opopanax from Syria, the souls of flowers imprisoned in sealed jars, all things that enchanted life, that hailed the gods. I believed that I could identify the aromatics of Babylon that Herodotus sings about, or that perfume of the city of Mendes that Plutarch celebrates. I heard the balsamic notes giving way to floral symphonies, a few hints of amber ceaselessly spreading out, dilating more and more, and even more... Dear Baroness, do you remember, we inhabited what that throne of incense carried along; we devoured a God who wasn't present but who was everywhere; we drank his blood, we died with him, we recovered the solitudes and the pains offered to the light, and we combatted demons in the looping motions of the thurible as it diffused the great perfume... "It was the only way to keep from staying in this coffin!"... the Baroness sighs. *"Make sure that hell doesn't have dominion over her!"*...

If you pass
There will be the chicken fricassee
The Noilly Prat that sings
And two-or-three marinades for a chiquetaille of stars.

After the Church hymns, the calm of the Lamentin cemetery welcomed sorrows that had been prolonged and anesthetized. Since the *Toussaint* holiday wasn't far off and the tombs had just been restored, they were admirably white. The cemetery is situated in the middle of town; its surface is limited, its space well optimized. Tombs are aligned on a checkerboard of cement alleyways. In the corner reserved for indigents, the tombs of children, and the tombs of the old and impoverished, crosses are planted above a shell of concrete or a circle of conch shells. Most of the vaults are covered with a roof that protects them from the wind and rain; it also protects steles and bouquets from plunderers and ensures that candles will burn all the way down. At these times, when someone comes to bury a relation, or to bury a part of himself, each tomb comes alive, gives substance to a soul that is now alert, marks out each unit of a vast unknown family that has suddenly become part of a fraternity. Each tomb watches you pass by, communicating the experience of a wavering peace in which the wake of Bazil can still be felt. Those tombs that have been abandoned are witness to the exile of a lineage, the extinction of a species; they remain like bays in the swell of a time that no longer knows which way to go. The cemeteries recapitulate a part of those times when the dead still wandered among us: times of stone, times of dust, times of immobile wind and residual yellow water under the blackened bouquets... The cemetery worker stuffs the interstices of the tombstone with newspaper, then hides the crack under a trail of mortar. He seals out of reach what could still compete with memories. Here, closing the tomb is like ringing the gong of a grandiose age that quiets sounds that are too loud, that deafens all living things, that leaves behind only a wrenching pain in which one inadvertently finds rest.

On laundry days Man Ninotte would sing—undoubtedly an old habit she picked up in her hometown, where the washerwomen sang their little songs from the riverbed. There were also those who, instead of singing, would babble much like the *raras* prayers during Holy Week, those who echoed the most beautiful couplets, and still others who could surpass them and start humming on their own, inspiring a silent admiration in everyone there. Singing while doing laundry can have a great variety of functions: it allows you to keep quiet when confronted by a clingy gossip; to taunt an enemy by declaring your pleasure in being alive, and thus tossing her back on the acidity of her hatred and jealousy; to express that surge of joy you feel when the body is engaged in something simple and the mind doesn't suffer from the great misfortunes it has had to trundle around. Man Ninotte sang in all these ways—under the sun, no hat, her arms bare, her dress lifted up to her thighs, seated on a stool in front of two enormous basins, one in which the dirty laundry had been soaking since the night before, and the other that served as a receptacle for the laundry after passing through her expert hands. The cadence of the song often matched that of the washing. The laundry was scrubbed, rinsed, twisted, beaten, and scrubbed again until that magical moment when she would squeeze it and a stream of soap would gush out: *Tssssit!* That whistling sound marked the beginning of a new cycle for the energetic handling of the laundry, and, no doubt, it was this *tssssit* that so often recalled the song of Tino Rossi, *O Catalinetta bella! Tchi-tchi, listen, love calls you Tchi-tchi...* until the *tchi-tchi!* of the singer mingled with the *tssssit!* of the washing, transforming this obscure task into a prolonged joy.

An orchid murmurs your name
In the patience of its emerging blooms
For a splendor of a thousand years.

The practice of placing conch shells around tombs is disappearing. I saw very few that day at the cemetery. Still, my eyes searched the sites in the way one might attempt to solve a mystery. The conches only appear on the tombs for indigents. It's always a strange feeling to see these old conches, vestiges, for me, of a "de-appeared" people. Glissant used this term *de-appearing* to evoke the Amerindian genocide in the Caribbean Islands. The use of the word "genocide" for this instance is contested; nevertheless, for some time after the arrival of the colonizers in Martinique, there remained very few of the autochthonous people, scattered about into disorganized encampments or dispersed and wandering. The survivors would end up taking refuge on the Island of Dominica, reassembling as best they could, and conserving in this way a Trace of what they had been. The handful of individuals who remained in Martinique melted into the amalgam of the new populations. And yet, their culture could be found in the practices that the colonizers had to adopt because of their lack of knowledge of the American wilderness. This culture would also endure in those practices mobilized by the enslaved for their survival and their acts of resistance. Man Ninotte, like many others, said she had Carib blood. Those who affirmed it often tried to hide a Hindu ancestry, which was hardly valorized in the way we typically represented ourselves in colonial times. It is no less the case, though, that Amerindian genes can be seen in many of us—in a look, a high cheekbone, a nuance of the skin, a general allure.

De-appearing is not disappearance.

De-appearing retains the alchemy of a form of apparition, of an alternate revelation.

It indicates the complexity of a past time that moves into a time that is still there, that accumulates facets and folds even as it comes undone. With de-appearing, a term brought over from the English language, Glissant wanted to indicate the extent to which the Amerindian dimension persists, multiform, in words and titles, in the Creole garden, in everyday gestures, in names and local techniques, in our relations with the river, with forests, in the names of fish, in the rituals and customs to which fishermen devote themselves so as to attract good fortune and hold their head high in the face of the ocean's caprice. In the sand of the beaches or on the banks of the stream, you can easily find arrowheads, incense burners, carved bones, or even real tombs. Near springs, you can find stones standing up on end. Everywhere you can find boulders that were used for polishing, and others that display engravings… Before the arrival of the colonizers, the Caribs inhabited the land in complete austerity. Their gardens were interwoven with the trees. They resided in structures that were light and easy to construct, easy to abandon. Their navigational techniques helped them envision the entirety of the archipelago, and they were in contact with so many islands at once that they probably couldn't understand what the Occidentals meant by "insularity," a word that attributed to them the misfortune of isolation. There is a film by Ridley Scott about Christopher Columbus that has an opening shot—if I remember correctly—of the foot of the conqueror sinking into the sand of one of our region's beaches. This step, which should have been soundless, instead resounds at great length, like a death knell. In this death knell, I hear all the Amerindian genocides, the destructive epidemics, the screaming and the massacres. But above all, I hear the naming of peoples who would take their place in our anthropological alchemy, forsaking proof of their presence, like the wind, like a shudder of the earth, like the light, and like the densities of time.

In my garden, close to Christmastime, there is a plant that crops up, spreading out in all directions like a proliferating skeleton. The plant ends each of its shoots with minuscule white and round flowers that the bees and the suckers adore. All you can see are these tiny cottony bursts of white, floating like a mist of vegetal fireflies. The plant, after its celebratory eruption, disappears as quickly as it appeared, until it is forgotten, provoking surprise the next time it emerges. I can tell myself to keep it in memory, to be there for its demise, and I can vigilantly await its return. But it's always in vain. The plant disappears completely only to appear completely again.

The dry savanna
The backwater and the duck
And a cherry season
Babbling a counterpoint to the snails

In the days following our trip to the cemetery, the nine days of the novena prayer had turned over the desert earth and the rock gardens that lay within us. Those days had cleared out small oases under the clear light of the sun. It was as though songs and gestures of familiarity had taken over, and since nothing resists magic, since nothing can escape its command, a fringe of repair was appearing at the edge of the lacerations. The novena was stemming the tides of the invisible that had begun to surround us. Hymns and prayers had risen like incense smoke, lightening the load of the sky that was beginning to crush us. Hymns were once again purifying the world. An obscure ferment that had seemed too close since the moment of her departure was coming up against the ramparts of well-executed protocol. I, who believe in nothing, had found myself taking part in the propagation of ancestral beliefs. These beliefs involved establishing the right symbols, containing the most fragile in the net of a ritual, lending all necessary care to the women singing the verses, contemplating the wreaths, accentuating the virtues of flame and light, and confronting point by point, in a conscientious fervor, the abyss that threatened us from within. Placed in reach of these timeless mysteries, *I had participated in them.*

It was like recapitulating the most ancient of adventures. At first, I wandered through the different levels of consciousness that must have arisen in the various types of living being. Almost spontaneously, I wanted to bury myself in the rapture of those first organisms that know only the ocean of life, that float in a perfect fusion of shadow and light, blind to that intention that was dividing life into an infinity of emerging forms. *They were participating!* Alas, in that original soup that concentrates everything imaginable, submitted to life's dangerous plan, these simple organisms felt the need to combine, blending their perfect unconsciousness and their cellular plenitude to create more complex beings. They augmented their capacities of being, of acting, and of making themselves distinct as they separated from a future-less union in favor of life's intention. I had attempted in vain to rediscover that original fusion, that perfect unity, which must be inscribed in the immemorial history of the strategic Sapiens mind. Next, I saw myself tip over into the big brain of that poor Sapiens, where I underwent the aberrant irruption of the bolt of thunder that permitted Sapiens at once to see the world and to distinguish himself from it, to be in it but no longer of it.

Consciousness, dear Baroness, is like an impact: it reveals you to yourself and by doing so detaches you from everything else, as if you were an orphaned moon. Consciousness isolates you right away. You suddenly perceive yourself as detached from all forms of existence; you lose your natural relation to the world. And since you don't understand what you are, the impulse is to want to melt once again into the comfortable totality of all existing things. Not being diluted in the oceanic and inexplicable presence of things produces great terror, whereas unconscious life is far more navigable. The initial anguish is at once the damnation of consciousness and the source of its marvelous power: consciousness finds itself trying to comprehend what is not or is no longer within its reach. To comprehend and to explain—that's like searching for the key to the inaugural fusion. It is the *immense desire...* I believe I have glimpsed that desire in myself...

But this fragile light of consciousness would amplify Sapiens' awakened state. It would take him from one discovery to the next, and each one would produce new meanings. Over the course of centuries and generations, a consciousness like the one we have, or that many of us have, would eventually have to discover death: that abrupt opening onto the beyond. Death is something inconceivable that consciousness would be forced to block out by inventing graves. These graves allowed Sapiens to reintegrate death into the world, lending it in this way a comfortable and controllable coherence. On the side of life—thanks to spirits, gods, and demons—we were no longer cut off from anything; we were no longer strangers to anything, there was no empty and indifferent gap visible beyond us, everything became a bit more reassuring, everything found a place in the continuity of the same meanings, everything was in us, and we were in everything. Functioning once again as a group, *we had rediscovered this participation that had existed since time immemorial*, almost intact and almost as alive in our breathing and the beating of our hearts.

If the sun winks
Each moon puts it to rest
And the nights have learned to reinvent it

There is a mystery surrounding these Sapiens who saw no god in the forces of nature or in the all-powerful animals. Those who, while experiencing an intuition of the divine, of the sacred, did not transform them into any dogma or any Church. Those who received this primal amazement of consciousness like a happiness to be gathered. Those who didn't allow themselves to be colonized either by wheat or barley or millet, plants that rooted humanity in agricultural rows, that harnessed them to houses and property and delivered them over to armies and wars. Those who made friends with the animals without ever restraining them within fences and pasturelands. Those who were able to acknowledge the abyss of the beyond without wanting to hide it. Those who could accept that the abyss would remain wide open and who could preserve their original relation to it, half-terrified and half-amazed before inexplicable splendors and disasters. Those who kept this point of juncture open to an open earth, with no limits, no enclosures, ready for voyages without end and with a taste for discovering the plains where the winds go, a desire to know the landscapes where the sun sets, and vowing to visit all the shores where the sun rises each morning. Yes, truly, those who were able to cultivate a presence on earth similar to that of water, a cousin to that of wind, a presence woven of night and shadow...

These were people of pure poetry...

Without having written a word, without having created anything or produced anything, they were poetry's incarnation.

By incarnating poetry, they remained invisible to the eyes of all the others. They constituted, unknowingly, the soul of all those who, having lost the initial magic, had sealed up the divine in altars or cathedrals, making the earth rigid with empires and armed frontiers, then relying on such absurdities as money, commerce, and merchandise... The people of pure poetry remained outside of Sapiens' dazzling projects; they were hardly visible, barely intervening, caring for neither conquest nor domination, like a people of no people, of no territory, but who would fertilize everything with a force that still resides in us. Glissant, who intuited their existence, who knew perhaps how to glimpse some of them, called them *Batoutos.* Can you imagine this participatory way of being in the world—to be of it, but not in it, and to be in it, but not of it?

Among certain peoples of the Americas, there were tribes that had no houses, no gardens or parkland or farming. Property was unknown to them. They didn't accumulate anything, and their tools were ephemeral objects. The person who became the chief of the tribe was merely at the service of the collective bond between members and between members and all those who were not members. Nothing was inanimate; the proximate and the distant were enmeshed; all was a space of life and of encounter, exchange, and association in a continuum marked out by signs and rituals. Groups were constituted to watch over specific species of plants, insects, birds, and other things. Women who cultivated yams or manioc spoke to them as though they were children, educated them until their maturity, and met their soul in the coils of their dreams. Nature was their culture, and their culture was made of a careful alliance with nature; and this weaving together benefitted from the attentions of an intense devotion. They remained thus half-effaced due to their all-encompassing participation in the great totality they had made sacrosanct. Can you measure the power of this self-effacement?

Participation weaves the nebulous fringes of consciousness into everything unconscious and everything inconceivable. All the forces—those of the elements, those of the vegetable kingdom, and those of the animal kingdom—could be mobilized in us, mobilized for us. The unalterable placidity of the mineral world could be mobilized as well. These forces would be used to usher in an extension of what we were, or to envision ourselves according to the implacable will of magical thinking. I explained to the Baroness the circles that started to ripple out from individual consciousness. Everything was organized around the participation of each individual in his or her community, each community in its environment, each environment in the infinite beyond sketched out by the Milky Way. The community was the basis of participation, instituting it, mastering all its modalities, and placing ready-made horizons in each empty, impervious, implacable window that death had opened wide. The community defined and delimited the visible world; that visible world opened onto an invisible one that the community also shaped. The community-based invisible world, now made into something accommodating, added to the reassuring comfort of the visible. To live in a state of devotion, to believe, pray, comprehend, to reach toward the mystical powers and magical gestures was, above all, to *participate* in the world. Individual consciousness paradoxically discovered its liberties and its prisons in the symbolic systems that propelled it into relation with all existing things. The force of each life—and its becoming—could be found here. You see that, don't you? The sweetness that comes from afar and that offers itself in the midst of confusion, when one is cornered, as we had been?

Thus, I rediscovered in myself this Man Ninotte who lived connected to the world, attentive to its signs. I rediscovered the arch of her eyebrows, creased in concentration. Man Ninotte, as you know, didn't admire nature, landscapes, or the beauty of the weather. She was content to evaluate the force of the rain, the damage of the heat, the possibility offered by one or another apparent or hidden circumstance. She functioned within a very dense fabric of sensation, the multitudinous threads of which had to be activated—sometimes several at the same time. This conferred on her gaze a fixity which I often took for vigilance, and, above all, for determination. All the *manmans* from here have these creases between their eyebrows. All of them possess this sharpness in their look, this force of attention, this alacrity of the permanently alert. Fearful trembling and the backwaters of doubt were stopped well before they reached the somber clarity of her eyes. They were conjured away by signs that kept bad luck at a low level of virulence. What she was able to see was what her life, her confidence, her hopes, and her everyday acts offered to her as a pathway through adversities. Her gaze in our direction—but only in our direction when we were sick or in difficulty—could soften to the point where it achieved a semblance of tenderness, but without ever leaving to tenderness the slightest chance of winning out... —"That's true," the Baroness acknowledges. "At that time, tenderness was not on the program... She had to hide herself, go about without showing herself... We had to live with her without really seeing her..."

Man Ninotte knew how to make use of the rain and the sun to whiten her sheets; it was what she called "sprucing up." Sprucing up was part of an ancient science. Rich people would call on laundresses to deal with their dirty laundry. These women would wash at the stream, in the brisk waters that came down from the foothills. Morning dews, spring waters, waters from ancient volcanos, waters from the woods, rainwater, storm water... all of them gathered in that stream. They beat, wrung out, and squeezed the laundry before putting it out to dry on the boulders and the bushes of the riverbanks. The prowess of a laundress could be judged by the whiteness of the fabric she achieved. The quality ranged across the spectrum from *dead white* to a splendid concert of *white revivified*. To obtain the revivified white, an entire stream had to be recruited, along with almost the totality of the sky and a good part of the elementary forces of the world. Over the course of centuries, there developed a singularly Creole science of this sprucing up. There were good and less good attempts: not too much sun and not too much rain, not too much shadow, nor too much heat, just a subtle atmospheric precipitation capable of exalting all that wasn't white and leaving to every piece of white cloth a memory of the sky, a solar effervescence, something aerial, like the wings of an angel painted by Paul Klee.

And so, sometimes Man Ninotte's washing ended with a sprucing up that prioritized the sheets. Back then, all sheets were white. When the proper conditions weren't in place (which she could judge with a glance at the sky), the sheets and the regular laundry were simply put out to dry in the sun. They came back like mummified skins. On the other hand, after a sprucing up, a sheet or a blouse gave off a fresh marine scent, all fluffy with a creamy haze and perfumed by the flowers nearby. At that time, there were flowers in the courtyards, on balconies, and on terraces; we lived among flowers, and flowers participated in that sprucing up. Dragonflies came to seize a bit of moisture and butterflies came to rest on a clean sheet, extended along a line and hanging from its pegs. The winds rising up from further off, heavy with salt and with the memory of the pollen coveted by bees, would permeate them. Volatile rains scintillating with sunshine, the source of those dews that don't stay wet, swept down to secure the magic and magnify an arcana of secrets in the deep profundity of the fibers. I loved to slide into the undulation of the spruced-up linens. They smelled like Marseille soup, washing bleach, and a shiver of oxygen. I also loved it when Man Ninotte recruited me to shake out a sheet. She took one end, with me grabbing the other, and we performed in concert this energetic, alternating movement that stretched the fibers and eliminated the creases. You could sense the enchantment that the sprucing up had lent to the white of the linens. The house filled up with their perfume, was cleansed by it... Man Ninotte achieved an active complicity with the soul of the world, one that was so well expressed by those beautified sheets! —"I see what you mean," the Baroness interrupts me. "What is more difficult than attending to the white! How do you judge it, and what are you judging? I'm not talking about that tremor that goes from gray to white; I'm talking about that invisible difference between the white that you call 'dead' and the white that you call 'revivified'! The laundresses knew the science of this slight difference..." Yes, dear Baroness, that's why they knew everything that was happening in this land, why their eyes and their ears traversed the visible and decoded the invisible. It's also why they told stories so well and sang so marvelously! Think also of the power of Paul Klee, that artist who, with one and the same stroke of the brush, was able to capture the emptiness, compose the white, and leave us to intuit the presence of an angel! Or again, think of Kazimir Malevich, who succeeded in crossing over the barriers of color, who could see in the white both cold and hot, a bit of blue or some ochre, offering us the infinite landscape of white on white!... They could have been laundresses!... —"Like Man Ninotte?" the Baroness asks me. —Like Man Ninotte... I reply.

If the winter yam
Has not offered a chance
The breadfruit of the dry season will gladly provide
You've understood

The women who selected the prayers of the novena enjoyed a direct access to the mysteries. Their gestures as they caressed their rosaries were silhouetted against the lightless sun that troubled our conscience. They personified an ageless injunction against annihilation. Their wisdom drew from a reservoir of hope: all was not lost, neither for her, Man Ninotte, nor for us, the children. It was still possible to act. Such progress toward the heart of hope stirred up in us a powerful reminder of the sacred. I was ready to believe anything. It would have seemed normal to me to see huge totems rise up around them as they sang the psalms. It was easy for me to imagine them in the act of quenching their thirst with the milk of rebirth, frolicking in the marvelous waters of the first clarities, spitting out strong flaming rum, eating flesh authorized or sanctified with cups of blood in the clearings of catacombs. It would have seemed almost normal to see them dining on bread and beer near the fields of Sekhet-Aaru, on the altar of Ra, following the detours of the barque of Re or that of Atoum, between the cyclical threats of the giant serpent. They would have felt no fear of Baron Samedi of the Haitian Vodou *hougans* or of Ankou of the large scythe feared by the Bretons. They would not have been moved by the bloody bones harbored by Mictlantecuhtli under his owl feathers, nor by these unseeing eyes that serve as his necklace, nor even by the stiff wind of the knives that the Aztecs fled. Some of them would have been able to ordain dances dedicated to astral enigmas or turn away swarms of grasshoppers just by batting their eyelashes. Others struck me as capable of hypnotizing enormous sacrificial bulls, or of laying on altars the jasper lambs mummified in sulfur. They might even climb back up the hallways of Yamapu in the processions led by the dogs of Master Yama (whose flute we hear, but who remains invisible under a red tunic)… They displayed a total confidence that was without rhyme or reason, beyond time or season, actualized at every moment, a bit like Muhammad facing Izrail, that angel of the ultimate day, whom he welcomed with open arms and without emitting a word. Their force of persuasion had been sharpened over millennia of disbelief and persecution, and thus they maintained themselves before Bazil, never trembling with doubt, as if in ecstasy, carried over by their strength alone: *they believed!*… and we clung to them, I as much as anyone, as though to the branches of a gigantic lotus where the apsaras waltz… *ah wake up and sing for joy, poor inhabitants of the dust!*…

Prayers arose from bodies that had become solid blocks which nothing could disturb or dissipate. These absolutes of force seemed to incline the universe toward a request that was also a celebration. Nothing seemed able to resist them. Yet after each of their volleys, there reigned an astounding silence. It dissipated in a new assault of songs and prayers. Each time, silence returned. Silence rushed back in. Silence was the only response. It wasn't a silence like any other silence; they weren't awaiting it, didn't question it, and weren't troubled by it. Rather, it seemed as if silence had been summoned there solely by the authority of their voices to ornament the intensity of expression they had become. Each wave of this spectral silence established another degree of certitude that reinforced the salvo of supplications to come. I thought I saw them take hold of the silence to chisel it into infinity, to extend it as far as possible in a mixture of airy humility and stolid pride, until it would retract and return to them in a mass as dense as they had become...

The prayers and songs were adapted to the silence of the gods. It is true that peoples have opposed a thousand spectacles to that silence: the soothsayer, the diviner and the Pythia of Delphi, sibyls, magi, augurers, visionaries, and sleepwalkers who hear the future. All of them could sense, see, and decipher something that was not made manifest... They provided the theater for that which cannot be explained, for what dreams don't reveal, for what the teachings of suffering don't clarify. They replied to signs with the extended shapes of their bodies, with the emotions of their eyes. They manipulated languages that were of the same stuff as the silence, of the same indefinition as the darkness or as a dazzling light, and because of that they could resound into infinity inside of each and every one of us. They are still among us, using almost the same tools, but with other names. The signs, premonitions, and intuitions of Man Ninotte furnished thousands of responses to circumstances that came together and came apart under the fire of her vigilance alone. This practice of divination organized her choices; it filled the unalterable silence of fortune's dangers, the impenetrable passageways of destiny that opened at every moment of the day. She lived in that great silence, truly nourished herself with it. And so, it is possible to understand what the Haitian singer Althiery Dorival means in his song *Anba tonèl* when he cries out: *Man kout'e man kout'e, man pa wè nouvel, dadou!*... "I've listened for a long time, but I've never *seen* news of you, Dadou!"

Miles Davis had understood that certain musicians would refuse to face the silence. These musicians filled the moments they thought the weakest with a profusion of notes. Or else they captured with a great horde of sounds the prey pursued by their inspiration. In contrast, Miles had intuited that music is already in silence. He learned to stay with the indecipherable silences of the vertigo and the void until he arrived at the exact instant when one sound could make them resonate even further. At that point, he restrained the notes so as to intensify the rarer ones; he was not afraid to see them reach their end and fade away. He turned his back on the public and extracted himself from their grip, almost effacing himself. During his solos, he frequently commanded the piano to be silent, to the point where he provoked the rancor of that genial monster, Thelonius Monk. Miles then placed himself directly in front of the drummer to confront the immense clamor of the polyrhythms coming from a lost Africa, from an obliterated Africa. The extravagant commotion of the rhythms stirs up spaces and times, makes them fluid and permeable, deforms existence through notes and beats that overlap, assemble, explode into difference, opening all portals of perception. The rhythms instantly mobilize memories of the body that have preserved the echoes of the most ancient rituals. They speak all languages, call all languages. You can't choose them or organize them; you liberate them in yourself, you liberate yourself in them, you compose them. They call for the living fire of improvisation.

Polyrhythm opens onto participation.

Miles, at the heart of this alchemy, started to surveil the moment, to capture its intelligence, to weave silence into a fabric of scattered, unpredictable, and unusual notes that were fabulous because many more than necessary. He left the stage without a word, sometimes without even returning, as if to achieve an ultimate form of silence in the music that kept going without him... Participation is a music that lives, I say to the Baroness, stammering; she looks at me, unmoved.

You can find the same kind of symbiosis between Coltrane and the drummer Elvin Jones, one of the geniuses of the 20th century. Jones didn't accompany anyone; he didn't submit himself to anyone. From the end of his drumsticks, sometimes held upside down, and while visualizing whole tempests of color, he set off a rhythmic storm for his partner with thunderclaps of autonomous sounds and incomparable cymbals that leapt out from everywhere, creating irreducible sonic meanings that were not only human but also inhuman, not only rational but more than that—implausible, woven with shocks and small miracles. The authority that he displayed in the face of Coltrane's musical intention compelled him to labor without the anchor of a firm foundation, to go beyond the initial impulse and to clarify that impulse while at the same time pushing it toward its outermost edges. Their harmony maintained in separation the appearance of two violent wills that, through confrontation, transcended each other while requiring the acuity of each one, so that together they could produce something new.

They entered into participation!

When Coltrane stopped playing and Jones continued solo, Jones would rush to go where Coltrane hadn't yet ventured, in the direction of what he had perhaps pointed out but hadn't explored, or toward what he had invented solely by means of a shockwave of divination. Keeping in memory both the melody and Coltrane's intention, Jones radiated them out into these never-promised lands that their confrontation had brought into existence, and that Jones was ultimately the only one to glimpse...

Two colliers-choux
Three chaînes-forçats
And the chest to wear them
Given well

Among the masterpieces of Haitian music, in the category known as *Compas*, there are two emblematic songs: "Patience" and "New York City."

They are arranged in an identical manner.

"Patience," by M. Robert Martino and the Gypsies of Pétion-Ville, begins very simply in praise of patience, affirming it as the basis of all success in life. Once this idea is established in the song's opening, the singer falls silent and the word disappears into the musical instrumentation until the return of the opening couplet, which will assume the identical form but this time rich with the energy of celebration. "New York City" recounts how the musicians of the Tabou Combo Orchestra experience exile in New York. They feel the absence of their far-off land, their beloved Haiti. In an overture, the singer identifies sadness, melancholy, and anguish before exclaiming: *How am I going to return to the land?* Then he gives himself over to the celebration.

At that point, in both songs, the musicians explode, expressing in the first instance their hymn to patience and, in the second, their lament for the chains of exile, according to the theme of each one. When these songs were first performed, they were no doubt improvisations. But the improvisations would become standards, reprised as such by those who, across the generations, wanted to celebrate patience or lament homesickness. The two songs carry you away on magic carpets. Your body lets loose unfamiliar gestures, feel-good twists. You allow yourself to be intoxicated by the keys that spring up, that contract, and that rebound in proliferating sheaves. The music turns, it waltzes, it hops, it punctuates, articulates, disarticulates. The perspective spins about, circling around patience or exile, figuring a slow implosion, soliciting the same inexpressible intuition from diverse angles. Sometimes, one of the musicians displays the color of his own soul; at other moments, the group comes together as a single entity to support the dance, to carry the body away on a propulsive wave. Sometimes, one rhythm alone does the work and strives to reach the bones, far beneath the muscles; at still other times, it is a simple ritornello, half percussive and half melodic, which sucks you into a round and delivers you from far away to an enchantment of ricochets and lines of flight. Patience and homesickness are completely absorbed by this enchantment. You forget to follow them, but you dance them and you experience them. The body deserts its habits and takes flight, inspired by sensations of energy and celebration, joy and hope. *You participate.* "Patience," by the Gypsies of Pétion-Ville, fixes itself like a star in the most profound depths of your spirit. And if, on the very last note of "New York City," the lost country is not recovered, its healing presence is still among us.

To hold on is not enough
It's holding on tight that counts

For Glissant, the hold of the slaveship functioned as an abyss would have functioned: it instigated a major rupture.

A rupture with Africa.

A rupture with our former ways of being in the world, our ways of perceiving the world.

A rupture in our means of individual actualization.

The number of slaveships was in the thousands. For centuries, from one crossing to the next, each hold was added to the others to constitute this Abyss which, for millions of the deported, would transform lost Africa into a collection of Traces.

The idea of the Abyss cancels out any notion of return or continuity.

This idea requires that we explore a beginning.

Traces will subsist in those who survive. These miraculous

survivors were, for Glissant, *naked migrants*. Nakedness is a kind of container that magnifies the little that remains. At the same time, it compels you to imagine everything else. Traces will enter the creative drift, engendering inextricable cultural emergences in the anthropological alchemy of the Americas and of our Caribbean Islands. They constitute the dynamic out of which, through the shocks, encounters, and chaotic mixtures inherent to these sites, something new will be produced, something conclusive for the future, something—most importantly—*valid for all*. Remember, dear Baroness, the *quimboiseurs*, the dancers, the singers, the *tanbouyé*, the storytellers, the musicians from around here—they all had to compose starting from this lack, from this nakedness, and, ultimately, from this energy bestowed by Traces, and which made them crave (made them hungry and thirsty for) what was possible in the place where they had found themselves, what was possible in the world. It is truly the *naked migrants*—and not the others, dominant and well provided for—who will create the blues, gospel, jazz, tango, reggae, biguine, calypso... so much of what gives vitality to the contemporary world.

But let's come back to the ship's hold, which is now an Abyss. The individual has no other choice than to be born there, to be born to himself, to what he is, with what remains to him. The Abyss liquifies all prior experience. This experience doesn't disappear but instead transforms itself into a chaos of elementary components; let us call them "elementaries."

Our famous Traces.

The individual captive must commence his singular experience at the extreme point between death and life. To survive, he must realize—as quickly and as well as possible—who he is. It is as though the Abyss definitively charged them, him and his descendants, with the task of improvising dances, songs, sayings, stories, culture, and the expression of their existence, not under an identitarian diktat, but under the anguishing latitude of the everything-suddenly-possible, everything-suddenly-nebulous, everything-suddenly-effervescent. The liquifaction of origins, cosmogonies, myths, and other dogmas and certitudes plunges every individual into a *genesic soup similar to that founding sea that covered our planet, and where blossoms of life would surge forth*. This soup is a concentrate of elemental substances, as nutritious as they are energizing. These substances can be combined indefinitely, creating *reactions*, producing rich liaisons in which tiny organisms are nourished—absorbing this, rejecting that, feeding themselves at the will of chance, choice, and necessity. All display a strategy of persistance. All lead to experiences that end by differentiating each one from the others. *All are capable of everything.* Some will establish themselves in the most functional and efficient simplicities; others will advance toward the most adventurous complexities.

All will participate in the concert of life.

All will constitute the living.

The captives capable of effectuating such a leap of individuation will improvise on it.

There is no right way.

In the Abyss, everyone becomes a young poet, as Glissant believed.

Each person does what he can with what he is, with what he has, with what remains to him, with what he imagines. Each captive in his vice of chains will produce his own means of surviving the unliveable, then of embarking toward the unknown, then of regrounding the self on the dehumanizing plantations. Some, without prior consultation, in the midst of convergences and simultaneities during the crossing, will create groups like the clusters that we spoke of earlier; these will revolt, take hold of the boat, lose themselves in the ocean, or regain the first shore they encounter. Others, invisible during the two or three months of the terrible voyage, will be able to flee as soon as they arrive at port, or, after arriving at the plantations, will organize these individuated selves into active forces. These are the people who will trigger the forms of resistance capable of regrounding them, forms ranging from dance to *marronnage*, including the *quimbois*, the song, music, storytelling, and more…

Improvisation thus appears alongside the Abyss of the hold. It will be at the heart of survival strategies and of those life strategies that were reworked from generation to generation. Jazz musicians have shown us this: improvisation permits, in the most intense manner imaginable, the expression of what one is. Improvisation establishes the individual, an actualization as a person, as the principle structuring the possibilities for a newborn communal life. It permits an *elaboration*, an actualization of the self that swiftly places you in contact with everything. Jazz allows you to be fully, almost desperately, in the present. It allows you to seize, all at once and totally, what is. When you launch into an improvisation, there's a mingling of life and death. From then on, the improvisatory moment must be extremely concentrated; it has to advance forward in the most powerful way. *Let go.* The musician who improvises cannot be sectarian or hesitating, limited or closed off; he is the total gift, without a before or an after. He is the immense desire and the full grasp. His act of extended self-expression opens onto all the modalities of the Other, without hierarchy or distinction. We could have called it *participation*—that first fusion that exposes you to an encounter with everything in the mystical intelligence of abandon, in the horizontal relation to things. But Glissant will go further, exploring what happens in that oceanic night of the hold.

He believed that the Abyss of the slaveship hold was also the site of a Digenesis. That is, it was the site of a genesis that opens not onto the absolutes of a community but rather onto the realities of the individual forced to construct the self all alone: to become a person. This is a genesis that doesn't send you back to Africa but that opens you, *with Africa*, to the active diversity of cultures and civilizations, the adventures of their contact and the riches of their interactions. Such a genesis offers you the possibility of considering another possible mode of existence that can be lived as well as conceived. Glissant will call this the *Tout-monde.* The hold, like an enormous door that remains ajar, sent us all into an interrelated world, a world that became conscious of itself. The Tout-monde is first of all a relational energy: the shock, the rush, the encounter, the contact, and the exchange are decisive, even inescapable. This leads to the identification of another phenomenon that Glissant will designate with a capital letter: *Relation.*

These two words flash like bolts of lightning in Glissant's thought: *Tout-monde* and *Relation.* They can be linked, organically. The actualized world in its totality has become a relational flux of an almost atmospheric intensity, from which no one can escape. This intensity is of course fed by the digitalized cortex of the world, the technoscientific accelerations, the contaminations of the market economy, planetary mobility, and processes of individuation which allow each individual to construct his/her/their own personhood.

This arrival of the individual at the emergence of the person lets us experience in the bio-digital world a relational calculus that is potentially much more erratic, powerful, unexpected, fresh, and total than any archaic communal system could have forged.

When the world became a *Tout-monde*, it regained its own complexity. A world-consciousness was constituted, sparkling with each of our individual consciousnesses, which, from that point on, integrated the desirous imagination belonging to this totality. This world-consciousness (that we inhabited and that inhabits us, that makes us and that we make) assigns us an obligation to live in Relation, in an open, erratic, unpredictable availability, with all the diversity of the world and all imaginable possibilities. This is extremely difficult; it seems to us, at first, like a complete impossibility.

Glissant has never contested this impossibility. On the contrary. Refusing to eliminate or to simplify it by means of systematic thinking or thought-systems (with which we assure our comfort in the world), this impossibility has maintained us, uncomfortably, in a poetics. Rather than define the terms *Tout-monde* and *Relation* once and for all, he took care to *indefine* them. *Indefinition* is a poetic knowledge with a beautiful, delectable energy. It incites us not to fix the real in our conventional approaches—which do nothing more than deny the real and forbid us from approaching it more closely. Reality is a crystalization of our imaginary, and this crystalization is never the real. Just like the *Tout-monde*, the real is a silence that is unattainable. In Glissant, there is thus a profuse indefinition of the two terms. They are, properly speaking, "concepts"—one might say "poeticepts." The poeticept is a beautiful line of flight, a strange intellectual organism in which poetic fire brings out bursts of lucidity and moments of vivid awareness. Glissant considered that, accordingly, the highest object of literary creation, and even of creation itself, was none other than the exploration of the existential situation of these isolated individuals that we have become, individuals who must construct their personhood on the great relational stage of the world.[14] Glissant's strength was to remain in poetic indefinition: his was an open vision that altered without denaturing, an evolving vision that helped us to sense what we would have to experience, from that point on, in a state of endless questioning. In this way, he taught us to live with both the uncertain and the unknowable.

In *L'Esclave vieil homme et le molosse* [The Old Slave and the Mastiff], I told the story of this old slave who left the plantation to live as a maroon, not to try to rediscover a real or fantasized Africa, but to immerse himself in a way of life that he could not conceive in advance. It is this impossibility to conceive in advance that I alluded to (thinking of the philosophical stone of the alchemists) with the symbol of a Stone. At the end of his journey, the old slave encounters a symbolic stone that concentrates in its impenetrable matter all the presences, the "voices" and the "vectors" of the world realized as one object of consciousness. For me, this Stone was nothing other than the *Tout-monde* of Glissant. Transmuting the *Tout-monde* into a *Pierre-monde* was my way of saying that the *Tout-monde* emerges from the unknowable, and that we, like this old slave, must envision our refoundings, personal as well as collective, as centered on the mobile pedestals of something impossible, unpredictable, unknowable.

The globalization of the world has brought about encounters (massive, accelerated) among fragmented peoples, fragmented civilizations, fragmented cultures, fragmented imaginations, and individuals carried off in an anthropological maelstrom much more complex than a simple *métissage*. Shocks. Hybridizations. Syntheses, symbioses, and repulsions. Antagonisms and interdependences that are endlessly produced. This anthropological and environmental maelstrom is called *creolization*. The rapidity, volume, and condensed temporality of creolization make it a phenomenon that is infinitely unpredictable in its results and evolutions. In that sense, creolization also remains something unknowable, something that must now be experienced on a

---

14 See Patrick Chamoiseau, *L'Empreinte à Crusoé* (Paris: Gallimard, 2012). TN: See also the recent translation by Jeffrey Landon Allen and Charly Verstraet, *Crusoe's Footprint: A Novel* (Charlottesville: University of Virginia Press, 2022).

global scale. Creolization is what my old slave discovers as he is about to die (that is to say, as he is about to be *infinitely reborn in the beyond that the matter of his bones implies*). The old slave discovers creolization at the foot of the *Pierre-monde*, in the face of that impenetrable mystery that, for him, constituted the future, a future that is, for him, rigorously unknowable. The true Black maroon, the fundamental Black maroon that Glissant was, did not flee in search of new certitudes, or of a world rendered transparent. Glissant was the one who had the courage *via* the *Tout-monde*, *via* the *Pierre-monde*, to accept the great relational mystery and to confront the undeniable nature of what he could not even imagine or ever understand.

In the *Tout-monde* there's no actualization except "in" and "by" Relation.

Everything is connected to everything.

That is why the immense dehumanizations, the massive regressions (as in the hold of the slaveship, American style slavery, Nazi camps, ordinary genocides, or the damnation that Europe inflicts right before our very eyes on those who migrate toward her shores), or still more, the technoscientific advances, or even the outbursts of Beauty in the domain of the arts, once they have taken place, in whatever corner of the planet they are produced, remain, so to speak, like doors flung wide open before us all. They are vertiginous gaps that concern every single one of us, that connect us in this way. Such a placing into relation establishes dynamics of fluidity, of uncertainty and unpredictability in the world's consciousness and sensibility. Relation compels the convergence and coming-together of individuals and societies in the same way as the opposite reaction that takes place when walls, isolations, and murderous solitudes proliferate. *Then the Tout-monde functions like an extension of the consciousness of us all, as the vector of an everything-is-possible for us all.* When everything is interconnected to this extent, horror may still circulate, but a tremor of beauty, a lucid moment of hope, and an elegant ethics can spread at great speed to everyone everywhere... That is why it isn't futile to try to install at the heart of the relational, not "values" erected as a system, but rather a poetics for experiencing the world, for living in the world, for participating in it, for constructing it, and for actualizing oneself within it, governed by an ethics of sharing and a poetics of exchange-that-changes without losing or denaturing anything... —"Wouldn't the 'participation' you've been talking about so much be a primal form of Relation?" the Baroness asks me. —Participation seems to me quite close to mysticism. Relation, in contrast, would come more from a developed philosophy, from a flash of awakened consciousness, and from thought. If you wish, let's think of Relation as the more secular, the highest, the most vast, and the most decisive of participations...

LEGENDARY OF FORGETTING – The sealing of the coffin had endowed all the objects that belonged to her with a soul. The sealing of the vault cut what remained of the moorings. The objects started to radiate out—that is, to diffuse memories. They inspired mental activities that conduct curious inventories, digging around in attics and ruins, ramifying within us long tidal waves of sensation. A life can often be summed up in two to three small suitcases, a few papers, a few photos, some jewelry, some baubles, linens, and remaining clothes and shoes. In the eyes of those who inherit them, some of these things take on importance; others only just come alive. But all can be found at the center of a vibrating, sentient web like that of a spider that extends itself into an area of space much larger than itself. These objects threw out their traps and chose us, or else it was the Baroness who divvied them up by instinct. Another life slowly began again. The group came undone until it rediscovered ordinary, everyday life: a few phone calls here, a few family dinners there; the pretext of a birthday; an impromptu visit... And then it was oblivion, by which I mean the total dispersal of remembrance.

Constantly, in a corner of the commune, at the turn of a street, smack in the middle of an assembly, or on my Facebook wall, a woman or a man would greet me in the name of Man Ninotte. These were strangers from the neighborhoods of Lamentin or the streets of Fort-de-France who had known her well, who had seen her as a child in the schools of the village, and who took pleasure in seeing me so as to remember her.

Each time, aspects of her existence were presented to me, in details that will always be inaccessible to me, but that these strangers incarnated in their very person. They confided to me a few hints about the past that I hadn't asked for, and, even while keeping silent, they confirmed the scope of that life of which I was never but a small part. I never questioned them; I simply noted their name to pass on to the Baroness. What they knew belonged to them. I preferred to imagine them as guardians of this mystery, and I was content that they should bear it away with them, share it, and keep it alive in a way that remains elusive to me.

Other flashes of her appeared as the result of a nebulous vision, an imprecise mental image, a look, a smile, a silhouette, an imagining of what she was like as a little girl, splashing about in the stream, gathering up her mangos, tasting the cocoplums, crossing savannas where bulls with menacing horns threatened. Over the course of time, I measured how much forgetting had done its work. Scenes came back to me in their essential outline, without details, without coherence, rarely congruent, and with labile contours. I retained almost no specifics concerning the dresses she wore; their colors were lost, and all that remained was the form of the broad blouses in which she moved easily, the neckline bordered with that English lace she so adored. In my mind's eye, her shoes remained vague, as did her hairstyles. All that I could remember was the style she wore during that crepuscular period when the Baroness cut her hair, when she started to wear it short like a boy's. I still believe I can recall the timbre of her voice, but what comes back to me escapes me again as soon as I try to hear it better. Sometimes I surprise her gaze, but it fades the moment I become aware of it. Certain of her words shoot through me like lightning bolts when I use them; it is only after I pronounce them that I recognize that they were hers, but their wake of sensations is clear. Forgetting has sculpted whatever it is that I have retained of her. I no longer even know what it has erased, and I don't understand what it has preserved. Some images only produce sensations and the sensations mime images. All of these surge forth from nothing; they rely on the ordinary, milling about in the insignificant moments of my everyday life, as though escaped from a pit and emerging, for reasons I cannot grasp, in a game of impenetrable associations. I take it all up, smiling, feeling moved without thinking about it. When I am fully conscious of an image, a sensation, I allow it to subsist or to depart, as its music and its vibration require.

Never be prudent as you enter your dreams
Please

Our libraries only cause us *not* to read; they nourish forgetting—or, more precisely: they nourish us with forgetting. I have read so many books, flipped through so many books, breathed in the odor of so many books that it would be impossible for me today to count them all. Most of them have disappeared; those that remain do so in a tangible form that is never present to my consciousness, but that emerges when I write. My mind, placed on alert, turns over the crests and lifts up the sediment. Those books that have escaped from the trash, from losses, borrowings and gifts, are still around me, not always for good reasons, simply for that happy moment—an idea, a sentence, a scene, a character, an instant of pleasure that lingers like a lonely secret, sometimes as a guilty penchant, often as a sweet insignificance. Some have resisted forgetting because they truly shaped the foundation of my thinking; others are there like lands to discover where the excursions are brief, sporadic, always as a project begun and never accomplished. But by perusing them, by opening and closing them, I gain an unidentifiable knowledge that feeds who I am. I wouldn't know how to cite these hundreds of books in a knowledgeable way; I often haven't the slightest idea why I've kept one or another of them. When writing comes, I walk around, looking at the shelves, animating the sentiments that come back to me, that awaken old memory zones. It's a *sentimenthèque* that contains all the books I couldn't write, books that I would have so loved to have been able to write, and all those others that it might still be possible for me to write if they have not already been written, or that I will write in another way, perhaps, or that I will never write. But their substance is disseminated in these shelves, in the dust, in the paper eaten by mites, in the yellowed sheets and the ink lost to an oblivion that provides both substance and source.

A biguine without the sweat
And the quadrilles without leaders
And the only piquancy the points of the mazouk

I love these epiphanies that, ever since the procession to the cemetery, have become increasingly frequent for me: seeing myself on the road to the south of Martinique, during the drought of Lent, thoughtlessly contemplating the undulation of a hillside covered with cabouya grass. The grasses are long, swaying, yellowing, reddish, and their undulation fans out in tremors on the dehydrated flanks of the foothill. They seem to be scattered along the passage of a more vast and invisible entity. It is then that a verse of Césaire comes back to me, one that had been, until that point, indecipherable: *"When the Lenten seasons were pursuing through the mornes the strange herd of splendid russets..."*[15] I had often recited that verse, and then forgotten it, without attempting to elucidate it. But in this undulation taking place before my eyes, the poetic enigma suddenly assumes its full meaning. I like to leave to Césaire the alchemy of his mysteries; these are felt knowledges that transform you from the inside before effecting the sudden transmutation of landscapes that we share with him but that he contemplated better than us.

Another epiphany: On the Saint-Pierre road, in May heat that makes the flamboyants sing. I contemplate the lightning of bright colors: red with its varieties of pink, orange, or violet, with sometimes—but more rarely—some triumphal yellow. And then, suddenly, dominating the landscape, a tree that seems to be a flamboyant but that isn't one. The black pods are hooked to the branches, the flowers hang like little lamps. They are of a sumptuous yellow that is glorious in the sun, enchanting the arid cliffs and the scorched scrub-brush...

A marvel.

A presence.

I sense that this vegetal plenitude has been sublimating the volcanic venture of this island, an island born of fire and lava, fertilized by ash, winds, time, and a scattering of birds, until it transmutes into a teeming mass of lives... I was halted before that tree. In its unique splendor it condensed all the beauties of the month of May. Then the meaning of another verse of Césaire's

---

15 In *Ferrements* (Seuil, 1960 and 1991). TN: The line is from Aimé Césaire's poem "Pour Ina" ["For Ina"]: *"Quand les carêmes pourchassaient par les mornes l'étrange troupeau des rousseurs splendides."* I cite here the translation by Eshleman and Arnold, p. 1543.

surged forth, one that is uttered at the beginning of a poem, and that goes, very simply: *An entire May of cañafistulas.*[16] Its sonorities had struck me; it captured something all-encompassing. All by itself, it is a poem. I had habituated myself to its mystery. The verse had buried itself in this forgetting that remains on the lookout, nourishing my gaze, feeding what I could see of the land, like an anticipation delayed, mulling over its next leap, until it is released into meaning. This is the quintessence of celebration, the archetype of the enchanting moment, the incomparable gift that is nothing other than a month of May full of cañafistulas.

PRESENCE

An entire May of cañafistulas
on the breast of pure hiccup
of an island adulterous to its site
flesh taken with itself harvests its grapes
O slow among the volcanic rock
scattering of birds enflamed by a wind
in which the falls of time pass blended
the fire, plenitude of a rare miracle
in the ever credulous storm
of a non-evasive season.

Along the Caribbean coast, submitted to the rushing spouts of the sun, the sea is an alchemy of waters as phosphorescent as a jetty of vivacious glass fragments. To describe it, Césaire will

---

16 *Cadastre* (Seuil, 1961). TN: "*Tout un mai de canéficiers*" — the line is from Aimé Césaire's poem "Présence," originally published in *Corps Perdu*, illustrated by Pablo Picasso (Paris: Éditions Fragrance, 1950). I cite here the translation by Eshleman and Arnold, p. 484, slightly modified. The stanza that follows, titled "Présence" in Chamoiseau's text, is also from this poem. I quote the stanza in the original French here: "tout un mai de canéficiers/sur la poitrine de pur hoquet/d'une île adultère de site/chair qui soi prise de soi-même vendange/O lente entre les dacites/pincée d'oiseaux qu'attise le vent/où passent fondues les chutes du temps/le feu foison d'un rare miracle/dans l'orage toujours crédule/d'une saison non évasive."

say very simply: *The jangling sea of noon.*[17] Noon is a sun. The sparks coming off it become sounds of a metallic sharpness. These sounds reverberate in keys, in bracelets, and, no doubt (given the backdrop of Césairean visions), in slaveship chains. It's the sun that holds the keys and the bracelets, somewhat like a jailer. To see this sea of the Caribbean coast is to live a privileged moment in which Césaire's poem rises up to the surface of my mind, leaving its wake of meanings and prolongations in time that make me infinitely alive, attentive, and happy to be so. Another moment and another verse—How many times under the rooftiles of the apartment on François-Arago Street, at Man Ninotte's, I snuggled with pleasure in the warm sheets of my cabana while on the roof the force of a stormy shower was let loose, an experience that we all share and that could orient us toward tenderness or innocence of some kind. Césaire, anxious and always vigilant, will name it: *the rainy salvo of shadow.*[18] But what we must retain, I say to the Baroness, is that Césaire, in refusing the colonial vision, will always be suspicious of the professed beauty of our landscapes. For him, these spectacular realities were full of silence. They were cast on a flayed emptiness, an inaudible howling: the suffering of the enslaved, the dehumanizing of the colonized, the exploitation and misery that had become the norm. In a magnificent flower, he will see a *burst eyeball*; in a cluster of our cañafistulas he will hear the *rumour of those who have been lynched*; in the pods of the flamboyant, he will sense the menace of the *curved blade of a cutlass*; in the slashed leaf of the banana tree he will spy the *pathos of a Vodou priest*, and in its proboscis a purple penis, tumescent with the potential to rape. In his clairvoyance, the foothills will have

---

17 TN: "*la mer cliquetante de midi*" — this line is from Aimé Césaire's poem *Cahier d'un retour au pays natal*, the 1956 Présence Africaine version. Regrettably, it is not reproduced in Eshleman and Arnold's *Complete Poems of Aimé Césaire*, since they relied on the 1939 *Volonté* edition. The line does appear, however, in the translation by Clayton Eshleman and Annette Smith in *Aimé Césaire: The Collected Poetry* (Berkeley: University of California Press, 1983: pp. 80–1). I have modified their translation, which reads "by the clanking noon sea."

18 TN: "*les pluvieuses mitraillades de l'ombre*"— the line comes from Aimé Césaire's "Le Grand Midi" in *Les Armes miraculeuses*. I cite here the translation by Eshleman and Arnold, p. 140.

bandages of shadow, the houses will be *chapped with blisters*, and the sea will fold its *little falcon eyelids*.[19] He identified a founding lack that nothing had dealt with up to that time... —"I see what you mean," the Baroness interrupts me. "In fact, Césaire thought that the beauty here, the beauty of the landscapes, was deprived of substance if you didn't take into account the flows of blood and suffering." ... —Exactly, I tell her. The frills and flounces of the *doudouist* poets tried to make the landscape magnificent, obscuring the land, and thus completing its dehumanization. They were exploded by the violence that Césaire sensed in each link of the chain that got us here; this true humanity restored to the splendor of our earth, its gangue of shadows and human ruins. Each drop of blood risen from the depth of our histories will count, each drop will shift the landscape toward greater meaning. Césaire tells us that true beauty does not tolerate any lacuna; it is always total and full, terrible and overwhelming. It amplifies everything from the smallest instant up to the prophetic shores of the past. It reveals obscure and luminous plenitudes, and thus it has nothing whatsoever to do with prettiness...

The masters and the slaves, the enlisted, the merchants, and the servants of the Cross were all in exile. All bore within themselves the void left by a distant land that they had little chance of ever seeing again. Here, the foundational act would not recognize itself as such; acts of violence would aim only to dissolve these lacks. What would be born of their encounter would for a long time remain unknown, with each one living in the hope of a return to

---

19 TN: The line "burst eyeball" ["oeil éclaté"] is from "Élégie-équation" in *Corps Perdu* (translation by Eshleman and Arnold, p. 493); "bandages of shadow" ["pansements d'ombres"] is from the *Cahier* (translation by Eshleman and Arnold, p. 17); "chapped with blisters" is a rendering of a line from the *Cahier*, which reads "gerçant d'ampoules" (translation by Eshleman and Arnold, p. 25); and "little falcon eyelids" ["de petites paupières de faucon"] is from "Les Armes miraculeuses" (translation by Eshleman and Arnold, p. 107). The expression "un hougan pathétique" is by Régis Antoine, referring to Césaire in *Rayonnants écrivains de la Caraïbe* (Paris: Maisonneuve & Larose, 1998 [p. 64]); the translation is my own. The other two images — "the rumor of those who have been lynched" ["rumeur des pendus"] and "the curved blade of a cutlass" ["la courbe d'un coutelas"] have not been located and may be approximations of Césaire's lines. The translation is thus my own.

the source. For the Amerindian survivors, this source must have been composed of all those times before the arrival of the first caravel. For the colonizers, it was no doubt their original territory, elevated to the rank of the absolute essence of civilization. As for the enslaved, for a long time I envisioned this first generation that had to survive with the hope of returning to Africa, a generation that regarded the sea as impossible to cross and the land where they arrived as fundamentally uninhabitable. This generation would find itself floating, so to speak, between a dream-land—*the lost land*—and a land impossible to inhabit—*the land of suffering*. In their minds, it would remain a place of "transit." I imagine this generation bleaching out, drying out, transmitting its asphyxiated hope to its sons and to the sons of its sons. We had to wait until lost Africa ceased being the major reference, the place where one could live. We had to wait a long time for the practical gestures of survival and the identitarian anabases to bend creativity toward the riches of this land—its silences, its emptinesses, its ruptures, and its lacunae. It will be easy for the *doudouistes* to retain in their poetic imagery only the landscape, forgetting its histories, forgetting the people, incapable of comprehending the fact that they had made of that land a native land, one not given but seized by infraction—no, better, by *effusion*. Only the great poets, from Césaire to Glissant, will intuit this way of gaining a "Site," which is not a territory considered to be exclusive in the traditional way, but rather is a mixture of a lost country, a fantasized country, an intuited country, a composite country, a country finally coming into being. —"Would there be a way to inhabit a land without absolutes, to leave it in its multifarious plenitude, to experience it without certitudes, without barbed wire frontiers?..." the Baroness murmurs. —I believe these poets did just that...

Our house burned down, but for me, the street of the Syrians remains a site charged with emotion. Everything is there, but practically nothing is left of what I knew during those days of childhood. The façades are no longer the same; the old house built with wood from the north country has disappeared under the casings of zinc and plastic. Stores constantly change their fluorescent signs and their window displays. Air conditioners colonize balconies that are falling into disrepair. The only constant: the Syrians are still there, not those whom I knew and who spent hours gnawing away at an onion on the doorstep, below the edge of an iron curtain, or whom I heard unwinding their stories under our window in their language of mysteries. The current inhabitants of the street are newcomers, arriving directly from Lebanon, or from Syria itself, or from some other land of the Maghreb where the islands of the Antilles are known to exist. They behave like the ones I knew; they install themselves on their doorsteps, inviting visitors in, or else they pay a Black town-crier to do the job. Once again, they begin the same story, but without me and without Man Ninotte; this time it is with other characters. Their shops are always bazaars filled with merchandise from other corners of the world, competing for the same clientele as the Haitians and the Chinese.

But some old Syrians are still around.

The oldest ones can be found at the back of the shops. I glance in, I take a look at them, say hello. Some of them recognize me because of the TV; others don't make the connection between what I've become and the *négrillon* of Man Ninotte. For me, they are like a memory-well of images of Man Ninotte—she enters here, goes out there, stops to chat with this Syrian or does some business next to that shopgirl, negotiating an under-the-table exchange... She brings back pieces of canvas, a carpet, some lengths of cloth, basins in plastic, a shirt, or boxes of shoes. This harvest of things was often destined for her fishermen or for the merchants who gave her basic staples in return. These things circulated very quickly and constituted one of our means of survival.

Her resourcefulness was limitless.

When it was necessary to go pay the water bill I know not where and confront the infernal uproar in front of the narrow windows, she would take with her a pile of other water bills from the Syrians or the shopgirls—people from all over the street—and would complete the chore for all of them. When something like a line seemed to be forming, her technique was to install the Baroness in a good spot and then turn her attention to another urgent task, returning just in time to position herself in the spot that the Baroness had held for her, and which by now was almost at the head of the line. Conversely, if the usual chaos took an orderly form, she would first elbow her way in, shaking up the universe with a shove of her hip, leaning her entire mass to the right, swelling herself to the left, forcing open the gaps, taking hold of fate, cutting off chance, and entering into a motherless war with the counter clerk who would take fright—*But what is this?*—at that great pile of bills.

The act of forgetting establishes a framework for surprises. Quite often, when I'm not even thinking about her, the Baroness will be speaking to me, or one of my brothers is in my presence, and all at once I capture in them a gesture, a laugh, a look, or an attitude that brings Man Ninotte, or sometimes Papa, back to me. As I've grown older, what I didn't see before becomes clear: a resemblance to Papa or to her appears in a pout of the lips, an intonation of the voice, or the shape of a silhouette. These resemblances are like phantoms that inhabit and surprise each of us in turn, appearing first in one, then in another. Over the course of time, certain resemblances that had established themselves became blurry, allowing others, less pronounced but just as substantial, to appear. She had been for such a long time the unique light source for our perceptions that we had become infused with her presence; for us, some of her gestures had turned into deep feelings, emotions without cause, open landscapes. The group reformed in these fluctuations, resemblances, subtle proximities, shared succulences, close-knit memories, like a tenderness that wells up in everyone on certain occasions and that constitutes a fusional bond. A lost world of children and of unconscious moments crystalizes in our contact. One of us offers a part of himself to the others; one brings to the other an instant from childhood, a moment of sunshine and rain, a tiny complicity that is useless but that is nonetheless preserved like an old bell rustled by a soft wind. Something invisible draws us back over time, fills us with reflections and nuances, enlarges us beyond what we are, climbs back up the bloodline and loses itself in the species…

It is forgetting that guides me on François-Arago Street. I search for what I have forgotten. Details. Moments. Colors. Atmospheres. I am happy when something is still there and brings back some reminiscence that forgetting has made more precious. Often, forgetting resists, keeping a certain strangeness in what I know, establishing a distance between me and what I encounter and what is familiar to me. Here or there, it lets me sense that a transformation has taken place, a disappearance has occurred, without revealing what it is. I only feel that there was something there, that a part of me knows what is no longer there, and the perception of it welcomes me, so to speak, yet leaves me locked out. Before a place that is unfamiliar, my imagination plays tricks and tells itself anything whatsoever in order to reintegrate what I see into my story. But forgetting, unmoved, clues me in to imagination's artifice. Sometimes, it's a sudden, precise memory that points out some place where I fell, or where I sat. I know it, I remember it, and it is preserved before me, neutral, delivered just like that to the shudder of memory. The sidewalks, façades, and vestiges of balconies construct a familiar topography for me, but even in what has not been transformed, forgetting produces a de-activation: I contemplate objects that neither awaken nor reveal anything. Forgetting orients me in this street through the intuitions of a son and the bewilderment of a stranger.

LEGENDARY OF THE UNTHINKABLE – What happens in the oceanic night of the hold? What wound of our imaginary was suddenly opened by this Digenesis? Please consider, dear Baroness, what that night would produce. Since our origin as Sapiens, the first communities presided over initiation rituals meant to contain the calculus of the individual within a communitarian context. These rituals permitted each individual to confer meaning on the unfolding of his or her own life while submitting that life to an order maintained by the collective. Now, in this alternate origin that was, for us, the slaveship hold, the former initiation rituals were dissolved by a shock set off by death.

Not simply the death of the Other.

Nor even the death of the self.

But sovereign death, immanent death, the death that nothing can transcend.

In the hold, *it was the death of everything*.

There, Bazil became a sun without light. Bazil, or that thing that he inspires, mingled with all that palpitates, in the concrete world as well as the imaginary one, in the proximate as in the distant. Bazil steps into the light and assassinates the shadow. Veils fall. Vision is fixed, without eyelids. Nothing can explain or justify or envision what goes on there. At the bottom of the slaveship hold, there is nothing to get beyond, no possible way. There, consciousness finds itself once again *struck*, as it was the moment it appeared in those who would first achieve the human state.

Under the blow of such an impact, many of the captives were extinguished like lamps, flowing back body and soul into the cocoon of ancestral truths, which provided a reassuring limit. They were asphyxiated and they disappeared along with the former world.

Others would hold fast and discover a final dimension of *Digenesis.*

These captives set out on a strange route, one with no landing and no entrance, with neither front nor back, with no sign or ritual, without gods, without devils, and without demons, with the intensity of their lives reduced to the minimum or heightened to the utmost extremity of essence. They found themselves having to go on with no lines of flight, with no possible landscapes, no horizon. It wasn't just a matter of confronting a painful circumstance. Of surmounting a real or symbolic death before finding another state of the world. Of exchanging cultures or leaving behind one cosmogony so as to improvise what might be possible. No. It was a matter of persevering without advancing. Of going forward astride nothing. Of seeing oneself precipitated into a sort of immobility. In the deathliness of the slave boats, and in many of the succeeding "situations" of the slave plantation, there would be, ruling over them, the terror of *that thing*.

The thing outside any meaning.

The thing outside any paradigm.

Beyond the major absurdity, the unknown barbarity, the new perception of space and of the world, there is *something that hangs over the catastrophe and through which its impassive presence has been revealed.* He who can perceive it clearly senses that this thing was there before, that it will be there after, that it is beyond death, beyond life, beyond scarcity and abundance, beyond the capacities of the mind. The shock of the hold helps him recognize that this could not be a god (a horror without limits has unburdened him of gods), and that this thing is without evil or good intent, neither welcoming nor hostile.

It simply is.

The slave triangle, the hold, and American slavery (just as, later, the Nazi extermination camps) burned up the veils that had accumulated in front of the thing. They brought to our attention once again that *fundamental nudity* that provoked the initial terror of the Sapiens consciousness, and which had unleashed the immense creativity of our multiple forms of humanity.

It was the emergence of the unthinkable.

Like a return to the origin before origins.

The embryonic reflective consciousness of Sapiens was first transported by a profound, unalloyed joy. The pure happiness of being, the sumptuous flavor of being alive and of perceiving oneself alive. Then, there had been a part of consciousness that was amazed by the beauty of the world, by the great harmonious mysteries of the universe, and this initial amazement primed us for the feeling of the beautiful, and thus for an indescribable sacred, an unattainable divine, an immanent force that gave us the desire to bow down before it. But the experience didn't end there. No doubt, to the benefit of the unchaining of great natural forces, the inexhaustible rhythm of dangers of all kinds, this inaugural feeling was mixed with an apprehension due to finding oneself in the face of an immense unknown, a something-there that does not belong to the order of the knowable, a something-there upon which it was impossible to confer a spontaneous meaning. All this would be reinforced in the mind of Sapiens by the painful incongruity of death and decay—blind death, sudden death, violent death, and the deaths that are always unjust and that place every single life in a state of mute absurdity.

From unalloyed joy to the feeling of the beautiful—this ultimate effervescence—consciousness established its founding moment and moved on from there. It grew closer to something, as though approaching a star that gives no light but that remains above, right at the end of everything, and that consciousness begins to sense. This *beyond* attracts everything to it, implicates everything, indicates its existence through the sensation we have of something that cannot be transcended, the obscure certitude that we cannot and never will be able to conceive of that which—from the smallest of things to the inexhaustible totality—unveils itself, reveals itself, and ceaselessly escapes. Consciousness senses a without-horizon, silent, indifferent at the very heart of its awe.

Consciousness will remain forever thunderstruck by this contact with the beyond.

A shock will thus be at the origin of an inextinguishable desire to understand, to know. It will be at the origin of a natal terror responsible for engendering the spectrum of our emotions and the scintillating matter of our dreams. This beyond had to be rendered bearable. All the protections against the unthinkable and all the celebrations of that unapproachable mystery would be born from it. With the aid of magical thinking, of religions, of spiritualities and mysticisms, of gods, of demons and devils, of symbols and signs, of dances and chants, of dreams and artistic practices, of science and philosophy, of mathematics and its categories, of Reason and unreason... with all of these, Sapiens will seek to arm himself against the indifferent and mute presence of the unthinkable. He will strive to conceal the unthinkable with signifying systems, dictatorships of "meaning," an inexhaustible tableau of explanations or denials which will permit him to reassure himself and protect himself from this terrible *beyond-that-is-over-there*.

But the same shock will be repeated during the entire existence of Sapiens. The unthinkable will reappear in a host of circumstances. The death of loved ones will set off this endless unhinging of perception. Mystics, suddenly intoxicated by a whiff of the sacred, will espy the beyond in this gap. Many artists will sense it in the course of their quest for beauty. Unique works and certain exhilarating situations in life will trigger for some a feeling of the beautiful, the great expanse of which will point to the incomparable proximity of that beyond... And then, of course, the inconceivable—the hold of the slaveship, Nazi camps, and prodigious scientific advances—can tear open many of the veils and destroy many of the ramparts protecting the most human among us.

In literature, the conjuring away of the unthinkable will provide the story, that lovely story that leads a bit of the real back to the comfortable paths of the conceivable. In principle, fiction is always a construction that the mind can accept: one imposes a measure on the immeasurable nature of existence. This measure confers the illusion that life can be understood, that one can master the world, that one can possess its meaning, and thus that life has a meaning. In principle, every story attempts to organize the world and to reassure us that there is a limit to the ancient terror. As for the work of art, it strives to persist beyond death, to construct something permanent that is situated above the uncertain and the unpredictable. The work of art lends significance to the life of the artist who wishes to achieve posterity, to traverse centuries, to create a work that in itself constitutes an unalterable truth. *In the face of the unthinkable, the recourse to meaning functions like a fear, a refuge, and also like an impoverishment.*

Our consciousness extends outward. We forget less and less frequently that we are plunged into a pool of mysteries, into the inexplicable nature of life, the unknown essence of death, the uncanniness of the galaxies and of their becoming, the big bang, or, perhaps, the simple rebound of a universe that might be eternal. The infinitely large and the infinitely small never cease to engender enigmas, pointing us toward that same region of the unknowable. Both our understanding and our unconscious confront the inexplicable substance of what constitutes our universe. To that are added major distortions. *The slaveship hold functioned for centuries. Slavery in the Americas damned an entire segment of humanity. Auschwitz occurred at the heart of Europe...* The slow progress of consciousness toward the center of the mind emptied the world of enchantment, a world that had been hyperstimulated by that fear of the unthinkable. The veils and the various modes of concealment now struggle to resist today's growing lucidity, a lucidity submitted as if to its own intoxication, disarray, and despair. Privileged peoples regress to weak mysticism or defunct reasoning. Democracies become denatured under dreadful populisms. Archaic peoples, drowned in their own environment, ejected from their myths and protective symbolic systems, take up alcohol, drugs, or the stupor of collective suicides. Fanaticisms, desperation, and confusion, omnipresent stress, the return of archaic miseries, the de-ritualized use of drugs, social disengagement, and the quest for an absurd accumulation of riches—none of these have ever been as powerful as they are today. In the Mediterranean, right there, under our very eyes, children of migrants die every minute; men and women pursuing their last hope are swallowed up each day on the shores of a Europe of great abundance, which pays billions for an indecent tranquility... Whether or not one is aware of it, the fact is that the unthinkable is there; it stares at us in indifference, reaches the edge of our eyelids, erodes the banks of our spirit, and blasts through the escape route of the contemporary illusion that, until that point, had been leading nowhere.

Our greatest, most courageous act would be to stare back at it, without trembling.

I am going to tell you why.

Creation is never as powerful as when it is *exposed to a major lack as though to the excitations of a source.* In all that is living, it is voids, ruptures, and confusion—much more than abundance or excess—that produce the decisive evolutions of cellular organisms. Irruptions of genomes, the integration of new genes and their mutant combinations in these organisms are less responses to full plenitude than reactions to implacable crises and substantive shortages. Life is maintained over billions of years by these structural instabilities, huge volcanic catastrophes, gaseous mutations, cosmic scatter-fire, massive extinctions, and swooping dances of the climate. Life has always pursued itself, renewing and complexifying everywhere, specializing here, diversifying there, not *against* all that, nor *despite* all that, but *with* and *thanks to* all that. Absence, disequilibrium, and disorder have encouraged an agile new dynamics, opened up unpredictable paths, allowing those creatures who could to improvise astonishing horizons. Exaggerating just a little, one could say that in the living thing, plenitude (perfect equilibrium, blissful, unchanging stasis, effort that doesn't tremble with fear) is death. (But death itself is a process that is inscribed in life and constantly inaugurates new cycles!) The plenitude I often speak of with respect to the way the individual becomes a person would not be the summit of achievement. Rather, this plenitude would consist in the optimal capacity to confront voids, ruptures, disequilibriums, disorders, and lacks, at whatever intensity they may be found, and to transform them into opportunities. The climate upheaval currently taking place only clarifies this challenge: it will extinguish many things, stabilize others, and catalyze even more. But what remains to be determined is how we will manage to position ourselves. Is the right amount of plenitude available to us?

In literature, the power of the text derives more than ever from its proximity to the inexpressible, its vow to express the unspeakable. Description can only nourish itself when staying close to all that evades description. In its essence, philosophy only deals with the question of what cannot be philosophized. Extreme lucidity, not that which despairs but that which can re-enchant Reason's relevance, now approaches the banks of our mind; it must face, most importantly, voids, ruptures, and lacks.

Speaking of our enslaved ancestors, William Faulkner used to say, quite simply: *they endure.* Glissant meditated on this understatement for a long time. Its meaning is inexhaustible. Today, I tell myself that Faulkner wanted to suggest that our ancestors had *received the impact of the unthinkable.* They underwent a brutal enlargement of the human spirit, an extreme derailing of sensibility. They had to survive in annihilation, to resist without knowing exactly what they were resisting, *to be resurrected with the abyss.* Faced with the everyday, the sayable, the expressible, or the already thought, one recounts, fabricates, remakes, glosses, perseveres... Faced with the unthinkable, and having to be reborn with it, one is reduced to ash, or else one *seizes*, mobilizing all imaginable means. One plunges into the indeterminate; one fears neither the indefinite nor the opaque; one activates improvisation, thoroughly attentive to the improvisation of the Other; one links back together what has been undone or what is opposed and enters into combat; one plunges into the only nourishment one has, the moment itself, until it is possible to obtain a singular experience, irreplaceable, complex, often not renewable, and always in a state of becoming... That which receives the impact of dehumanization's blow will always reverberate with the vast rebounding force of humanity. American slavery showed us: *receiving the impact of the unthinkable tends to lead to remarkable resurgences of beauty.* You see now why I have spoken to you for so long about the enslaved, storytellers, jazzmen, men of the biguine of salsa, of reggae, players of *ka*, masters of *lewoz*, the Majors of *danmyé*, the troubadours of Haitian *kompa*...

All of them know this tendency and illustrate it perfectly...

The great poets do so as well.

Confronting the unthinkable allows the splendors of uncertainty to persist, allows us to expect the unpredictable and to act in concert with it. It allows us to orient ourselves in a state of wandering. To consider the inextricable. To go toward totality without totalitarianism. Creativity can be found there. The rejuvenation of the imaginary happens in the same way. This renunciation of meaning as a place of refuge marks out the ultimate migration of consciousness toward the mind's center. *Migration itself is what gives meaning; it is like danger, or like being placed on alert.* All the incontestable joy, the immanent joy that consciousness has known while discovering itself, while discovering the imponderable fascinations of the real, can be reactivated in this way, like lightning bursting forth from everything-everywhere, and striking everything-everywhere, as much in terror as in felicity.

It is there that the feeling of the beautiful endures!

The poetics of Relation proposed by Glissant as a prolongation of *Digenesis* reconciled us with the Other, the stranger, with difference as a fundamental building block, with the multiplication of our intimate personhood. It is here that our unified self is created. The poets of Relation reconciled our human nature with nature, allowing us to establish our proximity to the animal and to other ways of being. This poetics allowed us to understand that it was pointless to oppose the shadow to the light, the local to the global, or the individual to the collective. It taught us to connect what is dissociated, to undo fusions and confusions so as to better understand the Diverse. The *horizontal plenitude of the living*[20] can be conceived as a better way of being human within the equilibrium of our biosphere. We did away with the artifices that coddled our perception, that falsified its borders, and that anesthetized every wound brought closer to the sun. But now we have accepted our limits: perception is only slightly functional, and the imaginary is infinite. It is only the imaginary that will allow us to take the ultimate leap of Relation: *to make of the unthinkable a singing presence.* To build it up by inspiring new creations. To constitute it by establishing another stage of humanization, the most profound because the most humble, and the most just because the most naked.

The unthinkable
Not to renounce
But to desire, again, completely, in full force

---

20 See Patrick Chamoiseau, *Les Neuf Consciences du Malfini* (Paris: Gallimard, 1993).

—"If we had not concealed the unthinkable, perhaps we would have no magic, no religion, no divine, no sacred, no arts, no philosophy...?" the Baroness asks me, not really convinced.

—How can we know what would have happened? Perhaps everything that serves us as a crutch, a refuge, or a veil would have disappeared. What would have remained no matter what, I believe, is a feeling of the beautiful, which would have nourished poetic and artistic ways of knowing. And no doubt, also, the scientific mind, open-ended Reason, and philosophy in its essential form...

In your name
This coconut palm whose soul is a navel
And whose heart is to be consumed
And fragile, climbs, risking exposure to the sun and winds

I walk back up François-Arago Street. I regale myself with impressions—the street is still there, but it is a former reality slowly being erased. The street seems much narrower. The stores are still as numerous, but nobody lives upstairs anymore in the rooms that have been transformed into storage units. The no-longer-there accumulates everywhere and creates an atmosphere that is not unfamiliar. Small things subsist, old doors and old locks, part of a hallway here, an old window with Persian blinds there, a street sign, the detail of a façade... these tiny remainders terminate in folds of dust, seem to survey from afar and to watch me fixedly the entire way. As I advance, other streets criss-cross: Perrinon Street, Ernest-Renan Street, Lamartine Street, Victor-Hugo Street... All these streets saw me as a little boy in the shadow of Man Ninotte. Each possessed a unique affect that I rediscover every so often in a raggèd shudder. The gutters are plugged now, the clocks few and far between, the colors new. Some ruins and some abandoned fragments exhibit their old tints, but for me, they are in exile. Man Ninotte is not in this exiled place; she is elsewhere, precisely in that which is no longer there but which, for me, confers on this zone its curious texture. She is in the patina of this wan sun and in the morning shadows that bathe both the old and the recent with a renewed freshness, one that I recognize, that has not changed, and that I perceive much better than before. The arrival of the Syrians in the 1940s must have seemed like a cataclysm of modernity that would never come to an end. Thanks to them, the street became a large open window onto the fantasies of the universe, a temple of nylon, polyester, enamel casseroles and cocottes-minute, perfumes and rolls of fabric, cheap metal jewelry, hats not to be believed, and polished cowboy boots. The chairs, tables, tablecloths, engravings, and religious icons that would invade our homes came exclusively from their stock. When I was born, our street had already established itself as the source, the proud udder of things, an obligatory site of passage. With the exception of Sundays and Saturday afternoons, it was never empty, never mute, never completely put to sleep. The incessant fever of the street had no doubt fascinated Man Ninotte, who was elated to have left her sluggish quarter of La-Bélème. Even if she lived like a country person, she knew better than anyone how to take advantage of the urban bustle, somewhat like those hunter-gatherers who ceaselessly roam about a land of living things and who, over the course of seasons, through chance and opportunity, are able to bring back an inexhaustible abundance.

I remember that anthropologist who had embedded himself in one of those tribes. Its members gave him the sense that they were always satisfied with whatever the rounds of the day had brought them. If the hunt for racoons had been successful, they shared the catch, consumed it right there, put nothing aside for later, experiencing to the limit this feast that left no remainder. When the anthropologist was astonished at how little prudence they showed, the hunters declared that they would capture as much the next day, and the day after. In fact, the next day, they came back with just a little something: some insects, a skinny bird. They shared what seemed to be this small harvest with as much exaltation as if the successful hunt had occurred all over again. Their abundance consisted in celebrating what had been found, whatever that might be. To bring back nothing appeared just as normal to them; they waited without impatience, in a state of gaiety and festivity, for their good luck to return. It always came back one way or another and, since they were cheerfully vigilant, the hunters were always grateful for what came, however it came. Man Ninotte liked this state of being on alert similar to that of the hunters, a state that was required by the *En-ville*. Nothing was given; everything circulated within the reach of desire. Nothing was free, but the solidarity of those who simply make do multiplied the exceptions to the rule. One only had to shift gears, accelerate on all the turns, rush down the slopes and circumnavigate the walls, come and go like that every day, and every day bring back a *what-the-good-lord-sent-you* in your baskets or in your cooking pots. What caused her some passing concern was that nothing was ever good enough or abundant enough for her children. That's why some days, before a *blaff* that was somewhat less well garnished, she would cross her forearms above her head.

The unthinkable
To begin again the astonishing and radical audacity of questioning

The people from the countryside still proceed down this same François-Arago Street. The commercial malls haven't managed to depose it. The sight of so many people walking down that street brings Man Ninotte back to me. I see her climbing back up toward the Mercure superette. I see her going along the Levassor Canal to reach the spot where the fishermen dock. I see her leading the charge toward the vegetable market to obtain the spices for her *blaff* and our meager evening soup. I also see her engaging once more in her little contraband, going from one shop to the next, from one shopkeeper to the next... An imperceivable framework subsists, sketching out nothing precise, transmuting everything into a kind of sensation. These sensations are like mental images, the grain of which draws its texture from each fiber of my being. Whatever shows itself to me immediately escapes again. Whatever can be seen calls for the reparatory work of the imagination. I can only move forward in something that is dissipating, but that nonetheless fills me with sensations and memories. The disappearance of Man Ninotte has made me much more apt to see what persists in what has been lost, to take into account the degree to which what has been erased still affects the data of my consciousness and my attention... I realize that the Baroness (who nods her head while listening to me) knew these streets long before I did, and that the little that I preserve of them must be insubstantial compared to what she would be able to perceive... She tells me, indulgently: "We didn't see and we still don't see the same things. But what you say creates memories for me..."

Artistic knowing
It is precisely what, although arched over itself,

Can no longer envision
The beyond of the unthinkable

The Syrians were not the only ones to instruct us in the unknown.

The trinket-traders led us there as well. They were born here but without the slightest mooring to tie them down, somewhat like those savanna blackbirds that only care for the wind. They used to travel ceaselessly throughout the Caribbean, haunting the shores of the continent, exploring mountains and going down rivers. They came back (with a load of small suitcases and woven sacks) to keep up their mobile commerce. We weren't familiar with the things they sold us. Flashy clothing. Fanfare hats. Mother of pearl buttons. Silk bobbins. Enticing lace. Trinkets coming forth from limbo to present themselves as useful things. The innumerable items of their merchandise could be stuffed into a suitcase or lodged in the hollow of a sack. These sacks couldn't be too heavy, because the matrons had to carry them around on boats and in airports, crossing over the trenches of incredulous customs officials. They didn't stock themselves from the same sources as the Syrians. Their booty came instead from the world of Hispanic fashion, English houseware, Byzantine ready-to-wear lace, and Aztec wonderlands of ribbons and knots. They also brought back British medicines, bay rum or lunar concoctions, and tinctures that were unknown to our pharmacists. They were no longer part of us, while still being from here; they had seen other shores, other cities, other ways of being and not being, had explored other loves and other friendships. They knew other ways of eating, dancing, doing their hair, and dying. They dressed in unusual ways. Their hats were flowing banners. Their jewels didn't come from our stale-headed jewelers but from gods without temples, joyful and forgotten. They barged in, surrounded by an aura of scandalous audacity and indecent authority. They spoke other tongues. An accent from nowhere deformed their speech. They were always new and always interesting because they would suddenly disappear for a long time, leaving behind an afterglow of mirages that offered nothing to hold onto. They said nothing about it, but the distance that had been established between them and us thickened with more and more impenetrable mysteries. Bound to nothing either before or behind them, needing nothing more than themselves, they frightened the men, enchanted the women, and terrified the creatures hovering ambiguously between male and female. Man Ninotte, who had often dreamed of great journeys, must have eyed with envy these *manmans*-women who emerged at the edge of the market like flocks of turtledoves in flight. They were of the same type as she, with the same make-do energy; but they weren't burdened with little kids, were bound to no dead-weight men or unmoving earth. They were queens of the wind, practicing departure as a principle, disappearing with no address and no certainty of return. Did they even have a birth certificate? We couldn't guess. At the end of their life, the essential quality of which was to remain invisible, they would sometimes come back to the land, just to die at home, loaded down with as many memories as the bark of a mango tree. And we were witness to their strange aging, occurring as silently as an urn weighted down with oil, freed from material cares, but intoxicated with that missing part of the world that still lapped under their misty eyelids. Those who did not come back, who died somewhere else, were immediately transformed into memories in the minds of their far-away intimates; or else they expired in the second-hand dreams of whoever had met them, even just once, during their lifetime.

This same energy that the trinket-vendors spread across the Islands, Man Ninotte also released inside the house from four o'clock in the morning on. The light was turned on in the living room, the dishes were being done, the noise of rattling pans could be heard, a broom was sweeping the kitchen, and the aromas of milk and coffee were wending their way through the house. The door would open and then close again; you could hear the creaking of the hallway, and, further on, the squeaking of the stairway. The hens and the pigs in cages in the courtyard honked and squealed with pleasure while she tended to them and set right a catastrophe caused by the cats or the rats, finished a basin of dirty laundry, or spruced up a sheet... Instead of waking us up, that intangible concert cradled us back into serenity. It told us that Man Ninotte was on the ramparts: all was in order! When we emerged from our pillows, nothing of the evening's disorder remained; all was ready for the business of the day. During our recess in the courtyard of the Perrinon school, which was at the very heart of the city, I would see her, watching over us no doubt, passing back and forth en route to I know not where, coming back from I know not where, sometimes finding the time to bring me a comforting sweet. Over the course of a day, she would appear in the house, pile something on the kitchen table, and then disappear just as quickly. The frequency of her comings and goings was a sign of how much good fortune she'd encountered. She'd drop off baskets of vegetables, a cluster of rare fruit, a rabbit, some gourds full of fish, products from the Syrians, a bouquet of fresh flowers... Toward the end of the week, at the moment when the butchers completed the slaughter in the alleys of the slaughter-house, she would bring back some stew meat or a steak, or some giblets, some ends of beef hide, spiced and cooked on a grill, that Papa and his buddies would relish at punch time. The basin that we had seen filling up around eleven o'clock with wriggling fish could be found around noon full of fish bathing in a brine flavored with lemons and large red peppers. Or else a stewpot would start to simmer on the little fire of the gas stove set at minimum strength, steaming with lentils, or rice, or beans, emanating the scent of yam or dasheen, until the moment when Man Ninotte reappeared to finish the meal before we returned from school. During the hottest hours of the day, she could more frequently be seen devoting herself to a bit of sewing, sorting through rice or lentils, or shelling peas for us, before taking off again to find the evening merchants to buy watercress and fried fish. Nothing stopped her or slowed her down, from sunrise to her bedtime, no cold or *malcadi* could block her; she was engaged in a perpetual activity that could absorb without fuss whatever opportunity, emergency, or catastrophe presented itself. The old house resounded with all of that creaking and crackling, sounds that traverse me still and that come back to me in full force when, in a wooden house, I hear the hissing of the floorboards or the moaning of a partition wall laboring under pressure. Old wooden houses still move me. I know that they are living, that they are singing with the life energies they've conserved... The rich mixture of Antillean marinades, local vegetables, and all the seasonal fruits that populated my everyday life, and that I often didn't like, and that I never really thought about, today capture my attention, spark the immediacy of flavors on my voracious papillae, and let loose waves of images and desires on all the shores of my mind.

My only still life painting: a packet of scallions, a red pepper, a green pepper, two lemons, a few leaves of satinwood, a bunch of parsley and a bunch of thyme, salt, pepper, a large French onion, all placed on a waxed tablecloth.

Consider the long process of individuation. In that original magma, the living organism created for itself an inside and an outside: the evolutions of its metabolism, the recourse to the genome, were aimed at making it less and less dependent on the conditions of its environment. The brain and consciousness achieved this differentiation. Like all-encompassing filters cast over the exterior world, the brain and consciousness analyzed that world, structured it, predicted its variations so as to optimize the adaptation of the organism. They would even go as far as to endow Sapiens with a purely imaginary environment, making it the most bizarrely autonomous of living creatures. As a species, Sapiens grows further and further away from that oceanic indistinction of life-forms to carve out an autonomous collective way of being. These cultures based on communal living, which constitutes a second level of collective organization, build on the dictates of the species to create higher levels of sophistication: love, for instance, goes beyond the need to reproduce; the ear is employed to listen to music and to savor song; and receptive organs can be moved by the poetic and can evolve with it... Progressive individuation takes us out of our communal straitjackets, while our advance toward personhood under the category of the individual structures our ultimate autonomy. Beyond that autonomy is another, one that confers to each of us the capacity to confront the unthinkable. In the face of the unthinkable, each of us is alone, distilled down to our most elemental being—that is to say, a being like the young poet... and like the artist, most of all.

As for the Baroness, whose morphology seems quite different from Man Ninotte's, it is our mother's attitudes that return in her, the fluctuating expressions, such as the blackness of a look, a nod of the jaw. Also the care given to plants, this preference for economy—you don't throw out bread, an over-ripe fruit calls out to be made into jam—the stocking of almost everything, this refusal to believe that a thing could be useless, this constant vigilance so that the mischief of misfortune can be confronted head on, this tender care for the state of the clan, this constant attention to what is not going well for one person or another, and these rat-a-tat orders to set you straight in the universe and to straighten the universe around you... These reflections of Man Ninotte in the Baroness reveal to us what had never been evident when we had them both side by side, arguing with each other and opposing each other over the course of a discreet war. Now, within the context of that fundamental absence, these reflections offer proof of a similarity that is manifested in unpredictable and inescapable ways.

When Christmastime returns, the Baroness once again takes out the *santons* of our childhood, the shepherds, the donkey, the oxen, the angel, the Three Kings, and the little Jesus—all of them the same, without alteration, in their cocoons of old paper, and she constructs a crèche before the amazed eyes of these little children, who look at her as we used to look at her long ago. Constructing this crèche is better than a tradition; it's a ceremony that belongs only to us, and we are nourished by its impeccable execution. Building the crèche was the job of the Baroness. Man Ninotte, who never held back from anything, would eclipse herself at the moment of the crèche, satisfying herself with scrutinizing the work of the artist from the corner of her eye, simply making sure that no *santons* were missing. They were very costly, given her pocketbook; nevertheless, year after year, one by one, she found them and handed them over to the Baroness. I no longer have any occasion to attend the ceremony of this installation, renewed every year by the Baroness. But I always make a careful detour just to contemplate what she has been able to offer up. Today's crèche no longer has the same breadth; the wrinkled paper that represented the rock no longer goes on forever at the angle of the two partitions; the grotto is just a normal size, coiled around the Infant and his humble companions as though everything that still needed to be evoked now resides in these antique figurines. They had composed so many crèches and known us for so many years that they could tell many more stories about us, and tell them so much better, than could the narrative volume of a mountain of paper. I know that, but I protest—just for form's sake—without ever making the Baroness budge: *But it's too small!*...

It wasn't until the advent of old age and disease—its heavy ransom—that the massive body of Man Ninotte started to lose its round curves. The Baroness claims that she had always been round and compact while demonstrating an airy mobility and the strength of a bulldozer. The Baroness contends that this was not obesity, that it was nature, like those very dense, round breads called *massifs*. I, the last to arrive, had always known her with this strength, this roundness of the shoulders, the width of her arms under the well-padded armpits, the waist lost in the width of her hips, and legs capable of supporting the weight of those huge loads coming from the Factory François. Everything was firm and muscular; nothing about her was soft or had given way to languorousness or was dangling down like bad lard. You have to imagine a large hat, with a wide brim that protects from the sun and covers almost the totality of the shoulders, and then adapt it to that silhouette that I waited for at the window as a child experiencing my first anxieties. Over the course of the years, that silhouette labored without pause up and down our François-Arago Street, until, in the end, it pretty much summed her up for us. There's not a single curvaceous lady and no wide-brimmed hat that I don't gaze upon with tenderness, not for the details, nor to savor a resemblance to her, but just to catch a glimpse of that energetic shape that holds what was most precious to me, what was strongest and most fragile.

Something invisible inhabits our landscape. *Keep the trance of every passage of every landscape intense*, said Césaire.[21] He had been confronted with that invisibility thrown over the land by the sheer force of colonialism. The triumphal discourse of the Western colonizers had eliminated the Amerindian presence, forcing Africa to disappear and washing away whatever creativity survived from the resistant uprisings of the enslaved and their descendants. In the shock of these contacts, of apparitions and disappearances, an emerging landscape was born. The colonizers deforested, hollowing out here, raising up there. Amerindian blood bathed the beaches. The colonizers buried the enslaved wherever. Plants were brought over, some chosen by the colonizers, others privileged by the slaves. The shoreline was reserved for the exigencies of the King. Cultivation invaded the flat zones. The liberated slaves found and sculpted shelters in the shoals, the ravines, the slopes, and the heights. Generally, the high points and the great forests were sites

---

21 TN: *"De tout paysage garder intense la transe du passage"* from "Wifredo Lam"; translation is by Eshleman and Arnold, p. 773.

of maroon liberty. (Amerindians, indentured workers, or slaves found refuge there over the centuries, fleeing oppression.) Streams remained at the heart of practices linked to the fellowship required for everyday survival... From this long alchemy there arose a landscape that was also an archive. Colonial memory, exclusive and dominant, was never able to efface it, nor even to express it; instead, colonial memory was content simply to ignore it. Tourist imagery managed to diminish this archive even further by burying it under a paradisical prettiness, peeling away its depth—which is to say: all its beauty.

Like Glissant, Césaire found himself faced with this hollowed-out landscape. To intensify the landscape is to lead it toward a state in which we can divine the very substance that is gestating within it. This transmutation of the landscape intensifies horizons inside the self as well; interior vistas are enlarged and, at the other extremity, the world is encountered. Thus, in order to represent the inextricability of the *Tout-monde*, Glissant mingled and intermingled landscapes. Our flowers, our trees, our plants, and our bushes—which often come from all over—were plunged into bayous and deserts, steppes and ice floes, and their outpourings (everything from magnolias to sweetgrass) were created for those who knew how to envision *a new region of the world*: a chaos, strange to conceive and just as strange to inhabit. It is only by accepting the strange that we attain the most beautiful visions.

The colonizers, taking possession of the land, initially inhabited the coast, first with military quarters, then with the big plantations. The heart of the country, its volcanic heights, remained what they called, bitterly, the *lost country*: these were unexploited zones, unexploitable zones, a piece of *terra incognita*. The colonizers' wide roads in the lowlands linked only the villages that served as landing docks for their products. The connections that were established from one site to another, from one coast to another, in all directions, toward the high points and toward the low points, were little paths that the Amerindians had dug out to climb this terrain, to which were later added the trails made by the enslaved to access their secret gardens, as well as the passageways forged by the maroons and the digressive routes, walks, and various individual explorations... These paths twisted about in the foothills, the ravines, and the forests; they ran alongside the coastline, linking springs and following streams. They disappeared and reappeared, persisting through intense use and long abandonment. Their chaos, impossible to map out, bore witness to the inscriptions left in the silt of this country by the arrival of people still unsure of who they were. The Creole language called these inscriptions "traces." Glissant repurposes this term, conferring on it, with the capital letter, a breadth of meaning that we now recognize. Since then, these little "traces" rejoin the great ones, becoming for Glissant an access to the famous *lost country* of the colonizers, but also, more generally, to the *unsuspected country*, the dream country that constructs itself beneath the colonial triumph. This furrowing was amplified until it engraved something impalpable that the landscapes would integrate like a bony structure that is subtly visible to our great poets. It is the first of the doors that open onto the not-visible of our world.

There is that poetics that Victor Segalen declaimed, a poetics that makes you attentive to what is no longer, to what was, to what is not yet, to what founds and prolongs what is.

That was the sign of the great poets who came from here.

Their manner of regarding the landscape did not come from any militant act, any effort to bend the natural splendors to the shape of a preeminent human trajectory. They were simply in search of beauty, a beauty that doesn't reassure, that isn't afraid to frighten, that presents itself as always full of sublimity and terror, that always inspires exploration beyond the real and that welcomes the most overwhelming vision of what could be. This ethical regard, companion of the most evolved among us, nourishes us with pleasures that are reinforced as future epiphanies emerge.

LEGENDARY OF DIAMANT – Since the disappearance of Édouard Glissant, something invisible has been growing within the commune of Diamant. Glissant, who explored so deeply the Trace, left one of his own in what we have shared on this beach, in front of this boulder, in the sand that is sometimes gray, sometimes black. Something trembles in this wind, magnifying the landscape.

Whatever exists that is tender and sensitive, in this sunshine and on this sand, has agreed here to inhabit the shadows. He who knows it finds himself transported by it, and to see it stationary beneath the protection of the round leaves makes one think that it is withdrawing, whereas on the contrary, it is going right to the heart of things, persisting in the quick of life. Under the sun, veiled at times, the sand accentuates the light gray of forbearance, the dark black of memories; it alternates in this way between lost times and spaces to which no one holds the key. But in pinpoints of light, at bursts of the conch, out of old quartz and salt, the sand arranges a single and smooth carpet under the muddle of imprints that chance has selected. Alone, from foam, a bright trembling preserves the first intuition and the last sign of what remains, mildly, in the moving sand where nothing can remain.

Here too, in the selfish patience of the sands, in this memory that swallows things up, one sees vestiges of cities that glimmer, eyelids that open, passing innocences in the renewed archive of imprints. We imposed evanescent monuments here, monuments whose bases distinguish and use what is most solid in forgetting. Since that time, and for a long time after, in the name of memory, a diffuse constellation has marked the presence of ancient Amerindians, the wrecks of slaveships, and the colonial furies in the violet of the grapevines. And now, for me, memory adds and celebrates, here, near the ground, this part of the firmament that has come down to us. At the edge of the foam, the crabs are white or pale yellow. Under the manchineel trees, their vigilance is red. If they ignore what the poet said, tirelessly maintaining their holes in the ceaseless ruin of the sands, they still live in the fire of this vigilance. They hold their ground.

Too many bees are dying in the foam. I often watch their little deaths, performed to the ovation of the landscape. The wind appears joyous to be able to pull the sun from the eclipse of the clouds; it knows how to hear both the breaks and the flows of the long, sweeping passage. The play of the foam and of the waves is trying to conjure away the void. It is a song that anticipates what here becomes permanent, neither interrupting nor troubling anything. You must wait, wait for the ripening of the seagrapes, their ripening and the ripening of seasons. You must wait until you hear the blue hum of sugar under their violet robes and their budding tenderness. Then, the encounter begins, and the encounter continues.

I can also remember those strange moments when the waves fall silent, when all that remains is an oily surface that mirrors the sky in its commerce of different blues. Then, what glitters in us, what glitters around us, is nothing other than fleeting smiles, the slow ebb and flow of contentments accompanied by two wands of truth: the legs of the poet.

Oala, on the beach, crabs and caterpillars, zandolie lizards and insects remember. They say that what has happened, what has passed through us, marking this landscape with an intangible memory, comes from a solar lineage, a companion of lights and graces, like certain shadows and other signs. All have sung about this lineage as if they were deciphering in its wake abandoned hearts and lingering passions. Now, the pride of this old volcano comes down to nothing more than a boulder, a tragic humility that creates beauty in the rock, offering its nest to nests of bird populations. And all these different shades of blue from which it builds a bower are (in the tortoise nests that occupy my mind) nothing other than the guardians that have been offered to protect this place.[22] They hold a vigil just this side of eternity.

And if one day the algae return—in this fermentation that creates the sargasso—if these algae bring back to us their skeins of red-headed beauties, sooner or later the sand will swallow them up, the tradewinds will dissipate their acidity, and under what

22 TN: In the French, the word "bleu" ("blue") can also mean "bruise." It is therefore possible to give a second, more metaphorical reading of the passage that would describe how injuries—the history of the region—may be conserved like a precious treasure, amassed in a kind of case ("*écrin*"—"case" or "bower") that guards that history. However, the mention of the "different blues" at the beginning of the paragraph leans me toward the more literal meaning. René Hénane writes that in the French Caribbean, "bleu" can also refer to "blue blood," or the mixture of European, African, and indigenous peoples (*Glossaire des termes rares dans l'oeuvre d'Aimé Césaire* [Paris: Jean-Michel Place, 2004]).

remains of them (that great scorching of the drought) there will just be unalterable memories and this boulder against which, from now on, forgetting will hurl itself and break. Forgetting renounces and departs without saying a thing, leaving nothing behind, neither stitch nor sprig.

From Man Ninotte to the soul-bestowing splendors of the poet, I made an inventory of the signs that create substance. A city of fireflies, a kapok tree that, in the month of May, seems to marry the flamboyant, yield to the magnolias, invent the jasmine, and make off with the perfume of the sweetgrass, which, returning from its voyages, arrives to enchant the route toward Diamant.

LEGENDARY OF THE INVISIBLE CITY – Now that my mind has agreed to shift its attention, I like to walk in this town that the volcano has mercilessly destroyed. There are two towns in Saint-Pierre: an invisible town and another town that is visible, still in a state of becoming. The invisible town lies beneath the one that can be seen. The visible town channels the former one through its old markings, serving as a substructure and spreading a diffuse charm that is tragically exact.

Great ruins, vestiges, and dream-like paving stones (moulded in ancestral lava) seem to brood over the memory of an ancient catastrophe. But, if you look harder, you see that no recollection supports them. They're only stones, carved stones, stones of fire, and there is no identifiable consciousness that would transmute them into a ritual memorial, that would honor those who died so suddenly, the immense array of those suffering thousands. Rising up from a tragedy with no record, from an event with no memory, they represent elements of an impalpable presence: the strange density of an absence.

Ruins and vestiges move me in this way. They sketch out ancient forms, suggest volumes, and construct spectral edifices. They inspire me to imagine what is missing, to complete, elsewhere, their aborted arc. My imagination, which fails to materialize that arc, then reaches a blank; it retracts, bending my consciousness toward this tragedy without cries or clamor, this tragedy without memories that nonetheless persists and insists.

The town was removed from all administrative maps. The immense tomb underwent the ordeal of a decade of abandonment and an eternity of indifference. The block of remains was broken up and, for the most part, erased in a sort of frightening and sustained pillage. The town that appeared (made by builders of fortune, by conquering miseries, and by disorderly grabs) began to swallow up the ruins and deconstruct them. This went on for a long time. All that was left were the distended forms—splintered geometries, eviscerated volumes, stones united or reunited in indefinition, tiles of clay and old marble—the deterioration of which seems to find its only source in eternity. What had been a field of destruction was then transmuted into a *presence* composed of localized stagnations, small, sudden protuberances, isolated slabs, stairways going nowhere, arcades and porches celebrating nothing, and windows that frame only gradual vertigos. You rest your elbows on these tilting surfaces; you look from there at the lines of flight.

Great ruins and vestiges are like a city in an old person's dream. Here, visibly, the ruin has slowly risen far above itself. The stone has formed a substance, and the substance, in a game of broken and repeating mirrors, summons secret echoes.

Thick walls and large stones resolve into an archipelago of immobility and silence.

Don't just look at them. Touch them too; allow the hand to respond. The salience of silence, sharp carvings, gnawed corners, the texture of dead moss, spots of shadow, shuttered depths, sweet and patient warmth recalling the sun and a primal burning. Audible fermentation and the fragrance of ancient things. Time imprisoned. Palpable space disseminated along a strange archipelago.

A blind burning of the light on the drama of overturned pillars. An entire tragedy takes in breath. Here, the pigment comes from the fire. Light circulates in the irremediable fatality of shadow. It almost seems as though shadows were *searching*...

I imagine the catastrophe. The cauterizing effect of the fire, almost instantaneous, and then the meters of ash that would forever imprison the totality of this extraordinary town. How much time had to pass before there appeared the first blade of grass? And what became of the stone under the flames, the live cinders, the spores of abandon, the fecundations of pollen and of animal dung? What became of the stone when it had to take on, all by itself, the role of impossible remainder? From what high density does it now reemerge?

For a long time, I imagined this reconquest of the destroyed town: the street-sellers who came back to the beach of Mouillage, and who, over the years, conquered the great shroud of ash; these fishermen who established a foothold on the coast, attracted by the startling maritime fecundity of the zone—the vitality of a chain of predators nourished by grilled flesh and, no doubt, melted gold. These huts, then these shelters, and then these rock gardens they assembled, these supports of sheet metal and wooden crates, these fragments of wall to lean against, this ash on which you could rest things without seeking to awaken what lies moaning beneath: new abodes in the enclosure of the ancient ones... This reconstruction with no inventory required at first the immense task of destroying the ruins, decomposing a past that had become illegible, effacing it under new layers. The act of rendering something invisible would respect the constraints of the old boundaries. The cartography of the earth that resisted the infernal flattening out would impose its checkerboard pattern; streets and alleyways would remain, just like the foundations and their vestiges, just like the fragmenting walls. Façades, redistributed to supply building material, would serve as foundation, binder, and suture. Today, these façades can still be glimpsed like a bit of dead lace. The old order holds the new order in the grip of its jaws, breathing into it a soul by which I am moved.

The plaster coating has given way, leaving the authentic ardor of the rubble held together under torn fringes, a solidity as massive as it is haggard: an infinite fragility. The rubble asserts a lost truth.

The former town has been laid waste. Bodies and souls, furniture and jewelry, customs and manners, mute stupefactions and barely formulated terrors. The town burned for a long time—its northern wood, the liquors of the distillery accompanied by, I assume, the filth and the horrors of the Amerindian genocide, of slavery trailing in its wake the age-old exploitations. Such a shock affects more than just stone. A lid of ashes holds down more than just the combustive matter. No doubt, there are also acts of respiration that have been stilled, glances that have been disengaged from eyelids, clusters of last thoughts, final smiles, and piles of little sparks leaping from this massive extinction of the human. This is what articulates and sustains the tragedy, not the lost form, or simply failures of the imagination, but, properly speaking, what was, what is no longer, and what subsists as something that cannot be deciphered.

Rain confers on the remains a gleaming that becomes like a skin trembling in the light. When these gleams are extinguished, the density of their presence gathers in on itself. Total.

Nothing hides itself, and nothing escapes. All is offered and nothing is given. The lack leads its flock of ghosts and the void consolidates.

I like this idea of a sudden blow coming from something unthinkable. At the time, it must have been impossible to conceive of such a burning cloud, to understand that what is striking *you* is that *thing*: a sudden death that has not even been identified as such. This shock must have permeated every one of these stones, thus *animating* them, conferring on them that irremediable immobility, those haloes of silence that no wave of temporality can encompass. And so, I cherish this evidence: each ruin is a *concentrate*.

Everything seems to converge toward the cemetery of Mouillage and to radiate out from it. Nested in the heart of that other cemetery, which is now the town itself—always preceding and pursuing it—the cemetery of Mouillage seems to arise from a more ancient eternity and from another future. Carved grillwork outside of time, old enameled marble, crosses, curious virgins, and wandering saints. Oblivion, sweet playmate of the mosses, takes care of the fissures and nourishes the old grass, dirties these names that no longer name anyone, these shipwrecked regrets, these eternal thoughts that have dried up... What has been arrested here is of another origin, of another dust of pain and suffering, and there subsists a supplementary calm born of this field of small deaths that came before (since the nights of the very first invader), the vast, sudden death, abyss-death, death without *manman*, death like a river without a bank, and without a prie-dieu for lamentation.

This cemetery of Mouillage resembles a little island of death arranged in the midst of the immeasurable bedraggled pile of the dead. After the eruption, a special team worked over the ruins, hollowing out ditches of compassion, making the great logs creak. Heaps of half-carbonized cadavers added their concluding embers to the triumphant ash, contributing a little dust from their eyelashes and from their hair to the stares and skulls of the lonely tombs. They brought an embarrassment of bones back into this old cemetery, raising an ossuary that is now deserted. Fecund matter of the bones. Archive and living stone.

A cemetery has significance only when it's at the heart of a circle of the living. It bears witness for the living and acts for them too. And when the surroundings collapse and destruction arrives, when no memory calculates the number of deaths and regrets, when memory can't even recall them, the cemetery suddenly palpates with confusion. It becomes meaningless; it subsists only in the odd elegance of old tombs, their cares belonging to an age that has passed, their details obsolete, the whole thing coming undone bit by bit, becoming drawn and gaunt, a shipwreck without a boat in an abyss without an ocean. The town of the present has brought back convoys of new dead; it has thus reconstituted meaning. Yet this cemetery of all cemeteries remains isolated, removed, unpleasantly persisting, focused on its own deterioration, organized around its voids and hollows, lost in its ancient origin, without a lingering memory to accord it respect. A mess of bones and marble vows.

The old town contained a population of almost nineteen thousand inhabitants. They accumulated in the cays of Mouillage. People stayed outside for a good part of the day, most moving about on foot. The work was a constellation of diverse activities, and the rhythm was slow with localized areas of intensity. Even if the slowed-down time and the general stasis created shadows and secret depths around the great ruins, now, when you're near them, within their intangible circle, you glimpse only a very little of the exposed town's new life. It is as though that life had been deafened, repressed, and made blurry at the margins of an ancient order that no longer exists but continues nonetheless to dominate.

The ruins are like specters of a former splendor, of a lost light taking refuge somewhere in the tender coat of moss and the impatience of the vegetal cushioning. That immobility precedes no flight, prepares no leap. It is a poetry dispersed in the fluctuating hues of shadow and light.

From everywhere, you can see the mountain. Between the stones, at the end of useless staircases, under the yawning arcades, the mountain reveals itself, looms above, emerges, signals its presence, velvety with green cream, strikingly beautiful. An imperial presence that the old town could never diminish. The smallest break, the slightest angle, the least perspective—all these still recall and point to the coming of a magnificent and monstrous force.

Shadow is an intention questioned by light.
Uncertainty circulates.

That mosaic of ruins and vestiges constitutes a presence that is unknown to us, a declaration of what no longer is and what remains to be revealed, an indifferent mass that proclaims the fragility of all things. Everything was so frangible; everything was so solid. What's left now was already present in the time of its splendor, the ruin already existed there in its proud form; and that form haunts each vestige, each piece of debris, with a residue of vanity that has become illegible. A pathos sustained.

Presence as an energetic weaving. A dislocation that knits together immobility and silence, the shadows and light patterning the recesses. A lightness.

Standing before these ruins and vestiges, the first stage is to imagine what's missing, what was there, how it existed. The second stage is to proceed toward compassion, to sense the catastrophe, to imagine this drama without living it. *How can one imagine blazing matter, matter leaping out, matter that carbonizes and that levels and that... bam!! evacuates all oxygen?* Finally, there comes the lucid perception that is also a form of compassion, *a noble compassion*, not an imagining but a sensing of this mixture made of elevation and sudden collapse, this clamor and this silence, this formless eruption that exposes all forms. The challenge of a true visitation is to advance toward this magic—serene, humble, cleansed, purified, yet still unalterable, truly unalterable—a magic that fills you at once with a sense of gravity and a sense of endless joy: profound, subtle, and calm. High compassion brings together these two extremes: sadness without pain and joy without folly.

The serenity of the great ruin welcomes, in a unique celebration, obscurities and vibrancy, past depths and present infinities; it makes the instant into an enigma. It is a vast, scarred-over wound that has never closed up again and that distorts everything known.

Each great ruin is a peaceful scene, a space of urban theatricality, followed by silence and murmuring. One truly senses that these are not monuments. No one has assigned to them a memorial function, something that would preserve an official memory, that would put into order a collection of memories. These are not Trace-memories either, the kind that emerge from forgetting, from the forgotten, from the impossible, from the dominated. Rather, they bear witness in a horizontal, open, multifarious way. These great ruins of Saint-Pierre and its vestiges have something in common with both the monument and the Trace-memory. Like a crack in colonial memory, the skeleton of a vast collapse, they have come close to the labile fragility of the Trace while their origin, their function, has slowly been erased from memory. Chips of paint remain, the famous ochre yellow among the mosses, and courageous plants extend their impressive manes. The plaster sealants have given way and a blackish skin rises from the burns and the volcanic rock. A palpable patina distances them yet a bit more from what they were before. Since these ruins have nothing else to do, they absorb the nocturnal variations and the blades of the sun, creating ephemeral intimacies, breathing in the crevices that are only partially visible, and sometimes seeming to echo the sighs of souls arisen from the ashes that form the ground.

The Trace-memory comes back from below. These great ruins and vestiges that come from on high constantly fan out in an infinite retraction. They signify nothing, give no account of anything. They are content to capture the spirit of those who encounter them, to fascinate the sensibilities of those who visit them, and to exist in that way until they become *creation*.

Creation doesn't display and it doesn't hide. Creation *indicates*, infinitely, and thus it liberates us. Augments us. What is restored provides a stage for what is absent, like a fossil coming detached from a lost alphabet.

Situated between the monument and the Trace-memory, these immobile masses, these broken expanses, peopled with spent sounds, reflect memories, shudders of memories, edges of forms, a floating movement of meanings that also derive from the illegibility of a becoming. And he who still says "the theater", "the church of the Fort", "Rise-to-the-Sky Street", "depot of the Fig tree" abandons these names very quickly when—if he assumes the risk, if he accepts the adventure—all of a sudden, these presences start to awaken in him.

Sometimes, pieces of a tile floor call out to us, remind us of something we cannot name. They demystify and mystify in equal measure.

I need to take long, slow walks in the town to perceive, like a distant murmur, the density of an impalpable presence. There's not a single millimeter that isn't woven with ashes, bones, and stone, not a space that doesn't contain a bit of loosened rubble. Everywhere, a glance detects a bit of wall, the fragment of a staircase, a tile that tattoos the ground. And then there's an indecipherable mass, inhabited by the wild grass that rearranges it, and which seems to have imprisoned slabs of tranquility and *impossible things*. This sight is only accessible to a sensory letting-go, a true errancy of the imagination that is kept ready in wait. Certain ruins have resisted the invasion; no house has covered them over. They have preserved narrow slits of coherence that the proliferation of green magnifies in an abandoned garble. This mixture of mossy stones and wild proliferating grasses, these bits of mortar that spring up, these bouquets of freely growing flowers invoke the intimation of an ancient wisdom, of a contraction of several ages that have gone back to the wild.

The lack does not come from nothing; it is the persistence of a presence undone, one that we still don't know how to transcend.

Hollow basins and gutters are everywhere. Only streams of light remain, the stony flickering of a motherless warmth. That is where the flow begins.

Faced with these ruins, the historian stays at the surface. The archeologist follows several trails, but he stops short at the doors of the imagination. The guide, for his part, is forced to fall silent. All that remains to the free spirit is that tranquil contact with the inexpressible, the perception of an invisible town that lives on an archipelago of atmospheres, of mad situations, of dysfunctional sites and spaces that are impracticable for ordinary life and that attract trash and waste too easily, as though this indefinition staggered a mind nourished by certitudes, forcing it to the point of insult. The visible town of today struggles in the thick of an invisible town that exists without functioning, that resists in its absurd geography, and that imposes itself in this way: through the *triumph of an emergence.*

The black stone, the gray ash, the moss of abandonment... the colors of the invisible town, spread out on the ground, wander between black and white. The shards of light, the omnipresence of the blue sky and the blue sea, the effusive green of the tufts of grass and vines—all these seem to rise up from the stark reality of the visible town. Ruins and vestiges, they too—although exposed to streams of light—seem above all to distill mystery, or rather, the depths of something immobile that is undergoing a slow metamorphosis, of shadows that ferment, and of an unformulable utterance that is accompanied but never reached by the dazzling sun.

After the departure of Man Ninotte, I learned not to name the ruins. I learned to see only their indecipherability, to walk, my senses open, among these vestiges that formulate no audible word. The most vertiginous ruins are the staircases, sometimes suspended in the void, always leading if not to nowhere, then at least toward something missing. Each step is like a composition, a condensation of details that must have once been useful, each paving-stone a song that recalls nothing; their collection constructs something like a dispersed path that would make the stroller into his own destination.

These stones have left colonial memory behind to draw in and distill all the silences: those of the Amerindian, the enslaved, the freebooter, the pirate and the sailor, the merchant and the musician, the immigrant and the nomad, and now these new inhabitants of Saint-Pierre who have led the conquest of miseries that gave birth to this town and whose lineage has not been captured by history. Everything is there, in a dense mass that only the stone supports, that only the stone manifests.

It is the only place in Martinique where the work of colonialism has left such a concentration of *presences*. Here, the grand story of the dominator met its defeat, ceaselessly collapsing, vanquished by a blazing bolt of lightning. Our indifference has achieved and intensified the slow metamorphosis of this vast destruction... I say to the Baroness: This lack calls us; this presence compels us.

LEGENDARY OF TOUSSAINT – Traces always reveal to me a source that is more expansive, a source of precious ambiguity. They operate at a level of the real that they point out and transform, all at once. They form the spreading line of our forward advance, like chemical vertebrae that construct more than memory. They establish, ceaselessly, what makes us what we are.

There are Traces in the place where I live: Man Ninotte's plants that I rediscover in a corner of the garden, mite-eaten photographs, fish bladders, suitcases, a table, an armoire, a couple of chairs that still cross my path... All that has been transformed into infinitesimal flickers linked to the Traces that, for me, make up this land. They capture my attention, project me toward myself and into what I see. They trouble the flow of images, all interconnecting in memories and sheets of sensation, in intangible propagations. The same phenomenon is set off in me at the sight of certain fruit trees, certain vegetables, certain fish, or when I smell certain scents... The kind of perception thus opened by Man Ninotte is neither vision nor hallucination, just an imperceptible *disconnect* in which precision offers as much as indefinition, a contemplative immobility as much as the burst of a sudden intuition. From this point on, the disconnect can provide the hint of a melody in the tumult of the day. The blossoming of a lemon tree surprised by a bee, a grandiose half-tone in a sunset, or the passage of an angel in a pearl of rain. I can see a dream of gold and straw in the light of an ordinary morning, and take the time to experience it... Never ruling over me, the dream is just the softest wave on which I can move forward, trembling. Nor is it truly new: I have always been sensitive to these bones of the enslaved that resurface in the mud of November's cyclones; to the Amerindian ceramics forgotten in the sand. And I am just as sensitive to the colonial ruins that trigger in me a continual swirl of emotions. But today a different sensibility inspired by their encounter offers them to me bathed in a cordial radiance, in a possible access to this particular instant, as if it were the totality. They permit brief glimpses of the real, there where time contracts and diffracts all at once. These moments lead me back almost to the totality of what I perceive. These moments lead me back to Man Ninotte and to her Traces; and her Traces propel me out toward everything.

It is during the week of Toussaint that the group reassembles.

Under the impetus of the Baroness, we have instituted this ritual: on the early morning of November 1st, before the great rush of the crowd toward the graves of the dead, we gather around Man Ninotte's tomb. To clean it. To change the flowers. To place some orchids on the walls nearby. To speak about her, to speak to her, to reactivate her Traces. To find ourselves together again, forgetting what she had to become. It's the Baroness who makes sure that everyone is there. She brings the flowers and replaces last year's plants, which were stolen or have died. The others take charge of the candles and of what's needed to remove the dust. The tomb is in the cemetery of Lamentin. A little edifice in the old style surrounds the vault and protects it with a roof. It is found in a spot where the sheltering walls meet with the barbed wire, creating a corner that is seldom visited. The darkness and the quiet remain there, motionless.

On those mornings, the little cemetery is the site of a pleasant bustle.

You can hear the buckets striking each other, the water that dribbles, the faucets squeaking, the brushes churning in an odor of bleach and disinfectant. Itinerant painters refresh the whitewash of the tombs or revive the eternal regrets. Some tombs come back to life near those that have been abandoned and that suddenly appear mournful under the dance of wild grasses. The alleys, the recesses, and the passageways are tidiness itself; it is as though they have had to witness the passing of multiple processions of saintly souls. A wagon gathers things that have faded and regrets that have been left behind. Flowers—false or real—are radiant. The living are happy to take care of those who are no longer there, those who, nonetheless, continue to circulate like a breeze among us. Our ritual doesn't last very long, certainly less than an hour or so. Wiping down the tiles once more. Arranging the flowers just so, for no reason. Cleaning up the area around for no one. Brushing up the entire area, one way or another. Being thoroughly absorbed by it all while watching oneself doing it. Consciously abandoning oneself—that is the essence of the moment. Then, to get pleasure from entrusting I know not what to the flame of two or three candles. The whole thing taking place in the flow of words that come to us, about Man Ninotte, about Papa, about some memory or other, a chuckle, a passing worry, a protest against whatever, or delicious tidbits of gossip. Finally, we close the grill with the care of those gestures that protect and also caress. We don't come back in the evening when the cemetery will be invaded by the crowd and the rising tide of burning candles. We prefer these mornings lit by sunshine or depopulated by rain, not to dwell on what we've lost, but to celebrate in true innocence what was given to us.

"Those who live a long time are nourished by absence," the Baroness repeats to me in this new early morning of November. We are down to just the two of us. The rest of the group isn't there. Life's emergencies; life's lassitudes, too. I go down the alley of the cemetery with her, toward the exit. As usual, we have taken care of the tomb, arranging the flowers, lighting the candles. We expressed our sorrow about the grillwork that shelters the vault and that had been broken into by some junkie in a state of delirium. We had just encountered two or three elderly people weighed down by bouquets; the Baroness, always friendly, exchanges a few words with them. At each step she recognizes someone, greets them enthusiastically, and

enters into some serious bantering about banalities. As usual, the cemetery is beautiful, pervaded by a somewhat unreal efflorescence, each inch cleaned, *cleared out*. Those who are there are well worn with age; a few young people escort them, but they entertain so many certitudes that they seem to come from another type of humanity. The morning visit is the affair of those who have grown closer to the mysteries, who have lost parts of themselves, who have recovered them in another way, who are acquainted with the seasons of tears and the seasons of laughter, and who, when there's nothing left to wait for, know only patience. The happiest of them sometimes partake of the blessèd bread of plenitude, standing high on a pedestal purified of desire. In whatever light, their body projects only a little shadow, at most, a few glintings of mother of pearl, and their steps, supported by wings of experience, produce the slight touch of a ladybug. It has rained, but the sun is there. The sun makes the shower's pearls glisten. A little wind's freshness glides between the grills of the tombs. Shimmering. Glistening. Light is everywhere. It seems to arise from the headstones and fall from the entirety of the sky. I can see that transparency that Chinese wisdom names the *transparency of morning*:[23] a light that remembers the night, that retains its mystery, that spreads out, that is spared the heat that will come soon after, that is exempted for a time from the dustiness of life, and that draws out from each thing an immanent clarity. The Baroness speaks to people, communicates her vitality to them, dissects them with her glance... *"Those who live a long time are also gnawed away by absence... gnawed away by absence..."* she says yet again, a dreamy shadow in her eyes.

Near the tomb of Man Ninotte, we had, as usual, spoken together. This time, the conversation had been different. I had said to her everything that passed through my mind, all that I thought I had understood, all that I had become since the impact of her disappearance. I had revisited the event, experienced so many years before, when the Baroness had shared with us the news about Man Ninotte. That moment, which we believed we had lived through so intensely, had now escaped us forever. I had needed those silences, those spaces of forgetting, and the ultimate forgetting, so as to live

---

23 See François Jullien, *Philosophie du vivre* [Philosophy of Living] (Paris: Gallimard, 2011).

it at last, to relive it with her, and to realize what had happened. Something, unbeknownst to us, had changed us in different ways. In the past, these experiences of grief that opened a wide gaping hole in our lives had been entrusted to the symbolic systems of long-established communities. *These griefs became thresholds.* They gave access to a form of rebirth, transmuting grief through rites of initiation whose customs have been lost. Ever since the Abyss of the slaveship—which still gapes wide open—nothing structures our journey through life's desires, loves, anguishes, transformations. Nothing circumscribes our encounters with the shocks of the unpredictable, the senseless, and, finally, the unthinkable. Nothing helps us to limit that fearless, indifferent beyond that often rips apart our everyday consciousness. We approach these unnamed thresholds without a set of controls. We cobble together individual solutions, often imperceptible to others, successful or not, which might, in fact, be initiations.

Or, more precisely: *auto-initiations.*

The old communal symbologies used to give substance to these thresholds in our consciousness. The hold of the slaveship, that bonfire of the unthinkable, the *Tout-monde* and its relational power—these have made everything explode. Not only for us, but for the entire world. Today, those of us who have been exposed to the great stage of the world, educated only by our experiences, still find that, despite everything, what came before and what comes after fall into some kind of sequence. Beginnings and re-beginnings flow on beneath our blind sense of continuity; they come from nowhere, offer no way out, and remain invisible. Thus, we construct who we are, on our own, according to the will of what is worst and what is best in a tangled confusion. While we were scrubbing down the tomb, I had said to the Baroness: We have so much to do in this time when peoples and individuals are regrounding themselves. We're responsible for creating an auto-initiation, an auto-organization, an auto-ethics, an auto-foundation, with solidarities born solely of our own riches, our relational practice with respect to all things... *everything is to be done by oneself in this immense work of Relation!* We have to live for a long time just to begin the process. We have to lose so much just to be able to nourish ourselves and gather a harvest from something that isn't there. There is so much to dispel before we can return to the opulent sobrieties of simple perception. So much courage to find if we are to confront things without making an attempt to give them meaning, an attempt that makes us lose them. So much to survive and to unlive before we can understand that living offers us nothing more than the occasion to celebrate each second as it arrives, and that that only happens here, in this exact place.

What makes us able to identify the nourishment we receive from the moment, to grasp it thoroughly, is sadly that which suddenly evades us: a sense of bewilderment. Otherwise, the seeming continuity lulls our mind, and Heraclitus finds us sleeping. Without full access to what we are experiencing, all reality, all abundance, is out of reach, and life escapes us. When a tension is created over this acknowledged void, this contemplated hollow, this rupture without panic, this accepted lack, then life starts again, as in a staging by that esteemed director, Peter Brook. The tension is what allows us to feel more thoroughly what it is to be alive. It is always desire that makes what is lacking into an infinite substance, a source in which one can lose oneself, but from which one can also genuinely emerge again into oneself.

I had to recapture all the moments lost during the great impact in a whirlwind of confused impressions. I had sorted through them there, in this cemetery, one by one, examining them, then interweaving them, enlarging each second, re-exploring our great origins, attempting by means of a complicitous distance and a free imagination to experience at last what had never been experienced. This event concerning Man Ninotte had neither a beginning nor an end. From the start, it had become inaccessible under the weight of its own intensity. It had established itself in a blinding and blind continuity, abruptly made present, conserved as a present even while disappearing, and maintaining itself in our life through all these years in a deafening intensity, to reveal itself when I started once more to envision it, with you and for you, to experience the event not simply in order to live it and lose myself in it again, but to feel that ferment of life, to better envision the poetics that it sanctioned.

The event had ejected us from that inaccessible region that weighs on the ordinariness of everyday life. It had propelled us onto the stage of an immense erasure in which we still had to exist. Something had thus been given to us, and we had taken it in. For all those years, I needed to discover in myself another degree of sensibility, apparitions I couldn't anticipate, transparencies that were revelatory, by which I mean: *trans-apparitions*. Today, these allow the least little event in the field of my consciousness to achieve the status of an advent. The trans-apparition surges forth from all things, traverses all things, and links all things to one another.

During these long years, the shock had wandered through me without leaving a trace, except for a few hardly perceptible, always awkward clues. The shock installed itself somewhere in the geology of my existence, not like a memory, but like an enlarged space, *a clearing*, which sharpened my immediate perceptions and helped me to glimpse facets of life that until then had been marginal. This clearing, this supreme source, brings me the riches that we are given to experience, instants of beauty detached from any specific cause. With that assistance, I attempt to understand what it is that I know, what matters to me, what comes from the origins, what surges forth from this land, what comes together and what comes apart in these sudden jolts of the planet. I found better access to myself and to the world by means of this searing passage, this transition that has already happened, but that is always present, forgotten yet serenely unforgettable.

What started to blossom from this immense crater can now be understood and considered to be a threshold of experience. It inaugurates a consciousness moved by what we are living at each instant, at every moment, a celebration that mobilizes the senses, that transcends them and offers us the possibility of discovering the face, no longer terrifying, of the unthinkable. With that, I contemplate the infinitesimal. I circumscribe the inexhaustible. I circumscribe what is always beginning and endlessly changing. I circumscribe what cannot be summed up, what it will be impossible to encompass. I envision that there is nothing more urgent than to live, without waiting any longer, at the highest possible and most complete intensity. With this, I make little assemblages of words, which mean nothing. A language of sensations, an alphabet of small mental tremors. I know this misfortune—to not be a poet—and also this grace that I am not one, which allows me to continue to desire.

What is lacking fills us with desire; this desire persists, it takes its life-force from our life, allowing us to live in a burning tension, thus harnessing us to what we will become. This lack confers a substance to what we have as much as to what we don't have. Or what we no longer have. Lack releases a shiver of the imagination. It calls upon all that remains around us, all that we perceive in our depths, inclining it toward the site where poems, impossible to write, are forged. These are poems that have a life of their own. What poets write constitutes merely the rubble of what they have been able to experience. And what they have been able to experience is only the froth at the edge of what they have been able to sense, the absence of which remains throughout their lifetime like the afterglow of an illumination. Here, the auto-initiation, if we are to retain that notion, would in no way be an integration into the absolutes of a community but rather an introduction to epiphanies—great or minuscule—dispersed into the swelling wave of a solitary mind, the tide of a life pursuing its own experience. This auto-initiation would give us access to intensities—past, lost, and present, above all, present in amplitude, and thus in becoming—which we would not be able to access without its electrifying power. The auto-initiation would be a transmutation of the improbable matter of absence.

We leave the cemetery in the beautiful light of morning. Light creates something like a weightlessness; it passes through everything, opens each thing to the most expansive landscape. It dissipates and reveals. It is an innocence that is unafraid of what the past reserves for us, and that is unafraid of what the future has already brought. I would have wanted to speak more with the Baroness, to explain to her what I feel, but I have rambled on so much that I fear I would annoy her. Until now, she has exhibited a benevolent willingness to hear me, listening in the way one listens to a confession, and she has disguised her annoyance despite my flood of explanations. No doubt, she has caught in my verbiage only the delirium of the former *négrillon*, the one who had to be reassured when he began to hear zombies. Still, I say to her: There. The cemetery is behind us. The impact has not swallowed us whole as I thought it would when we first began, nor has it removed us from the flow of existence. On the contrary. We have been projected into a vertiginous recapitulation of human possibility, into all the hopelessness that lies within the hope that has been animated. At the height of this maelstrom, each of us has had to keep going as he could, with what he has, and, above all, with what he is. Each of us has had to pursue what we had thought we had lost of the symbolic rebirths of former times. But these rebirths occur within an intimate horizon, an infinitesimal, sometimes impalpable horizon. The thresholds that are now crossed are no longer crossed under the great arch of the absolutes, but instead in the vertigo of a trembling consciousness, detached from facile illusions, and still capable of holding on in the face of the unthinkable, which is also held wide open, not like a terrifying slash but like a precious source and resource. Resolute.

The Baroness murmurs:
—"Do you remember what Jojo l'Algébrique said in front of Man Ninotte's coffin? At that moment when all forms of language abandoned us?..." —No, I tell her. It was undoubtedly a poem, I don't know which one, but I've done everything I could so that you'd remember... —"It was some verses of Segalen; they already said what you're trying to say..."
—Oh really? I say to her, innocently.
Smiling, she then recites for me:

> Let this, therefore, be marked with no reign...
>> but that of this unique era, with no date & no
>> end, of unutterable characters, which every
>> man founds in himself & salutes
>
> That dawn he becomes Sage & Regent of his
> heart's throne.[24]

Que ceci donc ne soit point marqué d'un règne mais de cette ère unique, sans date et sans fin, aux caractères indicibles, que tout homme instaure en lui-même et salue, à l'aube où il devient Sage et Régent du trône de son coeur...

Favorite, 2016

---

24 TN: The quotation comes from two different stanzas of Victor Segalen's *Stèles*, translated by Timothy Billings and Christopher Bush (Middletown, CT: Wesleyan University Press, 2007: p. 77).

Glossary

anneaux-créoles: a kind of necklace made of links like a chain ("anneau" means "ring," or "loop," in French).

atoumo: considered a miracle plant with a fruit that looks like a small pumpkin. It can be used to cure headaches, flu, and indigestion.

barracoon: an enclosure in which slaves were confined on the plantation.

béké: refers to the whites, usually the planter class, in Martinique.

bèlè: a dance for couples integrating African dance and French quadrille dance traditions. Popular in Martinique, it is taught and studied at La Maison du Bèlè near Fort-de-France and Gros-Morne.

brisée: soursop, a fruit with a high vitamin C content.

chaînes-forçats: a kind of necklace shaped like a chain with links; literally "chains of the prisoner."

chien-fer: a hairless dog with iron-gray skin, not appreciated in Martinique.

chiquetaille: a hash or crumble of fish or vegetables. The term is used here to mean a hash or mash-up of things (e.g., references).

colliers-choux: a necklace made of rows of hollow beads, often in gold gilt, that can be wrapped around the neck several times.

danmyé: a Martiniquan martial art form, also known as *laghia* or *ladja*, brought to the island by slaves from Africa. "*Danm*" means "to initiate" and "*yê*" means "group."

détour: this is a concept developed by Édouard Glissant in *Le Discours antillais* (*Caribbean Discourse*); he writes of a "poetics of detour," which he differentiates from a "poetics of retour [return]."

doudouistes: refers to a group of poets writing at the beginning of the 20th century (and thus immediately before Aimé Césaire's generation) who tended to paint the Caribbean islands as an exotic, feminized paradise.

En-ville: this is a term Patrick Chamoiseau invents in *Texaco*, his award-winning novel about the transformation of Martinique over generations, to refer to the city, Fort-de-France. "*En*" means "in" and "*ville*" means "city."

féroce: a kind of purée made with avocado and fish.

filibos: colorful candies made from sugarcane, indigenous to Martinique.

fleurit-noël: a plant with small white flowers, used to treat upper respiratory maladies.

gros thym: broad-leaved thyme.

hougan: a Vodou priest.

langues-de-boeuf: a buttery, flaky pastry named after a cow's tongue. One side is covered in melted candied sugar and the other side in sugar crystals. Once the buttery dough bakes, it has a bubbly spotted pattern resembling a cow's tongue.

langues-poules: a herbaceous plant found in rice fields. "Poules" means "hens."

macadam: a dish made with codfish.

madous: lemonade or orangeade made with cane syrup.

malcadi: an epileptic seizure.

manjé-kouli: the cuisine of the Hindus who came to Martinique ("*manjé*" is like the French "*manger*," "to eat," and "*kouli*" was a term for people from India).

manmans: a Creole name for mother, similar to "*mama*" in English or "*maman*" in French. I have kept the original so as to preserve the masculine-sounding "man" and use it as the prefix for "Man Ninotte" and the other "Man," or mothers, who appear in the text.

marronnage: an escape from the plantation to rural, forest, or mountainous areas. A "marron" is a "maroon," someone who has escaped from the plantation.

mazouk: a partner dance that emerged in the former French colony of Dominica involving precise foot work.

métissage: the mixing, or coupling, of ethnicities.

morne: the name given in Martinique to the steep foothills of the volcanic formations rising up from the coasts on the island.

moubins: a fruit that has curative properties, e.g. for sores in the mouth.

nègre: this word is impossible to translate into English. It has a wide variety of meanings, from "Negro" to "Black." Translators of francophone authors such as Césaire and Chamoiseau have often chosen to use different translations, depending on the context. Rose-Myriam Réjouis and Val Vinokurov, the translators of *Texaco*, choose to translate "*nègre*" as "blackman." The word "*nègre*" should be contrasted with the French word "*noir*," which was a less offensive term at the beginning of the 20th century but has now been replaced for many in France by the Anglo-American term "Black."

négresse: the female version of the above.

négrillon: the child version of the above, here intended to be an affectionate nickname.

pieds-piments: a West Indian chili pepper plant. "*Pied*" in French means "foot."

pieds-pois: the pea plant. The *pois-d'Angole* is a pigeon pea.

pieds-zicaques: the icaque (cocoplum) tree.

Pierre-monde: a concept Chamoiseau has proposed in order to build on and nuance Édouard Glissant's concept of *Tout-monde* (see below). The Pierre-monde (from "*pierre*," "stone" in French, and "*monde*," "world" in French) gives a mooring to the "unthinkable" of absolute relationality contained in the notion of the "*Tout-monde*." Chamoiseau writes that the "Pierre-monde inscribes points of view," providing a solid grounding when faced with the vertigo of relational possibilities; see Chamoiseau, "Mondialisation, mondialité, pierre-monde." *Littérature*, 174:2, August 2014: pp. 92–103.

quimboiseur: an Afro-Creole sorcerer/healer; the *quimbois* is an object thought to have magic powers.

roucou: achiote, the source of annatto, a kind of sweet peppery condiment.

santons: means "little saint" in Provençal. It is the name for the little figurines (traditionally in wood) used in a crèche as part of the Christian ritual of Christmas.

sentimenthèque: one of Chamoiseau's inventive portmanteau words from the French. *"Bibliothèque"* means "library," or the "shelves of a library," and *"sentiment"* means "feeling." Thus, a *sentimenthèque* is a kind of library that you feel, or a set of books with sentimental value.

tambours-ka, tambours-bèlè: long drums played during the *bèlè* dance, originally made from tree trunks and then from barrels. *Gwo-ka* is a type of music played by the *tambours-ka*.

tété-négresse: gold jewelry in the shape of a woman's breasts.

thé pays: an herb with tiny white flowers with medicinal properties; an infusion is used to treat diarrhea, inflammation, hypertension, and joint pain.

Toussaint: La Toussaint is the equivalent of All Saints' Day. It normally falls on or near Halloween.

Tout-monde: a concept related to Édouard Glissant's poetics of Relation. The infinite diversity of the world is contained in the *Tout-monde*; see Glissant, *Treatise on the Whole-World*, translated by Celia Britton (Liverpool: Liverpool University Press, 2020) and *Tout-monde* (Paris: Gallimard, 1993).

vache-qui-rit: the cow-that-laughs is a kind of processed cheese made in France and often given to children.

vers bleus: a kind of pimple, usually caused by acne, appearing on the face. When the pimple reaches a certain point of maturity, it turns blue. At that moment, it should be pinched to eliminate the pus, otherwise a scar will be left on the face.

yéyé: a groovy dude. Originally, yéyé was a style of pop music that emerged in Europe in the early 1960s. The French term *yé-yé* is derived from the English "yeah! yeah!", often heard as a refrain in songs by groups like the Beatles. It has also been linked to types of clothing—the mini-skirt, tight pants, belted jacket.

zeb-mouton: the prefix *"zeb"* designates a medicinal plant used as an herbal remedy. *Zeb-mouton* is a leaf infusion for high inflammation, diabetes, and other ailments. *Zeb-mal-têt* is a remedy for headaches (*"mal"* can mean "pain" in French and *"têt"* is Creole for the French *"tête,"* or "head" in English).

www.ingramcontent.com/pod-product-compliance
Lightning Source LLC
Chambersburg PA
CBHW020107030726
47498CB00006B/1985

* 9 7 8 1 8 0 2 0 7 2 1 0 5 *